Praise for the authors of *'Til the World Ends*

Julie Kagawa

"Kagawa wraps excellent writing and skillful plotting around a well-developed concept and engaging characters, resulting in a fresh and imaginative thrill-ride that deserves a wide audience."
—*Publishers Weekly* on *The Immortal Rules,* starred review

"Kagawa has done the seemingly impossible and written a vampire book...that feels fresh in an otherwise crowded genre. Mix[ing] paranormal and dystopian tropes to good effect, creating a world that will appeal across audiences."
—*Kirkus Reviews* on *The Immortal Rules*

"Julie Kagawa is one killer storyteller."
—MTV's *Hollywood Crush* blog

Ann Aguirre

"A gripping survival story set in an apocalyptic future.... This is a tense, action-packed dystopia with intriguingly gray characters."
—*Booklist* on *Enclave*

"A dark, haunting read.... Ann Aguirre has me hooked!"
—*New York Times* bestselling author Gena Showalter on *Enclave*

"The world Ann Aguirre has created is a roller-coaster ride to remember."
— #1 *New York Times* bestselling author Christine Feehan on the Sirantha Jax series

'TIL THE WORLD ENDS

JULIE KAGAWA

ANN AGUIRRE

KAREN DUVALL

HARLEQUIN® LUNA™

'TIL THE WORLD ENDS

ISBN-13: 978-0-373-80349-1

Copyright © 2013 by Harlequin Books S.A.

The publisher acknowledges the copyright holders of the individual works as follows:

DAWN OF EDEN
Copyright © 2013 by Julie Kagawa

THISTLE & THORNE
Copyright © 2013 by Ann Aguirre

SUN STORM
Copyright © 2013 by Karen Duvall

Recycling programs for this product may not exist in your area.

Printed in U.S.A.

www.Harlequin.com

CONTENTS

DAWN OF EDEN

JULIE KAGAWA

In the summer of my twenty-third year, the Red Lung virus began its spread across the eastern United States. Flulike symptoms evolved to raging fever, necrosis of the lungs and finally asphyxiation, as victims choked and drowned in their own blood. By the time government officials knew anything was wrong, the virus had already made its way overseas and was rapidly decimating Europe and parts of Asia, with no signs of slowing down. A worldwide emergency was called; towns had been emptied, cities lay in ruins and the virus continued its deadly march toward human extinction.

We thought Red Lung was as bad as it could get.

We were wrong.

"Kylie! It's Mr. Johnson!"

I spun from Ms. Sawyer's cot, nearly beaning Maggie in the nose as I whirled around. The intern looked frantic, her eyes wide over her mask, her face pale as she pointed to a cot along the far wall. Two masked interns were struggling with the body of a middle-aged man who was spasming and coughing violently, trying to throw them off. Blood flecked his lips, spattered in vivid patterns across his sheets and hospital robes. His mouth gaped, trying to suck in air, and his breathing tube lay on the ground in a pool of blood and saliva.

I rushed over, snatching a syringe from my lab coat and dodging the intern, who stumbled back as the man flailed. Grabbing the patient's arm, I threw my weight against him, which didn't do much as Mr. Johnson was a big guy and frantic, and I weighed about one hundred ten sopping wet.

"Hold him down!" I called to Eric, the intern who'd been flung back, and he pounced on the man again. Blood streamed from the man's nose and flew in arcing ribbons across the bed as he coughed and flailed. I uncapped the syringe and plunged it into his arm, injecting eight mms of morphine into his veins.

Gradually, his struggles ceased. His eyes rolled back, and his head lolled to the side as he passed into unconsciousness.

At this stage of the infection, he would probably never wake up.

I sighed and brushed away a strand of ash-blond hair that had come loose from my clip during my struggles with Mr. Johnson. My hand came away sticky with blood, but I was so used to that now, I barely noticed. "Keep an eye on him," I told Eric and the other intern, Jenna, who looked on with weary, hooded eyes. "Let me know if there's any change, or if he wakes up."

Jen nodded, but Eric made a disgusted sound and shook his head, his dark curls bouncing.

"He's not going to wake up," he said, voicing the fact that everyone knew but was too numb to think about. "We've seen this a thousand times, now." He turned accusing eyes on me, gesturing at the unconscious patient. Though he slept now, we could hear the gurgling in his throat and lungs, the rasp of air through a rapidly flooding windpipe. "Why did you even waste a shot of morphine on him? We're almost out, and it could've been used on someone who has a chance. Why not put the poor bastard out of his misery?"

"Keep your voice down," I said in a cool, even tone, giving him a hard glare. Around us, our patients coughed or slept fitfully, too drug-addled to really understand what we said, but they weren't deaf. And the other interns were watching.

They were just as discouraged and frightened and exhausted, but I could not show weakness, especially now.

"It's not our place to say who lives or dies," I said quietly, looking at Eric but speaking to all of them. "We have a responsibility to these people, to fight for them. To not give up. That's why we set up this clinic, even though all the hospitals in the city have probably shut down by now. We can still help, and we will not abandon them."

"You're crazy." Eric finally looked up at me, his face bleak. "This is crazy, Kylie. Everyone is gone, even Doc Adams, and he set this whole place up. You might not want to accept it, but it's time to face facts." He nodded at Maggie and Jen on the other side of the bed. "This is futile. We're the only ones left, and we can't save anyone. We lost. It's time to throw in the towel."

"No." My voice came out flat, cold. "This isn't a stupid boxing match. These are people's lives. I'm not going to abandon them. Even if I can only give them a peaceful last few days, that's better than doing nothing." Eric snorted, and I stared him down. "But I'm not keeping you here." I pointed past him at the entrance to the makeshift clinic, the opening covered with plastic strips. "You can walk out anytime. If you want to leave, there's the door."

He glared at me before he reached up and tugged down his mask. I could see the grim line of his mouth and jaw, and my heart sank, but I kept my expression calm.

"You expect miracles," he said, taking a step back. Glancing around the small, cloth-walled room, the patients huddled beneath the bloodstained sheets, he shook his head. "You can stay here until the city crumbles around you, and the stink of dead bodies makes your insides rot. You might not have a family, but I haven't seen mine in weeks, and I don't even know if they're still alive." His face crumpled with worry and fear, and I felt a stab of guilt before he curled a lip and sneered at me. "So you stay here with your cadavers and the virus until one of them kills you. I'm done."

He spun on his heel and walked across the room, pushed through the door in a swoosh of plastic, and was gone.

I wanted, badly, to sink into a chair, to rub my tired eyes and even get a little sleep, but that wasn't an option. Glancing at the two remaining interns, I gave them what I hoped was an encouraging smile.

"Maggie, go check on Ms. Sawyer," I said, and she nodded, looking relieved to do something that didn't involve large, violent patients. "Jen, why don't you check the supplies, see what we have and what we're running out of. I'll keep an eye on Mr. Johnson."

They hurried off, and I hoped I'd managed to hide the worry and constant strain of keeping this clinic alive, the despair that another had gone, given up, and the secret fear that he was right. I noted the hopeless slump of their shoulders, the exhausted way they carried themselves, and knew they wouldn't last much longer, either.

Walking to our tiny operating room, I turned on the sink and ran my arms beneath the cold water, letting the dried blood swirl into the basin. I glanced up, and a thin, pale girl stared back at me from the mirror, blood speckling her face and streaked through her fine blond hair, which hadn't been washed for days. Dark circles crouched beneath green eyes, the telltale marks of exhaustion, her cheeks gaunt and wasted.

"You look hideous," I told my reflection, which nodded in agreement. "You're going to have to sleep sometime or you'll be fainting on the patients."

But there was no time for rest, no time to take a break, especially now that Eric was gone. This small clinic, hastily set up on the edge of urban D.C., was the last hope for those infected with Red Lung, the virus that had decimated the city and turned the downtown area into a war zone. Makeshift clinics had been constructed around the city to help with the overwhelming number of sick, but it was never enough. As more people died and civilization broke down, chaos and riots had spread rapidly with nothing to stop them, the worst of mankind coming to the surface. All the other hospitals had closed down, the dead left to rot in their rooms, or laid out in rows in the parking lot. As the city had emptied, even the other clinics had begun to vanish, the doctors and staff either dying or giving up in despair. As far as I knew, this was one of the last, but there were still infected people out there, and they deserved some kind of hope. Even if it was very slim.

Splashing water on my face, I rubbed my tired eyes. Now, if I could just cling to a bit of that hope myself.

"Hello?" A deep voice cut through the beeping machinery and coughing of patients. "Anyone here?"

I jerked up. Hastily I dried my hands, scrubbed the towel over my face and hurried out to the main room.

Two strangers stood just inside the entrance flaps, both young men, one leaning on the other with an arm around his shoulders. I blinked in shock; the second man had on a stained white lab coat much like mine. He had light brown hair and glasses, and even across the room, I could see he was badly hurt; his shirt was torn, especially his sleeve, and his arm looked as if he'd stuck it in a meat grinder. The other was tall and broad-shouldered, holding his friend's weight easily. His shirt and jeans were stained with blood, though I suspected it wasn't his own. His gaze met mine, dark eyes appraising beneath a mess of short, mahogany-colored hair.

"Can you help us?" he asked, his voice rough with worry. "We saw this place from the road. Is there a doctor around?"

"I'm in charge," I said, stepping forward. "But this is a quarantined zone. You can't be here—you'll both be exposed to the virus."

"Please." His brown eyes grew pleading, and he glanced down at his friend, who seemed barely conscious, hanging from his shoulders. "There's nowhere else to go—the other hospitals are empty. He'll die."

I sighed and gave a brisk nod. "In here," I ordered, and he followed me into the operating room, hefting his friend onto the table as gently as he could. The other moaned, delirious, and his arm flopped to the counter. His skin was flushed, feverish, his face tight with pain.

I cut away his shirt and coat, revealing an upper torso that was pale and slightly overweight, but he didn't seem to be wounded anywhere else. I would examine him thoroughly later, but the arm was the most pressing concern. Gently, I lifted the mangled limb from the table to study it. Several torn, bloody holes ran up the limb from wrist to elbow. The flesh around the wounds was hot and puffy, deep punctures well on their way to infection.

"These are teeth marks," I said, frowning at the strangely symmetrical patterns through the mess of blood and shredded skin. "What attacked him?"

"I don't know." The voice behind me was husky, evasive, but I wasn't really listening. I studied the arm further, trying to match the bite patterns with what I'd seen before: dogs, cats, even a horse, once. Nothing fit.

Except...

"These...almost look like human bite marks." But that wasn't right, either, not with this type of deep puncture wound. The thing that had left these marks had long canines like a predator. Human teeth were not capable of this.

The stranger's voice was stiff, uncomfortable. "Can you save him?"

"I'll try." Turning, I fixed the stranger with a firm stare. He gazed back, eyes hooded. "What is your relation to this man, Mr....?"

"Archer. Ben Archer. And we're not related." He nodded to the body on the table. "Nathan and I... I worked for him. He's a friend."

"All right, Mr. Archer. Not to be rude, but you can either help me or get out. I can't be tripping over you every time I turn around. If you think you can take direction and do exactly as I tell you, you're welcome to stay."

He nodded. I pointed to the counter behind us. "Get some gloves on, then. This is going to be messy."

He turned, and I blinked. Blood covered one side of his shirt, and the fabric was torn, sticking to the skin. Several deep gashes were raked across his shoulder blade, still raw and bloody, though he didn't seem to notice them.

"What happened to your back, Mr. Archer?"

He jerked up, wincing. "Ah," he muttered, not meeting my gaze. "Nathan was attacked and...I got it when I went to help. It's nothing, not that deep. Please, help him first."

"I intend to, but as soon as we're done here, you need to let me take care of that. And you *are* going to tell me what happened when we're done, Mr. Archer."

He nodded, and we worked in tense, determined silence, broken only by me barking orders, directing my helper to hold this or fetch that. I didn't mince words or attempt civility; my focus was on saving this man's life. But my impromptu assistant took all direction without comment until the task was complete.

"There." I pulled the final stitch shut, tying it off with a short jerk. The man lay on the table, disinfected, bandaged and sewn up the best I could manage with such limited supplies. "That's it. We'll just have to keep an eye on him, now."

Ben Archer stood behind me. I could feel his hooded gaze on the table in front of us. "Will he make it?"

"He's lost a lot of blood," I said, turning around. "He needs a transfusion, but there's no way we can do that now. The wounds haven't gone septic, but I'm mostly worried about his fever." The man's face fell, and I offered a kind lie out of habit. "We'll have to wait and see if he survives the night, but I think he has a chance of pulling through."

"Thank you," he murmured. He seemed relieved but shifted restlessly at the edge of the counter, as if he expected something to come lunging through the operating room doors any second. "I didn't get your name, Doctor...?"

"Just call me Kylie." I really looked at him for the first time, seeing the stubble on his chin, the haunted look in his dark brown eyes. His shoulders were broad, his arms muscular under his shirt, as if he was used to hard labor.

"Miss Kylie." He shot a glance at the tiny window, at the late-afternoon sun slanting in through the glass. "I'm grateful for your help. But we have to go. Now."

"Excuse me?"

"We have to leave," he repeated to my astonishment. "We can't stay here. I'm sorry, but we have to go."

I scowled at him. "You're not going anywhere, Mr. Archer. Your friend is still badly hurt, and you don't look so good yourself. What you're *going* to do is sit down, let me take care of those lacerations on your back, and tell me what the hell happened to your friend."

He flinched, one hand going to his shoulder, but shook his head. "No," he whispered, and the guilt on his face was overwhelming. "We can't stay here," he protested in a stronger voice. "We have to leave the city." His gaze flicked to

mine, intense. "You should come with us. Everyone should—
everyone who can still walk needs to go. It...isn't safe out
there anymore."

"When was it ever safe?" I murmured. He took a breath to
argue again, but my voice grew sharp. "Move him now, and
your friend will die," I stated bluntly. "With that fever and
those wounds, he'll be dead by morning. You leave, you kill
him. It's as simple as that."

He slumped, the fight going out of him. I gestured to the
stool, and he sank down, his posture defeated. "If you would
take your shirt off, Mr. Archer," I urged, trying to remain
businesslike as I fished a needle and thread from my coat pockets. He blinked, pulling back a little, and I sighed. "I don't have
the time or patience for modesty, Mr. Archer. And we ran out
of hospital gowns the first week we were here. So, please." I
gestured with the needle. "Take off your shirt."

Wearily, he complied, pulling the garment over his head
without so much as a wince. I kept my expression professional,
but my gaze roamed over the tanned, powerful shoulders and
sculpted chest as he dropped his shirt to the floor. Things were
bleak, but I wasn't blind. Ben Archer was gorgeous; you didn't
need a Ph.D. to see that.

He didn't move as I walked up behind him, examining the
five deep lacerations that ran from his shoulder nearly to the
center of his back. They looked like...claw marks. I shivered.
Something was very wrong here.

"What happened to you and your friend?" I began, dabbing
the wounds gently with an alcohol wipe. He didn't flinch,
though the lacerations were quite deep, and I knew the alcohol stung. "Did you hear me, Mr. Archer?"

"Ben. Just Ben."

"All right, Ben." I wiped the last of the blood away and
reached for the needle and thread. "You still haven't answered

my question. Those bite wounds on your friend, they aren't normal. What happened?"

I felt him hesitate. My voice grew a little harder. "Don't lie to me, Mr. Archer. If I'm going to help him, I need to know exactly what happened. Any information you withhold could end up killing him, or my other patients. Now—last time—tell me what happened."

"We..." Ben paused, as if fighting himself, struggling to get the words out. "Nathan and I...we were attacked," he finally admitted.

"Yes, that I gathered," I said, gently touching his shoulder. His skin was warm, and he finally flinched at my touch. "I'm going to start stitching now, so brace yourself."

He nodded.

"So, something attacked you," I continued, sinking the needle into the smooth, tanned skin, talking quickly to keep him distracted. "What was it?"

"I...I don't know."

"What do you mean, you don't know?" I frowned as I pulled a stitch closed, seeing him grit his teeth. "Something obviously savaged your friend and tore the hell out of your shoulder. What was it?"

"I didn't see it very clearly," Ben muttered. "It was dark, and the thing moved so fast." He shrugged, then grunted in pain as the motion pulled at the stitches. "I thought it was human, but..." He trailed off again, and I frowned over his shoulder.

"Ben, your friend was bitten by something with canines at least an inch long. Humans don't have teeth like that."

He raised his head just as I looked up at him, and for a second, our faces were inches apart. Guilt, horror and fear lay open on his face; he had the look of a soldier who had seen far too much and would be eternally haunted by it.

"You should leave," he whispered once more, his voice like

a ragged, open wound. And my stomach flip-flopped at the look in his eyes. "Don't ask questions, Kylie, just trust me. Get out of here as soon as you can. Go home, leave this place, and don't look back."

I took a deep, steadying breath.

"I can't leave," I told him firmly. "I won't leave my patients, so that's out of the question. Besides, I don't have a home to go back to." He looked away, and I wished I could turn his head back, force him to meet my gaze. "You're not telling me everything," I said, and his face shut down into a blank mask. My eyes narrowed. "What are you hiding?"

"Miss Kylie?"

Maggie appeared in the door. Seeing Ben, she blushed and looked down at her feet. "Ms. Sawyer was complaining that it hurt to breathe. I gave her a shot of morphine for the pain and a sedative to help her sleep."

"Good girl," I said, feeling a lump rise to my throat. The final stages of Red Lung, before the victim began coughing uncontrollably and drowning in their own blood, was difficult, painful breathing.

I felt Ben's eyes on me, sympathetic and knowing. Suddenly self-conscious, I drew away. I didn't need his pity or his advice to leave—as if I could just walk out. And it was clear I wouldn't be getting anything further out of him, at least not now. "I have to get back to my patients," I told him, beckoning Maggie into the room. "I'm sorry. Maggie, would you mind taking care of Mr. Archer, please?"

"Sure." Maggie smiled at Ben, and he gave her a tired nod. I left them together and wandered back to the main room, checking the rows of patients along the makeshift walls. For now, everyone seemed okay; comfortable and in no pain, at least. Except for Ms. Sawyer's raspy breathing and the occasional bloody cough that I couldn't do anything about, the clinic was quiet. An event that occurred less and less, as Red Lung continued its war on the human body and continued to win.

I pondered what Ben had told me. He and his friend had been attacked, there was no mistaking that. It wasn't uncommon, sadly. With the breakdown of normal society, human beings reverted to their base instincts and started preying on each other. In the early days of the plague, not a day had gone by that I hadn't heard gunshots, screams or other sounds of distant chaos. I didn't doubt they'd been attacked, but the wounds on Nathan's arm and Ben's shoulder didn't look like anything I'd seen before.

What was Ben Archer hiding? What wasn't he telling me?

"Kylie." Jenna appeared as I made another circle through the rows of cots. The intern had been training to be a nurse and was older than me by several years, but always took my instructions without fail or complaint. Her gaze was sympathetic as she pulled me aside. "You're exhausted," she stated, blue eyes appraising, and I didn't argue with her. "How long since you slept last?"

I shrugged, and she patted my arm. "Go lie down. Maggie and I can take care of things for a few hours."

"I don't know. Ms. Sawyer—"

"You've done everything you could for her," Jenna said in a low voice. "Seriously, Kylie, get some sleep. While you still can. You're going to fall over if you don't rest soon, and no one can afford that. I promise, we'll come get you if anything happens."

I nodded. It was getting close to eighteen hours with no sleep, and I *was* tired. But before I left the room, I made a note to check on my newest patients, make sure Nathan was comfortable at least. And maybe, I could get the last of that story out of Ben Archer.

I didn't quite get that far. Instead, I went to Doc Adams's old office and collapsed on the cot against the far wall, pulling the sheet over my face. I thought I wouldn't sleep with all the dark thoughts swirling through my head, but I was out almost before I touched the pillow.

It seemed only a few minutes had passed before someone touched my shoulder, jostling me awake. Blearily, I opened my eyes and glanced up at Maggie, who stood over me with a half-worried, half-reluctant expression.

"Yeah?" I mumbled, struggling to sit up.

"Sorry, Miss Kylie." Maggie bit her lip. "But, I wanted to let you know, Mr. Johnson just passed away."

I sighed, scrubbing a hand over my eyes, grief and anger and disappointment flaring up momentarily. "All right, I'll be right out. Thank you, Maggie."

She nodded and scurried away. Standing, I put my fingers to my temples, massaging the headache pounding behind my eyes.

Dammit. Another one lost. Another life taken by the plague, and I couldn't do anything about it. Eric had been right; this was futile. Those people out there, coughing and gagging and fighting to breathe, they wouldn't survive. Not at this stage of the virus. But I couldn't abandon them. I'd promised my patients I would fight to the end, and that was what I was going to do.

Grabbing my coat, which I'd tossed on the desk before falling into unconsciousness, I walked out of the office.

And ran smack into a large, solid chest as I emerged, yawning and rubbing my face. With a yelp, I stumbled back, looking up into Ben Archer's worried brown eyes.

"Sorry." His deep voice held traces of alarm, and I gave

him a wary look. "I need to talk to you. Something is wrong with Nate, and I don't know what to do for him."

My head pounded. The stress, disappointment, and looming sense of pointlessness were starting to get to me, but I put my feelings aside to focus on what I had to do.

"Walk with me." I started down the hall, and he followed at my side. The clinic was dark now, as evening stole in through the door and cloaked everything in shadow. I could hear the generators out back, humming away, but we were running out of gas, and not much power was left for lights.

We reached the spot where Nathan was being kept, one of the smaller rooms that was separated from the main wing, away from the sick. A chair stood in the corner, probably where Ben had been sitting. Jenna hovered next to the patient, looking grim.

The man on the bed groaned, sounding delirious. He was definitely paler, and blood had soaked through the bandages on his arm. But what was most worrying was the red fluid seeping from beneath his eyelids. It oozed slowly over his cheeks, cutting two crimson paths down his skin, and it could be only one thing.

I swabbed it with a cotton ball, just to be sure. Yes, it was definitely blood. Ben came up behind me, peering over my shoulder.

"What's wrong with him?"

"I...don't know." Though I hated admitting it. Peeling back his lids, I shone a light over his pupils, checking for wounds or scratches. Nothing. "The only thing I can think of is a sub-conjunctival hemorrhage, or Ebola, as unlikely as that is. Sadly, the only way to know for sure would be to conduct blood tests, but we don't have any way to do that here. We'll just have to keep him under surveillance and see what happens."

I caught a whiff of something foul, rotten, like the stench

of a decaying animal, and my heart sank. Frowning, I shooed Ben out of the way and bent over the wounded man, gently unwrapping the gauze to see the wounds on his arm.

The wounds were clean. The skin around them was still puffy and red, but the bites themselves looked fine. Or at least not infected. And yet, I could still smell the faint stench of rot and decay that suggested gangrene or wounds that had gone septic.

Then I realized it wasn't coming off his arm, but the body as a whole.

Puzzled, I cleaned and rebandaged the arm, feeling Ben's worried eyes on me the whole time. Nathan groaned and tossed restlessly, and I finally gave him a shot of morphine to calm him down. As his tortured thrashing stilled and he drifted into a drugged sleep, I heard Ben take a ragged breath.

"He's getting worse."

I turned to face him, wiping my hands. "There's no infection, as far as I can see. His fever is getting worse, yes, but we've done all we can for him now. We just have to wait and see if he pulls out of it." Ben sagged, looking lost and hopeless, unsure what to do. Sinking into the chair, he ran both hands over his face and sighed.

I hesitated. Then, not really knowing why, I walked over to him and put a hand on his shoulder. "I'm not giving up," I told him softly. "And you shouldn't, either. Why don't you get some sleep? There's an extra cot in the office if you need it. I'll let you know if there are any changes."

He looked up with a faint, grateful smile. "Thank you," he murmured. "But, if it's all the same, I'd like to stay. I should be here if…anything happens to him."

"Miss Kylie." Maggie walked into the room. The petite intern smiled shyly at Ben before turning to me. "Sorry to interrupt, but Jenna wanted to know if you'd like us to move Mr. Johnson's body to the back lot now or down to storage."

I stifled a groan. "I don't think Mr. Johnson will fit in any of the storage units we have down there," I said, aware of how morbid this must sound to Ben. It had become so common-place to us now, we didn't even think about it anymore. "If you and Jenna will get him on a gurney, I'll take him out back."

She nodded and padded away, and Ben gave me a worried look. "Out back?"

"There's an empty lot we've been using for body stor-age," I said tiredly. "When the freezers downstairs get full, we move them outside. This place was set up pretty fast, so it didn't come with a proper morgue. We've had to improvise."

"You're going outside? Now?"

"I can't leave a cadaver lying on a bed all night."

He rose swiftly, his gaze narrowing. "I'll come with you."

I frowned at his sudden change of mood. "There's no need. I'm capable of handling a dead body by myself. Besides—" I glanced back toward the bed "—I thought you wanted to stay with your friend."

"Please." He took a step forward, not intimidating, but in-tense. "Let me help. It's the least I can do."

There was more to it than that, I thought. I wasn't stupid. He was still hiding something, and I was going to find out what. Just not tonight. I was tired, my head hurt and I didn't want to fight him. "All right," I sighed. "If you think you can stomach working with a dead body, then I'll put those muscles of yours to work. Follow me."

We walked back to the main room, where Maggie and Jenna were struggling to load the body onto a gurney. In times past, I'd had a couple of the male interns perform this task. But they were gone now; it was just the three of us left.

Plus Ben. Who didn't flinch as he hefted Mr. Johnson onto

the cart, handling the body like he might a sick calf. His face remained businesslike as he laid the corpse down gently, and Jenna and Maggie gaped at him.

As I covered the body with a sheet, I caught a faint hint of rot coming off the corpse. What the hell? It hadn't even been an hour since Mr. Johnson had passed; there was no way the body would start to decompose so quickly.

"What is it?" Ben asked quietly. I shook my head.

"Nothing." I flipped the sheet over the body's head, and the smell vanished. Maybe I'd imagined it, or maybe I was smelling something else: a dead animal outside. I maneuvered the gurney around him and the interns, ducked through the curtains surrounding the bed and headed out the back door. Ben followed.

Outside, the temperature was cool, chilly even. Which was a good thing, given the number of dead things lying everywhere around us, hidden away in houses and beds; the ones who had died alone and forgotten. As it was, the stench coming from the back lot was always there, drifting in the clinic when the breeze blew just right. If it had been high summer, the smell would've been unbearable.

As we made our way down the sidewalk, I was struck again by how quiet everything was. Not long ago, the sounds of sirens and cars, screaming, gunshots and breaking glass, had been constant. Just across the river, in monument D.C., the city had been a war zone. Now, an eerie silence hung over everything, and the buildings around us were dark. Of course, our small clinic was located just outside the city limits, so I didn't know what was happening closer to downtown. Occasionally, I heard screams or the roar of a distant car engine, signs that there was still human life somewhere out there. But the city seemed abandoned now, left to the desperate and the dying.

I sneaked a glance at Ben, walking beside me, one hand on

the corner of the gurney. His gaze scanned the buildings and the shadows around us, every fiber of his body on high alert. The same look he'd had in the clinic when night was starting to fall, only amplified a hundred-fold.

He didn't come out here to help me, I realized with a cold feeling in my stomach. *He's afraid there's something out here now.* I pulled the gurney to a halt in the middle of the sidewalk. "Ben..."

Something big slipped from the shadows into our path, making us both jump. I flinched, but Ben lunged forward and grabbed my arm as if prepared to yank me behind him. A stray dog, big and black, drew back when it saw us. It dropped what it was carrying and darted out of sight between two cars, its tail between its legs.

Ben relaxed. Quickly, he dropped my wrist, looking embarrassed. "Sorry," he murmured, staring at the ground. "I'm not usually this jumpy, I swear. Are you all right?"

I rubbed my arm, wincing from the strength in those hands. "I'm fine," I told him, and was about to ask him why he was so twitchy. But then I noticed what the dog had been carrying and stifled a groan.

"Is that...an arm?" Ben asked, peering past the gurney.

"Yeah." I sighed, knowing where the dog had probably gotten it. As we got closer to our destination, the smell began to permeate the darkness around us. That familiar knot of dread, guilt, sorrow and anger coiled in my stomach. "Just a warning," I told Ben, "this isn't going to be pretty. Steel yourself."

"For what?"

I smiled humorlessly and turned the corner of the alley.

From the corner of my eye, I saw Ben straighten, though he didn't say anything. The drone of insects was a constant hum over the hundreds of bodies lined up in neat rows up and down the empty lot. Most were covered with sheets and tarps, but several covers were torn off or had blown away, leaving the corpses to stare empty-eyed at the sky. And, from the looks of the older, "riper" corpses, the scavengers were already gathering en masse.

Ben made a sound in the back of his throat, as if he was struggling not to gag. For a moment, I was sorry for bringing him out here, letting him see the stark reality we faced every day. But he set his jaw and walked with me to the edge of the last row, where I'd laid three people—a mother and her two sons—side by side last week. I tried not to look at them as we lifted Mr. Johnson's body up in the sheet and set it on the pavement. But it was hard not to remember. I'd stayed up countless nights with that family, trying desperately to save them, but the virus had taken the mother first and the boys hours later, and that failure still haunted me.

Ben was quiet as we left the lot and pushed the empty gurney back to the clinic. He didn't say anything, but instead of scanning the streets and shadows, he appeared deep in thought, brooding over what he had just seen. It *was* pretty sobering, when you realized how much we had lost, how insidious this thing was: an enemy that couldn't be stopped, put down, reasoned with. It made you realize…we might not make it through this.

"How do you do it?"

I blinked. I'd gotten so used to his silence; the question caught me off guard. Strange, thinking I knew a man after only a few hours with him. His brown eyes were on me now, solemn and assessing.

"Because you have to," I said, ducking through the back door with him behind me. "Because you have to give people hope. Because sometimes that's the only thing that will get them through, the only thing that keeps them alive."

His next words were a whisper. I barely caught them as

we moved through the main room into the dark hall beyond. "What if there is no hope?"

I shoved the gurney against the wall and turned, pinning him with my fiercest glare. "There is *always* hope, Ben. And I will thank you to keep any doom-and-gloom observations to yourself while you're here. I don't need my patients hearing it. Or my interns, for that matter."

He ducked his head, looking contrite. "I'm sorry. It's just... it's hard to keep an open mind when you've seen...what I have." I raised an eyebrow at him, and he had the grace to wince. "And...you've seen a lot worse, I know. My apologies. I'll...stop whining, now."

I sighed. "Have you had anything to eat lately?" I asked, and he shook his head. "Come on, then. We don't have much, but I can at least make you some coffee. Instant, anyway. You look like you could use some."

"That would be nice," Ben admitted, smiling, "but you don't have to go to the trouble."

"Not at all. Besides, *I* could use some, so keep me company for a while, okay?" He nodded, and we headed upstairs to the small break room and dining area that hadn't seen much use since the clinic opened. The fridge and the microwave hadn't been used since the power had gone out and we'd switched to the generators, but the gas stove worked well enough to heat water. I boiled two cups of bottled water, spooned in liberal amounts of instant coffee and handed a mug to Ben, sitting at the table.

"It's not great, but at least it's hot," I said, sliding into the seat across from his. He smiled his thanks and held the mug in both hands, watching me through the steam. Taking a cautious sip, I scrunched my forehead and forced the bitter swallow down. "Ugh. You'd think I'd get used to this stuff by now. I think Starbucks ruined me for life."

That actually got a chuckle out of him, and he sipped his drink without complaint or grotesque faces. I studied him over my mug, pretending to frown into my coffee but sneaking glances at him every few seconds. The haunted look had left his face, and he seemed a bit calmer. Though the worry still remained in his eyes. I found myself wishing I could reach over the table, stroke his stubbly cheek and tell him everything would be fine.

Then I wondered what had brought *that* on.

"Tell me about yourself," he said, setting the mug down on the table, suddenly giving me his full attention. "No offense, but you're awfully young and pretty to be running a clinic alone. And you don't wear masks like the others. Aren't you afraid you'll get sick, too?"

Absurdly, I blushed at the compliment. "I caught Red Lung early," I told him, and his eyebrows arched into his hair. "From one of the patients at the hospital where I worked. Kept me in bed for three days straight, and everyone thought I would die, but I pulled out of it before my lungs started disintegrating."

"You're a survivor?" Ben sounded shocked. I nodded.

"One of the lucky sixteen percent." I looked down at my hands, remembering. Lying in a sterile hospital room, coughing bloody flecks onto the sheets. The worried, bleak faces of my colleagues. "Everyone was surprised when I pulled through," I said, taking another sip of the stuff that claimed it was coffee. "And afterward, I felt so grateful and lucky, I volunteered to help Doc Adams when he set this place up. Especially after..." I trailed off.

"After?" Ben prodded.

I swallowed. "After I found out that my family all passed away from the virus," I muttered. "They got sick when I was in the hospital, only they never recovered. I found out when

I was released and planned to go home, only I didn't have a home to go back to."

I thought of the little home in the suburbs, the place I'd spent my childhood, with its tiny front yard and single-car garage. My mom's small but perfect flower garden, my dad's ancient leather armchair. My old room. It had just been the three of us; I didn't have any brothers or sisters, but I'd never been lonely. I'd had friends, and my parents had filled whatever void was left, encouraging me to chase my dreams. Dad had always said he knew I would become something big, either a doctor or an astronaut or a scientist, and pretty much let me do whatever I'd wanted. I'd left for college as soon as I'd graduated, eager to see what was out there, but had always come home for breaks and holidays. Both Mom and Dad had been so proud, so eager to hear of my life at school. It had never crossed my mind that one day they would just be...gone.

When I'd returned to the house after my parents had died, I'd stood in the living room, with its empty armchair and ticking clock, and realized how much I had lost. Curling up in my Dad's old chair, I'd cried for about an hour, but when it was over, I'd left the house with a new resolve. I couldn't save my parents, but maybe I could save other people. Red Lung, the silent killer, was my enemy now. And I would do whatever I could to destroy it.

Across from me, Ben was quiet. I kept my gaze on the table between us, so I was surprised when his rough, calloused hand covered my own. "I'm sorry," he murmured as I looked up at him. I smiled shakily.

"It's okay. They went quickly, or at least that's what the doctors said." My throat closed, and I sniffled, taking a breath to open it. Ben squeezed my palm; his thick fingers were gentle, his skin warm. A shiver raced up my arm. "What about you?"

I asked, as Ben pulled his hand back, cupping it around his mug again. "Where's your family? If it's not too personal?"

"It's not." He sighed, his face going dark as he looked away. "My family owns a big farm out west," he said in a flat voice. "Nathan and I were on our way there, to see if anyone survived. They're pretty isolated, so we were hoping the outbreak hadn't reached them yet. I don't know, I haven't seen them for a while."

A farm. That fit him, I thought, looking at his broad shoulders and calloused, work-toughened hands. I could imagine him slinging bales of hay and wrestling cows. But there was something else about him, too, something not quite so rough. "What were you doing in the city?" I asked, and his face darkened even more. "You said you haven't seen them in a while. How long has it been?"

"Four years." He set his mug down and put his chin on his hands, brooding over them. "I moved to the city four years ago, and since then I haven't even talked to my folks. They wanted me to take over the farm, like everyone before me, but I wanted to finish school at Illinois Tech." He gave a bitter snort. "My dad and I got into a huge fight one day—I even threw a punch at him—and I walked out. Haven't seen them since."

"I'm sorry, Ben." I thought of my family, my dad who had been so proud I was going into medicine. My mom who always told me to dream big. "That has to suck."

He hung his head. "I haven't spoken to them in years. Mom always sent me Christmas cards, telling me how the farm is doing, that they miss me, but I never answered. Not once. And now…" His voice broke a little, and he hunched his shoulders. "With the plague and the virus and everything going to hell, I don't know how they're doing. I don't…I don't even know if they're alive."

He covered his eyes with a hand. I stood, quietly walked around the table to sit beside him, and put my arm around his shoulders. They trembled, though Ben didn't move or make a sound otherwise. How many times had I done this; comforted a family member who had lost someone dear? More times then I cared to remember, especially with the rapid spread of the plague. But it felt different this time. Before, I had been there to offer support when someone needed it, not caring if it was from a virtual stranger. With Ben Archer, I truly wanted to be there for him, let him know there was someone he could lean on.

I still didn't know where this was coming from. The man was a virtual stranger himself; I'd known him only a few hours. But I stayed there, holding him and saying nothing, as he succumbed to his grief in the small, dirty break room of the clinic. I had the feeling he'd been holding this in a long time, and it had finally broken through.

Finally, he took a ragged breath and pulled away, not looking at me. I rose and went to refill our coffee mugs, giving him time to compose himself.

"Thank you," he murmured as I handed him the filled mug again, and I knew it wasn't just for the coffee. I smiled and sat down, but before I had even settled myself, footsteps pounded outside the door, and Maggie rushed into the room.

"Miss Kylie?"

I stifled a groan even as I rose quickly to my feet, Ben following my example. "Yes, Maggie, what is it?"

"It's Mr. Archer's friend," Maggie said, and Ben straightened quickly. The intern shot him a half-fearful, half-sorrowful look and turned back to me. "I'm so sorry. He slipped into a coma a few minutes ago, and we can't wake him up."

• 3 •

"We've done everything we can for him."

I wiped my hands on a towel, gazing wearily at the man beneath the covers, so pale he could have been made of paper. His limp hair and clothes were the only things of color left, and the skin on his face had shrunk tightly to his bones, making him look skeletal. His bandages had been changed again, IV tubes had been put in and I'd given him several shots of antibiotics to try to help with the fever. The smell—that ominous, disturbing smell of rot and death—still clung to him, though I'd checked and double-checked for any sign of gangrene. There was none that I could see, but that wasn't what worried me most.

Nathan lay on his back beneath the sheets, his shallow and raspy breathing the only indicator that he was still alive. Blood flecked his lips, making my stomach knot in dread. Jenna's sad, knowing eyes met mine over the patient. I didn't need to listen to the gurgle in his chest to know. He was infected with Red Lung. The virus had gotten him, too.

Ben stood in the corner, looking on with hooded eyes. I didn't know how to tell him. "Ben…"

"He has it." Ben's voice was flat, his eyes blank.

"I'm so sorry." He gave no indication that he'd heard. "We'll keep him under surveillance and make him as comfortable as we can, but…" I paused, hating that I had to say the next words. "But I think you should prepare yourself for the worst."

Ben gave a single, short nod. I shooed the interns out of the room and walked up to him. "Does he have any family that you are aware of?"

"No." Ben sank down in the chair, running his hands over his scalp. "Nate's family all lived here and…they were gone before we started out." I put a hand on his shoulder, and he stirred a little. "Sorry, but could I have a few minutes?"

"Sure," I whispered, and walked out, leaving him alone with his friend. As I ducked through the frame, I heard the thump of his fist against the armrest, a muffled, broken curse, and swallowed my own frustrated tears as the door clicked behind us.

Maggie and Jenna looked so disheartened when I returned to the main room that I told them both to get some sleep.

"I can handle the patients alone for a few hours," I said as Jenna protested, though Maggie looked ready to fall over. "They're not going anywhere, and I'll call you if I need assistance. Get some rest."

"Are you sure, Kylie?" Jenna asked, even as Maggie stumbled away, heading for the few extra cots upstairs. "Maggie and I can take turns, if you want one of us down here with you."

I opened my mouth to answer and caught the subtle hint of rot, drifting from the beds along the wall. My stomach turned over, and the scent vanished as quickly as it had come.

"I'll be fine," I told Jenna firmly. "Go get some shut-eye. Lie down, at least. That's an order."

She looked reluctant but left the room after Maggie. When they were gone, I hurried over to Ms. Sawyer, slipping through the curtains to the side of her bed.

Her skin was chalky white, and the faint smell of decay clung to her, as it had to Nathan. Looking at her face, my blood ran cold. Though her chest rose and fell with shallow, labored breaths, her eyes were half open, and red fluid seeped from beneath the lids.

Just like Nathan.

As I went to wipe the blood from her other cheek, Ms. Sawyer jerked in her sleep, lunging toward my hand without opening her eyes. A short hiss came from her open mouth, and I yanked my hand back, heart pounding, as she sank down, still unconscious.

She didn't move again, and about an hour after midnight I woke Jenna, helped her move the body onto a gurney, and took it down to storage. Then, because the freezers in the basement were full, we woke Maggie and began the painstaking task of moving all the bodies to the back lot, freeing up space for future victims. We didn't know then how soon we would need it.

The epidemic began several hours later.

It started with Ms. Sawyer's bed neighbor, a middle-aged man who had been clinging stubbornly to life and who I'd hoped had a good chance of pulling through. An hour or so before dawn, he started bleeding from the eyes and rapidly went downhill. He was dead two hours later. Then, one by one, all the patients began weeping the bloody red tears and coughing violently, causing Jenna, Maggie and me to scurry from bed to bed, trying desperately to slow the flood. By the time the late-afternoon sun began setting over the tops of the empty buildings, half our patients were gone, with the other half barely holding on to life. We didn't even have time to move the corpses from their beds and resorted to covering them with sheets when they died. As evening wore on, the number of bodies under sheets outnumbered the living. With every death, my anger grew, until I was swearing under my breath and snapping at my poor interns.

At last, the flood slowed. The patients still bled from the

eyes, and the smell of decay had permeated the room, but there was a lull in the storm of coughing and gasping and death. As the sun set and the light began fading rapidly, I called Jenna and Maggie into the hall. Jenna looked on edge, and Maggie had succumbed to exhausted tears as I drew them aside, fighting my own frustration and the urge to lash out at everything around me.

"Where is Mr. Archer?" I asked in a low voice. I'd never seen a roomful of patients decline so rapidly, and I had a sneaking, terrible suspicion. I hoped I was wrong, but I needed answers, and there was only one person who could give them to me.

"I think he's still in the room with his friend," Maggie sniffled. "We haven't seen him all day."

I spun on a heel and marched down the hall. Blood from the eyes, the strange bite marks, the rotten smell without the infection. Nathan's symptoms had spread to my patients, and Ben knew what it was. He knew, and I was fed up with this hiding, keeping secrets. Less than a day after Ben Archer had stepped into my sick ward with his friend, I had a roomful of corpses. He was going to tell me what he knew if I had to beat it out of him.

I swept into his room, bristling for a fight, and stopped.

Ben sat slumped in the corner chair, eyes closed, snoring softly. Exhaustion had finally caught up to him, too. Despite my anger, I hesitated, reluctant to wake him. Sleep was a precious commodity here; you snatched it where and when you could. Still, I would have woken him right then if I hadn't seen what had happened to the body in the room with us.

Nathan lay on the bed, unmoving. Unnaturally still. The faint smell of rot still lingered around him, and in the shadows, his skin was the color of chalk. I moved to his bedside, and a chill ran up my spine. His eyes were open, gazing sightlessly at the ceiling, but his pupils had turned a blank, solid white.

The chair scraped in the corner as Ben rose. I held my breath as his footsteps clicked softly over the linoleum to stand beside me. I heard his ragged intake of breath and glanced up at him.

He had gone pale, so white I thought he might pass out. The look on his face was awful; grief and rage and guilt and horror, all at once. He gripped the edge of the railing in both hands, swaying on his feet, and I put a hand out to steady him, my anger forgotten.

"Ben."

He glanced at me, a terrifyingly feverish look in his eyes, and his voice was a hoarse rasp as he grabbed my arm. "We have to destroy the body."

"What?"

"Right now." He looked at the corpse of his friend and shuddered. "Please, don't ask questions. We need to burn it, quickly. Does this place have an incinerator?"

"Ben, *what are you talking about?*" I wrenched my arm from his grasp and glared up at him. "All right, this has gone far enough. What are you hiding? Where did you and Nathan come from? He was sick, wasn't he?" Ben flinched, and my fury rose up again. "He was sick, and now I have a roomful of dead patients because you're hiding something! I want answers, and you're going to tell me everything, right now!"

"Oh, God." If possible, Ben paled even more. He glanced down the hall, running his fingers through his hair. "Oh, shit. This has all gone crazy. I'm sorry, Kylie. I'll tell you everything. After we destroy the body, I'll tell you everything I know, I swear. Just…we have to take care of this now. Please." He grabbed my arm. "Help me, and then I'll tell you anything you want."

I clenched my fists, actually tempted to hit him, to strike him across that ruggedly handsome face. Taking a deep breath to calm my rage, I spoke in a low, controlled tone. "Fine. I don't know what this is about, or why you want to deface your friend, but I will help you this one last time. And then, Ben Archer, you are going to tell me what the hell is going on before you leave my clinic forever."

He might have nodded, but I was already marching back into the hall, fighting a sudden, unexplainable terror. The unknown loomed around me, hovering over Nathan's corpse, the sick ward full of the newly dead. The body on the table looked…unnatural, with its pale shrunken skin and blank, dead eyes. It didn't even look human anymore.

The sick ward was eerily silent as I walked in, searching for the gurney I'd left at the edge of the room. In the shadows, bodies lay under sheets in their beds, mingled with the few still living. Jenna glanced up over a patient's cot, her cheeks wasted, her eyes sunken. Lightning flickered through the plastic over the front door, illuminating the room for a split second, and thunder growled a distant answer.

Something touched my arm, and I jumped nearly three feet. Bristling, I spun around to come face-to-face with Ben.

"Sorry." His gaze flickered to the darkened sick ward, then slid to me again. "I just… How are we going to do this? Do you need help with anything?"

I yanked a gurney from the wall. "What I *needed* is for you to have told me why you were here the first time I asked, not when all my patients started bleeding from the eyes and dying around me." He didn't respond, too preoccupied with the current tragedy to take note of my anger, and I sighed. "We'll transport the body to the empty lot," I explained, pushing the cot back down the hall, Ben trailing after. "Once we're there, you can do whatever you want."

"Outside?"

"Yes, outside! Preferably before the storm hits. I'm not starting a fire indoors so my clinic can burn down around me."

He seemed about to say something, then changed his mind and followed me silently down the hall, our footsteps and the squeaking of the gurney wheels the only sounds in the darkness.

I sneaked a glance at him. His face was blank, his eyes expressionless, though I'd seen that look before. It was a mask, a stoic front, the disguise of someone whose world had been shattered and who was holding himself together by a thread. My anger melted a little more. In my line of work, death was so common, but I had to remind myself that I wasn't just treating patients; I was treating family members, friends, people who were loved.

"I'm sorry about Nathan," I offered, trying to be sympathetic. "It wasn't your fault that he was hurt, that he was sick. Were you two very close?"

Ben nodded miserably. "He was my roommate," he muttered, briefly closing his eyes. "We went to Georgetown together. I was working on my Masters in Computer Engineering, and he got me an IT job at the lab where he worked. I was never about that biology stuff. When the virus hit, the lab threw everything else out the window to work on a cure. They kept me on for computer stuff, but Nathan was with them for the really crazy shit. He couldn't tell me much—everything was very hush-hush—but some of the things I heard..." Ben shivered. "Let's just say there were some very dark things happening in that lab. Even before the—"

He stopped in the doorway of the last room, his face draining of any remaining color. Blinking, I looked into the corner where Nathan's bed sat, where the corpse had been lying minutes ago.

The mattress was empty.

I stared at the empty bed, the logical part of my brain trying to come up with a way for a dead body to vanish from a room in a few short minutes. One of the interns must've come in and moved it. Perhaps Maggie had whisked it down to storage, by herself, without a gurney. Improbable. Impossible, really. But that was the only thing that made any sort of sense. It wasn't as if the corpse got up and walked out by itself.

Ben staggered back, shaking his head. I could see he was trembling. "No," he muttered in a low, anguished voice. "No, it isn't possible."

"I'm...I'm sure there's a rational explanation," I began, trying to ignore the chill creeping up my back. "Maggie probably took it away. Come on." I turned, suddenly eager to leave to room. The silent, empty bed, sitting motionless in the shadows, was starting to freak me out. The once-familiar walls of the clinic seemed darker now, closing in on me. "We'll check storage," I told Ben, leading him back down the corridor. It seemed longer, somehow. I could hear the groans of my patients, drifting to me from the main room. "This is nothing to worry about. She's probably down in the basement right now."

Ben didn't answer, and my words felt hollow as we reached the stairs to the sub-basement level. The door at the bottom of the steps was partially open, creaking faintly on its hinges, and the space beyond was pitch-black.

I fished the mini-flashlight from my coat and clicked it on, shining it down the stairwell. That faint smell of rot lingered in the corridor, but it could be coming from the bodies in storage.

I pushed the door to the basement open and was hit by a wave of cold, dry air that made me shiver. As usual, the scent of death was thick down here, like stepping into a tomb, and tonight it seemed even more ominous. There was no light, no need for electricity except to keep the freezers running, and everything was cloaked in suffocating darkness.

"Maggie?" My voice was a whisper as I eased inside, Ben following at my heels. The door groaned as it swung behind us, closing with a soft click. I swept the flashlight around, scanning the rows of cluttered shelves, the thick white columns that held up the building. I'd never thought about what a maze this place was until tonight. Against the far wall, barely discernible in the weak light, the huge freezers with their grisly contents gave off a faint, low hum.

"Maggie?"

Something clinked to the floor nearby, and an empty can rolled out from between the aisles, stopping at my feet. It caused a chill to skitter up my back.

"Maggie!" I hissed again, sweeping the light around. "Are you down here? Maggie!"

"Yes?"

Ben and I both jumped, swinging around as Maggie stepped between the aisles, holding several sets of folded sheets, a mini-flashlight stuck between them. She frowned at our reaction, looking confused. "Sorry, Miss Kylie. We ran of sheets to cover the bodies, so I came down to get some more. Are you all right?"

"Geez, Maggie!" I released Ben and slumped against the wall, my hand going to my heart. "You scared me half to—"

Something lunged between shelves and slammed into the girl, dragging her down with a screech. Her flashlight spun wildly, clinking to the floor before flickering out. Stumbling back, I caught a split-second glance of a spindly, emaciated creature that faintly resembled a man before it bent its head and sank its teeth into Maggie's throat.

I screamed. Maggie's body jerked and flopped to the cement, twitching, and the coppery smell of blood filled the room. My mouth gaped again, but nothing came out. In the flashlight beam, the thing raised its head and stared at me with Nathan's face, no recognition in its dead white eyes, nothing but the flat, glazed stare of a predator. It hissed, and I couldn't tear my gaze from its gleaming, jagged fangs, smeared with the blood of my intern.

My mind had gone blank. This wasn't happening. That thing couldn't exist, it was dead! The stress had finally gotten to me, and my mind had cracked.

Frozen, I stared at it, subconsciously knowing I was about to die. But the thing turned and started savaging Maggie's corpse, tearing her open with long fingers, ripping into her with its fangs. Blood splattered everywhere, painting the walls with wet ribbons, and I threw myself backward, hitting the edge of a shelf.

Something grabbed my wrist, yanking me away. I cried out and fought to break loose, hitting the arm with the flashlight, barely conscious of what I was doing, until I realized it was Ben. He dragged me across the floor and up the staircase, his eyes hard, his mouth pressed into a thin white line.

We ducked into the stairwell, the smell of blood clogging our nostrils and the sound of ripping flesh following us out. Ben slammed the door behind us and leaned against it, gasping. I stood there, shaking, trying to gather my thoughts. Rain pounded the ceiling overhead, and lightning flickered erratically over the wall, reflecting the pulse at my throat.

Maggie. Maggie was gone. And that *thing*, that horrible,

pale thing, had been Nathan. It couldn't be real! I had seen him die. I knew he was dead, but now...

This had to be a nightmare.

"Kylie." Ben's voice was low, hoarse. I blinked, attempting to focus. "We have to get out of here, now. Do you have anything you have to take, anything you absolutely can't leave behind?"

"Leave?" I stared at him, still reeling. "I can't leave. What about Jenna?"

"We'll take her, too."

"But my patients! What about the survivors? I can't leave them—"

"Kylie!" Ben pushed himself off the door and took my upper arms, forcing me to look at him. "They're dead," he whispered, his eyes dark with sorrow and guilt. "Everyone here is dead, or they will be. There's nothing you can do for them anymore. But we have to get out of here now, if we want to survive ourselves."

A crash from the main room startled me upright. Lightning danced over the walls, the flash revealing eerie dark spatters that hadn't been there before. Fear, cold and acute, stabbed through me. Ben followed my gaze, his muscles coiled tight beneath his shirt.

"Come on," he whispered, leading me down the hall. "My truck is out front. Let's find Jenna and get out of..."

He stopped. I looked down the hall, and everything inside me went cold.

Ms. Sawyer's gaunt, wasted body stood silhouetted in the doorway to the sick ward, still in the hospital gown she had died in. Blood stained her face and hands, smeared around her mouth and the fangs that protruded from her upper jaw. She carried something in her hands, something round and dripping, the size of a basketball.

Lightning flashed again, and I saw that it was Jenna's head.

I might have gasped, or gagged, for the thing that had been Ms. Sawyer looked up, and her dead, blank eyes flashed to mine. Her mouth opened, fangs gleaming, like jagged bits of glass. She screamed, a wail unlike anything remotely human, and charged toward us.

Ben yanked me across the hall, ducked into Doc Adams's office and slammed the door. A booming thud rattled the frame just as he threw the latch and looked frantically around for something to brace it with.

Another bang on the door, followed by the screech of the thing on the other side. I fell back in terror. Ben pulled me aside, dragged the old wooden desk from the corner and shoved it across the tile, pushing it up against the door.

"Kylie, come on!" His voice snapped me out of my daze. Crossing the room, he yanked back the curtain on the window, revealing the full fury of the storm outside. "Hurry, before it claws its way in."

The door jumped inward a few inches, scraping the desk back, and nails clawed at the opening. More voices joined the one beyond the frame, terrifying shrieks and howls, as if a whole pack of the things were clustered outside. The door shook and began to open as pale arms and shoulders shoved their way inside.

Ben threw up the window with a blast of rain-scented wind. "Come on!" he yelled at me, and I threw myself forward. His hands grabbed my waist as I scrambled for the opening, pushing me through. I fell on wet pavement, gasping as my elbow struck the hard ground, and then Ben collapsed beside me, rolling to his feet.

He dragged me upright, and through the window, I saw the door burst inward and a host of pale, shrieking bodies spill into the room. Former patients, people who had died that very afternoon, reanimated and somehow transformed into bloodthirsty monsters. Their empty white eyes scanned the room, catching sight of us outside the window, and they lunged forward with vicious wails.

We ran.

My shoes splashed over the wet concrete, cold rainwater soaking my hair and clothes. The storm raged around us, forks of lightning slashing the sky over the buildings. Behind me, I heard the monsters' savage cries as they leaped through the window and skittered after us.

I followed Ben around a corner, dodging a rubble pile, and nearly ran into a small white pickup parked between two buildings. I waited, heart hammering, as Ben fiddled with the keys, hands shaking as he tried to unlock the door. A monster leaped to the top of the rubble pile, hissed when it saw us and sprang forward.

Ben yanked open the door, reached in and pulled a shotgun out of the front seat. The monster leaped onto the hood, snarling, as Ben aimed the muzzle at it and pulled the trigger point-blank.

A flash and a deafening boom rocked the alley, nearly making my heart stop. The creature was hurled away, crumpling into the wall and slumping down, a bloody mess. But then it staggered to its feet, hissing, though there was a massive gaping hole that went right through its chest, showing jagged ribs. It shrieked again, sounding more pissed than hurt, and lurched forward as several others came around the corner.

Ben pushed me into the truck and lunged in after me, slamming the door just as Ms. Sawyer crashed into the glass. She shrieked at us, clawing the door with bony talons, as Ben jammed the keys into the ignition and the truck roared to life. The monster with the bloodied chest scrambled onto the hood again and lunged at me. Its head bounced off the windshield, and a spiderweb of cracks spread out from the impact. More creatures crowded the truck as Ben threw it into Drive. The vehicle lurched forward, striking several monsters as it roared out of the alley. The creature on the hood slipped and rolled off the side as Ben slammed his foot onto the gas and sped into the road.

I turned to look through the back window, watching the clinic and the pale, spindly creatures swarming from it like ants, until Ben turned a corner and the building was lost from view.

• 5 •

We drove for nearly an hour in frozen silence. Ben kept his gaze on the road, swerving around rubble and debris, easing through oceans of dead cars that had clogged the street. The city loomed above us, dark and menacing in the rain. Except for a few flickering streetlamps and several dying traffic lights, the streets were black, the buildings empty and dark. I remembered, when I first came here, how bright and busy the city had felt, even at night. Now, it was like driving through a war zone. Most everyone had fled or succumbed to the virus. There were a few stubborn hangers-on, those who had nowhere to go, or worse, those who stayed behind to prey on what was left. But for the most part, the city was empty of life, and just a few short months after the catastrophe hit, it was already beginning to crumble.

But *things* moved in the shadows, pale and terrifying, skirting the edges of the light. They skittered through alleys and between aisles of dead cars, sometimes alone, sometimes in small packs. Every time I saw one, my stomach convulsed in dread, and I couldn't move. How long had they been here, roaming the city, with me oblivious to the monsters right outside my door? Or was this something new, some awful, mutated side effect of the virus?

We drove on, through the city limits, though progress was slow. The road out of the city was clogged with cars, crashed into railings and each other, some upside-down or on their sides. Hundreds lay in ditches, and a few sat burned and blackened in the middle of the road. After weaving around this endless obstacle course of steel and glass, Ben finally pulled his truck off the pavement and drove through the dirt and trees.

It seemed to take forever, but the sea of cars finally thinned, then stopped altogether. After a few miles of nothing, Ben took the next off-ramp and parked the truck at an abandoned gas station.

"Stay here." His voice was hoarse. Turning off the engine, he grabbed the door handle, not looking at me. "We're almost out of gas. I'll be right back."

"Ben, wait!" My words came out harsh and sharp, startling us both. Ben flinched, then slowly took his hand from the door, turning to face me. His eyes, his face, his entire body, were slumped and resigned, as if he'd been waiting for this moment, dreading it.

"You promised me answers," I whispered. The numbness inside was fading, the horror and fear slipping away into something that felt close to rage. I could barely force the words out, but I did. "You promised you would tell me what's going on. I'm not going another step with you until you start talking."

"All right." Ben took a deep breath, let it out slowly. "All right, Kylie, I'll tell you everything I know. I don't have all the details, because I wasn't close to it, not like Nathan. But what I did find out…well, you'll see why I couldn't tell anyone."

"You know what those monsters are," I guessed, and it was an accusation. Ben hesitated, then nodded slowly.

"I've seen them before," he began, gazing out the window. "It was one of those things that attacked Nathan, in the lab." He looked at me, suddenly pleading. "I swear, I didn't know it was transferable. Not like that. Nathan was bitten, but I didn't know the disease could spread to others, Kylie. If I'd known that, I would have never brought him in."

"Disease?" My mind was spinning. "Ben, what *are* those

things? I just watched my dead patients come back to life and attack me! Are they...some sort of zombies?" The words sounded ridiculous out loud, but what else could I think? I'd only seen this happen in horror movies.

"No." Ben rubbed the stubble on his chin, clearly uncomfortable. "Not...zombies. From what I understand, they're more of a hybrid. Of human, and..." He trailed off, bring his lip.

"And?" I prompted.

"Vampire."

Ben grimaced, even as he said the word. I blinked. The implication hung between us, impossible. Ridiculous. Vampires didn't exist. They were movie monsters, Halloween costumes. Never mind that a second ago I'd seriously considered the zombie apocalypse. My logical doctor's brain scoffed at the idea of fanged, undead creatures that came out at night and drank the blood of the living to survive.

And yet...I'd been attacked by people who had died. I'd seen the corpses, lying in their beds that very afternoon, before they'd sprung to life. Corpses that moved at lethal, frightening speeds. That had ripped apart two humans as easily as paper, that had smelled of death and rot and decay. Corpses that had fangs.

"Vampires," I said slowly, still trying to decide what I thought about this, whether to accept, question or scoff at the claim. "You mean...like Dracula? The drinking-blood, turn-into-bats kind?"

Ben sighed. "I know how it sounds," he muttered. "And that's why I couldn't tell you before. You would've thought I was insane. But...yes, vampires are real. They don't turn into bats or wolves or mist, as far as I know, but everything else— the drinking blood, the coming out at night—it's all true." My face must've betrayed my disbelief, because he shook his head. "I know. When Nathan told me, I thought the chemicals in the lab were affecting his brain. I told him he needed help. But then he showed me, once, what they were keeping behind closed doors." He visibly shivered. "And that was enough to convince me."

"Why…" I couldn't believe I was asking this. "Why were they keeping vampires down there, anyway? I thought you said Nathan was part of a team searching for a cure."

"He was. And they were." Ben looked disturbed now, his brows drawn together in a frown. "I didn't get this out of Nathan until later, but…they were experimenting on the vampires. They were using vampire blood to try to develop the cure."

"Why?"

"Because vampires were immune to the Red Lung virus," Ben replied solemnly. "Nathan told me they didn't know if it was because the vampires were, technically, dead, but none of the specimens they acquired could be infected with the virus. They were hoping to duplicate the vampire's natural immunity to disease into something that could combat Red Lung." His gaze darkened, and he gripped the steering wheel tightly. "But something went wrong," he said in a near whisper. "The virus mutated. The 'cure' they gave infected patients—*human* patients—killed them. And turned them into those…things." He shuddered, running a hand through his hair. "I was there the night they escaped. No one knows how it happened, but Nathan was attacked, bitten. Everything was chaos. We got out, came here. But I had no idea the mutated virus was airborne, that it would spread just like Red Lung."

"Then…" My stomach felt cold as the implication of what he was really saying hit me like a load of bricks. The virus was airborne, seeping across the country like a spill of blood.

"Then, you're saying that everyone who is already infected with the Red Lung virus..."

Ben didn't meet my gaze. His hands gripped the steering wheel so hard his knuckles turned white. His face was ashen, and for a moment, I thought he might actually pass out.

"Oh, God," he whispered, closing his eyes. "What have I done? What have *we* done, Nate?"

My hands were shaking. I clenched them in my lap and took a deep, calming breath. I'd seen what Red Lung could do to a person, I knew how fast it spread, I'd heard how entire communities and towns had vanished off the map in the space of a week. I imagined those towns now, only instead of bodies lying in their homes, I could see pale, screaming abominations filling the roads, destroying anything they came across.

And it had started right here. With the person in the seat next to mine.

No, that wasn't entirely fair. Ben Archer hadn't performed those experiments on—I stumbled over the word—*vampires*. Ben hadn't created the retrovirus that was spreading across the country, turning the sick into bloodthirsty undead. He wasn't responsible for the creation of those monsters, he wasn't even a scientist. I knew that. My doctor's brain accepted that.

But the part of me that felt responsible for Maggie and Jenna, that had worked like a dog to save those patients, that viewed Red Lung as an enemy that had to be destroyed—that part of me hated him. He'd brought a hidden virus into my clinic, and because of him, my patients were all dead. Worse than dead, they were monsters, rabid beasts. If Ben Archer had never darkened my doorstep, they would still be alive.

My heart pounded. Anger and rage coursed through my veins, turning them hot. Ben's shotgun lay on the seat between us; without thinking, I grabbed it and flung open the door of the truck, leaping to the pavement.

"Kylie!"

Ben scrambled after me. I heard his footsteps round the hood of the truck, and though my hands were shaking, I planted my feet, spun around and raised the muzzle of the gun, leveling it at his chest.

He stopped, raising his hands, as I took a step backward, glaring at him down the barrel.

Lightning flickered, distant now, the storm having moved on. The lingering rain felt like cold spider webs falling across my skin.

Ben took a slow, careful step forward, still keeping his hands raised. I bared my teeth and shoved the muzzle at him, and he stopped.

"Stay back!" I hissed, knowing how I must look: wild and desperate, the whites of my eyes gleaming in the darkness. I felt crazy, out of control. "You stay right there, Ben Archer. Don't move, or I swear I'll kill you!"

"Kylie." His voice was low, calming, though he didn't move from where he stood. "Don't do this. Please. You can't survive out there alone."

"You," I snarled, curling my lip back, "have no right to tell me anything! You brought this down on our heads. My patients are dead because of you! Maggie and Jenna are dead because of you! The whole city, the whole world, maybe, is going to hell. Because of you!" With every accusation, he flinched, as if my words were stones smashing into him. My throat closed up, and I took a breath to open it. "All my life," I whispered, "I wanted to help people, save people. That's why I became a doctor, so I could make a difference. I wanted to beat this thing, so badly. And all it took was you waltzing into my clinic with your demon friend to destroy everything I worked for!"

"Then shoot me." He dropped his arms as he said it, regarding me with dead, hooded eyes. I blinked at him in shock, but he didn't move. "You're right," he said in a quiet voice. "What we did, what happened at that lab, there's no excuse. We unleashed something that could destroy everything. And if I..." He paused, closing his eyes. "If I deserve to die for that, if killing me will make things right for you, then...do it." Opening his eyes, he met my gaze, sorrowful but unafraid. "If this will bring you peace," he rasped, "for Maggie and Jenna and everyone, then do what you have to. No one will fault you for pulling that trigger."

My arms shook, and the gun was cold in my hands, the curved edge of the metal trigger pressing into my skin. It would be so easy, I realized—a quick pull, barely a motion in itself. I gazed down the barrel at the body in the rain, my throat and chest tight, my mind spinning. No one would hear the gunshot this far from the city. And even if they did, no one would care.

Ben stood there, unmoving, the rain falling lightly around his shoulders, waiting to see if I would kill him.

God, Kylie, what are you doing? You're really going to murder this man in cold blood? Horror, swift and abrupt, lanced through me. I was a doctor, sworn to save lives, regardless of circumstances or personal feelings. Ben had saved *my* life. If he hadn't been there when those things attacked, I would be a pile of blood and bones on the clinic floor. Just like Maggie and Jenna.

And then, all the fear, frustration, sorrow and guilt of the past three days rose up like a black wave and came crashing down. Tears blinded me, my throat closed up and the world went blurry. The gun dropped from my limp grasp, falling into the mud, as, to my horror, I started to cry.

Strong arms wrapped around me a moment later, pulling me to a broad chest. For a heartbeat, anger flashed, but it was immediately drowned by everything else. I had failed. I had lost everything, not only the patients whom I had sworn to save, but my family, my friends and, very nearly, my humanity. And now, the world was filled with monsters and things I didn't understand, I had nearly been *eaten* by my dead patients and I had nowhere to go, nowhere left that was familiar. I leaned into Ben and sobbed, ugly, gasping breaths that blotched my face and left the front of his shirt stained with tears.

Ben didn't say anything, just held me as I cried myself out, the rain falling around us. My back and shoulders were cold and damp, but my arms, folded to his body, and the side of my face where his cheek pressed against mine, were very warm. Eventually, the tears stopped and my breathing became normal again, but he didn't let me go. One arm was wound across the small of my back, the other rested near my shoulders, holding me to him. His head was bowed, and I could feel rough stubble against my cheek.

My arms, trapped against his chest and stomach, began to wind around his waist, to pull him to me as well, but I stopped myself. *No,* I thought, as my senses finally returned. *Just because he saved you, do not excuse this man for what he has done. Jenna and Maggie are dead. If he'd never come to your clinic, they would still be alive.*

I stiffened, and Ben apparently sensed the change, for he let me go. I stepped back to compose myself, wiping my face, pulling my hair back, deliberately not looking at the man beside me. Because if I glanced up and met those haunted, soulful brown eyes, I wouldn't be able to stop myself from reaching for him again.

The shotgun still lay in the mud between us, and Ben casually reached down for it, as if it had simply fallen and hadn't been aimed at his chest a few minutes earlier. I looked at the weapon and shuddered, appalled at myself, what I had almost done.

"What now?" I whispered, rubbing my arms as the rain started to come down hard again. Ben hefted the shotgun to one shoulder, staring out into the darkness.

"I'm going home," he said without looking back. "Back to the farm. It's been…too long since I've seen everyone. If they're still there." He paused, then added, very softly, "You're welcome to come with me. If you want."

I nodded, feeling dazed. "Thanks. I…I think I will. Come with you, I mean." He finally glanced back, eyebrows raised in surprise. I shrugged, though I was a little surprised at myself, as well. "Might as well. I don't have anywhere else to go."

He didn't say anything to that, and we walked back to the truck in silence. Ben pulled open the passenger door, and I slid inside, blinking as he handed me the shotgun as if nothing had happened. Shivering, I placed it on the dashboard and watched Ben use a rubber tube to siphon fuel from one of the abandoned cars into a gas can. It was a slow, tedious process, but it couldn't be helped. Many of the everyday conveniences—like ATMs, smart phones and gas pumps—were no longer working since the plague and the collapse of society. There was no one left to keep the grids going, no one to man the towers and the internet servers. It was a wake-up call for everyone, to realize how much we relied on things like electricity, running water and easy communication, and how crippling it was to go without.

When he was done, Ben slid into the driver's seat, closed the door, and sat there a moment, staring out the glass.

"Are you sure you're okay with this?" he asked in a near whisper, glancing at the weapon on the dashboard. "I won't force you to come with me. I can drop you off anywhere between here and home."

"No." I gave my head a shake. "Like I said, I have nowhere to go. And I don't want to be by myself right now, not with what's happening out there. Not if those things could be spreading across the country like the plague." Ben looked away, hunching his shoulders, and I wasn't sorry. "I'll figure out what to do next when we get there. If your family doesn't mind me hanging around…"

"They won't. Mom, especially. She'll be thrilled I finally brought home a girl."

That tiny bit of humor, forced as it was, finally coaxed a smile from me. I settled back against the leather seat and pulled down the seat belt, clicking it into place. "Then let's not keep them waiting."

Ben nodded. Turning the key in the ignition, he eased the truck down the ramp and onto the empty road, and we roared off toward our destination.

• 6 •

We drove through the night, down a road that was desolate and empty, snaking through the darkness. No cars passed us, no headlights pierced the blackness but our own. Ben and I didn't speak much, just watched the quiet, primitive world scroll by through the glass. Out here, far from cities and towns and dimly lit suburbs, it truly felt as if we were the only humans left alive. The last two people on earth.

I dozed against the window, and when I opened my eyes again, Ben was pulling into the parking lot of a small motel and shutting off the ignition. The streetlamps surrounding the lot were dead and dark but, oddly enough, a Vacancy sign flickered erratically in the window of the office.

"We're stopping?"

"Just for a bit." Ben opened the door, and a gust of rain-scented air dispersed my drowsiness a little. "It's almost dawn. I need a couple hours of sleep, at least, or I'm going to drive us off the road. This looks safe enough."

It might've looked safe enough, but he snatched the gun off the dashboard and handed me a flashlight before walking up to the office door. I followed closely, peering over my shoulder, shining the beam into windows and dark corners. We stepped up to the porch, and my heart pounded, imagining gaunt, pale faces peering through the windows. But they remained dark and empty.

After several moments of pounding on the office door and calling *"Hello?"* into the darkened interior, Ben raised the shotgun and drove the butt into the glass above the door, shattering it. Ducking inside, he emerged seconds later with a key on a wooden peg, jingling it with weary triumph. I trailed him down the walkway to a battered green door with a brass 14B on the front and watched as he unlocked the door and pushed it back. It creaked open slowly, revealing a small room with an old TV, a hideous pink-and-green armchair and a single bed.

"Damn," I heard him mutter, and he glanced over his shoulder at me. "Sorry, I was hoping to get one with double beds. I'll see if they have the keys to another room—"

"There's no need." Bringing up the flashlight, I brushed past him through the doorway. The room was stale and dusty, and the carpet probably hadn't been cleaned in years, but at least there was no stench of death and blood and decay. "We're both adults," I said, attempting to be pragmatic and reasonable. "We can share a bed if we have to. And I...I'd feel better not sleeping alone tonight, anyway."

"Are you sure?"

"Ben, I'm a doctor. You don't have anything I haven't seen before, trust me."

My voice sounded too normal, too flippant, for what was happening outside. I felt like a deflated balloon, empty and hollow. Numb. I'd seen patients with post-traumatic stress disorder, having lost a loved one or even their whole family, and wondered if maybe I was heading down that same road. If perhaps this eerie calm and sense of detachment were the beginning.

The door clicked shut behind me, plunging the room into darkness. I whirled with the flashlight, shining the beam into Ben's face. He flinched, turning his head, and I quickly dropped the light.

"Sorry."

"It's all right." He looked up, and I saw that his stoic mask had slipped back into place. I shivered a little. If anyone was suffering from PTSD, it was probably Ben.

I turned from that haunting gaze, shining the light toward the bathroom in the corner. "I'm…going to see if the water still works."

He didn't say anything to that, and I retreated to the bathroom, leaving him in the dark.

Miraculously, the water still ran, though the temperature barely got above lukewarm. I told Ben I was going to take a bath, then filled the tub halfway, sinking down into it with a sigh in the darkness. The flashlight sat upright on the sink, shining a circle of light at the ceiling, turning the room ghostly and surreal. A tiny bar of complimentary soap sat on the edge of the tub, and I scrubbed myself down furiously, as if I could wash away the horror, grief and fear along with the blood. I heard Ben stumble outside the door and felt guilty for hoarding our only light source, but after a minute or two I heard the door open and close, the lock clicking as it shut behind him.

Uncomfortable that he was going somewhere alone, I counted the seconds, the silence pressing against my eardrums. After a few minutes, though, the door creaked open again. I heard his footsteps shuffle around the room before the bed squeaked as he settled atop it, and finally stopped moving.

I finished my bath, slipped back into my dirty, disgusting clothes, and left the room, keeping the flashlight low in case Ben had gone to sleep.

He hadn't. He was perched on the edge of the mattress with his back to me, head bowed, slumping forward. His tattered shirt lay in a heap at the foot of the bed, and the flashlight beam slid over his broad shoulders and back. As I paused on the other side of the mattress, I saw his shoulders tremble, and heard the quiet, hopeless sound of someone trying to muffle a sob.

"Ben."

Anger forgotten, I set the flashlight down and slipped around to his side, touching a bare shoulder as I came up. A nest of bloody gauze sat on an end table, next to a bottle of peroxide. His stitches had torn open, and the claw marks were dark, thin stripes down his back.

Sympathy bloomed through me, dissolving the last of the anger as my logical doctor's brain finally caught up with my emotions. Ben was hurting, not from his wounds, but from the guilt that was tearing him apart inside. I wasn't quite ready to forgive what had happened to Maggie, Jenna and my patients, but I knew, really knew, that the horrible night in the clinic was not his fault. And if he hadn't been there, I probably would have died.

"Would you…help me?" Ben didn't even bother trying to hide the wet tracks down his cheeks, though he didn't glance up. He gestured to the peroxide and an open first aid kit on the nightstand. "I found those in the office, but I can't reach it on my own."

Silently, I picked up the first aid kit and scooted behind him on the bed. His skin was cold, but the area around the slashes was puffy and hot, though it didn't look infected. I gently wiped away the dirt and blood, watching the peroxide sizzle into the open wounds, bubbling white. Ben didn't even flinch.

"I don't blame you, you know." My voice surprised me, even more that I found it true. Ben didn't answer, and I pressed a gauze pad to the wounds, keeping my voice low and calm. "What happened back in the clinic, in the lab with Nathan, that wasn't your fault. I just…I freaked out. I reacted badly and I'm sorry for that, Ben."

"You have no reason to apologize," Ben murmured. "I should have been straight with you from the beginning, but…I didn't know what you would think. How do you explain zombies and vampires to someone without sounding like a raving lunatic?" He scrubbed a hand over his face, and now I felt a tiny prick of guilt. If he had told me that in the clinic, I probably *would* have scoffed at the idea, or assumed he was on drugs. Whose fault was this, really? "But I should have told you," Ben went on. "Nate…he was the smart one, the one who could explain anything and have it all make sense. In fact, I was hoping he would wake up so he could tell you what was going on. If that's not a selfish reason…" A soft, bitter laugh, ending in a muffled sob. "It should've been me," he said in a near whisper. "I should've been the one who died."

"No." I slid off the bed and walked around to face him. Crouching down, I peered at his face, putting a hand on his knee for balance. "Ben, look at me. This isn't your fault," I whispered again, as those tortured eyes met mine. "It isn't Nathan's fault. Ben, the virus is killing us. The human race is facing *extinction,* though no one is willing to admit it. Something had to be done."

"Something was," he muttered. "And now things are even worse. I don't know if we can survive this. And just thinking that I was there when it happened, that maybe if I'd done something a little different, I could've stopped them from getting out—"

"You couldn't have known what would happen." I kept my voice calm, reasonable, my doctor's voice. "And those scientists, they were only doing what anyone would do to save our race. We had to try something. It isn't our nature to roll over and die without a fight." I smiled faintly. "Humans are stubborn like that."

He held my gaze, the light reflected in his eyes. Very slowly, as if afraid it would scare me away, he reached out and took a strand of my hair between his fingers. I held my breath, my heartbeat kicking into high gear, pulsing very loudly in my ears.

"I don't know how you can stand to be around me," Ben murmured, staring at his hand, at the pale strings between his fingers. "But...don't go. Don't leave. You're the only thing keeping me sane right now."

Maggie and Jenna's faces crowded my mind, angry and accusing. My patients rose up from the darkness to stare at me, their gazes vengeful, but I shoved those thoughts away. They were gone. They were dead, and I couldn't honor their memory with anger and blame and hate. The world was screwed, monsters roamed the streets and I had to cling to my lifelines where I could. I was sure everything would hit me, hard, when I had the chance to breathe. But right now, I had to make sure I—we—kept breathing.

Gently, I placed a palm on his cheek, feeling rough stubble under my fingers. "We'll get through this," I promised him, feeling, absurdly, that I was *his* lifeline right now, and if I left he might take that shotgun and put the muzzle under his chin. "I'm not going anywhere."

For just a moment, Ben's gaze grew smoldering, a dark, molten look that swallowed even the anguish on his face, before he straightened and pulled back, looking embarrassed.

Turning away, he gingerly bent to scoop up his shirt. "I'll take the chair," he offered in a husky voice, rising to his feet. I stood as well, frowning.

"Ben, you don't have to—"

"Trust me." He slipped into his shirt, grimacing. "I think I do."

I didn't think I would sleep, but I did drift off, listening to Ben's quiet snores from the chair in the corner. I awoke the next morning to sunlight streaming in through the dingy curtains and Ben emptying a bag of junk food onto the table.

"Morning," he greeted, and though his voice was solemn, it lacked the despair of the night before. "I thought you might be hungry, so I raided the snack machines by the office. I, uh, hope you don't mind Doritos and Twinkies for breakfast."

I smiled and struggled to my feet, brushing my hair back. "Any Ho Hos in the bunch?" I asked, walking up to the table.

"Mmm…no, sorry." Ben held up a package. "But I do have Zingers."

We smiled and ate our hideously unhealthy breakfast without complaint, knowing food was an unknown equation. The days of easy access were over. Places like McDonald's or Wendy's, where you could just walk in and order a hot breakfast, were a thing of the past. And many of the big superstores had been raided, gutted and picked clean when the chaos began. I wondered how long it would be before things went back to normal. I wondered if things would ever go back to normal.

"How far is it to your parents' farm?" I asked, once the chip bags were empty and plastic wrappers covered the table. Ben handed me a Diet Coke, and I washed down the cloying sweetness in my throat.

Ben shrugged. "About a fourteen-hour drive, if the roads are clear. We should get there by this evening if we don't run into anything."

Like rabid zombie vampires. I shivered and shook that thought away. "You'll be home soon, then. That's good."

"Yeah." Ben didn't sound entirely convinced. I glanced up and saw him watching me intently, his chin on the back of his laced hands. A flutter went through my stomach. Abruptly, he stood and started cleaning up the piles of wrappers scattered about the table, before he stopped, shaking his head. "Sorry. Old habits. Mom would always have us clear the dinner table for her. Come on." He grabbed the shotgun and opened the door for me. "Let's get out of here. The sooner we're on the road, the sooner we'll arrive."

We piled into the truck, after stashing the shotgun safely in the backseat, and Ben stuck the key in the ignition. "Home," he muttered in a voice barely above a whisper, and turned the key.

Nothing happened.

My heart stood still. Ben swore quietly and turned the key again. Same result. Nothing. The engine lay still and cold and dead, and no amount of jiggling the key or pumping the gas pedal seemed to revive it.

"Dammit." Ben jumped out of the driver's seat and stalked to the front, opening the hood with a rusty squeak. I watched him through the window, obeying when he told me to slide into the driver's seat and try the ignition again. We worked for nearly twenty minutes, but the old truck remained stubbornly silent.

Ben dropped the hood with a bang, his face sweaty and grim. I peeked out the driver's side window, trying to stay calm. "No luck?"

He shook his head. "Fuses are blown, I think. That, or the battery is dead. Either way, I'm not going to be able to get it started without jumper cables and another running engine. Dammit." He rubbed his jaw. "Looks like we're hoofing it."

"To Illinois?" The thought was staggering. "A fourteen-hour drive will probably take us a week or more of walking, and that's if we don't run into anything."

"I don't see any other way, do you?" Ben looked around helplessly, hands on his hips. "We'll look for another vehicle down the road, but we can't stay here. I know, it scares me, too. But we have to get moving."

Daunting was the word that came to mind—hiking across a lawless, empty, plague-ridden country, where society had broken down and humans were just as likely to turn on you as help—it was a frightening thought. Especially now, with those...things out there. But Ben was right; we couldn't stay here. We had to continue.

Ben dug an old green backpack out from under the seats, and we raided the broken vending machines again, stocking up on sweets, chips and soda, as much as the pack could carry. Hefting it to his back, slinging the gun over one shoulder, he beckoned to me, and we started down the empty road, feeling like the only two people left on Earth.

The highway continued, weaving through hills and forest, past side roads and off-ramps that led to unknown places. Occasionally, we passed cars on the road, pulled over on the shoulder, abandoned in ditches, or sometimes just stopped in the middle of the lane. Once, I thought I saw a person in one of the cars in a ditch, a woman slumped against the dashboard, and hurried over to help. But she was long dead, and so was her little boy in the backseat. Sickened, I turned away, hoping their deaths had been swift, and the images continued to haunt me the rest of the afternoon.

Ben inspected every car we came across, searching around the dashboard and glove compartments, hoping for a lucky break. But except for the dead woman's car, none of them had keys, and hers was too damaged to use. Another, a van, seemed to be in good condition, but the tires were flat. I asked him once if we could hot-wire a vehicle into running, but neither of us had a clue how to do that. So we kept walking as the sun slid across the sky and the shadows around us lengthened.

"Here," Ben said, handing me an open can of Sprite when we stopped for a break. I took a long swig and handed it back as he sat beside me on the guardrail. We'd been hiking uphill for what had seemed like miles, and I could feel the heat of his body against mine, our shoulders and arms lightly touching. My stomach did a weird little twirl, especially when his large hand came to rest over mine on the railing.

"I think we're coming up on a town," he said, after finishing off the can and tossing it into the ditch. "If we are, it might be a good idea to stop and look around for a car. And food. Real food, anyway." He glanced at the backpack, lying open at our feet. Twinkies, Snowballs, chips and candy wrappers stood out brightly against the dull gray of the pavement. "I might slip into a sugar-induced coma if I eat one more Twinkie."

I smiled, liking this lighter, easygoing version of Ben. Out in the sunlight, away from all the blood, death, horror and despair, things didn't look as bleak.

I grinned at him, bumping his shoulder, just as he looked back at me. And, very suddenly, we were staring at each other on a lonely, empty road, miles from anywhere.

The late-afternoon sun slanted through the branches of the pine trees, turning his hair golden-brown, his eyes hazel. I could see rings of amber and green around the coffee-colored irises. They were beautiful, and they held my gaze, soft and tender, and a little bit afraid. As if Ben was unsure where we stood, if this was all one-sided.

My heart pounded. Ben waited, not moving, though his eyes never left mine. The ball was in my court. I licked my lips and suddenly found myself leaning toward him.

The growl of a car engine echoed, unnaturally loud in the silence, making us both jerk up. Gazing down the road, I saw a flash of metal in the sun, speeding toward us, and my heart leaped. Ben stood, grabbing the shotgun from where it lay against the railing, as a rusty brown pickup roared around the bend and skidded to a halt in a spray of gravel.

My senses prickled a warning, and I moved closer to Ben as the doors opened and three big, rough-looking guys stepped out into the road. They looked related, brothers maybe, blond and tanned, with the same watery blue eyes. I caught the stench of alcohol wafting from the cab as they sauntered to the edge of the pavement and grinned at us.

They all had guns, one rifle and a couple pistols, though no one had raised a weapon yet. My stomach clenched with dread.

"Hey there." The closest guy, a little bigger than the other two, leered at me. His voice was lazy and drawling, and a little slurred. I saw his gaze rake over me before he turned a mean look on Ben. "You two lost? Kind of a bad spot to be stranded—never know what kind of crazies you'll run into out here."

The other two snickered, as if that was actually funny. Ben nodded politely, though his arms and shoulders were tense, his finger resting on the trigger of the shotgun. "We're not lost," he said in a cool, firm voice. "We're just going home. Thank you for your concern."

They hooted with laughter. "Ooh, listen to him, all dandy and proper," one of the others mocked. "A real gentleman, he is."

"Now, now, be nice, Bobby," the leader said, turning to grin at the one who'd spoken. "They said they're trying to get home, so let's help 'em out." He turned and smiled at me, blue eyes gleaming, as inviting as a snarling wolf. "We'll take you home, darlin'. So why don't you just hop in the truck, right now?"

Ben's weapon came up instantly, as did the other three. I gasped as a trio of deadly gun barrels were suddenly trained on Ben, who had his own pointed at the leader's chest.

Time seemed to stop, the air around us crystallizing into a silence that hovered on the edge of chaos and death. I froze, unable to move, shocked at how quickly the situation had descended into another horror film. Only the guns pointed right at us were real.

"Ben," I whispered, placing a hand on his arm. My legs shook, and a cold, terrified sweat dripped down my spine. "Stop this. You'll be killed."

"Listen to your girlfriend, boy," the leader said, smiling as he leveled the pistol at Ben's face. "There's three of us and only one of you. Odds ain't in your favor." His eyes flicked to me, and he jerked his head toward the open truck door. "Just come along quietly, missy, and make it easy on you both. Unless you want your dandy boyfriend pumped full o' holes in about two seconds."

"I'll go," I told both of them, though my eyes still pleaded with Ben. I felt sick, knowing what they wanted, what would happen to me the second I went into that truck. But I couldn't let them shoot Ben. "Ben, don't. Please. They'll kill you."

"Stay where you are." His voice, low and steely, froze me in my tracks. He hadn't moved through the whole encounter, and his stare never wavered from the man in front of him. "There's three of you," he agreed, still locking eyes with the leader. "But I can still kill one of you before the others get their shots off. And the odds aren't in *your* favor, are they?" The leader stiffened, and the barrel moved with him, just enough to keep him in its sight. "Do you know what happens to a body shot point-blank with a shotgun?" Ben asked, his voice cold as ice. "You'll have to be buried with your truck, because they'll never get all the pieces out of it."

"Fuck you." The leader pulled the hammer on his pistol back, aiming it at Ben's face. Ben stared him down over the shotgun, not moving, never wavering, while my heart hammered so hard against my ribs I thought I might pass out.

Finally, the leader slowly raised his other hand, placating. "All right," he said in a soothing voice, and lowered his weapon. "Everyone just take it easy, now. Relax." He shot the other two a hard look, and they reluctantly lowered their guns. "This is what we're gonna do. Give us that pack full of stuff, and we'll be on our way. That sound like an okay trade, boy?"

"Fine," Ben said instantly, not lowering his weapon. "Take it and go."

The leader, still keeping one hand in the air, jerked his head at one of the other two, who edged around the truck and snatched the bag from the ground. Ben kept his gaze and his weapon trained unwaveringly on the leader, who smirked at us and slipped back into the truck, slamming the door as the others did the same.

"Well, thank ya kindly, dandy boy." He grinned as his friends hooted and pawed through the bag, snatching at Twinkies and cupcakes. "You two have fun, now. Run on home to mommy. It'll be dark soon."

The truck peeled away in a squeal of gravel, the echoes of their laughter ringing out behind them.

Ben let out a shaky breath and finally lowered the weapon. I could see his hands shaking as he leaned back against the rail, breathing hard. "Why did you do that?" I whispered, my heart slamming against my ribs. "You could've been killed."

"I wasn't going to let them take you."

My legs were trembling. I took a shaky step toward him, and he reached out with one arm, pulling me close. I felt his heart, beating frantically through his shirt, and wrapped my arms around his waist, clinging to him as fear and adrenaline slowly ebbed away, and my heartbeat slowed to normal. Ben leaned the shotgun against the railing and held me in a fierce, almost desperate embrace, as if daring something to try to rip me away. I relaxed into him, felt his arms around me and, if only for a moment, let myself feel safe.

"Come on," he whispered, finally drawing back. "Let's try to make town before nightfall."

It wasn't quite dusk when we stumbled off the main highway, following an exit ramp into the ruins of a small town. The late-afternoon sun cast long shadows over the empty streets and rows of dark, decaying houses, their yards overgrown with weeds. We passed homes and streets that must have been a nice little suburban community. Yards had been well-tended once, and the driveways were full of station wagons and minivans. I kept looking for signs of life, hints that people still lived, but except for a small orange cat, darting away into the bushes, there was nothing.

"What are we looking for?" I asked Ben, my voice sounding unnaturally loud in the stillness. The sun hovered low on the horizon, a sullen blood-red, like a swollen eye. Ben gave it a nervous look, then gestured to a building as we reached a crossroad. "Something like that."

A gas station sat desolately on a corner, windows smashed, gas hoses lying on the ground. We approached cautiously, peering through the shattered glass, but it was empty of life and most everything else. Inside, the shelves were stripped clean, glass littered the floor, and most of the displays were tipped over. Others had been here before us. Fleeing town, perhaps, when the plague hit. Though I didn't know where they thought they could run. Red Lung was everywhere, now.

"Been pretty picked over," Ben muttered, stepping around downed shelves and broken glass. He nudged an empty display that had once held energy drinks and shook his head. "Let's not waste too much time looking; I want to get out of here soon. This place is making me jumpy."

Me, too. Though I couldn't put my finger on why. The town seemed lifeless. We rummaged around and found a few meat tins, jerky rolls and a bag of Doritos that had been missed. We tossed our findings into a plastic bag, the rustle of paper and plastic the only sounds in the quiet. Outside, the sun dipped below the horizon, stealing the last of the evening light, and a chill crept through the air.

"All right," Ben said, rising to his feet, "I think we have enough, for a little while, at least. Now, I wonder how hard it will be to find a car…?"

A woman shuffled past the broken window.

I jerked, grabbing Ben's arm, as the figure moved by without stopping. My stomach lurched. "Hey!" I called, hopping over shelves and broken glass to the door, peering out. The woman was walking down the sidewalk, stumbling every few steps, and didn't seem to have heard me.

Abruptly, she put a hand against the wall and bent over as violent coughing shook her thin frame. Blood spattered the ground beneath her in crimson drops, and I stumbled to a halt.

Ben came up behind me and took my arm, moving me back. The woman finally stopped coughing and slowly turned to face us. I saw the thin streams of blood, running from her eyes like crimson tears, and my insides turned to ice.

"Oh, my God." I looked at Ben, saw the same horror reflected on his face, the realization of what was happening. Not Red Lung. The other thing. It was already here. "How could it spread this fast?"

He grabbed my wrist as the woman gagged on her own blood and collapsed to the gutter, twitching. "The whole town could be infected. We have to get out of here, now!"

We turned and fled, our footsteps pounding the sidewalk, echoing dully in the stillness. Only…the town wasn't as empty and still as I'd first thought. As the light vanished from the skies and streetlamps flickered to life, things began moving in the darkness and shadows. Moans and wails crept from dark houses, doors slammed open and pale, shambling figures stumbled out of the black. Terror gripped me. We were out in the open, exposed. The second that one spotted us, we would be run down and torn apart. The only saving grace was that the creatures seemed groggy and confused right now, not completely alert. If we could get to the edge of town without being seen—

Ben jerked to a halt in front of a line of cars as one of the creatures, long and thin and terrible, leaped onto the roof with the ease of a cat. It peered at us with blank white eyes and hissed, baring a mouthful of jagged fangs. My heart and stomach turned to ice. Gasping, we turned to run the other way.

Three more of the monsters leaped over a fence, hissing and snarling as they crept forward, blocking our path. One of them had been a woman, once; she wore a tattered dress that dragged through the mud, and her hair was long and matted.

Oh, God. This is it, we're going to die.

One of the creatures screamed, sounding eerily human, and rushed Ben. It moved shockingly fast, like a monstrous spider skittering forward. Ben barely had time to raise the shotgun, but he did bring the muzzle up just in time, and a deafening boom rocked the air around us. The creature was flung backward, landing in the bushes with a shriek, and wild screeching erupted from the shadows around us. Pale things scuttled forward, closing in from all directions, teeth, claws and dead eyes shining in the darkness.

"This way!"

The deep voice rang out like a shot, startling us both. Whirling around, I saw a tall, dark figure emerge from the shadows between two houses, beckoning us forward.

"Hurry!" he snapped, and we darted toward him, following his dark shadow as it turned and vanished between houses, seeming to melt into the night. The shrieks of the monsters rang all around us, but we trailed the figure through a maze of overgrown yards and fences until he fled up a crumbling set of stairs into the ruins of a brick house.

The door slammed behind us as we ducked over the threshold. Gasping, we watched the figure throw the lock, then stalk to the front windows and yank the curtains shut before turning around.

Muffled silence descended, broken only by the shrieks and wails outside. I blinked, my eyes slowly adjusting to the darkness. The man before us was enormous; not overly tall or heavy, just physically imposing. He wasn't that much taller than Ben, but he possessed a definite quiet strength, the bearing of someone who knew how to handle himself. His skin was the pale color of a man who spent all his time indoors, someone who didn't see a lot of sun, though his broad chest and corded muscle hinted at the power underneath. His hair was dark, and his eyes, when they turned on us, were blacker than the shadows that surrounded him.

"Stay back from the windows," he said in that deep, powerful voice. "We should be safe here, but the rabids will tear down the walls if they see us. Move back."

"Rabids?" I whispered. The man shrugged.

"What some have taken to calling them." His piercing gaze lingered on me, assessing. "Have either of you been bitten?"

"No," Ben said, holding his shotgun in both hands, I noted. Not pointing it at the stranger but not relaxing it, either. I held my breath, but the stranger didn't press the question. He simply nodded and moved away from the door, heading toward the dilapidated kitchen.

"If either of you wish to be helpful, you might want to start covering any windows that you find." His voice drifted back from the hall. "Just don't let the rabids see you, or we'll have to find a new place to hole up. I'm afraid you're rather stuck here until morning."

Ben and I shared a glance, then did what we were told. For several minutes, we concentrated on fortifying the house, making sure there were no windows, gaps or open spaces through which the monsters—the rabids—could climb in or see us. When we had made the house as secure as we could, closing curtains, shoving furniture in front of doors, we returned to the kitchen, which was small and had no windows to speak of. The dark stranger was there, leaning against a counter, watching us with fathomless black eyes.

"You might want to turn the flashlight off for now," he said, nodding at the light in my hands, the feeble ray barely piercing the shadows. "There are candles in the drawers if you need light, but be cautious where you set them out. Make sure they are in a spot where the rabids cannot see them."

I watched him carefully, shining the light for Ben as he rummaged through the drawer across from the stranger, pulling out three short candles and a book of matches. He stood there, motionless as a statue, his stark gaze not even on us anymore. He seemed distracted, as if we were only shadows, moving around him, not part of his world at all.

There was the sharp hiss and sizzle of a match flaring to life, and I clicked off the flashlight as Ben set the lit candles on the counter. The stranger's attention finally shifted back to us, and he looked almost surprised that we were still there. Ben stared back, his expression cautious, all the muscles in his body rigid.

"You can relax," the stranger told us with the faintest hint of a smile. "It was pure coincidence that I stumbled upon you this evening. I did not lure you here to kill you in your sleep." His smile faded, and he turned away. "I mean you no harm tonight, I give you my word."

Tonight? I thought, not knowing why that sounded odd to me. *What about tomorrow night, then?* "We don't mean to be ungrateful," I said, as Ben slowly relaxed his grip on the shotgun. "It's just been a rough couple of days."

"Yes, it has." The man scrubbed a hand across his face, then pushed himself off the counter. "There's food in the cupboards," he announced, sounding tired. "And I believe the stove is gas. It might still work. I'd advise you *not* to open the refrigerator—the electricity has been out for a couple weeks, by the looks of it."

"Thank you," Ben murmured, setting the gun on the counter as the stranger moved toward the door. "I'm Ben, by the way, and that's Kylie."

The stranger nodded. "I'll check the closets for blankets," he continued, as if Ben hadn't spoken at all. "Make yourselves as comfortable as you can."

With a nod to me, he turned and left the room, making absolutely no noise on his way out.

He didn't, I noticed, offer his name.

I found several boxes of macaroni and cheese in the cupboard, along with a few cans of vegetables, and cooked them in the darkness with Ben hovering beside the stove. I found myself wondering who had lived here before, what had happened to them. Had they fled town, leaving their house and all their possessions behind? Or were they now a part of the horror…outside?

"Your carrots are boiling over," Ben commented, and I jerked up with a whispered curse. Water was bubbling over the rim of the pot and flowing down to the stovetop. "Sorry," I muttered, moving it to a different burner. "Cooking is not my strong suit. Most of my dinners come in microwave boxes."

The macaroni suddenly followed the carrot's example, hissing as it overflowed its container. "Dammit!"

"Here." Ben gently moved me out of the way, turning down the heat and maneuvering the pots around with the ease of familiarity. I watched him stir in the cheese, spoon the noodles and carrots onto tin plates, and wondered at the surreal normalcy of it all. Here we were, cooking macaroni and having dinner, while outside the world was falling to the vampire-zombie apocalypse.

No sleep for me tonight, that's for certain. Think about something else, Kylie.

"Wow," I said, as Ben put the bowls on the table, "a man who can shoot a gun *and* cook? Why are you still single, Ben Archer?"

I couldn't be positive in the flickering candlelight, but he might've blushed. "Mac-n-cheese is *not* cooking," he said with a small grin. "And, I don't know. I've never found the right girl, I suppose. What about you?"

"Me?" I sat down at the table, picking up the spoon left on the cloth, hoping it was clean. "I never had the time for... anything like that," I admitted, as Ben sat down across from me. "It was either work and study or have a life, you know? I never thought about settling down or having a family. I wanted to concentrate on finishing school, getting a good job. Everything else sort of took a backseat."

"What about now?" Ben asked softly.

I fidgeted. He was giving me that intense, smoldering look again, the one that made my insides do strange twirly backflips. "What do you mean?"

He gave me a you-know-what-I-mean look. "What do you want to do, now that the world is screwed over?" He jerked his head at a window. "Everything is different, and it won't be normal for a long time, I think. Do you..." He paused, playing with his fork. "Do you ever think you'd want to…settle down? Find a safe place to wait this out and start a family?"

"You mean pull an Adam and Eve and populate the world again?" He didn't smile at the joke, and I sighed. "I don't know, Ben. Maybe. But I also want to see if I can help. I know everything is screwed up right now, but I'd like to help out where I can." I shrugged and prodded my food. "I haven't really given it much thought, though. Right now, all I want to do is stay alive."

"An admirable plan," came a voice from the doorway.

We both jumped. The dark stranger stood in the frame, the light flickering over his strong yet elegant features. I hadn't even heard him approach; the space had been empty a moment before, and now he was just *there*.

"Next time, though, perhaps you should avoid going into any towns or settlements at night," he said. "The rabids are everywhere now, and spreading. Just like the virus. Soon, nowhere will be safe, for anyone."

His voice was dull, hopeless, and though his face remained calm, I could see the agony flickering in his dark eyes. As if his mask was slipping, cracking, showing glints of guilt, horror and sorrow underneath. I recognized it, because Ben had worn the same mask when he'd stepped into my clinic that day, a stoic front over a mind about to fall apart. This stranger looked the same.

Ben gestured to the chair at the end of the table. "There's plenty of food, if you want it," he offered.

"I've already eaten."

"Well, join us, at least," I added, and that black, depthless gaze flicked to me. "You sort of saved our lives. The least we can do is thank you for it."

He paused, as though weighing the consequences of such a simple action, before he very slowly pulled out a chair and sat down, lacing his fingers together. Every motion, everything he did, was powerful and controlled; nothing was wasted. His eyes, however, remained dark and far away.

A moment of awkward silence passed, the only sounds being the clink of utensils against the bowls and the occasional shriek of the rabids outside. The man didn't move; he remained sitting with his chin on his hands, staring at the table. He was so still, so quiet, if you weren't looking directly at him, you wouldn't know he was there at all.

"Where are you headed?" the stranger murmured without looking up, an obvious attempt at civility. Ben swallowed a mouthful of water and put the cup down.

"West," he replied. "Toward Illinois. I have family there, I hope." His face tightened, but he shook it off. "What about you? If we're headed the same direction, you're welcome to come along. Where are you going?"

For a few seconds, there was no answer. I wasn't sure the stranger was even paying attention, when he gave a short, bitter laugh. My gut clenched with horror and fear. In that moment, his mask slipped away, and I saw the raw agony beneath the smooth facade, the glassy sheen in his eyes that hovered close to madness.

"It doesn't matter," he rasped. "Nothing matters anymore. No matter where I go, I'll be hunted. I could flee to the other side of the world, and they would find me. I thought..." He covered his eyes with a hand. "I thought I could change things. But I've only made it far, far worse."

"What do you mean?" I asked.

The stranger drew in a deep breath, appearing to compose himself. "I've...done something," he admitted, lowering his hand. He stared down at the table, the candlelight reflected in his dark eyes. "Something I will never be forgiven for. Something that will likely cause my death. A very painful, drawn-out death, if I know my kin." Another of his short, bitter laughs. "And it will be completely justified."

Outside, something shrieked and slammed into the side of the wall. We froze, holding our breath, listening, as the body scrabbled around the base of the house, watching its jerky movements through a slit in the curtain. Finally, it shuffled off, vanishing into the night, and we started breathing again.

I glanced at the stranger. "Whatever it was," I began, knowing he probably wouldn't tell me the details, "it can't be *that* bad, right?"

No answer. Just a tight, bitter smile.

I took a breath. "Look," I began, wondering why I wanted to help him, to ease the darkness in his eyes, on his face. Maybe I was trying to return the favor, or maybe I felt that I was seeing only a hint of the agony beneath that cool, flinty shell. The reasons didn't matter; I reached out and put a hand on his wrist. "Whatever you've done, or think you've done, it's over now. You can't go back and change it. What you do about it, right now, from here on out, that's the important thing."

I felt Ben's eyes on me and realized I could be talking to both of them. And myself. I *couldn't* go back and change anything. Maggie and Jenna were gone. The world was full of monsters, or it would be soon. I could not dwell on the past, what I had lost, who I had failed. From here on, I could only move forward.

The stranger blinked, staring at my fingers on his wrist as though surprised to find them there. His skin was pale, smooth and oddly cool.

"Perhaps…you are right." He straightened, giving me an unfathomable look. "I cannot escape what I have done, but perhaps I can make up for it. I still have time. It shames me that a…stranger…must tell me what should be obvious, but these are unusual times." He stared at me, and that faint, bemused smile flickered across his face. "Incredible, that after all these years I can still be surprised."

He rose, startling me with the smooth, quick motion. "There are stairs to a finished basement down the hall," he said, back to being matter-of-fact, his mask sliding into place once more. "It will be the safest place for you to spend the night, I believe. If you want to get some sleep, I would do so there."

"What about you?" Ben asked. The stranger gave one final faint smile.

"I will be up all night," he said simply, and left the room.

Ben put the dishes in the sink, despite the futility of it all, and in the flickering candlelight, we found the stairs leading to a bedroom on the lowest floor. I caught sight of the stranger as we left, sitting in a living-room chair facing the door, his fingers steepled in thought. Strangely, the notion that he was on guard duty made me feel that much safer.

The walls downstairs were made of concrete, with no windows and a single queen-size bed in the corner. It was dry and cool, the cement floor covered with several thick shag rugs, muffling our footsteps. It felt more secure than any place we'd been so far. I set my candle on a nightstand by the bed and clicked on the flashlight to see better, shining it around the room. Ben shut the door, locked it and then pushed the dresser up against it, the scraping sound making me grit my teeth.

"There," he muttered, once the heavy piece of furniture was butted firmly against the wood. "Only one way in, and if anything tries to get through that, at least we'll hear them coming."

He turned just as I did, shining the beam right into his face, and he flinched away. "Sorry!" I whispered, lowering the beam. "I'm not doing that on purpose, I swear—"

I stopped at the look on his face. He crossed the room in two long strides, took the flashlight from my hands and pulled me to him, pressing his lips to mine.

His lips were warm, soft and hard at the same time, and something inside me, some dam or wall or barrier, shattered. I thought I'd be shocked, at least surprised, but my arms wrapped around his neck, and I rose on tiptoes to kiss him back. Ben groaned, sounding almost like a growl, and crushed me to him, nearly lifting me off my feet. I met him with equal passion, fisting my hands in his thick hair, pressing my body to his. My brain jangled a warning, but it was rapidly shutting down; I had to say something before it powered off completely and my body took over.

"Ben," I breathed, as his mouth dropped to my neck, searing the flesh along my jaw. "Wait, we shouldn't…there's still that guy upstairs. And the rabids. If they hear us…"

"I can be quiet," Ben whispered against my skin. His hands were roaming down my ribs to my thighs, and mine had somehow slipped beneath his shirt to skim his muscular back. "But it's your call," he panted. "Tell me to stop, and I will."

Yes, stop! my logical doctor's brain was screaming. *This is crazy! You don't know this man, the house is surrounded by zombies and there is a scary, I-might-be-a-serial-killer stranger in the front room. This is not the time for…this!*

I ignored the voice. God, I *did* want this. I wanted *him*. If only to feel something again, to convince myself that I was alive. The past few days—hell, the past few *months*—had been a nightmare, and I'd felt like a zombie myself, shambling from place to place, numb. Barely alive. Ben had reawakened something inside me, and I didn't want to let it go. Dammit, I'd nearly been killed tonight. One night of letting go wasn't too much to ask.

"No," I rasped, clutching at him. "Don't stop. We just… have to be quiet."

Kissing me fiercely, Ben drew back just enough to push my coat off my shoulders and tug my blouse over my head. I did the same, freeing his shirt from the waistband of his jeans and pulling it from his broad shoulders. He bent over to help, shrugging free, and his tanned, muscular chest and stomach were suddenly bared in the glowing candlelight.

Oh, my. I scarcely had time for a complete thought before he was on me again, kissing, nipping, devouring. His strong arms wrapped around my waist and lifted me off my feet, moving me back to the bed. I braced myself to be dropped, but he laid me on the quilt very gently and straddled my head with his elbows.

I looked up at him, at his face inches from mine, at the hazel eyes gone dark with passion and want. But he was hesitant now; a little of that worry had trickled back, filtering through the desire. He licked his lip and drew back, his expression shifting to guilty concern.

"Are you—" his voice was a little ragged "—okay with this? I don't want you to—"

Frowning, I slid my hands into his hair and pulled his lips down to mine. He sucked in a breath, and a low groan escaped him. "You're not being very quiet," I whispered against his mouth, and he moaned again. "Less talking, more kissing, Ben. Now."

"Yes…ma'am."

With deft fingers, Ben undid my bra and shifted it off, tossing it over the bed. His mouth left mine and trailed hot kisses down my neck, my collarbone, between my breasts. I arched my head back, biting my lip to keep from gasping, knowing especially now, we had to be silent. His lips closed over a nipple, teasing it with his tongue, and I clutched at the quilt beneath me, whispering his name. I felt alive, my body glowing, afire with every stroke of Ben's artful fingers, every brush of his lips across my skin. I trailed my hands up his arms, feeling his hard triceps, and lightly raked his back with my nails.

He jerked up, wincing, as my fingers scraped across the claw marks on his shoulder. I instantly yanked them back.

"Shit! Sorry!"

"It's all right." His voice was a ragged whisper in the darkness. "You didn't hurt me." His gaze roved over my face and bare chest, heavy with passion, as he lowered himself down. "God, you're beautiful," he breathed into my ear, making me shiver. "If I were allowed to talk, I'd tell you how gorgeous you are. But since I'm not..." His lips closed on my earlobe, and I squeaked, feeling his smile. He seemed different now, more playful and less guarded, perhaps lost to desire, same as I was.

Once more, he raised his head, mouth and hands skimming my stomach, moving slowly downward. I closed my eyes as he reached my navel, right above the hem of my jeans, and raised my hips as he undid the button and eased the fabric down. My panties and shoes hit the floor with my jeans, and I was laid out before him, naked and aching for his touch.

Abruptly, he scooted forward again, taking my lips with his own, thrusting with his tongue. I whimpered and arched into him as Ben caressed my breasts, my stomach, then very slowly moved his fingers down, slipping them between my legs, into my wet folds. I gasped into his mouth as he stroked lightly, circling gently with one finger, and I nearly came apart in his hands.

Oh, yes. I moaned softly and writhed beneath his stroking fingers. *Yes, more. I want to feel more. Shatter me. Make me feel alive.*

Somewhere outside, a rabid screamed, chilling and terrifying, but I was too far gone to even care. Ben was circling my bud; this was sweet, exquisite torture, and I could feel myself tightening, tightening...

"Come for me, Kylie," Ben crooned in a velvet whisper, and I erupted, throwing my head back and biting my lip as my insides fluttered and convulsed and I melted onto the quilt, shuddering with release.

As I lay there, reeling, Ben rolled off the bed and stood, slipping out of his jeans. The mattress shifted as he clambered back on, a smooth, muscular jungle cat. I felt his length graze my stomach as he moved between my legs, positioning himself over me, and trembled in anticipation. *Protection,* my logical doctor's brain objected, a faint, weak plea, but I shoved it aside. The world outside was ending. I was not going to worry about the future. All I wanted to feel was the *now.*

With one quick, masterful stroke, Ben slid inside me. I stifled a cry and rose to meet him, arching off the bed as his arm snaked under my back, pinning me to his chest. We began a slow, rolling rhythm that quickened and intensified with every gasp, every panting breath and muffled groan. I buried my face in his neck, biting his hot skin to keep from crying out, as every thrust brought me closer to the edge again.

The white-hot pressure building inside released, and I couldn't contain the shriek that tore free as waves of pleasure radiated out from my core. Ben gasped and followed me over, crushing me to his chest with one arm, the other braced against the mattress as he poured himself into me.

We slumped to the quilt, panting. Ben carefully eased out and settled behind me, wrapping his arms around my waist, pulling me to his chest. My body was still tingling from the aftershocks, and I could feel his warm skin where it pressed against mine. The crazy whirlwind of emotion and passion faded, and I shivered as, just outside the walls, I heard the rabids, shuffling around. Still out there.

Ben kissed my bare shoulder, blew out the candle, then pulled the quilt over us both. "Don't think about them," he whispered as the warmth and darkness closed around us like a cocoon. "They can't get in, they don't know we're here. Try to get some sleep."

I shouldn't be feeling this safe, but I believed him. Of course, that could be because I was completely spent, warm and satisfied, and the quilt combined with Ben's body heat was making me drowsy. I felt protected here. Ben held me tighter and, wrapped in the nest of his arms, I faded into a dreamless sleep.

· 8 ·

The next morning, the dark stranger was gone. He left nothing behind, nothing to indicate he had been there at all, except a short note on the kitchen table.

Apologies for the sudden departure, but I could not stay. There is a vehicle in the garage with enough fuel to get you where you need to go. The rabids cannot be out in the sun and will sleep when it is light out. Travel only by day and seek shelter before night falls.
I will remember your words about the past and making things right. You will likely never see me again, but you've helped me more than you know. For that, you have my gratitude.
-K

We took the van, which had the keys in the ignition, probably left by our mysterious friend, and got out of town as quickly as we could. The streets and roads were eerily deserted, though subtle signs of the monsters' presence lingered: broken windows, doors with claw marks slashed across their surface. The bones and shredded carcass of an animal lying in a dark stain on the side of the road.

Rabids, the stranger had called them. It fit. I wondered where he was now, where he was going. I hoped, wherever it was, he would find his peace.

We drove all afternoon and through the evening, following the deserted highway as it wound its way through a desolate, empty world. I sneaked glances at Ben, at his rugged profile, and every time my skin flushed and my stomach squirmed. Last night…I didn't know what to make of it yet, what had come over us. I didn't know if our lovemaking had been brought on by our hopeless circumstances, a desperate need to connect to another human being when we thought we could die, or if it had been…something more.

Did I want something more…with Ben?

I didn't really have much to compare it to. I'd been in relationships before, of course, even thought I was in love, once, at the ripe old age of fifteen. But when I'd left for college, boyfriends and relationships had taken a backseat to my future career. I didn't have time for a serious commitment; my life revolved around my work and school. The couple guys I did go out with soon realized they played second fiddle in my life, and ended things after a few months. I barely gave them a second thought.

But Ben…was different.

We stopped a couple times for gas and other necessities, siphoning fuel from abandoned cars and raiding gas stations and minimarts for food. As the afternoon wore on, Ben grew increasingly nervous and quiet, brooding over the steering wheel with his gaze far away. I asked him, once, if he was afraid we wouldn't make it before nightfall, but he shook his head and said we would get there before the sun went down. When I pressed him further, asking if anything was wrong, I received a mostly empty smile and the assurance that he was fine, that it wasn't anything I should worry about.

Of course, that just made me worry more.

We stopped one last time at a gas station atop an off-ramp, and Ben siphoned gas from an old tanker while I answered a call of nature inside, despite the fact that the toilet was beyond disgusting. We hadn't spoken for nearly an hour, and I'd given up trying to draw him out.

When I returned, Ben was screwing the cap back onto the tank, so I moved past him to the door, ready to get on the road. He called my name as I went by, but I ignored him, opening the door to slide in.

He caught me by the wrist and drew me to him, wrapping his arms around my waist. I stiffened but didn't have it in me to push him off.

"Hey." His voice was quiet, apologetic. "I'm sorry. I know I've been distracted. I didn't mean to ignore you." His hand came up, brushing my hair back. "It's not you, I promise."

I slumped a bit in relief. "What's going on, Ben?"

"It's just…" He sighed. "My family. I haven't seen them in so long, I don't know what they're going to say when I come back. If they're alive at all." His face darkened, and he gazed out over the trees. "God, I hope it hasn't spread that far. I would rather they be…dead…than turned into those things." Shivering, he held me tighter. "I don't think I could handle seeing them like that."

My heart ached for him, and I reached up to stroke his cheek, bringing his attention back to me. His eyes softened, and he leaned down, kissing me gently. It was not like last night, hard and desperate and needing to feel something, anything, to remind ourselves that we were still alive. This was tender and thoughtful, a promise without words and a hint of something more, something that could be forever.

"We'll figure it out when we get there," I whispered when I could breathe again.

The road wound on, and the sun continued to sink toward the horizon, making me check its position every few minutes. It felt strange, watching the once-cheerful sun slip away like sands through an hourglass, feeling tiny flutters of panic the lower it dropped and the longer the shadows became. I was contemplating telling Ben to stop for the night, to not risk pushing further into the evening, when he suddenly turned off the main highway and onto a smaller road. We drove through a small town, chillingly empty, and continued down several winding, one-lane roads. At last, as the sun became a brilliant orange ball on the horizon, he turned off the pavement onto a bumpy dirt path that snaked between a field and a line of trees, and the van lurched to a halt.

Ben stared down the road, his face lit by the setting sun. I glanced past him out the side window and saw a battered mailbox nailed to a fence post, soggy letters hanging out the front and rotting to mush in the grass below. The side of the mailbox read *Archer* in faded white paint.

Ben drew in a deep breath, and I reached over to lay a hand on his leg. He looked at me, managed a sickly smile, and started the van again.

We bounced down that tiny path for quite some time, until we rounded a bend, and a monstrous old farmhouse rose from the sea of grass. Perched atop a hill, it looked ancient and foreboding and desolate, a faded gray-white structure against a backdrop of clouds, glaring down at the tractor supplies and rusty cars scattered around its base. A collection of whimsical statues in the front yard did nothing for its somber appearance.

"Looks deserted," Ben whispered in a voice that was half terrified, half relieved. We inched up the driveway, gravel crunching under the tires, until we reached the first of the rusty shells of cars left to disintegrate in the grass. Ben parked the van and opened the door, gazing up at the farmhouse. I followed his example.

"Hello?" Ben called, slamming the door. The sounds echoed thinly over the silent fields. "Anyone here? Hello?"

A metallic click made my hair stand on end.

A man slid out from behind a car, and another followed on the other side of the driveway, blocking our path. Both held rifles pointed in our direction. Our weapon still lay on the backseat of the van.

Ben raised his hands as the men glared at him, their faces hard. One was lanky and rawboned, the other grizzled and huge, but they both looked dangerous and unfriendly. "Don't know who you are," the big one growled through a thick brown beard, shoving the gun barrel at Ben, "but you can get in your car and drive back the way you came. We got nothin' here for the likes of you."

My heart was pounding, but Ben stared at the man with a faint, puzzled frown on his face, as if trying to remember something. The man scowled back.

"Hey, you hear what I said, boy? If you and the little lady know what's good for you, you'll hightail it outta here, before I put a lead slug in your stupid—"

"Uncle Jack," Ben breathed. The man stopped, squinting at him down the gun barrel, then his thick eyebrows arched into his hair.

"Damn. Benjamin Archer, is that you?" He snorted and lowered the rifle, and I nearly collapsed in relief. "Last I saw of you, boy, you were this sulky teenager always trying to get out of heavy work." He shook his head and gave Ben a piercing look. "We heard you ran off to the city an' broke your mama's heart, swearin' you'd never come back."

Ben shifted uncomfortably, not meeting my gaze. "Yeah, well, things change. Are Mom and Dad around?"

Before he could answer, the screen door banged open, and a man stepped onto the porch. I swallowed, glancing between the two of them. He looked like a grizzled version of Ben, with gray streaked through his brown hair and a neatly trimmed beard. Dark eyes raked over us both, hard and cold, lingering on Ben. He didn't smile.

Ben stepped forward, approaching the front door. "Dad…"

"Get out."

The command was unyielding. My stomach plummeted. Ben came to a halt a few feet from the steps, gazing up at the older man, his voice pleading but calm. "We have nowhere else to go."

"You should've thought of that before you went traipsing off to the city and left the rest of us to pick up your slack." His cold eyes flicked to me, and one corner of his lip curled. "Now you come dragging yourself back, with a pregnant girlfriend most likely, and expect us to welcome you home like nothing happened? After what you said to me, and your mother?"

I bristled, stepping forward, as well, but Ben gave me a pleading look, warning me not to get involved. "You want me to say it?" he asked, turning back to his father. His hands rose away from his sides in a hopeless gesture. "I'm sorry. You were right, and I was an ass. I should have never left."

"Four years too late, Benjamin." Mr. Archer's expression didn't change. Neither did his uncompromising tone. "You made it very clear that you are no longer a part of this family. As far as I'm concerned, you can go back to whatever city hole you crawled out of. You have no place here anymore."

I couldn't see Ben's expression, but the way his posture slumped hinted at the devastation on his face, and my blood boiled. Stepping around the van, I marched up the driveway, coming to stand next to Ben. "What the hell is wrong with you?" I demanded, and all four men stared at me in shock. I ignored them and faced Ben's father, seething, as he turned that cold glare on me. "Don't you know what's happening out there? People are dying! Cities are empty, and you're going to stand there and tell your son that he can't come home? Because of some stupid argument you had four years ago?"

"Who the hell is this?" Mr. Archer asked, not speaking to me, but to Ben. "Some tramp you picked up off a street corner?"

I took a step forward, raising my chin. "If by 'tramp' you mean 'doctor,' then yes, I am," I answered before Ben could speak. "Ben came to my clinic when his friend got sick, so let me tell you what I've seen before he showed up. I've seen people puking blood in the streets, right before they drown in it, and their bodies lying there because no one is alive to take them away. I've seen infected mothers smother their own infants with a pillow so they won't have to suffer a long, painful death. I've seen piles of bodies rotting in open pits, because there are too many to bury and everyone is too busy dying to dig more graves. *That* is what is happening out there now, and *that* is the world you're going to send Ben into. So if you want to be a heartless, stubborn bastard over something that happened *four years* ago, that's your decision. But I will tell you this right now—you're handing out a death sentence. To your son. Send him away, and you kill him."

I didn't mention the rabids, not wanting to look like a raving lunatic in front of these people we needed to convince. I suddenly understood Ben's reluctance to talk about them at the clinic; it did sound like something from a horror movie. Ben's father still wore a stone-faced expression, no crack in his flinty mask, but the other men looked rather pale and concerned, yet still unwilling to step in for us. I felt Ben's gaze on me but didn't dare turn to face him.

The tension mounted. Then the screen door banged, startling us all, and a woman rushed onto the porch. Tanned, bony, her steel-blond hair coming loose of its bun, she took one look at Ben and flung herself down the steps with a cry.

"Ben!" I stepped back as she embraced him fiercely, almost wildly, and he hugged her back. "Benjamin! Oh, you're home! Thank God, I knew you'd come home! I prayed for you every night. Samson, look!" She turned to beam tearfully at the man on the porch. "Ben's home! He's come home."

Tentative hope blossomed through me. Ben's father pursed his lips as if he'd swallowed something foul, turned and vanished inside, slamming the door behind him. Ben winced, but the woman, his mother I presumed, didn't seem to care. I felt a tiny twinge of longing, watching them, and swallowed the sudden lump in my throat. I would never see my parents again.

"Mom." Ben freed himself from her embrace and turned to me, holding out a hand. "This is Kylie. She helped me get here." His eyes met mine, solemn and grave. "I wouldn't have made it this far if it wasn't for her."

"Bless you, dear." I was suddenly enveloped in the thin, steely arms of Ben's mother. She pulled back, holding me at arm's length, sharp blue eyes appraising. "Thank you for bringing him home."

I shot Ben a desperate look, and he cleared his throat. "Mom," he began as she turned back, releasing me from her wiry grip. "What's happening? Is everyone all right?" He paled, looking back toward the house. "Rachel. Is she…?"

"Your sister is fine," Mrs. Archer said firmly, and Ben slumped in relief. I gave a little start, not having known he had a sister. "And if you're talking about that horrid sickness, we heard what's been on the news, before all the stations went down. That's why your uncle Jack is here." She nodded to the two men, who were walking back to their posts. "He lost everyone," she whispered, her voice sympathetic. "Your aunt Susan, his three boys, all the farmhands. Except Shane, there. It was so horrible." She shook her head, and tears filled her eyes. "I just thank God that it hasn't spread out here, yet. I guess because we're so isolated."

Ben relaxed, as if a huge weight had been lifted from his shoulders. "Where is Rachel?" he asked, a smile creeping onto his face. "Did she move into my old room, like she always wanted?" He looked toward the house again, excitement and longing peeking through the worry. He looked very big-brother-ish then, and I smiled.

"She went to feed the goats a few minutes ago," Mrs. Archer said, beaming. "Your sister has turned into quite the little goatherd, Ben. There's an orphaned kid who follows her around like a puppy. It's adorable, though we could do without her letting the thing sleep with her at night. But Samson can't tell her no." She sighed and pointed a finger over the distant hills, where a sliver of red hung on the horizon. "She's probably out in the far pasture right now."

A chill went through me, and by the blood draining from Ben's face, he was thinking the same thing. At that very moment, it seemed, the sun slipped behind the tree line and shadows crept over the fields like grasping claws.

"Rachel," Ben whispered, and took off, running toward the pasture and the darkness looming beyond the fence line.

9

"Ben! Where are you going?"

Mrs. Archer's cry rang out behind us, but Ben didn't slow down, his long legs hurrying across the field. I scrambled to keep up as he strode through the tall grass to the pasture surrounding the building and leaped the fence without breaking stride.

Squeezing between the boards, I followed. Sheep and goats scattered before us with startled bleats and watched us curiously from several yards away. A massive shaggy dog, pure white with a huge thick head, eyed us warily as we rushed across the field, but it didn't appear threatening as long as we didn't bother its herd.

In the farthest pasture, a small group of long-eared goats milled around a figure with a pair of buckets, bleating and trying to stick their heads into the containers. Just beyond them, beyond the fence line, the forest crowded forward with long, dark fingers.

"Rachel!" Ben called, and the figure looked up, a skinny girl of about twelve, light brown hair braided down her back. She gasped, dropping her buckets, which the goats swarmed over immediately, and sprinted into Ben's arms.

"Benji!"

Ben hugged her tightly, then pulled back a little, shaking his head as I came up. "Hey, Scarecrow. I told you I hate that name— Ow!" he yelped as the girl hauled off and slugged him in the arm with a small fist. "What was that for?"

"Jerkoff!" Rachel snapped, scowling at him, though her eyes were bright and glassy. "You never showed up for my birthday, or Christmas, or anytime you said you would. Stupid jerk, making Mom cry." She hit him again, and this time he accepted it, his expression going solemn. She glared at him, fists clenched, ready to continue the abuse. "Are you back for good? Or are you going to be stupid and leave again?"

"I'm back for good," Ben told her. "I'm not going anywhere this time, I promise."

That seemed to placate her, for her curious gaze suddenly shifted to me. At that moment, I noticed a small white creature sniffing around my legs: a baby goat with black legs and dark splotches down his back. It nipped the hem of my jeans, and I squealed.

"Davy, no." Rachel freed herself from Ben and gathered the goat in her arms. "He's not trying to be mean," she explained. "He's just curious."

"Benjamin? Rachel?" Mrs. Archer's voice cut across the field, and the older woman came striding up, shielding her eyes. "Are you three all right?" she asked, giving us all a worried look. "What's going on?"

Ben cast a nervous glance at the forest and took a deep breath. "Let's go inside," he suggested, leading us all away from the trees and the shadows beyond the fence. "We…Kylie and I…have to tell you something. And everyone needs to hear it."

"That's the biggest load of bull I've ever heard."

I bit the inside of my cheek to keep back a frustrated, snapping reply and faced Ben's father calmly. "That is the truth, Mr. Archer. Believe it or not, but it's true. We've both seen it with our own eyes."

We were in the Archer family's kitchen, huddled around the table. All of us, which was pretty impressive. The Archer clan, it seemed, was quite the large, extended family, with aunts, uncles, brothers and sisters, cousins, in-laws, nieces, nephews, even some farmhands, all packed into one room. When the plague had hit and people had begun dying, the Archers had sent out the call for everyone to come home, bringing the family under one roof.

Ben had not received this call.

"You're talking about zombies," Samson Archer said in disgust. "Walking dead people. Movie monsters." He sneered. "You must think we're mighty stupid."

"They killed my friend," Ben said softly, though I could hear the quiet anger below the surface. "They killed him, and he came back to life and attacked me. I have the scars to prove it." He looked around the table at the grim, skeptical faces, and his voice grew even harder. "This is real. These things are real, and they're out there, and they're coming. If we're not ready for them, they'll tear this place to pieces and everyone here will die. That's the truth of it."

Silence fell as the reality of everything sank in. I could understand their skepticism, their disbelief. One person they might've shrugged off as crazy, but two accounts made them hesitate. Even if I was a stranger, I was still a doctor, and I was from the city. And then, Ben pulled up his shirt, revealing the still-healing claw marks down his back, eliciting a horrified cry from Mrs. Archer, and that was enough to convince them that *something* was truly out there.

An older woman, one of Ben's many aunts, spoke up, her voice shaking. "Shouldn't we leave, then? We're all alone here—"

"No." Samson Archer's voice cut through the suggestion like a knife. "I'm not going anywhere," he said flatly. "This has been our home for eight generations, and I'll be damned if some zombie apocalypse will drive me off my own land." His steely gaze went around the table, and most everyone looked away. "Anyone who wants to leave, leave. Right now. Because the only way I'll leave this place is in a long wooden box."

Or in a rabid's stomach, I thought ungraciously, but didn't voice it out loud.

Ben stood up. "We're not ready for them, not yet," he said. "We have to get this house fortified if we're going to stand a chance when they show up. We should start right away—I don't think we have a lot of time."

"Since when did you become the head of this family, boy?" Mr. Archer asked in a low, dangerous voice. "Last time I checked, *I* owned this land and this house, and you were the one who didn't want anything to do with us."

Ben paused. He took a slow breath, then met his father's gaze. "Fine. What would you have us do?"

"We'll start with the house." Samson Archer raised his voice for the rest of the group, taking charge. "Fortify the doors, board up the windows. See if we can't attach some of that old rebar to the frames from outside. After that, we'll work on the barn—the livestock will need to be protected, as well. We'll set up watches at night, and we'll have a safe room the women can retreat to if something gets inside. Everyone got that?"

Everyone did. I was surprised and, reluctantly, a little impressed. Samson Archer might be a mean, sexist sonofabitch, but he knew how to protect himself and his land. However, as everyone at the table rose, preparing to carry out his instructions, Samson gave both of us the coldest, most withering glare yet, and I knew that, even if we survived the rabids sweeping across the land, our biggest challenge was going to be the man standing in front of us.

That first night, nothing happened. We fortified the old farmhouse, nailing boards across windows and installing a bar across the front door. The next day we continued to secure the house, creating a room in the basement that we could fall back to and lock from the inside if needed. When night fell, we set up watches on the porch and the roof, as the hilltop farm offered a fantastic view of the fields all the way to the woods. If anything came shuffling out of the trees, at least we would see it coming.

Nothing happened on the second night, either.

When the house was secure, we moved on to the barn where the goats and other livestock would be kept at night, closing all windows and reinforcing the heavy sliding doors. The barn became a virtual fortress; the livestock had to be just as well-protected as the humans, as they were the key to our survival now that the outside world was in turmoil. No more running to Walmart for steaks, eggs and milk. At least, not for a long time.

After the third night, people began to mutter. What if we were wrong? What if the house was too isolated to be in any real danger? What if all this work was for nothing? As the nights wore on, tension flagged, nervousness disappeared and people began to revert to their old habits and routines.

Ben and I kept pushing, however. Just because the rabids hadn't found us yet didn't mean they weren't out there. During the day, Ben helped the men fortify the property, while I stayed in the farmhouse and helped the women as they gathered food supplies, water, medicine, candles, soap and other necessities. At night, when Ben wasn't on watch, I would curl up with him beneath the quilt in the guest bedroom and we would make love, pressed tightly against each other in the darkness. And I would fall asleep wrapped in Ben's arms, listening to his slow, deep breathing and basking in the warmth of his body.

One morning, about a week after we'd come to the homestead, I walked out onto the porch to find Ben and his father standing in the driveway. By Ben's frustrated, angry gestures and Samson's cold glare, it was obvious they were in the middle of an argument.

"And I'm saying we shouldn't leave the farm," Ben said, stabbing his finger down the driveway. "Dammit, you haven't seen these things. You don't know what they can do, how many of them are out there. Sending people into town is going to get them killed."

"We're low on ammunition," Samson said in his flinty voice. "And the women are complaining that we're running out of certain things. We need more firepower if we're going to defend this house from your monsters. The town isn't far— if we leave now, we can get the supplies we need and make it back by sundown."

"You're going to get everyone killed."

"I don't need your opinions, boy." Samson narrowed his eyes. "This is happening, whether you like it or not. I've seen no evidence of your walking zombies, and the people in this house have to eat. We're going into town, so get out of the way."

"Fine." Ben raised a hand. "Then I'll come with you."

"No, you will not." Samson's mouth curled into a sneer, and Ben took a breath to argue. "I won't have you whining at us the whole trip," he said, overriding Ben's unvoiced protest. "We don't need you. I'm taking Jack and Shane, and you can stay here with the women. I'm sure they can find something for you to do."

Without waiting for an answer, Samson spun on a heel and continued down the driveway, where Jack and Shane waited in the back of an ancient-looking pickup. Ben watched them, fists clenched at his sides, until the truck bounced away down the gravel drive and disappeared around a bend.

"Dammit!" Ben turned and kicked the ground in a rare show of temper, sending gravel flying. "Stupid, stubborn old man!" He spotted me then, watching from the porch, and winced. "Hey. Did you hear all that?"

I nodded and stepped off the porch, slipping into his arms. "I'm sure they'll be okay," I told him, peering up at his face. "Your father is a bastard—sorry—but he knows how to take care of himself. And he knows not to stay out past sunset."

Ben frowned. "I know he's looking out for everyone, but he shouldn't compromise people's safety just to put me in my place." He sighed and gazed down the driveway. "I wonder if he'll ever forgive me for walking out on them."

I didn't have anything to say to that, so I just held him as we stood in the middle of the driveway and watched the road, as if we could will the truck and its occupants into appearing, safe and unharmed.

"I guess I should get back to the barn," Ben muttered at last. Glancing down at me, his eyes softened. "You have apple peels in your hair." He picked a sliver of red skin from my ponytail. "What have *you* been doing all morning?"

I grimaced. "Busy discovering that I became a doctor for a reason, since the mechanics of turning fruit into preserves is completely lost on me. I think your aunt Sarah was just about to ban me from the kitchen permanently."

Ben laughed. Pulling me close, he kissed me deeply in the middle of the driveway. My stomach did a backflip. I slid my hands up his back and held him tight, feeling the hard muscles shift through his shirt. I wanted to take away his pain, the guilt still lingering in his eyes. Because, even though he was home, he wasn't part of the family; as long as Samson kept him at arm's length, he would always be an outcast. Just like me, a city girl and an outsider. Someone who didn't know the first thing about goats, or chickens, or making preserves.

That was fine with me. I could learn. And Samson would eventually forgive Ben, or at least start treating him like a human instead of the mud on his boots. And if he didn't, that was fine, too. We would be outsiders together, and maybe together we could save this stubborn family.

Ben suddenly pulled back, his gaze intense. One hand rose to stroke my cheek, sending little flutters through my stomach. "Kylie, I—"

"Kylie, dear?" Aunt Sarah appeared in the doorway. In one hand she held a long wooden spoon, covered in bits of fruit mush. "Oh, there you are. Are you ready to give this another go?"

We both sighed.

"You go on," Ben said, reluctantly pulling back. "I have some work to finish." He caught my hand as I drew away. "Will you tell me when Dad and the others get back? I'll be checking in every five minutes, otherwise."

"Sure."

He looked as if he wanted to kiss me again, but Sarah was still watching us, so he gave me a quick peck on the cheek and left, striding away toward the barn. I stifled a groan and returned to the kitchen and the torture of canning.

The afternoon wore on, and Samson did not return.

A tense silence hung over the farmhouse that evening. Everyone knew the three men had gone into town, and by now, even if they didn't quite believe the rabids were out there, we had at least made everyone nervous about the sun setting. Said sun now hovered over the distant hills, dangerously low and sinking lower with every minute. As Mrs. Archer and some of the women bustled about the kitchen making dinner, I busied myself with setting the table, finally free from my disastrous canning attempts. But every thirty seconds or so, someone would glance out the window and down the road, searching for headlights or listening for the rumble of a distant engine. Dinner was solemn, and afterwards, as the kids and women cleared the dishes, some of the younger men began arguing about sending a search party. Surprisingly, Ben was the one to talk them down, saying that we had to give them until sunset, that if we left now, we wouldn't make it back before dark.

Restless, needing to get out of the tension-filled farmhouse, I wandered onto the front porch, breathing in the cool evening air. A breeze whispered through the grass, moaning through the trees surrounding the field, and I shivered. Rubbing my arms, I glanced toward the sun and found only a half-circle of red, sliding behind a cloud. As I watched, unable to look away, it shrank to a crescent, then a sliver, then finally vanished altogether.

"Kylie?"

I jumped, spinning around at the deep voice. A shimmering blob of color hovered in front of my vision, and I had to blink several times before I could see who it was.

"Geez, Ben. Sneak much?"

"Sorry." He joined me at the railing. "What are you doing out here?"

"Just needed some air." I rubbed my arms and nodded to the darkening sky, trying not to shiver. "Sun's gone down, Ben."

"I know."

"Your father isn't back yet."

"I know." He ran his fingers through his hair, looking uncomfortable, as if there was something he didn't want to tell me. I was afraid I already knew what it was.

"You're going after them, aren't you?"

Ben nodded. "I figured we'd give them until sunset to make it back," he said, glancing at the fading orange glow on the horizon where the sun had been. "But we can't leave them out there now, even though it'll be full dark when we make it to town. We have to go look for them."

"You know I'm coming with you."

"Kylie—"

"Don't you dare give me any crap about this, Ben Archer." I glared at him. "I am a doctor, and it's my duty to help people. What if someone is injured, or bleeding? I am not going to sit here and wash dishes while you go off to face these things alone. So save your 'I am a manly man' speech, because you're not getting rid of me that easily."

He looked torn between amusement and exasperation. "I know that," he snapped, matching my glare with his own. "I wasn't going to tell you to stay here. I already told Donald and Chris that you'll be coming with us. That's not what I was going to say."

"Oh," I said, faintly embarrassed. "Well…what were you going to say, then?"

For some reason, this seemed to fluster him more, and he scrubbed a hand over his face, wincing. "Christ, this is going badly. Kylie…I know we've just met, and everything has gone crazy, and I probably shouldn't even be thinking of this right now, but…" He looked down, swallowed, then met my eyes. "I want to know what your plans are…with me."

"You?"

"I'm staying, Kylie." Turning away, he gazed over the fields, resting both hands on the railing. "I want to build a life here, if I can," he murmured. "No more running, or fighting with my past. I'm done. Dad can rake me over the coals all he wants, but I'm staying here. This is where I belong."

I was glad to hear it. Family seemed important to Ben, even if certain members made life difficult for everyone. But despite the tension and occasional argument, this was a strong community, and I was glad that he had found his place, that he was finally home.

"Except," Ben continued, facing me again, "I don't know what your plans are. You once said you didn't know if you could settle down. And I wouldn't force you to do anything, but...you could have a place here, if you wanted it. With me."

"What do you mean?"

My heart pounded. This sounded very much like a proposal without the words. I didn't know what to say or think. Ben wanted to build a life together...but was it only because he recognized the need to keep the family strong? We'd only known each other a short time, barely more than a week. What did Ben really want from me? And what did *I* really want, from him?

Ben moved closer, sliding his hands up my arms. "Kylie, I..."

A shot rang out in the darkness.

We jerked, all senses rigidly alert, listening as the echo of the gunshot faded away. Ben's hands were clenched on my arms, squeezing painfully, but I barely noticed.

More shots, several this time, rapid, frantic. Ben released me, ran into the house and emerged seconds later with the shotgun. My heart clenched as he leaped off the porch, sprinting down the driveway. After a second's deliberation, I followed.

"Kylie, go back to the house!" he growled, sparing a glance over his shoulder. I ignored him, and he spun, grabbing my arm again, his face tense.

"Don't!" I snapped before he could say anything. "I'm coming with you, so don't waste time telling me I'm not."

His eyes darkened, but then the shots came again, closer this time, followed by a scream of anguish. Ben gave me one last angry look and sprinted down the driveway again, me trailing doggedly behind.

We neared the road, and I gasped. Samson and Ben's uncle Jack were staggering up the driveway, weapons drawn, gasping for breath. Samson was covered in blood, though he didn't look injured, and Jack's face was so pale it almost glowed in the twilight. As Ben jogged toward them, I looked around, hoping to see their final member limping frantically up the driveway, but he was nowhere in sight.

"What happened?" Ben demanded, taking Jack's weight as the big man stumbled and nearly fell. "You were supposed to be back hours ago. Where's Shane?"

Samson's eyes were huge, scary orbs in his bloody face. His beard and hair were streaked with crimson as he pointed down the road.

"Truck broke down a few miles from town," he panted, shaking with gasps as Ben grabbed his arm. "We had to abandon the supplies...try to make it back on foot. They were everywhere, came right out of the fucking ground. Shane... didn't make it." His face crumpled with anger and grief, before he shook himself free. "Hurry, I think they're right behind us."

"Samson, you're hurt," I said, remembering, for one horrible moment, Nathan's snarling face as he'd lunged at me, eyes empty of thought or reason. I remembered the wound on his arm, the seeping bite mark that had been the start of everything. "Did one of them bite you?"

"Dammit, girl! There's no time!" Samson gave me a wild glare and started limping up the driveway. "Get everyone inside!" he ordered as we hurried to catch up. "Lock the doors!" he bellowed as several people crowded onto the porch, wide-eyed. Mrs. Archer and Rachel were among them, with Davy, the goat, peering at us from behind her legs. She scooped him up and fled inside. "Secure the barn," Samson continued as we staggered up the steps. "Close the windows, and get all the women and kids into the basement!" He turned to me and Ben, his dark eyes intense. "Everyone grab a weapon, because I think there's a lot of them."

An eerie wailing rose from the trees around us, making my hair stand on end. We lurched through the door and slammed it behind us as the chilling cries drew closer, and we prepared for what might be our last night alive.

10

They slid out of the darkness like wraiths, a pale, monstrous swarm, cresting the rise at the top of the driveway. Even huddled behind a window, peering through the slats in the boards, I could see their faces, their dead white eyes and slack jaws bristling with fangs. Most of them still wore the clothes they had died in, torn and filthy now, some with darker, more ominous stains spattered across the fabric.

"Mother of God," one of the men swore beside me. Shuddering, I drew away from the window and turned to where Samson was giving orders a few feet away, one hand planted against the table to keep himself upright.

"Douse all the lights," he hissed at a nephew, who scrambled to obey him. "Make sure everyone has a weapon, but, for the love of God, don't fire unless they're coming in through the walls! Let's keep our heads, people!"

"Samson," I said, stepping between him and Ben. "You need to let me examine you. If you've been bitten—"

"I'm fine." Samson smacked my hand away. "Get downstairs with the rest of the womenfolk, girl. You'll just be in our way up here."

I bristled, but Ben put a hand to the small of my back. "She can help," he said quietly. "She knows how to shoot, and if anyone gets hurt she can patch them up quicker than anyone here. She stays."

Samson glared at us both, then snorted. "I don't have time for this. Fine, give the woman a gun if she wants, and tell her to stay back from the windows. Everyone else, *shut up!*" His voice hissed through the room, quieting the mutters, the terrified whispers that we were all going to die. Silence fell, and Samson glowered at the small group of frightened humans. "We all knew this was coming. You all had the choice to leave, but you stayed. We are not going to lose our heads and make stupid mistakes. The survival of this family depends on us, and we will make our stand here."

A soft, drawn-out creak echoed from outside, as the first of the rabids eased onto the porch.

Everyone froze or silently ducked behind cover, as the pale, hissing swarm crowded the front door. Ben and I peeked around the kitchen doorway, seeing them through the slats over the windows, watching as they poked their claws between the wood, testing it. No one moved, not even when one of the rabids pressed its face to the wall and peered in with a bulging white eye, scanning the room. With a hiss, it pulled back and shuffled off, and the mob on the front porch slowly cleared out. We could still hear them, though, stalking the perimeter of the house, searching for a way in. But, for now at least, they hadn't seen us. I hoped they couldn't smell us, though it was obvious they knew something was inside. Maybe they had no sense of smell if they were already dead? I didn't know, and right now, I couldn't worry about it. Samson was hurt, and stubborn ass or no, he needed help.

"Ben," I whispered when everything was still again. "I have to check your father. He needs medical attention, whether he likes it or not. You saw what happened...with Nathan."

He nodded stiffly. "I know." For a moment, that ugly pain was there again, darkening his eyes. Then he shook it off, and an iron determination took its place. "What do you need me to do?"

"See if you can get him into the bathroom. There are no

windows there, and I'll need a light to see what I'm doing." I peeked into the front room again, checking for rabid silhouettes in the windows. "I'll need to go to our room and get my medical supplies. See if you can convince the stubborn fool to let me take care of him before—"

A thud echoed through the darkness, and everyone jumped, raising their weapons. Ben and I rushed into the room to find Samson collapsed under the table, moaning softly. The rest of the men gaped at his body and at each other, looking lost.

Ben stepped forward, smacking one of the men on the shoulder as he passed. "Dale, help me get him up. The rest of you, go back to your posts. The rabids are still out there. Kylie..." He glanced back at me, and I nodded.

"I'll get my bag."

Minutes later, the three of us huddled on the bathroom floor, with Samson slumped against the tub and Ben shining a flashlight over my shoulder. The older man had regained consciousness, but seemed oddly complacent as I cut off his shirt, only commenting once that a knife would work better. Ignoring him, I gingerly peeled back the fabric, revealing a dark mass of blood and mangled flesh below his ribs. Ben drew in a sharp breath.

"Dad, what the hell? Why didn't you say anything?"

Samson Archer sighed. "Because I didn't need the lot of you worrying over me when we had fucking zombies coming up the driveway."

"What happened?" I asked, liberally soaking a towel in disinfectant before pressing it to the wound. Samson hissed through his teeth, clenching his jaw.

"One of the bastards grabbed Shane. He started screaming, and I went back to help him. Then another one of 'em came right out of the ground, right under my feet. It latched on, and by the time I got it off, they'd torn Shane to pieces."

"Dammit," Ben growled behind me. "Kylie, can you tell what kind of wound it is? Is he…" He trailed off, and Samson narrowed his eyes.

"Am I what?"

"I don't know," I said, moving Ben's arm to hold the light at a better angle. The ragged flesh and blood made it difficult to determine what kind of damage it was. "Samson, do you remember if the rabid bit you?" I wasn't entirely certain how the virus spread, if it was passed on through the saliva or blood or something else. But Nathan had been bitten, and everything at the clinic started with that, so I wasn't taking any chances. "Did it bite you?" I asked again, firmer this time. "Or did it just grab you with its claws?"

"Shit, woman, I don't know. I was just trying to get the bastard off of me. I didn't ask what it was doing."

I pulled my last syringe of painkiller from my bag. I'd found it in my coat pocket a few days ago when I was gathering our clothes to wash. "This is morphine," I told Samson, holding it up. "It will help with the pain. It will also put you to sleep, so don't be alarmed if you get drowsy or light-headed."

"Don't want to sleep," Samson growled, waving me off. "Can't sleep now. Who will look after everyone with those things out there?"

"I will," Ben said quietly.

Samson's lip curled. He glanced at Ben and took a breath to scoff, but stopped when Ben didn't look away. Father and son gazed at each other for a silent moment, and I didn't know what passed between them, but I took advantage of the moment to slip the needle into Samson's arm, injecting him with the painkiller. He jerked, glaring at me, then sighed.

"Stubborn, intractable woman," he muttered, though I thought I caught the faintest hint of reluctant respect below the surface. He snorted. "Know what's best for everyone, do you? Just like this insufferable idiot. You two are definitely made for each other."

I didn't answer, not wanting to snap at an injured patient, though I could feel Ben's anger behind me. Tossing the needle away, I was reaching for the gauze when Samson's bony fingers fastened on my arm.

Startled, I looked back to find him leaning in, staring at me intently. "Take care of him," he rasped in a voice almost too soft to be heard. "If I don't make it, watch out for him. Don't let him do anything stupid. You're the only one he listens to now."

He slumped against the tub, all the fight going out of him. I sat there a moment, shocked, pondering his words. Anger flickered. Samson had no right to demand I look out for his son, not when he'd done such a dismal job of it himself. And I didn't need his orders. I didn't need anyone telling me to take care of Ben. Maybe Samson had to be reminded that you took care of the ones you cared for, even if they'd hurt you in the past, but I already knew that. I was here because I cared for Ben. I was here because...

The reason hit me like a load of bricks, and I nearly dropped the bandages. Because...I loved him. Even after such a short time. I loved his strength, his loyalty, his fierce protectiveness when the need arose. The way he looked at me as if I was the most precious thing in the world, the way his hands slid gently across my skin. Even his faults, the guilt and inner torment, the darkness that he retreated into sometimes. I loved all of that. I couldn't live without him.

I was in love with Ben Archer.

I finished bandaging the wound, my body and hands acting on autopilot, but my mind far away. Then, still feeling as if I'd been blindsided, I helped Ben move Samson into our room and laid him out on the bed.

Samson's eyes were closed, and he seemed dead to the world, which was a small kindness considering the pain he must've been in. However, when we drew back, he stirred and raised his head, muttering something insensible. Ben glanced at me, then knelt beside his father and bent close, as Samson whispered something only they could hear. Ben gave a solemn nod, and Samson's head fell back onto the pillow. He finally drifted into unconsciousness.

"I'll stay with him," I whispered as Ben stood, looking grave. "You go out there and let everyone know what's going on."

He nodded gratefully and paused as if to say something, then seemed to think better of it. Spinning around, he grabbed a long wooden box from the top shelf, set it down, and carefully opened the top.

A revolver lay there, glimmering dully in the shadows. For a second, Ben stared at the gun, a tortured expression briefly crossing his face. But then he yanked the weapon from the case and turned to me.

"Here," he said, flipping it over and holding it out to me, handle first. "Just in case."

"Ben..."

"Take it, Kylie." Ben's eyes pleaded with me. "In case I'm not here and he... Just take it. Please."

Gingerly, I reached out and took the gun.

"Ben?" I called as he went through the door. He turned, raising his eyebrows, and I bit my lip. *Just tell him, Kylie. You might not get another chance. Tell him you want to stay here. That you want to be part of this family.*

That you've fallen in love with him.

But that question still lingered, plaguing me with indecision and doubt. Was Ben's offer based on love, or the need to continue his family line? Did he genuinely want me, or was this a joining of convenience? Ben had admitted that he needed me, and that he didn't want me to leave. He hadn't said anything about love.

I forced a smile. "Tell one of the boys to boil some water for me? I might need to do some stitching later."

He gave me a puzzled look but nodded and vanished silently into the hall.

It was a long night.

The monsters never gave up. All through the night and into the early-morning hours we heard them, circling the house, clawing at the windows and scratching at the walls. Sometime after midnight, we heard a wild screeching outside and realized that the rabids had discovered the livestock in the barn. The swarm had surrounded the building, tearing at the walls, and we heard the frantic bleats of the goats within. But there was nothing we could do except hope that our fortifications and the reinforced doors would be strong enough to keep the rabids from slaughtering everything.

Samson continued to worsen. His skin grew hot, and the wound turned puffy and red, fluid beginning to seep through the bandages. I kept close watch on his eyes and mouth, mentally preparing myself to see bloody flecks on his lips or worse, red tears streaming from his eyelids. Apart from the shuffle of the rabids outside and the occasional cough or shift from men in the living room, the house was eerily silent. Ben was a ghost, gliding from room to room, checking on everyone and calming nerves. "We're almost through this," I heard him murmur to a relative once. "They'll go away when the sun comes up. We just have to survive till then."

And then what? I thought. *What happens tomorrow night, and the night after that?*

Ben came silently into the room, startling me. I looked

up from my chair as he handed me a mug that steamed and smelled heavenly of coffee.

"Thought you could use this."

"Lifesaver, Ben." I took the offered mug and sipped deeply, welcoming the hot jolt of caffeine. Ben set his ever-present shotgun aside and perched on the ottoman, regarding me with tired eyes.

"How's Dad?"

"Hasn't changed." The same answer I'd given him the past three times he'd come by. I gazed at his haggard, tousled face and had the very strong urge to kiss it. I restrained myself and sipped my coffee. "How's everyone else?"

"Tired." Ben rubbed his forehead. "At least, everyone up here is exhausted. Rachel and some of the others downstairs actually managed to get some sleep. Kylie, you never answered my question last night."

I choked on coffee, sputtering and spilling it down my chin. Setting the cup down, I wiped my mouth with the back of my hand and stared at Ben's serious expression. "Is...is this the best time to discuss that?" I whispered.

He closed his eyes briefly, as if pained. "When will I get another chance?" he murmured, scooting closer. "We're surrounded by death, afraid to even move, and they're not going to go away. This..." He let out a heavy sigh. "This will be my life, every night. Fighting these things, trying to keep my family alive. And I realize it's not fair to you. You shouldn't feel like you have to stay because of me. If the world hadn't gone crazy, I wouldn't ask anyone to go through this, especially you."

A scream echoed from outside, and on the bed, Samson groaned. Ben shot him a worried, hopeful glance, but he fell silent and didn't stir again.

"Kylie, I need you here," Ben continued in a low, intense

voice. "You're the most important thing in my life now. As much as any member of my family, maybe more. But…I won't ask you to stay if you aren't certain you want to. It's your choice."

"Why do you want me to stay?" I whispered.

Ben blinked. "I…thought it was obvious."

I shook my head. "You told me you wanted to settle down, maybe even start a family. That sounds an awful lot like a proposal, Ben. But, you haven't said…how you feel about me. And I need to know, before I decide anything. I need to know if this is some partnership of convenience, or if you want me to stay because…"

Because you love me as much as I love you.

"Kylie." Ben sighed, running his hands through his hair. He looked embarrassed, uncomfortable, and my heart sank. "We've only known each other a couple weeks," he stammered, as my heart plummeted to my toes. "And after the whole Nathan situation, I was certain you hated me. I thought if I said anything, it would be too soon. That I would come across as some creepy, desperate guy and it would scare you off. And I couldn't bear the thought of you leaving, so I stayed quiet."

My heart roused a little, a tiny flare of hope lifting it up. "What are you trying to say?"

Ben swallowed. "I wanted to wait a little while. I thought that if we came here, and I convinced you to stay, I would have all the time in the world to tell you how I felt." He glanced toward the curtained window, and his face darkened. "But we don't have much time anymore, and it's selfish of me to ask you to stay here, just because I—"

He stopped. My stomach was in knots, my heart racing, hanging on for those next few words. I wanted to hear them. I *needed* to hear them. "Because you…?"

Ben slumped, letting out a long breath. Leaning forward, he eased off the ottoman but didn't stand, dropping to his knees in front of me. His calloused hands took mine and trapped them in gentle fingers, while his gorgeous, soulful dark eyes rose to meet my gaze.

"Because I love you," he whispered, and my flattened heart swelled nearly to bursting. "I am completely and irreversibly in love with you, ever since that first night in your clinic when you told me you had survived. You are the most amazing woman I've ever known, and I can say with complete sincerity that I wouldn't be here if I hadn't met you. You pulled me out of the darkness, and I will be forever grateful for that. I honestly don't know what I'll do if you leave." He squeezed my hands, his gaze never wavering from mine. "I love you, Kylie," he murmured. "Stay with me. Till the end of the world."

My eyes watered. Sliding forward, I wrapped my arms around his head and kissed him fiercely, feeling his arms yank me close. I buried my fingers in his hair and pressed myself against him, and for a moment everything—the rabids, Samson, the circle of death surrounding us on all sides—all melted away, and the only thing that mattered was the man in my arms. Let the world fall; I had my sanctuary right here. My own pocket of Eden.

"Ben?"

A soft, hesitant voice broke us apart, and we turned to see Rachel standing in the doorway, a flickering candle in hand, staring at us. But she wasn't smirking or frowning; her eyes were wide and teary, and her free hand wrung the front of her shirt in quick, nervous gestures.

"Rachel, honey." Ben let me go and crossed the room, kneeling down to face her. "You're supposed to be downstairs with Mom and Aunt Sarah and the rest of them," he said, putting himself, I noticed, between her and Samson's body on the bed. "You need to go back to the basement, now."

"I can't." The child sniffled, biting her lip. "I can't find Davy."

"Davy? Your goat?"

A nod. "I think he slipped out when I came upstairs to use the bathroom."

Ben frowned. "Go back to Mom," he told her, and the girl's lip trembled. He smoothed her hair and gently tugged on an end. "I'll find him and bring him back, okay?"

She sniffed and nodded. Turning, she padded down the hall, and we listened until the creak of the basement door echoed to us in the silence. Ben stood with a grimace.

"Care to go goat hunting with me?"

A soft clink came from the kitchen before I could answer. Ben and I shared a glance and hurried quietly into the living room.

Sunrise wasn't far off. Instead of complete darkness, the slats over the windows let in a faint gray light, and the air held the stillness of the coming dawn. We could still hear the rabids, though, constantly shuffling around outside, sometimes passing in front of the windows, making the porch squeak. Ben had rotated the guard duty throughout the night, and the last watch huddled in the shadows and behind doorways, guns in their laps or beside them on the ground. It was lighter outside, the blackness losing ground to a muffled gray. We were almost in the clear, but we still had to be very, very careful.

I suddenly saw the kid, a glimmer of white in the shadows, trot out of the kitchen and into the front room. My heart stood still. Ben hurried forward, but before he could do anything, the frightened kid walked past one of the men, who instinctively reached out and grabbed it. The goat let out a startled bleat—and a rabid's face slammed into the window, mad white eyes peering in. It screamed, sinking its claws into the wooden slats, shaking violently, and more bodies flung themselves onto the porch. Blows rattled the doors and windows, filling the house with noise.

"Everyone, stay calm!" Ben ordered as the men jumped to their feet, grabbing their weapons. "Get down to the lower levels and block the doors. Use the staircase and the hall as a choke point if they get through." A slat ripped free of the frame, and a rabid's face became fully visible through the space, blank and terrifying. It screeched, and Ben's shotgun barked loudly, the flare from the muzzle searingly bright in the dark room. The rabid's head exploded in a cloud of blood, and it fell back, only to have several others take its place. More slats began to tear loose, and Ben turned on the men. "Move! Now!"

As they scrambled away, fleeing downstairs, Ben shot a sick, terrified glance at me. "You, too, Kylie. Go to the safe room and bar the door behind you. Don't open it for anything, understand?"

"What about you?" I gasped as he turned away. "Where are you going?"

"I have to get Dad!"

Ben fled down the hall, and I followed. Darting into the guest room, I slammed the door and leaned against it, panting, as Ben strode to the bed. Samson lay where he had all night, face up, eyes closed. But now, seeing him, I felt a chill go through my stomach. He was so very, very still. Too still.

"Ben," I warned, but it was too late. He had already grabbed Samson's arm to haul him over his shoulder. I watched, helpless, as Ben froze, staring down at his father, then slowly lowered the arm back to the mattress. His voice was a choked whisper in the shadows.

"He's gone."

Tears filled my eyes, more from the pain in Ben's voice than for the man on the bed. He would never reconcile with his father now. And Samson had been harsh, abrasive, stubborn and infuriating, but he'd loved his family and, in his own way, done everything he could to protect them. He might not have been a good man, but Ben had loved him, and had struggled hard to be forgiven and accepted.

Which made what I was going to suggest even more horrible.

"Ben," I said softly, hating that I had to bring it up. "We can't leave him like this." He gave me an anguished look, and I swallowed hard. "You have to…make sure he doesn't come back," I whispered. "You can't let him turn into one of *them,* like Nathan."

Understanding dawned on his face, followed by horror. I walked to the corner table and retrieved the revolver that Ben had given me that night. The metal was cool in my hands as I came back and stood in front of Ben, holding it out.

Ben's eyes were glassy. He looked down at the gun and drew in a shuddering, ragged breath. "I can't do this."

"Yes, you can." My own throat was tight, but I swallowed the tears and continued to hold out the gun. "He would've wanted this, Ben. It has to be done, and it has to be you. Go on." I lifted the revolver toward him. "Take it. Set him free."

A sob tore its way past his lips, but Ben slowly reached out and took the weapon from my hands. Turning stiffly, he raised the gun and pointed it at the corpse on the bed, aiming it right between the eyes. He was shaking, trembling like a leaf, but his arm was steady. "I'm sorry," he whispered, using his thumb to click back the hammer.

Samson's eyes flashed open, blazing white. Turning his head, he screamed, baring fangs, and the boom of the revolver shook the bed and the walls. Samson fell back amid a pool of blood, the top of his head blown apart with the violent explosion, and Ben fell to his knees.

An answering screech rang out beyond the door, making me sick with fear. They were in the house! I lunged across the room and locked the door, just as a bang from the other side made me shriek in terror. I stumbled back into Ben, on his feet once more, as the door shook and rattled, and the maddened wails from the monsters grew more numerous as they crowded forward on the other side.

We pressed back into the corner by the curtained window, watching as the only thing between us and death began peeling away, shuddering under the relentless assault. Surprisingly, I felt calm. So, this was it. This was how I was going to die. At least...I wouldn't be alone.

Ben's arms wrapped around me from behind, pulling me back to his chest. I felt his forehead against the back of my neck, his warm breath on my skin. "I'm so sorry, Kylie," he whispered, his voice shaking. I turned to face him, gazing up into those haunted brown eyes, placing a palm on his rough cheek.

"I love you, Ben," I murmured, and watched his eyes widen. "I don't regret any of this." There was a splintering crack behind me, as a rabid tore a large chunk out of the door, but I didn't turn. "You gave me a home, and a family, and if I had to do it all over, even knowing how it would end, I would still follow you anywhere."

Ben leaned down, pressing his lips to mine, crushing them. I pressed forward, trying to feel him with my whole body, to merge my soul to his. We kissed one last time in that dark bedroom, the rabids shrieking at the door, Samson's bloody corpse lying on the bed a few yards away.

Ben released my mouth, but he didn't pull back, his forehead resting against mine. "They won't take you," he whispered fiercely, a bright, determined gleam in his eyes. "I won't let them. You're not going to die like that."

The door shook again, rattling in its frame. They were almost through. Ben pulled back slightly, and there were tears in his eyes now, as I felt the cold barrel of the revolver under my jaw. It sent a shiver down my spine, but I wasn't afraid. Yes, this was better. No pain, no teeth or claws tearing me open, ripping me apart. No chance to rise as one of them.

"It won't hurt," Ben promised, holding my gaze. "You won't feel a thing, I swear. And I...I'll be right behind you."

He was shaking. I wrapped my fingers around his hand, holding it and the gun steady. He was watching me, waiting for my signal, to let him know I was ready. Behind me, the rabids screamed, almost as if they knew I was slipping away, to a place they couldn't ever reach me. I almost smiled at the thought.

"Ready?" Ben whispered, and I took a deep breath. Behind him, through curtains and the slats in the window, I could see the sky, a soft dusky pink.

The window. "Wait!" I whispered, tightening my grip on his. "Ben, wait."

I pushed at the gun, and it dropped instantly as Ben yanked it down with a shudder of relief. Taking one step around him, I reached for the thick, black curtains covering the boarded window and threw them back.

Orange light streamed between the cracks in the wood, bright and promising, throwing ribbon-thin slivers of light over the floor. "Ben!" I gasped, spinning toward him, but he was already moving. Snatching the shotgun off the floor, he slammed the butt into the window, and the sound of breaking glass joined the wild screeching of the rabids.

I joined him, using a book from the shelf to batter at the wood. Frantically, we pounded at the boards over the window frame, as the rabids wailed and screamed behind us. The nails held, and the boards loosened, though they stubbornly refused to give.

With a final crack, the door burst inward. Howling, the rabids swarmed the room, flinging themselves across the floor. I cringed, bracing myself, just as Ben gave the board one last blow, and it came loose, flying out and away from the window frame.

A bar of orange sunlight spilled over the floor between us and the lunging rabids, and amazingly, the monsters skidded to a halt. Ben pressed back into the corner, holding me tightly to him as the swarm hissed and snarled at the edge of the light. I clung to Ben, forcing myself to keep my eyes open, to face the monsters not five feet away. I could feel Ben's heartbeat, his breath coming in short gasps, the strength of his arms crushing me to his chest. The rabids hissed, frustrated, and one of them inched forward, out of the shadows and into the light.

There was a different sort of hissing as smoke erupted from its white skin. The rabid shrieked, flinging itself backwards. Clawing at itself and wailing, it turned and fled the room, the stench of burned, rotten meat rising into the air. The other rabids hissed and growled and gnashed their fangs at us, but slowly followed its example, filing out of the room. I peeked out the window and saw the pale forms scramble off the porch into the shadows outside, darting into bushes and trees, keeping out of the sun.

In seconds, they had disappeared.

A hazy mist hung over the distant woods and fields, pooling in low spots and coiling through the branches. Somewhere in the trees, a bird called out, and another answered it. The rabids were gone. They would be back tonight, that was certain, but for now, they were gone and we were still alive.

Or, most of us were.

I looked up at Ben and found him staring out the window, a bit dazed. He was still breathing hard, and his heart was still pounding, but he closed his eyes and, without warning, crushed me to him in a desperate hug.

I returned it. We didn't say anything. We didn't state the obvious: they would be back tonight when the sun went down. We just held each other, content to listen to our breaths and heartbeats mingle as the sun crept farther into the sky and touched every living thing with light.

We buried Samson that morning, beneath a single pine tree that stood tall and straight in the middle of the field. The sky was clear, and the sun blazed overhead, slanting through the branches of the pine, speckling the bare patch of earth at the trunk. Ben wore a borrowed tie and jacket, and standing beside the grave, his hands clasped in front of him, he looked solemn and serious…and very much like his father.

"I haven't been back long," he said to the semicircle of kin on the other side of the mound. "I remember, just a few years ago, I was so eager to leave this place. So desperate to get away. And I did, for a while. The city was exciting and noisy and crowded, so different than the boring little stretch of farmland I left behind. I thought I would be happy there, on my own. I was wrong.

"Now," he continued, meeting everyone's gaze, "I realize what Dad was talking about. This is our home. And we're going to defend it. We will stay strong, and rebuild, and start over. We will make a life here. Whatever it takes." His gaze dropped to the mound of earth at his feet. "Dad would've wanted it that way."

He bowed his head and stepped back. Rachel and some of the other women came forward to lay flowers over the grave. I held out my hand as he rejoined me, and he squeezed my palm.

Ben sighed and closed his eyes, tilting his head to the sunlight. I watched him a moment, then bumped his shoulder with mine.

"What are you thinking about?"

He looked at me, his eyes clear and direct, as if the light had finally burned away the last of the guilt and anguish, and I was looking straight down into his soul. "Just...that everything is beautiful in the sun," he said quietly, holding my gaze. "And that I'm home, finally, and I am going to take care of this family. That's what he wanted, anyway. The last thing he said."

I remembered Samson's last words, whispered into Ben's ear, and smiled. "Yeah?"

"Well, there was one more thing." Ben stepped forward, gathering me into his arms. "He also insisted we get married in the fall, like him and Mom."

I smiled through my tears. "Bossy, stubborn man. I guess we can't say no." Ben kissed me gently, a kiss full of promise, and love, and hope. Especially hope. Taking my hand, he laced his fingers through mine, and together we returned to the open arms of our family.

A full moon glimmered over the waves as they lapped against the dock, throwing fractured sliver light over the hull of the ship tethered there. Two figures stood at the end of the pier, speaking in low, intense voices. One was a sunburned, lanky man who smelled faintly of brine and was most at home on the open water. The other was a tall man with pale skin and eyes blacker than midnight. The pier bobbed up and down on the waves, and the lanky man shifted his weight subtly to compensate, but the tall stranger was as motionless as a statue.

"The pay was acceptable?" the tall man asked in a low, almost dangerous tone. His companion rubbed his beard and sighed.

"Yeah, it was fine. Last-minute, but fine. You're lucky—I turned down the last poor sap who couldn't pay up. Idiot thought I'd let him and his kid tag along for free. I don't run a fucking charity here." He eyed the stranger's empty hands and shook his head. "Long way across the ocean, friend. Sure you don't want to take anything? This ain't a pleasure cruise, you know."

"You don't have to worry about me, Captain." A ghost of a smile tugged at the stranger's lips. "I have everything I need right here."

"Eh. Whatever. Let's get moving, then. Time and tide wait for no man."

The captain walked off, leaving the pier and striding up the ramp without a backward glance. But the tall stranger stood on the dock a moment more, letting the breeze play across his face. He turned, looking back the way he'd come, from a rabid-infested town and a small house and two humans he'd rescued on a whim. The boy was unimportant; it was *her* words he would remember, her words he would take with him on his long, impossible journey. His kin were already looking for him, vengeance and retribution foremost on their minds. He was not afraid of their wrath, but he could not allow himself to be destroyed just yet.

"I will make things right," he whispered, a promise to her, to everyone. "The rabids are my creation, but I will atone for that mistake. And I will not stop until everything I have destroyed is returned to the way it was."

"Oy, mister!" The captain stood at the top of the ramp, glaring down at him. "You coming or not? I'm getting too old for this kind of stress."

The stranger smiled. *Don't worry, Captain,* he thought, gliding down the pier. *You won't have that concern much longer, be-*

cause this will be the last trip you and your crew will ever make. I did not lie when I said I have everything I need, right here.

Walking up the ramp, he nodded politely to the captain and continued inside. Ropes were tossed, anchors were pulled and the great ship slid easily into open water and vanished over the horizon.

★ ★ ★ ★ ★

What if life as you knew it was ending all around you?
Where would you go, who would you want by your side?

This novella is a prequel to Julie Kagawa's
BLOOD OF EDEN *series,*
published by Harlequin TEEN.
For more information,
visit www.BloodofEden.com.

THISTLE & THORNE

ANN AGUIRRE

If I didn't deliver the goods to Stavros by midnight, he would kill me.

He was the local bossman in our ward. Mostly I scavenged and pawned stuff, but I also had training from my dad, who had been a top-notch cracksman in his day. Back then I thought it was an adventure when he took me on a job. Now it was a nightmare. In the Red Zone, people robbed and murdered each other outright for half a sandwich or a bottle of water.

That meant my skills were worth something to people who needed the subtle approach. Generally, that demand was limited to people who lived in the fortresses, gated communities that had gone full lockdown after the worst chemical spill around thirty years ago. Fortresses offered everything the wealthy could want—lush green parks, clean air, filtered sunlight, entertainment, shopping—and the developments stretched on forever, one into the next, much as the city sprawls did, only with more desirable results. They were the best of the Computer Age, confined within heavily guarded walls.

Some inhabitants had inherited their fortunes; others came from criminal empires. There were entrepreneurs, as well, who owned sweatshops in Factory Ward, where children ran the tireless machines. According to my dad, all fortress residents maintained outside concerns. How else could they augment the wealth that permitted them to live in luxurious safety? Each complex had a corporate backer who owned the businesses inside and managed the employees. I'd heard they treated the staff more like slaves in exchange for the privilege of living inside the walls, but it was doubtful I'd ever discover the truth for myself.

A cold sweat broke out on my nape, despite the lingering heat from the day. It was dusk, and the pollution in the air dulled the purpling sky. Even the clouds were hazy from the adjacent Factory Ward. I'd promised my mother before she died that I wouldn't let them snatch the kids. I'd never known anyone to come back from the machines. Geezers talked about how they were chained up and left to work until they died. I'd heard mechs roved the ward, gunning down the runners.

I studied the wall before me, calculating the angle of my jump. There was no way I'd risk pissing Stavros off. A deal was a deal, and I hadn't survived for twenty years without learning the importance of keeping my word. In lean times, if you were a straight shooter, people were more willing to float a loan or cut a little slack. We were *all* thieves, of course, some more violent than others. Yet I shared a wary respect with those on my block, which was better than most neighborhoods. Since we had banded together, there had been less random crime. I did have to range farther afield for a score, as I never stole from people I knew. The community ran on a complex bartering system, though some people crafted goods, others planted and some scavenged. Everyone traded for what they needed.

When I did tricky work, I took care it didn't follow me home. As necessary, I spent hours ensuring my double life never rebounded on my siblings, Alonzo and Elodie. Like anyone who did dangerous jobs, I had multiple boltholes scattered throughout Snake Ward to keep anyone from uncovering my secret. So far, I'd managed.

But it was getting harder.

The fortresses had tightened security, making it all but impossible to pull off a heist. Under normal circumstances, I wouldn't have taken this job. Too risky when I had mouths to feed. I had refused Stavros's emissaries before—this was the first time I'd be working for him. But Alonzo and Elodie were exactly why I was perched on this ledge, smoky air swirling around me. I couldn't let the kids starve. Too few leads had panned out in recent days, rumors about pigeons venturing out of their armored roosts proving false.

We had little left to sell. Nobody had anything worth stealing. So when Stavros had made me an offer, I'd spoken his favorite words. *Yes, sir.* I'd be lucky if I didn't wind up with his boot on my neck permanently. He wasn't the kind of guy to be satisfied with less than total commitment.

Damn, it was a long way down, but I was too practiced to let my stomach lurch. I had been stealing for as long as I could remember. It put food on the table. In the fortresses, rich people ate well and enjoyed the protection of highly trained, highly paid mercenaries who reported to no government. Instead, they were loyal to the corporations that employed them. For folks like me, well, the expression "hand to mouth" meant a good day.

At the moment, there wasn't a single morsel in our cupboards. Which was why I was lifting an expensive bauble for Stavros, who would then deliver it to the idiot who coveted it. As long as the transaction went well, I'd get a cut and buy the kids something to eat.

But before I did any shopping, I had to achieve the impossible.

I checked the pads on my gloves and then launched myself from the ledge. Impact smarted, but I latched on to struts on the side of the Erinvale fortress, owned and operated by the

Yamaguchi Corporation. My lungs churned as I hauled myself toward the air intake. So many things could go wrong. Those whirling fans might make minced Mari out of me. That would leave Al and Elodie alone; they were fifteen and thirteen, not babies, but not old enough to fend for themselves, either.

So I climbed for them. Timing was everything. Dangling from the rim, I watched the fans spin and counted the seconds. I had three to slide into the ventilation system beyond. My arms burned. This was a definite security risk for Erinvale, but most thieves weren't small enough—or desperate enough—to go for this point of entry. There could be steam tunnels or any number of obstacles along the way.

Now.

Using my legs for leverage, I pushed off the side and scrambled onto the lip. There wasn't room to make myself comfortable, but I kept my balance while not thinking about all the open space behind me. For a few beats more, I counted, then dove. It wasn't graceful, but there was nobody to see me slam into the shaft belly first. Momentum carried me far enough not to have my feet shorn off, but I lost a few millimeters from the soles of my shoes. I lay there, trembling, horror scrambling over me like furry spider feet.

Soon, I got myself under control—not through strength of will, but due to necessity. In reflex, I touched the belt at my waist. Good, my tools were intact. They had been my father's, actually, and I hadn't sold them because they represented my only chance at freelance jobs. My line of work required more caution than a scavenge run to Junkland, which was dangerous enough. Determined not to fail, I pushed onto my hands and knees and crawled forward.

Everything I had done in the past three years had been driven by the need to look after my sibs. Things weren't getting better in the Red Zone, though. The land they'd left us when they'd built the fortresses was parched, fallow and, in some cases, poisoned. They might as well have salted it before they locked the doors. Now, due to risk of kidnapping, most dignitaries didn't leave their refuges. Instead, they sent emissaries. I hated the privileged few because they'd never gone hungry. They slept in palaces while the rest of us scrabbled to exist.

Occasionally, street rats like me infiltrated because somebody in Alphaville wanted a treasure being hoarded in Erinvale. The fortresses had borders, even against one another, with a complicated system of visitation privileges, and I'd heard rumors there was a designed DMZ where territories overlapped. My father had taught me everything I knew about corporate society in case I was desperate enough to steal from them. This was my first attempt.

Stavros had shown me some plans before I'd left for the job; I hoped they were up-to-date. On memory, I hung a left at the first T. I was gambling it would take the automated security measures a while to notice my presence. I didn't think there were weight or pressure monitors in the ventilation system, but they'd install them if they figured out how I got in. The tricky part would come in nabbing the trinket and then getting out alive.

It seemed I was always on the verge of dancing with death. Sometimes I heard his clacking knuckle bones as he tapped his fingers. *What's taking so long, Mari? The Red Zone got your parents. Why fight the inevitable?*

Because I have to. Screw you.

The Reaper could wait a little longer.

It was dark in the vent, punctuated with gusts of air that told me when I was approaching a fan. At the next turn, I came up against an unexpected blockade. Filters had been installed—not listed on Stavros's dated plans—and I couldn't get past without tampering with them. The security system would detect that immediately and dispatch drones to eradicate me.

I need a miracle.

2

I didn't get one. For hours, I wandered those shafts on my hands and knees, unable to proceed along the mental course I'd charted. Too many changes had been made to the system since Stavros's plans had been drawn up. So instead of going secretly to the target's room, I had to do something insane. Fear didn't begin to describe the chaos in my head as I went to work on the panel; I loosened the bolts from the back and then manually unscrewed them. If they had sensors to detect tampering—and they probably did—they'd discover the security breach in seconds. It was too small a window for me to find a place to hide and let the heat die down before I searched for the statuette the client wanted.

One problem at a time, I told myself.

First I had to get out of the ventilation system. I cut my fingers on the last bolt. It was stubborn and stuck, slightly oxidized because nobody ever performed routine maintenance. That might be a metaphor for fortress life for all I knew, beautiful on the outside, but breaking down within. I angled the grille so I could pull it through the opening, then I laid it quietly behind me. Terror spiked my movements, making me fast as I flipped down from the ceiling.

I'd never been in a room like this, pristine, expensive furnishings and electricity. People from the Red Zone knew about such luxuries, of course, but we weren't entitled to them. Unfortunately, there was a light flashing on the console that I took as an alarm; my father had told me stories about such things passed down from his grandfather. The Thistle family had been stealing for over three hundred years. I was just the latest in a long line of thieves, but if I didn't get moving, I'd be the last.

In my black clothes and cracksman tool belt, the guards would make me as a thief immediately. I darted into the hall; fortunately, most private residences didn't have a system that prevented people from *leaving* without authorization, though opening the door set off an audible alarm to match the discreet one.

My life just got so much worse.

I had no idea where I was inside the fortress, where the statuette lay from here. It seemed unlikely I'd ever find it; I had the habitation number, but the blueprints I'd seen hadn't included the living quarters. For obvious reasons, fortress officials kept that information secure. They hadn't been as careful with the specs for air quality design. As it turned out, there was a reason for that—the info Stavros acquired was years out of date. There was nothing I could do to change the bad break.

So I focused on staying alive.

In desperation, I ran down a random hallway. I was actually *inside* a fortress. Granted, I wouldn't be for long, at least not in one piece, if security caught me. Their booted feet rang out behind me, closing in from all sides. I shoved open a door and emerged into a moonlight paradise. The garden was verdant with blooming plants—spiky fronds and crawling vines, delicate petals that shimmered in the ethereal light. And there were trees, actual trees, stretching up toward the sky. The ones we had in the Red Zone were gnarled and stunted. Many grew sideways like humpbacked monsters with rot riddling their bark. Our world was nothing—*nothing*—like this.

Awe didn't still me for long.

I raced across the park and ignored my dread of what would

happen if they caught me. We had stories, of course, all of them awful. But silence was worse. There were always whispers of people who went missing, no reason why. Maybe Al and Elodie would never know what became of me. They'd think I abandoned them. Sure, my sibs could be a pain in the ass, but I loved them. I'd never cut them loose to fend for themselves.

"Stop!"

Obviously I didn't; I had enough self-control that I didn't even turn, but one of the security squad had gotten within spotting distance. This couldn't end well. Yet I didn't give up. I dodged around a half-wall that enclosed some flowers. In the Red Zone, they only looked like this because they'd crumbled and fallen over, and there were no sweet-smelling blooms to scent the night air.

"Over here. Hurry!" a feminine voice called.

Barely breaking speed, I evaluated my options. She didn't sound like someone who wanted to confine and/or kill me, so I wheeled in her direction. I had no idea who she was, but she pulled me into another hallway. The girl was around my age, slim and nondescript, and she didn't let go of my arm. Instead, she towed me toward another doorway. I was smart enough not to dig in my heels and fight someone who appeared to be helping me. Questions could wait.

We stopped inside what looked like a locker room, probably designated for staff use. For the first time, I noticed her uniform, which meant she was a maid. I wasn't sure I'd enjoy fetching and carrying for rich people; I might even hate it enough to prefer the Red Zone.

"Why did you help me? They could fire you. Or worse." I had no idea how fortress managers handled staffing issues, but their draconian policies made me think they didn't favor mediation.

"I owe Thorne a favor. You tell him we're square now."

"Who?"

Her face twisted with impatience. "He works for Stavros. Take this." She pressed a card into my hand. "It will get you outside."

"Won't me using it get you in trouble?"

For the first time, she smiled. "No, but thanks for caring. I stole it from a girl I don't like."

"I didn't realize staff ever left the fortresses."

"Who do you think they send when they need someone to travel on a whim? Certainly nobody with membership privileges." She shrugged.

Oh. No wonder she didn't mind sticking it to the authorities. They used her as if she was expendable, as if money made everything all right. Corporations had long since adopted that attitude; it hadn't taken long for it to infest the whole world.

"Do you live in a big apartment like the one I broke into?"

She shook her head impatiently. "My sleeping area's so small I have to lie down to fit inside it. What difference does it make?"

That was even worse than I'd imagined. "I was just curious. What's your name?"

"Kyla. Now *go.* Or you'll get us both killed."

"Thank you," I said. "I'll find a way to make this up to you somehow."

"Thorne already did. Ask him anything you need to know."

Who's Thorne, anyway? I didn't remember meeting him, but I'd only been in Stavros's HQ briefly, that one time. I turned then and hurried in the way she'd indicated. From behind me, I heard security shouting. They were nearby if they hadn't entered the locker room yet. I hoped Kyla made herself scarce before they found her. But maybe uniformed maids all looked alike to the guards; it had been dark, and it wouldn't be possible to tell one from another, even on camera. That was her best shot for eluding detection anyway. Whatever she owed this Thorne, it must have been big to take this risk repaying him.

The corridor became increasingly more industrial as I ran, until it terminated in a heavy-gauge steel door. Beside it was as an electronic lock I could never crack. Fortunately, I had the stolen passcard, which I used without a qualm. A green light came on, and the exit opened. They'd absolutely tie the other maid to the break-in, but that wasn't my worry.

I stepped out into the smoky, unfiltered night air and realized in the next breath that my problems had just begun.

3

Thorne was waiting.

Or I guessed it was Thorne because the man looked purposeful. In the faint light, I couldn't tell much about his features, but he was fairly tall. Ass-kicking boots. He beckoned. "Stavros is expecting us."

Yeah, he worked for the bossman, all right. But I didn't have the statuette. I dodged and made a break for it. I was a fair distance from Snake Ward where I lived, but if I ran all night, I might make it home before dawn. I could collect the kids and we'd move. It would mean leaving everything behind—

Quick as I was, he was faster. In a few strides he snagged my shoulder and spun me around. "Don't walk away from me."

"I wasn't walking," I muttered.

Truth. I'd been moving at a dead run, and he'd still caught me. That stung.

He planted himself in front of me, offering an introduction but not his hand. "Thorne Goodman. Don't let the name fool you."

Oh, I wouldn't. Anybody who worked as an enforcer for Stavros had coal for a heart and ice in his veins. I'd figure out how to slip his net later. "We should move. You have an escape plan?"

"This way." Thorne led me to a classic moto with sleek, powerful lines, antique if I was any judge of such things. It had silvered panels affixed to the side; they glimmered in the moonlight. He swung himself aboard and beckoned. "Get on."

I did. He had one helmet, which he gave to me. I strapped it on as he kicked the bike to life. I'd seen messengers riding these, usually from the fortresses. I'd assumed they must be important or they wouldn't be trusted with such expensive equipment. Though, if anything happened to a messenger, fortress authorities probably cared more about retrieval of property.

"Anything I should know about riding this thing?" I asked, as the heavy door in the side of the stronghold crashed open behind us.

He gunned the throttle. "Hold on, lean with the turns and don't fall off."

There was no chance to ask what he meant about leaning. I locked my arms around his waist and pressed against his back, more intimacy than I'd shared with anyone except my sibs for longer than I could recall. There had been a few guys passing through, but I came with a built-in family. Life was hard enough for one person in the Red Zone, and Snake Ward was worse than most.

Shots rang out. Bullets hit the ground behind us, throwing sparks, and I strangled a scream. I'd seen a few guns in my time, but bullets were strictly controlled. So on my block, people used old revolvers for pistol-whipping each other. There were a few geezers who knew the recipe for gunpowder, but casings required a blacksmith, and nobody could find the right chemicals or the equipment to process them. It was simpler to bludgeon and stab each other.

"Halt!" a guard shouted.

An automated tone came from the fortress itself. "Mandatory incarceration results from encroachment on Erinvale property. Yamaguchi Corporation offers a bounty on felons."

The tires screamed as Thorne slung us around a curve. He ignored the shouting guards and the fortress security AI. Until now, those had just been tales to scare little children. In childhood, I'd heard that computers ran the fortress systems, monitoring population and allotting resources with greater efficiency than humans could muster. *How long before that goes terribly wrong?*

If it hasn't already.

We zoomed along, leaving the security detail behind. The wind felt fantastic, not clean but fierce, and I loved every moment of this breakneck race, even if it might end in fiery death. In my normal life, I tried not to take risks. Could never forget that I belonged to my sibs as much as to myself.

I called, "If there's a computer running things, how come it didn't notice me as soon as I came in?"

"Do you know each time a new bacteria enters your system?" He pitched his voice to carry.

"What's bacteria?" I put my chin on his shoulder so I didn't have to yell. That, too, felt intimate, as if I was doing something more reckless than riding on a stranger's bike.

"A microorganism living in your body that you don't notice unless it makes you sick."

Okay, that was *horrible*. I wished I didn't know that. But I got the correlation. "You mean like when I set off the alarm coming from the ducts into the habitations."

"Exactly."

"How come the whole place didn't go into lockdown?"

"That would bother the residents. The AI tried to determine the threat level and how to trap you without inconveniencing anyone."

I laughed at that. "It failed."

"Because it didn't calculate bribery. It's an exploitable AI limitation."

"You mean Kyla?"

"Precisely," he answered. "The AI can't factor for favors owed or improbable risks."

Some distance alongside the fortress, another door opened, and a trio of vehicles emerged, nothing I'd ever seen, half car, half motorcycle, with a cockpit for one. They'd have weapons and targeting systems. I hoped Thorne was a good driver. I tightened my arms on him as he swerved, and the first boom rushed past us, striking the rutted road in a corona of cinnabar sparks.

"Relax," he called. "This bike can go places the cruisers can't."

There was nothing for it but to trust him and hang on, as he'd instructed. The shots came in hard and fast, but he dodged them, driving us through smoke and burning pavement that I thought should melt our tires. Certainly a hot rubber smell laced our flight as we hurtled forward. We sped out of Erinvale territory, and still the cruisers gave chase. They must have had orders not to come back inside until the intruders were dead. A lesson had to be handed down, so they fired again. Again. More explosions rocked the ground, so the moto shuddered, but he controlled it—and we didn't wipe out. I banished the mental image of my battered body skidding over the asphalt.

A hundred yards off, I spied a broken bridge with girders hanging like snaggle-teeth over the stinking river. At night, I could imagine it was clear and clean, not green-tinged and faintly smoking. The runoff from Factory Ward came straight our way, and there was no agency to make companies clean it up. So acid in the water would probably eat a body faster than the creatures that managed to survive in there. I'd heard there were three-eyed fish and things with tentacles, but if you liked your life, you didn't go down to find out after dark.

Thorne gunned the throttle. The moto growled a response, rocketing toward empty space. *Oh, no. He's going for it.* I didn't see how the bike could make the jump with two of us on board.

"Are you crazy?" I shouted.

We went airborne.

• 4 •

Sailing across the abyss with dark water and rocks below felt…
indescribable. A powerful cocktail, terror and exhilaration,
fizzed in my veins. I closed my eyes, unable to watch us
die. The moto hit the ground, bounced and slung sideways;
Thorne leaned, negotiated with the bike, which wobbled, but
he righted it and took off. Guards fired a few more rounds,
but they couldn't hit us from this distance, and they wouldn't
pursue us into the Red Zone. Outsiders were robbed and
murdered within seconds if they couldn't call on a local for
protection.

Still shaking from the insane getaway, I leaned my forehead against his back. It didn't matter that he was a complete
stranger. In some ways, that made it easier. I wouldn't see him
after tonight, so it didn't matter if he thought I was weak.

You might not see anyone *after tonight. Dammit.* I'd forgotten about Stavros, the guy who would cut off my hands and
watch me bleed out for failing to steal the statuette. *And this
guy works for him.* For a few seconds I pondered flinging myself
off the moto, but we were moving fast enough that I thought
landing might hurt me as bad as the bossman. This day just
kept getting better.

"What time is it?" I asked in Thorne's ear.

"Why?"

"I want to know how long I have left to live."

"It's 11:14." He didn't bullshit about the dire nature of my
situation—and for that I accorded him respect.

Not that I liked him any better for delivering me to my executioner. It made his rescue seem pointless; he could've left me to die in the hands of fortress security, but, no, Stavros couldn't let that happen. Like everyone else, he had to make a statement. *This is what happens to people who fail me.*

"You could take me home," I tried. "It's on the way."

"Not a good idea."

From his perspective, maybe, but from mine, it was my only play. I had to get away from him somehow, double back to the house and grab my sibs. They had convinced me they didn't need to stay with anyone for a one-night job, and they had been alone for hours already. Fear tightened into a hard core in the pit of my stomach. I had been in some tough spots, but this qualified as the worst. The bike zoomed along, carrying us deeper into Snake Ward. Here, the air smelled of industrial fumes and garbage, not flower petals. Two fires were burning, and as we rode by, I saw four muggings and a girl being dragged toward an alley. I recognized most of the thugs as working for Stavros, who offered beatings, extortion and terror as part of his regime.

Home, sweet home.

"He's going to kill me." I didn't imagine Thorne cared.

"I know," he answered. "That's why going to your place would be suicidal. You have to lay low until I figure something out."

Did that mean what I thought it did? People didn't just... save me. Ever.

"You're throwing in with me...why? What do you want in return?"

"We'll talk about that later."

"Forget it. I don't make deals without knowing the terms. I'll take my chances with Stavros." That was pure bluff. Even if I didn't know what this guy wanted, it couldn't be worse than death. Not worse than breaking my promise to my mother and leaving the kids. Somehow, I'd cope, even if he wanted me to break into another fortress.

'Cause, yeah, that went so well this time.

"You think you're in a position to negotiate?"

He had me there. "Look, we *have* to swing by the house. If we don't, I'm getting off this bike, whether you stop it or not."

"What's so important there?"

Here, I risked everything, but what the hell. I had nothing left to lose. My throat tightened as I confided my deepest secret to a stranger. "My brother and sister."

He swore, then asked, "If you have dependents, why'd you get mixed up with Stavros?"

"He doesn't exactly give people a choice." That much was true.

"Fine. Tell me where you live."

I gave the directions, hardly daring to believe my luck. There had to be a fly in the ointment, but I couldn't afford to argue. Not now. To my delight, Thorne wasn't such a good dog, after all. Apparently he was about to bite the hand that fed him. Whatever he had in mind, it should end better for me than severed limbs and slow death, which meant I was all-in.

He changed course, aiming us down a garbage-choked alley, where two of Stavros's goons were beating the crap out of an old man. His piteous cries rang over the purr of the moto. Part of me wanted to stop—to save him—but I squashed it. Al and Elodie had first claim to any heroics I mustered up tonight.

"Do you have somewhere to stash them?" Thorne asked.

"Yes."

After that, he drove in silence; we drew attention as few people could afford fuel or a vehicle anymore. Poverty trapped us in the wards we were born in. Nobody moved farther than they could walk these days, and when you had to carry everything you owned, it was a nightmarish prospect. Which indicated just how scared I had been, considering it with my sibs in tow.

As he pulled up in front of my house, I asked, "Why are you doing this?"

"If I walk in and kill Stavros for no apparent reason, I have to fight everyone who's loyal to him," Thorne replied. "If I save you from him, I get to say he's gone too far."

"I'm the justification," I realized aloud. *Excuse, really.*

I let that go for the moment as I swung off the bike, anxious to check on Al and Elodie. My neighbors were watching, and one of them came out, just to his doorway to limit his exposure. Edgar was around forty with salt-and-pepper hair and a rangy build. He rarely talked to people, but he liked me for some reason. We weren't close, but he'd said that he admired how I looked out for Al and Elodie. As a result, he kept an eye on my property, and I watched out for his when he went to market. He was also fairly skilled with mechanical solutions, like rigging a gravity shower or a filtration system using scavenged components.

He lifted a hand in greeting; his gaze flicked to Thorne. "Everything all right, Mari?"

"All clear," I said. "Any movement tonight?"

Ed shook his head. "Few of Stavros's thugs were prowling around earlier, looking for trouble, but nobody came near your place. They know better."

Unlike many, we lived in an actual house, an old one, granted, but our family owned the land—not that such claims mattered outside the fortresses. People took what they wanted, and if you couldn't defend your property, you lost it. With a nod of farewell to my neighbor, I unlatched the front gate. I wasn't the best fighter, but I had this place rigged with traps until it was impossible to go a foot without getting snared, strangled, impaled or beheaded. I led the way through the makeshift minefield, checking my triggers.

It all looked good. As Edgar had said, no trespassers to-night. There had been a few dead ones in our perimeter over the years, but they'd learned to avoid my territory. Thorne wheeled the bike along with us. *Smart.* I disarmed the front door and then opened it. Light fell across us in a diagonal swath. The solar lamps were on, shining from the windows; those had been my best find in the massive dump the locals dubbed Junkland. They were the kind someone had used in their garden once. If we put them on the roof during the day to charge, they provided enough brightness, along with the candles, so that we weren't squatting in the dark like fright-ened mice, waiting for the light to return.

"Will his people believe you give a damn about me?" De-liberately, I blocked Thorne from coming inside. He was big-ger than me. Faster. Those qualities wouldn't help him on my home turf, if he was playing me to snag the kids on Stavros's orders. He'd get to them over my dead body.

He shrugged. "Does that signify?"

"It does if you don't want to fight the others, anyway."

At that, he nodded. "You make a good point. And, yes, I can convince them you matter."

For a few seconds, I wished I did…because in that moment, I caught my first real glimpse of Thorne Goodman. He turned from parking the bike, sable hair tousled from the ride. His features were lean and sharp, like an old steel skyscraper. A few of them were still standing in Snake Ward, though they were missing windowpanes high up; I'd known people to go scavenging up inside, only to be blown out from fifty sto-ries, because unsealed, those places were like a wind tunnel. Looking at him made me feel like that, at risk and breathless. A silvery scar etched down his cheek, toyed with the line of his mouth. If I had to guess, I'd say knife fight; the attacker had nearly taken his left eye. His eyes gleamed with the same silver as the moon. He wasn't handsome, but he was compelling in the way of alkali flats, a haunting reminder and a dangerous trap for the unwary.

"The other guy's dead," he said.

In fact, I wasn't studying his scar, but his mouth. *Dammit.* I didn't have the freedom to be fascinated by someone who might double-cross or kill me. Or both. On a bad day, it was definitely both...and today qualified.

"I'm not surprised."

"What did Stavros send you to steal?" The question seemed random, but I could tell by his expression that it wasn't.

"A little figurine. He said it would be in a brown case. Why?"

Thorne pushed out a long breath. "I'm glad you didn't know."

"Know *what?*" Poised in my own doorway, I felt a frisson of fear.

"He marked your block for annihilation, Mari. You weren't stealing a little statue. Inside that case, there were chemicals, the last component he needed for the bomb he's building. He's decided to wipe this part of Snake Ward off the map."

• 5 •

I froze, unable to credit what I was hearing. "Even Stavros isn't crazy enough to—" I broke off…because in fact, the bossman was pretty damn psychotic. "But why?"

His expression was somber in the dim light. "Things are pretty good here, compared to other areas. You look out for each other…and you're part of the reason for that, I think."

"I am?" I had no idea what he was talking about.

"Your neighbor would've tried to stop me from hurting you, Mari. I've seldom seen that anywhere else."

A hot flush swept over me. I just tried to get by; it wasn't as if I'd rallied anyone to a watch program. Self-consciously, I shrugged. "We swap favors sometimes. It's better than stabbing each other in the back."

Thorne nodded. "More to the point, a few local traders have started refusing to pay protection money. And you know where that leads."

"The guy gets the shit kicked out of him, learns his lesson and doesn't do it again."

"Not this time. Stavros thinks a bigger example is necessary. He wants the populace to fear him completely."

"They already do," I protested.

If a bomb went off here, so many people would be caught in the blast. There would be collateral and structural damage, bodies everywhere and, depending on what kind of chemicals Stavros used, it might poison everyone in the ward. *Thousands* would die, if somebody didn't stop him. The sheer magnitude of the looming disaster locked me in place.

"I *will* destroy him," Thorne said softly. "With or without you."

"Is that why he hired me? If I fail, he kills me. If I succeed, he blows up my whole neighborhood." My voice went sharp and bitter. "That's win/win for him."

"I suspect that's why, yes. It amused him to think of you delivering the means of your own execution."

With some effort, I squared my shoulders. "Does Stavros think I'm responsible for my neighborhood being a little less horrible than the rest of Snake Ward?"

"Probably. He doesn't confide in me anymore."

"Did he ever?"

Some indefinable emotion flickered across his lean features. "Once, yes. Not now."

I made an instinctive decision. "Come in, quickly. But if you try anything—"

"You gut me like a chicken. Got it." He didn't have to sound so coolly amused at the idea I could do him harm. Just let him *try* to catch me in this house.

"I'm home," I called as I closed the door.

"Did you bring anything to eat?" That was Al's hopeful voice.

He was growing so fast. Already he was four inches taller than me, but he needed more food than I had provided lately. His arms and legs looked too long for his body, thin heading toward gaunt. A few seconds later I heard his footsteps on the stairs, and then he was in the front room with us. Al took a protective step in front of me, and I loved him for it.

"Who's this guy?" His tone was hostile but not threatening.

"Is Elodie asleep?"

"Yeah. Answer me."

"We're in deep shit," I said simply.

And then I summarized the sitch. Though I protected my sibs, I didn't lie to them. Al listened with worry dawning in his green eyes. He looked so much like our dad that sometimes I couldn't stand it—and more with every passing year. If he ever grew a goatee, I might burst into tears.

"So he gave you bad information to prepare for the job and now the whole neighborhood might blow up?" Al had a way of cutting to the heart of things.

I nodded. "That's about the size of it."

Al didn't bother complaining how unfair that was. "And him?"

"Thorne used to work for Stavros, but he's had a change of heart. He might join a monastery, meet up with the brothers in the Mojave." That would surely tempt a smile from his stern mouth.

But it didn't. Deadpan, Thorne offered, "Maybe someday, after my work's done here."

"What's the plan?" Al asked.

"I need you to pack some stuff, not everything. We'll be back." I hoped. "You can stay with Nat for a few days while I…" I choked. "While I think of a way to fix this." That sounded more confident than I felt, but Thorne must have a plan. If not, we were so screwed.

"Got it. I don't mind," my brother said.

No, he wouldn't. Al was totally in love with Nat, even though she was ten years older and had a kid. I didn't see that going anywhere for so many reasons, but try telling him that. Besides being Al's crush, she was also the only person on our block I trusted with my sibs. She'd successfully driven off seven squatters determined to take over her property, maiming two, killing three in the process. While her daughter napped. Yeah, it was a well-known true fact that you didn't mess with Nat. Her specialty was weapons; she could craft a beautiful knife out of scrap wood and metal, and she traded them to keep food on the table.

I just hoped she was willing to take on my two for a while. Though we were friends, she put her own family first for obvious reasons. There were so few resources that it didn't make sense to bond when you might have to turn somebody away down the line. Less hurt. Less guilt.

Therefore, I was prepared to bribe her. I ran upstairs behind Al, who was taking great joy in rousing Elodie. She fell out of bed from his tough-love tactics, but I didn't intervene. We needed to hurry. It wouldn't be long before Stavros realized Thorne had gone rogue.

Dropping to my belly, I squirmed under my bed, removed a loose floorboard and drew out a lockbox. In it was everything of value we had left. Most, nobody could afford to buy anyway, except those who lived in the fortresses, but there were fences who brokered deals for rare antiquities. Rich people loved collecting things; it was passive and safe and you didn't have to leave the comfort of your artificial habitat. I didn't trust anyone enough to sell this or I'd have pawned it long ago to fill our bellies; I wouldn't have done the things I had to keep body and soul together. I hoped Nat had better connections—that she could use the necklace. Otherwise…well, I wouldn't worry about it.

I threw some things in a bag and called the kids. "You guys ready?"

"What's going on?" Elodie demanded.

People said she looked like me, but I didn't see it. For one thing, she was pretty. I was small and squirrelly. On the plus side, I had great hands, nimble, quick, ace with all kinds of locks. I could scramble into spaces to scavenge gear other people had long since given up as impossible to recover.

I studied her worried expression and nodded at Al. "Tell her on the move."

They were great kids. Even my sister didn't argue as we hurried out of the house in the dead of night. We'd never pulled a runner before, but she trusted there was a good reason. In the dark, I led them to safety through the traps, and then I went back to help Thorne with the bike. As soon as we cleared the front gate, I broke into a run. I didn't check whether Thorne followed us to Nat's. He wasn't my concern at the moment—getting my sibs to safety was all that mattered. I heard his footsteps, though, coming behind us; he was smart not to fire up the engine just yet.

"How long will you be gone?" Elodie wanted to know, after she heard the story.

I was tired of thinking about it when I didn't know how it ended. "Not sure yet. Help Nat with Irena, do what she says, and don't piss her off."

"I won't," she said, wide-eyed.

"And stay out of Junkland."

Her mouth turned sullen. "I've found good stuff there."

"Yeah, but you could be killed, too. Thieves, other salvage crews...and some of the piles are unstable. If one of them crashed—"

"I'd be crushed like a bug."

Clearly I needed to work on varying my lecture material. But not tonight. I turned to Al as we drew closer to Nat's place. "You. No backrubs, tender glances, or anything else that makes her want to punch you in the face."

"Fine," he muttered.

"Wait here." Taking a deep breath, I slipped up to the door, dodging the triplines. I glanced over my shoulder, peculiarly reassured to find Thorne standing with my sibs. He looked as if he could handle himself in a fight, not just because of the scar.

A gentle tap on the door yielded quick results. There was no need for stronger measures; Nat was a light sleeper. In a few seconds, she stood in the doorway with her weapon of choice in hand, a simple claw hammer. Nat was fast and efficient with it, too.

"Trouble?" she guessed, glancing behind me at the kids.

"Yeah. It's bad. I wouldn't ask if it wasn't necessary," I began, but to my surprise, she held up a hand to stop me right there.

My heart sank. That was a no, then. *She won't even let me make the offer.*

"You took care of Irena when I was sick last year. Made me soup. I figure I owe you. Of course I'll look out for them, protect them like they're my own."

The tears surprised me. This was the first thing that had gone right in days. "Thank you." My voice came out strangled. "Take this." I pressed the lockbox into her hands. "If I don't come back, you can sell it. This should keep all of you for a while if you're careful."

"Don't talk like that," Nat muttered.

I went on, "You can't stay here." Quickly, I summarized the threat from Stavros, and I gave her directions to one of my boltholes. "I'm not sure if he can find the chemicals he needs to complete the bomb, but I can't take that chance. I need you out of here until I can be sure we've neutralized the problem."

Nat inclined her head. "I appreciate the heads-up. Are you telling everyone else?"

I hesitated, unsure if we had time. Finally I said, "I'll pass the word to Edgar. He can decide what to do about it, as we've got to move."

"Good call," Thorne said.

She wasn't one for long farewells, so in short order, I hugged Al and Elodie and sent them inside to wait while Nat collected supplies…and her daughter. I hurried down the street and called to Edgar, who went silent and fierce when he learned what Stavros was planning.

"Don't worry," Ed promised. "I'll keep it quiet on our end. We'll move off a few at a time so it's not obvious we're evacuating, until we hear from you that it's safe."

"Thank you." At last, personal business squared, I turned to Thorne. "I'm all yours. What're we doing about Stavros?"

• 6 •

"First, we get out of this neighborhood," Thorne said. "We won't give Stavros any reason to think you're hiding nearby."

I nodded. "Good thinking."

He led the way toward his bike. My worldly goods hung across one shoulder, so little, really. But the ability to travel light was an asset. I told myself that, anyway, to ease the sting of uncertainty. As I got on behind Thorne, I stared back at the house. It was hard to leave, even knowing my sibs were safe with Nat.

"We need to do something to draw his attention."

For what felt like the first time in forever, I smiled, liking the way he thought. "Something...memorable, maybe?"

"Exactly."

"How angry are we trying to make him?"

"For my requirements? He needs to be foaming at the mouth."

"That should help convince his other dogs that he needs to be put down." I wrapped my arms around his waist, marveling at how much easier it was the second time.

"Dogs?" He cast a sardonic look over one shoulder as he gunned the moto to life.

"That's what we call you, the bossman's dogs. Didn't you know?"

"It doesn't tend to come up when I'm stomping somebody's face."

I tensed, unable to believe I'd forgotten, even for a second,

who and what he was. Even if he'd drawn the line at blowing up a block, it didn't mean he was a nice guy. Disquiet and
shame whispered through me, chased by a pecking crow of
conscience. *Don't be an idiot. Don't let him in your head. You
might be temporary allies, but you can't trust him.*

Message received.

"I guess not," I said, as the bike jerked into motion.

After that, I didn't speak, but I held on. There were a few
roamers out, looking to roll somebody or try a property coup.
Squatters didn't usually kill you, but you wouldn't last long
after they ousted you into the street. I felt their eyes following
us, hot with envy. Good fortune got you killed in Snake Ward.

Stavros's men were out tonight, paying calls. We passed
a stall where a man bartered rotgut, and they were smashing up his stock. Maybe he was one of the guys who had refused to pay protection, but he didn't deserve the repeated
cudgel upside his head. By the time we left earshot, they had
him on the ground, crying in agony. Farther down, Stavros's
thugs slammed a girl against the wall, taking the only thing
she had left to sell. The sad part was, she didn't even protest
while the first bastard grunted on her. When we drove past,
her eyes were wide and empty, fixed on the smoky sky. Business as usual.

This has to stop.

Before long, we pulled up outside a tumbledown building. Hard to say what it used to be, but it had lights strung all
over it, drawing stolen juice from jiggered connections to the
Erinvale fortress, the one closest to Snake Ward. Only Stavros would be so bold; I had noted as much the last time I'd
visited his HQ. Which meant this had to be a setup. I leaped
off the bike before Thorne could spin and grab me. Though
he'd been kind enough to let me square my affairs, I wasn't
waiting for the knife in the back when he turned me over to

the bossman. I was a block away before I realized he wasn't chasing me.

Chagrined, I went back to find him waiting, arms folded. "You're skittish."

"Do you even know my name?" I demanded.

"Marjolaine Thistle, head of the Thistle clan."

"That's not funny."

He sighed. "Let's get this done, shall we? I've been patient, but..."

It wouldn't last forever. Wondering if I was crazy, I said, "Fine."

Thorne wrapped an arm around me. "Keep quiet, look helpless and play along."

He led me across the wreckage-strewn pavement. Two men lounged outside the building, and they shoved away from the wall at our approach. Both held weapons: a sturdy length of pipe and a couple of knives. They looked as if they might be Nat's designs.

"You're late," one of the dogs said, greeting Thorne. "Did she give you trouble?"

"Did you know Stavros gave her bad intel? That's like sending you to guard a shipment unarmed and then killing you because somebody jacked it."

The one who had spoken before shrugged. "I'm sure the bossman didn't realize it was out of date. He's talked about nothing but this score all day."

"Why does she have to pay for that?" Thorne drew me against his side, and I stayed there. His jaw tightened. "It's not right. Remember what he did to Veronica?"

The other man flinched. "I know she was like a sister to you...and I get what you're saying, brother, but you don't want to do this." The guy took a closer look at me. "Not for this splittail. She's not even tasty."

Like you'd stand up to Stavros for me, if I was the sweetest thing on two legs.

"It's gone on too long, Henry. This isn't the first time Stav's killed over something that was his own fault. He's gone blood-mad…got a taste for death. Soon he won't even pretend there's a reason."

Just then, screams rang out inside the building. They started loud and tapered off, as if the victim was losing blood and/or strength to resist. The smaller man, who hadn't spoken, the one armed with Nat's knives, closed his eyes and shook his head, as if that could block out the truth of what he was allowing to happen.

Henry seemed spooked, too, but it didn't alter his stance. "Maybe that's true, but I'm not going up against him. I like my head right where it is."

Thorne tightened his arm on me. "You tell him she's mine and I'm keeping her."

I felt like protesting, but I kept quiet as the other man took a step back. "I'm not telling him that."

"This will send the same message." With that, Thorne strode over to a vehicle parked nearby.

The other two didn't interfere, but they did go inside, presumably to alert Stavros. Thorne drew a tube from his coat, then siphoned some gas, holding it inside with deft maneuvering. I watched while he spattered the car with it. Next he inserted a slender cord, homemade and good for burning. Right away I grasped his intent; he'd just turned Stavros's ride into a bomb. He lit the fuse, grabbed my hand, and sprinted toward his bike.

"Why not just kill him now?" I asked.

"I need Henry and Mike to spread word that I'm going to war over a girl."

"Right. Otherwise they'll think this is just another take-over." I put on the helmet.

As the moto engine snarled to life, a boom rocked the ground. Smoke plumed toward the sky, and for the second time that night, we peeled away from men shouting and shooting at us. He drove toward the fringes of Snake Ward. To the east, we had Erinvale fortress. Junkland spread to the west. On the north side lay Factory Ward. And south, there was Burn Ward, called that mostly because its residents had a tendency to set things—and people—on fire.

"Tell me we're not going to Burn Ward," I called.

He shook his head. "I've got a place on the border. Stavros doesn't know about it."

"So we lay low while he rages and convinces everyone that he's nuts?"

"That's the plan."

"When you hear they're ready for a change in management, you step in."

"It sounds so cold when you put it like that."

Cold didn't describe it. *Icy, calculating*—those words came closer—but I didn't care about Stavros. He *was* a mad dog who needed a bullet to end his foaming. He couldn't be permitted to build and detonate a bomb that would kill thousands. Thorne's regime would be kinder to Snake Ward; he wasn't crazy, at least.

"I've heard that Stavros has crosses tattooed all over his body…that he believes he's some kind of messianic figure."

"Are you asking if I've seen him naked?"

"No." At least I didn't think I was. Thorne had a way of making me uncomfortable. It also felt as if this night would never end.

I was so tired. The feeling overwhelmed me, and I gave

up on conversation. I was a prop in his scheme, so it wasn't as though he wanted to talk to me anyway. Closing my eyes, I rested my face against his back, just letting the wind rush over me.

By the time he cut the bike engine outside an industrial build-
ing too big to properly defend as it had so many entrances,
I was on my last legs. Thorne helped me over the rough ce-
ment without making it a huge thing, and I appreciated that.
Maybe I didn't completely hate him, even if he was using me.
It could be argued I was using him right back.

Out of habit I scanned the area for squatters, potential
threats or witnesses who could be bribed for information.
This caution was second nature, and Thorne shared it. He
caught me making the same sweep; his mouth quirked into
a wry smile.

"It's how we keep breathing. Come on." He unfastened a
series of locks, complex enough that it would have taken me
a good five minutes to circumvent all of them.

Inside, it was a jumble of broken machinery, but on closer
inspection, I noticed many of the parts had been configured
into traps people wouldn't notice until they stumbled into
them. They were devious, expert, and a couple ideas I intended to steal, to implement them at my place. Well, if this
didn't go bad.

"I'll stay close," I muttered.

He cut me an appreciative look, registering that I'd seen
his traps. "Most people don't notice them until it's too late."

"I've got a knack for this sort of thing."

Soon we went up some skeletal metal stairs, coppery with
rust, and Thorne entered a room that must have been an of-

fice. He'd turned it into a functional apartment. Mattress on
the floor, a couple of chairs, but more important, the heavy
door had an excellent bolt. Between the locks on the door outside, the traps within and this final prevention, it was impossible anyone would get in here without us knowing about it.

"The other doors all have alarms on them," he said.

"Sound wires?" I guessed.

He nodded. It was simple enough to rig a line with noisy
things tied to it. If anyone disturbed the tension by opening
the door, the alarm jangled. Instant early warning system.

"Nice." I didn't often praise somebody else's setup, but this
was first-rate. Out of habit, I scanned the room, memorizing
the layout and potential weapons within my reach. Such care
had saved my life more than once.

"Get some rest."

In reply, I dropped to my knees on the mattress and then
rolled to my side. There was room for him to crash behind me
if he wanted to. I was beyond caring what he did. Every muscle
ached with weariness and tension. When sleep claimed me, it
was fast and dark; I knew nothing at all until the floor rattled.

Unused to waking in strange places, I scrambled out of
oblivion with my nerves tingling. Something was wrong. One
of the traps had gone off, and I didn't see Thorne anywhere.
It was dark, but the nature of the space made it impossible to
tell if it was day or night outside. From the way my body felt,
however, it was probably morning. I wasn't shaky-tired anymore, just grubby, hungry and worried.

There had been a knife on the desk shoved up against the
wall, close enough to the door that it could be used as a barri-
cade if necessary. I laid hands on the weapon; it hadn't moved
since I'd logged its location. Dropping into a stealthy crouch,
I unbolted the door and crept toward the fight I heard raging downstairs.

As I moved, I took mental notes. At least three combatants. If one of them was Thorne, then he faced multiple opponents. In a square fight where they saw me coming, I didn't always fare well, but if I came up quiet, in the dark, well, they never saw me at all. It was possible, of course, that these were just squatters who had stumbled into the building. Possible, but under the circumstances, not likely.

I hunkered down. From my higher vantage, I saw one man down, dead or soon to be, as a result of the traps. A second was on the ground and I recognized him. Damn, they had Thorne. Two more loomed over him. Stavros's dogs. They'd come in numbers, surprising him as he emerged from the office. He didn't have long. Once they finished taunting him, they'd drag him back for bossman justice.

Time to even the odds.

My weight wasn't sufficient to sound on the stairs, and I stepped lightly. I kept to the shadows, movements slow and careful, agonizingly so. I wanted to run down there and attack, but they had guns; Stavros could afford bullets. That meant I had to time this perfectly, or we were both dead. I didn't kid myself that I'd last long on the run with no allies and a bounty on my head from both Yamaguchi Corporation—if they knew I was the one who'd infiltrated their fortress—and the Snake Ward bossman.

Drawing closer, I saw these two weren't Henry and Mike from the night before. They were hired hands looking for a permanent place in the bossman's house. I couldn't blame them. There would be plenty of food, if nothing else. Not a bad deal in these times, if you didn't mind what you had to do to earn it. When one of them kicked Thorne in the face, I knew these two didn't. From the look of him, it wasn't the first time, either.

Closer now, the scent of fresh blood mingled with the stink

of unwashed bodies. I felt as if they should be able to hear my heartbeat as it thundered in my chest, but they were intent on the exchange with Thorne, who spotted my approach and kept their focus on him with a defiant lift of his chin.

His smile flashed, teeth red with blood, and he spat to the side. "That's all you got? I had worse beatings from my mother."

"You won't be so cocky when Stavros carves you up." The goon drew back a fist for one last satisfying hit, and I sank my blade below his ribs, above his hipbone.

A kidney shot took expertise, but I had practice. I twisted the knife, and the thug cried out. Pain immobilized him. I scrambled back, knowing he might be capable of fighting for five to ten more seconds. That moment of distraction was all Thorne needed; he launched himself at the other one. Bone snapped as he broke the guy's forearm. When the gun dropped, I scrambled.

I got my hands on it as the goon I'd stabbed fell over. Good, it had been clean. Occasionally I missed, and then the fights got messy. I didn't have the strength or training to throw down like Thorne. He had the last man on the ground, beating his head against the cement. When he finally stopped, he was spattered in red.

"I think he's dead," I said.

"That one, too?" He indicated the one I'd shanked.

"If not now, soon." People didn't recover from these kinds of wounds. There was no trauma center, no surgeon on call.

Not like in the fortresses.

I didn't let bitterness distract me. "I hope you have somewhere else for us to go. It looks like somebody knew about this place…and they told Stavros."

His bruised features tightened, and his silvery eyes held a haunted light. Fear and bitterness warred for supremacy, revealing the first vulnerability I'd glimpsed in him so far. "I know who it was."

Someone else would've said, *good, let's go,* but I had to know. *Why me, why this, why that look.* So I asked, "Who?"

"My mother."

· 8 ·

"Your mother? Was it safe here if she knew?" I'd have trusted my own mom with my secrets, so I wasn't wholly surprised. But I was worried on the woman's behalf.

"I told her about this place in case she needed somewhere to hide…or to locate me if she got in trouble when I was laying low."

That seemed sensible enough. "You think they got to her?" *Hurt her.* But I didn't say that out loud.

"It's more likely she sold me out," he said quietly, so quietly I almost didn't hear.

That shocked me. But even if they weren't close, she didn't deserve a bossman's wrath. "Did you *warn* her before going to war?"

"I sent a messenger to tell her she needed to head somewhere safe. Since they found us, I'm guessing she didn't listen." His face was odd, frozen, and I didn't know what to make of it.

Thorne took a step, and his leg nearly buckled. He swore, reaching for a nearby chain suspended from the ceiling to keep his balance. He hung, arms corded, putting little weight on the injured knee; by his reaction, it hurt pretty bad. The damage to his face was ugly but not indicative of permanent harm. This seemed more serious.

Without hesitation, I went to him and stepped under his arm. "Let go. Lean on me."

"Yeah, *that's* a good idea." Conflicting emotions warred in his expression. He didn't mind using me, but he hated needing me.

I shared his mistrust in a general regard, but since our fates were tied momentarily, this made sense. "Don't read into it. I'm just helping you to the bike. Can you drive?"

His tone was sharp. "I don't steer with my feet."

"They went after the kneecap, huh?" I stepped closer still, making it easy for him. For the moment, I let the matter of his mother go. I sensed there were nuances here that I didn't fully understand. Maybe I would, in time.

Thorne released the chain and encircled my shoulders with his arm. "At first. But I cunningly distracted them with my mouth, and they decided to knock my teeth out instead."

"How did that go for them?"

"Not well." A wolfish smile pulled his split lips back from not-broken teeth.

This time around, it took us longer to get outside. I scouted but didn't spot any enemies lying in wait. Which was good. I didn't fare well in fair fights, and he was in no condition to square off. Thorne threw his injured leg across the bike, and by the time he got it in position to ride, his face was pasty with pain-sweat. When I climbed on behind him, I put my arms around him gently, and he pressed his hand over mine, where it rested on his abdomen. His inhalations were too unsteady—poor pain management technique. I could tell it had been a long time since anyone had gotten the best of him.

"Breathe," I advised.

He peered at me over one shoulder, his black eye threaded with broken blood vessels. "Do you know me well enough to tell me what to do?"

"You could choose *not* to, but I don't see that performing well as a long-term survival strategy."

Thorne's shoulders shook, but I couldn't tell if he was laughing. Despite his injury, he managed the bike. The roads were in bad shape, barricaded here and there by enterprising people who'd built shelters in the middle of them and then demanded tolls for passage. In his hands, the moto was nimble enough to avoid those blockades. A man shouted and shook his fist as we went past, angling west toward Junkland.

"How much fuel do you have left?" I called, over the rushing wind.

"It's solar."

Wow. This bike was priceless. It could run as long as we had light, which nobody made us pay for. Yet. The gloomy thought put a smile on my face, as it was the kind of thing Al would say. Apart from Nat, he never saw a silver lining. I hoped my sibs were all right. Though I sometimes left on longer jobs, I'd never gone away without giving them an end date. My siblings were different as night and day; though Al was, by nature, a pessimist, he was also a gentle soul. Elodie, on the other hand, thought the promised land lay over the next hill, and she was a scrapper. Her temper sparked over little things, and I had to hold her away from Al sometimes. Not that he'd hurt her. But *she* might claw his eyes out.

It hurt to think about them, wondering if they were safe with Nat, so I focused on the view. Ramshackle houses gave way to towering piles of junk in the distance—and people lived in those like apartments. It was dangerous, of course, as the refuse shifted. Whole stacks could become unbalanced and crush anyone who lived at the base, bury those who dwelled at the top. Here, people often lived in rusted cars welded together, sometimes whole chains of them. There was a self-declared king of Junkland, but he was crazier than Stavros, though in a less terrifying way; he wore tattered robes and demanded travelers answer these riddles three in order to win passage through his domain.

The bike slowed; this was the far west end of Snake Ward. If this was where he'd grown up, it was a wonder he'd survived. Squatters who lived in Junkland were particularly vicious, and they respected no boundaries. They also didn't feel kindly toward scavengers, which was why I warned Elodie away. But my sister had a penchant for salvage. She hoped to find something valuable enough to change our lives. There were always stories of lost treasure, but I didn't put my faith in them. She shouldn't have, either, but she was a fighter who clung with both hands to her dreams, however unlikely.

"How'd they get the drop on you?" I asked, as we stopped in front of a shack near the border. He seemed like a man who could fight four opponents and win.

"I didn't expect Stavros to run us down so fast. They were waiting when I came out."

"Three against one is tough odds."

"If I hadn't been distracted—" He broke off, shaking his head. "It won't happen again. Thanks for your help."

His simple gratitude surprised me. "For the fight assist or afterward?"

"Both."

Thorne slid off the bike after I did; he held on to it as he straightened his bum knee. He had a solid poker face, but it didn't hide the pain. Since he wouldn't ask me for help, I didn't make him. I stepped in quietly, casually, and he reached for me this time with no words spoken. His arm around my shoulders didn't feel entirely wrong, either.

Check that. He's not a good man. He told you so himself.

Beside me, Thorne surveyed the weathered boards and half-rotten roof. Random bits of scrap tin had been used to shore the shack up, and barbed wire stretched around the sides, leaving a small pathway clear to the door. In the yard were posts

with dead animals nailed to them, all in various states of de-
composition, and the stink was…remarkable. I didn't say anything, but I wanted to ask about this place. But his face held
a grim, forbidding look, and I didn't know him well enough
to disregard it. So I said nothing as we approached the door,
which hung drunkenly from broken hinges. Yeah, Stavros's
men had definitely been here.

Inside, the stench was unspeakable. Like out in the yard,
there were dead animals everywhere; some were just hides
in various stages of tanning. Others looked as though grisly
work had been interrupted. Against the far wall, a woman
lay dead. She had a tangled mass of gray hair, and she wore
homemade leathers, stained dark with blood. Beside me,
Thorne froze.

By his reaction, I knew this must be his mother. For a moment or two, he didn't approach. He just stared. His fingers
curled into my shoulder, but he didn't realize what he was
doing. The pressure wasn't painful, just…kneading, as if I
was a lump of dough. His expression twisted between denial,
horror and…relief. The latter haunted me; it should *never* be
a weight lifted, seeing a parent so.

What had this woman done to him? Looking around, I imagined the worst.

At last he broke away from me, limped over to the body,
and laboriously lowered himself beside her. My instincts conflicted. With anyone else, I'd offer comfort. But maybe I was
making this too complicated. If Thorne found my gesture un-
welcome or too personal, he'd say so. I came up behind him
and rested my hand on his nape. His skin was warm, smooth,
but his shorn hairline prickled. He stilled and shifted to examine my face. Then, to my surprise, he tipped his head back,
so the base of his skull nestled into my palm.

It was a peculiar fraught moment beside his dead mother.

For brief, precious seconds, he closed his eyes and let me console him. But when he opened them again, his gaze shone with mockery. "Does this mean you'll be gentle with me, Mari?"

9

Yes, I thought, *and you need me to be.*

I didn't say that aloud. Instead I took the hint and stepped away. He was a man who equated touch with sex; I didn't mean to send him the wrong message. I wasn't looking for that, and *if* I were, it wouldn't be with Thorne, who intended to take over Stavros's kingdom.

"Is there anything you'd like to take with you?"

"From here? No." His tone was emphatic.

Thorne turned his mother's hands over and saw the blood beneath her nails. There was a weapon beside her on the dirt floor. Churned earth showed where they'd scuffled, where she'd lost. The pain must have been overwhelming. Even if they'd had a troubled relationship, this woman had given him life, and she was gone.

"She fought hard," I said. "Does that help any?"

I imagined her last moments of life, struggling until they had her on the ground, boot on her throat. Bruises were already darkening on her neck after death. They would have offered mercy if she gave up her son. In desperation, she had. And they killed her anyway.

"Not much," he said roughly. "Tell me, if Stavros took you, would you tell him where to find Alonzo and Elodie to save yourself?"

"No. I'd let him kill me."

He offered a weary, sardonic smile. "That's how family's supposed to be...or so I understand."

Given this glimpse into his past, I ached for him. Though I'd lost both my parents, they'd loved us. They'd done their best in a world gone to hell. Neither one of them would've sold me out for an extra second of life.

"Did you think they bribed her?" It was an awkward question, but he had been surprised to find her body; he'd expected to find a living woman to blame.

He tensed. "It was a possibility."

"Were you coming to…deal with her?" I meant execute, and he knew it.

"It doesn't matter now." His frozen expression hinted at so many things.

I took that as a yes. It was good that he hadn't been forced to kill the woman. Such trauma drove people crazy. Part of me wished I could believe he wouldn't have done it, no matter how she'd wronged him, but Snake Ward made monsters out of people on a daily basis.

Bending, I examined her body, and in her closed palm, I found a scrap of paper. It was the note Thorne had sent with the messenger, warning her to clear out. Crammed in her mouth, I found another, clearly a gesture of scorn from her killers. The words were smudged, written in a nearly illegible scrawl with no punctuation or capital letters, but I could make out the gist. I crushed it in my hand, unable to believe what I was seeing.

i know where he is come see me we'll make a deal.

She'd called Stavros's dogs, trying to benefit from Thorne's warning. I'd never had this feeling before, but it was so powerful, it had to be hate. I was *glad* the bitch was dead. If her recent actions spoke of her character, then she'd done unspeakable things when he was a child.

"Do I even need to ask what that says?" he asked mockingly.

"Thorne, you can't pretend this doesn't matter. She was your mother."

He raised a skeptical brow. "Do you want to hear about my childhood then?"

"If it will help."

His expression intensified, left me feeling as if I stood in a beam of sunlight. "Keep staring at me with those soulful eyes, and I'll decide you want me to kiss you."

For a few seconds, I fell into the fantasy. Even with bruised face, split lips and wrecked knee, he wouldn't be a tender lover; he'd be fierce and demanding, a little ruthless.

So not for me.

I smiled and shook my head. "Maybe later."

"Then, tempting as the offer of counseling is, we'd better burn the body and move on."

With chagrin I realized he was right. "Stavros might've left men in the area."

"I hate to ask, but…" Thorne canted his head toward the corpse.

Funerals were often informal. There were no services to handle them, and people disposed of their dead as best they could. It was a kindness that he didn't intend to leave her to be eaten by parasites and carrion feeders. Of course I'd help. Together, we built a fire, using the shack itself. That, too, seemed fitting. Nobody would move into her home after she'd gone.

"We can't stay to see her consumed," he said, after it was done. "It would take too long."

I nodded. "I'm surprised they haven't doubled back yet."

"Ironically, this will speed the process. Most of them have mothers, too."

Fortunately, the populace wouldn't know how evil she had been. Word would spread about the woman's murder, not that she had been the devil in female skin. As I aided him to the bike, I said, "I'm sorry about yours."

His reply was so faint that I almost didn't hear it. "Me, too. More than you'll ever know."

"How did you end up working for Stavros?" I had a terrible hunch.

His mouth quirked. "Isn't it obvious? She sold me to him."

There was nothing I could say to that.

Our next stop was somebody who owed Thorne a favor. I ran in, collected a bag, and hurried back out. As long as we kept moving, Stavros would receive conflicting reports on our location. But that mobility kept Thorne from resting his leg or getting any treatment at all. Doubtless he thought keeping it crooked up on the bike was good therapy.

"If you don't have anywhere for us to go, I do."

"Where? Is it nearby?" The strain in his voice made it obvious he needed to rest.

"Yeah." I gave him directions to my hidey-hole.

I used this one often when a job went south and I had angry owners gunning for me. Under those circumstances I never went home. The kids could be used as leverage against me, so I only returned when I was sure I was free and clear. This felt a little like giving Thorne the keys to my kingdom, but I didn't see many other options.

It's only one, I told myself. *You have more. Like one where Nat and the kids are laying low.*

He parked behind the building, which looked as if it would collapse any second. That was the beauty of the place. Inside, it was much better. The door was impossible to open, seemingly rusted shut—unless you knew the trick. And I did. With judicious push-pull pressure and perfectly timed jiggling, it creaked open, revealing a musty space with random odds and ends. This had been a theater once, long since fallen to mice and dust, since the people who'd paid to see shows only watched them in the fortresses now. The rest of us didn't have time for such things.

Our progress was slow as I checked my traps. Eventually we reached safety. I had no idea what this small room had been used for, maybe storage. My sanctuary wasn't as well-equipped as his, but I had built a nest out of old fabric and torn curtains; it was more comfortable than it looked. I supported Thorne, moving with him to the pallet, and I knelt beside him. His face was ashen by the time he settled, back against the wall.

"I don't have anything for the pain. Let me get what I do have."

I couldn't remember the last time I'd eaten, but dehydration was the more pressing problem. Fingers crossed that my emergency supply hadn't been looted. I gave him the gun I'd taken off the thugs; he held it as if he knew what to do. With luck, he wouldn't need it.

Nimbly, I went out a window and scrambled up the rusty metal staircase affixed to the side. Part of it had broken away, so climbing to the roof required springing off from the wall and pulling myself up with my arms. The effort left me dizzy. I hadn't cared for my body well enough to tax it this way.

When I saw my supplies still in place, I punched the air in triumph. Years past, my father had taught me a simple water purification trick: you only needed a container to catch the rain, a black roof and plastic bottles. If you took rainwater, put it in a clear plastic bottle, and left it sitting in the sun on a dark, hot surface, the heat was enough to make it safe to drink. Therefore, there was still clean water, left from my last visit. The roof was a safe place to store them, too; few looters could get up here. I stuffed the bottles in the loose waist of my pants, then retraced my steps.

10

"Who's your new favorite person?" I asked, tossing Thorne a drink.

"You, of course." As I shut and fastened the door behind me, Thorne unscrewed the cap and took a long drink. "There's food in my bag."

"Really?"

We made a meal of the dried meat and my sun-warmed water, more than I'd had in two days. I sighed in relief as I rubbed my stomach. Hopefully Nat had enough to stretch to four instead of two. Soup was a good bet, as you could add water and cook it a little longer. The facilities in the bolthole I'd directed her to were primitive, but at least they would be safe. I imagined Al staring soulfully at Nat while Elodie told Irena stories about Junkland's mythical lost treasure, riches enough to let an outsider buy her way into a fortress, where there was hot food every day and clean air to breathe.

After we ate, I moved over beside him. "Want me to check your leg?"

"And do what?"

"I've been looking out for my sibs for three years. I know something about injuries."

"Go ahead. But do be gentle." His mocking tone returned, as he referred to the last time I'd touched him kindly.

With some effort, I folded his pant leg over his knee. The joint was swollen, and bruises were already forming. I tore some cloth from the nest into strips and wrapped it tightly for support. Then I piled more fabric beneath his leg to elevate it. By the time I finished, he wore a bemused look.

"What?"

"You're mothering me. I don't know that I ever *have been* mothered."

"Not even—" I caught myself and broke off, as the woman who'd lived in that shack hadn't exuded maternal instinct.

She sold him to Stavros. Twice. Frankly, her death hadn't been painful enough.

"Especially not her."

Not knowing what to say, I changed the subject. "Is that better?"

He was pulling his pants down over the bandage. "Yes. It should help with the swelling."

"It's all I can do without medicine or ice."

Thorne laughed. "Where would you get either one?"

Stavros probably had an old cooling unit, powered by juice stolen from Erinvale. The rest of us had never even *seen* ice. But for the former, I had a connection.

"An herbwife lives on my block." I hoped Edgar had warned Seline, and she was safe. "Her people have been making remedies for centuries. I can't afford to trade for much, but her arnica cream is really good. I have some at home."

"Do any of your neighbors plant?"

Some did, if they could find clean earth, but the problem was, you couldn't always tell what was contaminated just by looking. Some chemicals didn't have color or odor, but they'd poison the food just the same, so people died of sickness, not starvation. There was a man in Burn Ward who had a kit to test samples, but that involved a lengthy journey with no guarantee of productive outcome. Most people preferred to scavenge.

"One guy has a bathtub garden."

"I don't know how you've survived this long without help."

"It's hard," I said honestly.

There was no point in pretending otherwise. If he had eyes, he knew what life was like for most. He got luxuries and privileges due to working for Stavros…and if he succeeded in this coup, he'd claim everything the man had stolen. Bossmen could make things easier for people in their wards, but they almost never did.

The rest of that afternoon, we rested. Whether Thorne admitted it or not, he was in no shape to ride. It indicated his discomfort when he didn't protest over hiding. We both slept in my nest, and I woke, disoriented, to find him watching me. His pale eyes shone in the dim light.

"Are you all right?" I asked groggily.

"Yeah." That wasn't an illuminating answer. Especially because he kept staring at me. "Are you familiar with the mouse and lion fable?" he added.

"No. But I gather I'm the mouse in this scenario?"

"You aren't a lion." Unexpectedly he smiled. "But the mouse saves the day in the end with her small, sharp teeth."

"I don't know how to take that. Did I bite you in my sleep?"

"Do you want to?"

I froze. Some men liked it when you got scared. I didn't think Thorne was one of those, but I didn't make any sudden moves, either. If it came down to it, I could kick his bad leg and run.

Somehow I made my tone nonchalant. "You must be bored."

"A little. But I'm starting to get the idea you're not interested."

"You're beautiful," I said. "You must know that. But I'm not in the market for a man."

I hoped he wouldn't take it wrong. Our partnership might

continue for a while. To my surprise, he fixated on the first part, not the polite rejection.

"Beautiful, am I?"

"Very." I stroked his vanity gladly in lieu of other things.

He touched his scarred cheek in reflex, as if he thought it made him ugly. In fact, it was quite the opposite. The mark identified him as strong in a world where the weak perished. If I wanted a man in my life, I'd look for one who could take care of himself. I was relieved when he let the matter drop.

Instead, thereafter, we laid plans...and when he felt up to it, we would implement them.

For days, we played with Stavros's men. Word on the street was, we had become a symbol, along with Thorne's martyred mother. If he didn't crush us, others would follow our example and defy him. Thorne was impatient with my admonitions to rest. It was important that they see us but be unable to catch us.

So we made regular supply runs, trading Thorne's stock-piled treasures for food, and my water filtration system kept us from going thirsty. People were nervous and shifty when we made the deals because it meant they could expect a visit from Stavros's thugs thereafter. Those with fixed stalls caught the worst of the abuse, so we stopped buying from them. Fortunately, Thorne knew several mobile markets, where folks bartered and moved on. There was no way to manage or dominate a migrant population entirely. Like rats in the walls, these folks had to be found before Stavros could crush them, and many knew Snake Ward better than the bossman.

Thorne bent beside his bike, peering at the ground. "The next meet's at Hazmat Square."

"How can you know that?"

"It's one of the few useful things my mother taught me." At my look, he explained, "Street people have always had a secret language. It used to mean simple things…like good water, danger, free food. It's more complex now. Messages are passed this way."

Fascinated, I crouched by him, wondering what he saw in the circles, angles and slash marks. I'd known there were permanent nomads; some people didn't see the point in defending a squat. It was easier to scavenge if you were mobile, but the kids made that prospect impossible. Maybe when they were older, I'd give up our home ground and move on.

"What does it say?"

He pointed to two small, conjoined circles. "This means *don't give up.*"

"And that?" I indicated a long box with a dot in the center of it.

"Danger."

It was dangerous, all right. Some might argue it was even suicidal, taunting Stavros this way. But there were whispers of revolt, too. People said he'd gone too far killing somebody's mother, who had *cooperated* with him. Those folks didn't live long. But making examples of those who opposed him only fed into the idea that it would be better for Snake Ward if somebody else took over. Via the grapevine, I'd heard that Edgar was leading the campaign, spreading gossip as fast as people could talk. There would never be a zone without a bossman running it, but he didn't *have* to be crazy. At the free markets, we heard all the gossip.

I looked forward to hearing today's news, even as I feared it. If I didn't get home soon—

No point in borrowing trouble. I already had more than I could handle.

• II •

At Hazmat Square, so named because there had been a chemical spill some fifty years before, they were already setting up the market. In the distance, I glimpsed the smog-blurred lines of the Erinvale fortress. Its hulking shape dominated the skyline, dwarfing the old and broken buildings left from the Computer Age. Decades ago, quakes had shaken through as a result of environmental fuckery, destroying most of the infrastructure. Failure to issue a timely emergency response and then to rebuild had resulted in the various wards, all over the Red Zone.

Apart from rare junkets to Junkland, I had never left Snake Ward. I'd visited migrant markets before, not often, because I didn't know the street signs. So when I found them, it was as a result of word-of-mouth. Instead, I traded with people who set up squats and stalls, running their business in one place. Middlemen, who didn't give me as good a trade as I might get here.

I watched as the peddlers set out their wares. Often they just had a bag or basket. Occasionally sellers had vehicles, converted to solar energy like Thorne's. After seeing their freedom, which made moving between wards feasible, obtaining a ride of my own became my chief ambition.

"Nice," Thorne said, catching me admiring a four-seater. "Lots of skill went into that retrofit."

"How much would something like that cost?"

"You'd just have to find something the owner wanted more."

True. Which made trading complicated. If you asked about an item, it flagged the vendor that you were interested, so they knew to price it high. But if you didn't ask, you had no idea what they were looking for. I'd probably never find anything valuable enough to swap for a vehicle anyway, but I could dream. Sometimes that was all you had left; and it was why I tried not to crush Elodie's fantasy of unearthing a lost treasure in Junkland.

He led me over to the local mouth, a grizzled old man named Lefty. "What's the word?"

"There was a fight over't Stavros's place. 'Pears one of his men questioned his decisions."

"Casualties?" Thorne asked.

"Just one. Fella named Mike."

He had been quiet, as I recalled. His partner, Henry, had said he wouldn't get involved in this mess, but Mike had. I expected to feel guilty; the feeling didn't come. Mike had made his choices, knowing the risks. He'd opted to speak up rather than watch Stavros run amok. Maybe it wouldn't comfort his family, but in my book, he died a hero.

Beside me, Thorne was silent. Lefty chattered on about disputes, territory scuffles and all notable migrations into Snake Ward. When the old guy stopped, Thorne paid him in food, the way most mouths eked out a living. Lefty served a dual purpose, too. The next thug who stopped him would receive a report on our most recent locale, which would lead to a raid on Hazmat Square, but the market should be long gone by then. That was the problem relying on street talk when tracking somebody down. As long as the quarry kept moving, it was hard to catch them.

Them, meaning us.

When we walked off, I touched Thorne's arm to get his attention. "Was Mike a friend?"

"Yeah," he answered tersely.

"Still worth it?"

He fixed a hard stare on me. "Mari, if you knew half of what Stavros has done, you wouldn't even ask."

Huh. Maybe it wasn't wholly about power. I remembered what Henry had said about Veronica, and I wondered about her. Thorne didn't strike me as a hero who cared only about making things better for others, but there was nothing wrong with combining community service with personal advancement. He'd lost folks in this fight already—his mother, Mike—and there might be more fatalities before we finished.

Just not Al or Elodie. Please.

That was my biggest fear. With effort, I put it aside. Despite the odds over the years, I had kept us all alive and together. This was just a minor setback.

Yeah, right.

At various vendors, Thorne traded for supplies in a hurry. I nudged him. "Can you afford to keep going like this?"

"I won't have much left by the time we're done. But it's worth it."

Yeah, he'd have Stavros's resources to call on then. I wished that didn't make me so sad; it seemed as if Thorne had the potential to do more, but in this world, what was there, apart from survival? Sure, there was a man who ran a mission in Snake Ward—and he had been robbed and beaten more times than I could count. Oddly, it didn't seem to discourage him. He just kept returning to his calling, which was what he dubbed it, and even the worst offenders didn't hurt him seriously because if they did, he wouldn't be able to gather supplies for them to steal. Which made no sense to me, given that he offered them freely to anyone in need. Some folks couldn't accept charity, but they could take from the weak…and *that* was a testament to how screwed up the world was.

Gunshots rang out, breaking up my thoughts. Bullets were rare enough that people panicked, packing their trade goods in wild haste. Precious resources fell to the ground, crushed and discarded. A woman screamed as a stray round hit her. Her man scooped her into his arms and tried to run, but the crowd got in his way. I couldn't see the shooter, but I knew who'd sent him.

"Stavros," I said. "How did he find us so fast?"

Thorne shook his head, deferring the question. "We have to get out of this mob."

For more than one reason. We were in danger of being trampled, but if people died here, because of us, it would haunt me. They hadn't made a decision to fight Stavros; they only wanted to exchange what they had for things they needed. I hated that the bossman would sacrifice innocents to bring us in. Maybe he thought if the cost grew too high, we'd surrender. On my own, I might, but not when Al and Elodie depended on me to keep them safe.

His face grim, Thorne grabbed my hand and towed me behind him, as fast as his sore knee let him. Resting it had helped, but he didn't move as fast as he had the first time he'd chased me. Good thing we were running *toward* somebody instead of away. The bad part? We were heading for a man with a gun.

I saw the enemy before Thorne, and I pulled on his hand. "Get down!" We dropped behind some rubble as a barrage of bullets hit the broken concrete. "Tell me you have a plan."

"I don't intend to die today, but that's not so much a plan as a goal."

From the other direction, more gunfire cracked; cries followed. There was a surreal quality about listening to a panicked mob you couldn't see. I wished I could help those people, but it was beyond my power. They had to look out for themselves.

"He's got friends," I muttered.

"Knowing Stavros, I'd be surprised if he didn't."

"Do you still have the gun we looted from the first crew?" I asked.

"I'm not shooting into the crowd, though."

That was reassuring. "What now?"

He leaned back. "Stay sharp and wait for them to come to us."

Thorne's plan made sense.

Charging men with deadly weapons didn't seem like the smartest move. Yet the wait was beyond frightening. I watched one side of the makeshift blockade while Thorne scanned the other. Unless they came straight over the top, which I didn't think was possible, we should have time to attack. That wasn't my strong suit, and Thorne was injured. But maybe the bad guys didn't know about his leg. We hadn't left survivors to tell, last time.

I heard the vendors fleeing; the guns fell quiet. No point in wasting bullets since we'd left line of sight. Over my thundering pulse, I detected footfalls crunching over chunks of cement, scraping over the pavement. Thorne shot me a look, questioning, and I nodded. I wouldn't get any readier.

They tried to come in quiet, but rubble made it impossible. Thorne wheeled around and shot one of them in the gut. Another circled, but I wasn't there. I moved fast, already laying hands on the blade I'd taken from the hideout. Using the concrete as cover, I crept around; I had more experience with stealth. Not with violence, however. That didn't stop me from pricking my knife at the base of his spine.

"If you move," I said softly, "I paralyze you."

"Which would be awful luck if I didn't have a gun to your head."

Dammit. There were *three* of them. Thorne had taken out one, and I'd stopped another. Fear lurched up into my throat

like a sickness, but somehow I kept my trembling to a mini-
mum. I'd never been in this position before. Never angered a
bossman this way...and these were just his henchmen.

"How did you find us?" I asked, buying time.

"I can read street sign, too. It stood to reason you needed
supplies."

Great, so he wasn't a dumb gun monkey.

He went on, "Drop the knife, little girl."

"I don't think so. If you shoot me, reflex might make me
stab into this guy's spine anyway. I like the idea of taking
somebody with me when I go. If he can't walk, he can't fight
well enough to please Stavros. I don't see that ending well." To
emphasize my point, I pressed the blade harder, deep enough
to draw blood.

The thug whined, "I think she's serious."

"So am I," the other one replied.

I couldn't even get a glimpse of Thorne. The gut-shot goon
moaned, and blood scented the smoky air with a copper sweetness, like pennies on a fire. There was nothing anybody could
do; Thorne had been cruel in his aim since his victim could
linger for days in agony and sweating fever as the wound went
putrid and he rotted from the inside out.

Come on, make a move, somebody.

Thorne said, "She won't back down. I've never seen her
drop something when she sinks her teeth into it." He gave
odd emphasis to *back* and *drop*.

If I was wrong, I was dead. I didn't hesitate; I couldn't, or
fear would get the best of me. I slammed my head into my
captor's chin, slashed the knife sideways along the other guy's
back, and then I dove to the ground. In the same instant, a
shot rang out. I heard a thump behind me. The cocky guy
was dead, and the one I'd wounded had his hands where we
could see them.

"Look," he said. "I don't want to go out like them. This is just a flesh wound." He cut me a look. "Hurts like a bitch, but I'll be fine. No hard feelings. I'll get out of Snake Ward."

Having failed Stavros, he didn't have a choice at this point. I let that go as I grabbed the gun. Though he had a bleeding slash on his back, this guy might not be out of the fight. The man took a step toward me, hands out as if to make peace. But he might be playing us, pretending cooperation while getting close enough to do some damage. I brought the revolver up. We made a decent team. Two of them were dead; we weren't. Sometimes that was the best-case scenario.

"I don't think so," I answered. "Thorne?"

"Take three steps away from her." He pushed to his feet and stood so it wasn't apparent he was walking wounded.

The goon complied. "I was just trying—"

"Save it. The only way you walk out of here is if you agree to carry a message to Stavros."

"That's the same as dying!"

"Pick one," Thorne said. "Now or later?"

I didn't intervene. Maybe I should have. But I watched and waited, my gun hand steady. I'd never fired one, but I understood the principle, and at this range, I'd hit the guy. Even if my aim wasn't lethal, a bullet *couldn't* be good for you.

"Screw this." A sudden lunge carried the thug toward Thorne, and I reacted. The gun jerked more than I expected, so I ended up shooting him in the leg.

He dropped with a groan, hands on the bloody wound. "You think this is over? Stavros will just keep sending people. Others can read street sign, too, so we'll find you…or you can go hungry. I doubt anybody would care if you starve to death—"

Thorne ended the tirade with a casual jab of his thumb into the bullet hole. "Do I have your attention now?"

An agonized nod.

"Excellent. You tell Stavros it doesn't matter how many men he hires. It won't end until he faces me. Which he's too chickenshit to do. He hasn't fought for this ward in ten years."

"Fine, I'll tell him. Then he'll shoot me. Again."

"Maybe it's time you considered a change of career," I suggested.

If looks could kill, I'd be a steaming pile of ashes on the ground. "You won't live through this. Thorne's never been known for his constancy. He'll get bored. Tired of you. And people will remember the things you helped him do. What're you gonna do when he's not around, protecting you?"

The same thing I've always done. Survive.

Before I could answer, the guy continued, mockingly, "And it's only gonna get worse. See, Stavros has a warning for you, too—he knows about those kids you got hidden away. He's coming for them."

My whole body iced over.

· 13 ·

How could he? I'd worked so hard to keep my two lives separate.

Thorne shut him up with a bullet to the face. Shock reverberated through me, even as I stared down at the ruined skull. No more taunting words would ever come out of his mouth. Nor could I ask anything about Stavros's plans, what he knew of Al and Elodie. Until this point, I had done well at keeping my family away from the attention of people who meant them harm. To the men I worked for, I was a ghost. No ties. Hardly even a person, more of a collection of useful skills.

"He was just mouthing off." Thorne tucked the gun away, remarkably composed. "Taking a shot in the dark."

I rounded on him. "If he was making a wild guess, it was pretty damn specific. And I thought you needed him to carry a message."

"I could see he was getting to you."

"So you killed him? That's crazy." But I didn't care enough about the dead man to debate it further. His words rang in my head.

He's coming for them.

I turned. Before I ran four steps, Thorne's hands clamped onto my upper arms; I fought him. I could think only of getting to the hidey-hole to check on Al and Elodie. They were counting on me, and while Nat kicked squatter ass, she might not fare well against more determined, better-armed foes. I couldn't let anything happen to her, Irena or my sibs.

He gave me a little shake. "This is exactly what Stavros

wants. You think he doesn't have others nearby? I doubt these three are the only ones he sent after us."

"Why? Why not just end it?"

"Leverage," he answered. "He thinks I care about you. So if he gets his hands on the people *you* love, then he hurts me more than if he just shot me."

"So he wants to make you suffer for challenging him?"

He shrugged in easy acknowledgment. "He'd make it last months if he could."

"I have to see them, just to be sure." I pulled against his hold, feeling the bruises form on my biceps.

"That's the dumbest thing we could do. Don't let him play you."

I curled my hands into fists and yanked away from him on the second try. "Easy for you to say. You don't care about anything but this grudge."

He cut me a cold look. "That wasn't always true. What do you think started this war?"

"I did," I said stupidly.

Thorne shook his head, dropping his hands away from me. "Never mind. Look, if you're determined to go, I won't stop you. I can finish this on my own."

"So if I leave, you're done with me?"

"You make it sound like we had more than a temporary partnership."

Dammit. I had, and I hadn't intended to. Not like that, anyway.

"I just meant, this has to play out your way, from A to Z, or you're out?"

"I'm not taking idiotic risks because you let some burner get in your head. The only way this ends for me is with a truce from Stavros's men and his dead body on the ground."

"What did he *do* to you anyway?"

"Killed my mother." But his mocking eyes said that wasn't the real reason, and he wasn't sharing, either. Our limited alliance only went so far. "So you tell me, Mari, are you going to be smart? Or do I ride off alone?"

"Do you get how hard this is?" I implored him for understanding.

"Inaction feels like abandoning your family when they need you most."

So he did grasp the crux of the matter. "And you still advise me not to go to them?"

"If he knows where they are, it's already too late. Therefore, I think that was a bluff. He's hoping you'll show him the way, by reacting just like this."

Already too late. My stomach lurched.

"You give a shitty pep talk."

"You wouldn't thank me for lying."

It was true; I wouldn't. If he promised me everything would work out, and then it all exploded, I'd have to kill him. This way, anything bad that happened was on my shoulders. He couldn't guarantee the goon had been bluffing. Stavros might have Al and Elodie already. But if he didn't, and I led him right to them, I'd never forgive myself.

Damn, this is too hard.

"How do you think he found out about them?" I asked as I considered.

"They broke somebody on your block."

Dammit. I hoped it wasn't Edgar or Seline. "I wish there was some way to check in without going in person."

Thorne flashed me a wry look. "Yeah, it'd be nice. Unfortunately…"

"Let's go." The decision burned, buzzing an angry futility in the back of my head.

Still, I led the way toward his moto, parked safely across the square. If the henchmen had been smart, they would've shot it instead of firing into the crowd. If they took out his bike, then they crippled us. So far, our survival had hinged on mobility, and Stavros was getting faster at hunting us down. He must be blowing through favors. Thorne climbed on, and I swung aboard behind him, strapped on my helmet and then saw the dark stain on his upper arm.

"You're bleeding," I said.

The engine purred to life. "Just a graze. They got me on a ricochet as we were running."

"You didn't say anything." His stoicism astonished me. His knee had to be hurting, and he'd just been shot. If toughness alone could carry him through, he'd kick Stavros's ass.

"Why, would you have kissed it better?"

"If you could reassure me that Al and Elodie are all right, I'd kiss anything."

"Really?" He drawled the word as the bike jerked into motion.

A hot flush suffused me. "That might've been an overstatement."

"No, the offer's on the table. Now let me counter."

Despite my worry, a zing of awareness pierced me. I was conscious of how I was pressed up against his back, arms around his waist. We had spent the past few days practically joined at the hip, and proximity often resulted in attraction. I couldn't afford a deep, dark well of a man like Thorne, but logic didn't block my reaction to him altogether.

"I'm listening."

"I'll find someone to check on them for you, someone Stavros won't know to follow. It's the best I can do at the moment."

It was, frankly, more than I expected, and the tension eased out of me. "Deal."

"You're not even going to ask what I want in return?"

Then I felt stupid, taking his joke at face value. Of course he didn't need to bargain for sexual favors. "What?"

He flashed me an enigmatic look over one shoulder. "I'll tell you when the time comes."

Oh, that didn't bode well for me at *all*.

According to Thorne's contacts, the kids were fine.

Which meant the goon had been bluffing, as predicted. Stavros might know about Al and Elodie, but he wouldn't live long enough to use the knowledge. His men had turned; this was the pivotal moment in Snake Ward.

Relief swept me, even as I listened to the offer. It came from the same guy who had looked in on Al and Elodie, carrying the message from Stavros's people.

"Henry wants to meet."

This was what we had been waiting for. I shifted against the wall, exhausted beyond bearing. No question but these had been the longest days of my life. I had lived on the back of Thorne's bike, catching sleep in corners and crevices, moving on before I felt rested. Others might thrive on chaos and conflict—not me. I missed my routine and seeing my sibs every morning. By the time I got back, I was gonna owe Nat so big I'd never be able to repay her.

"He can set the time and place," Thorne said. "As long as it looks clean, I'll be there."

"It's not a trap. I'll leave word in the usual place."

"What does that mean?" I asked after the courier left.

"I have a system. Notes left, answers retrieved. It's safe."

A day later, he was proved right when we set up a meeting at the border of Snake Ward and Junkland, far from Stavros's HQ—and out of the way enough—that nobody should catch Henry parlaying with the enemy. So weird to think of myself in those terms; I had spent so many years just trying to get by, but now there was no question I'd become one of the powers in the zone. Going forward, people would know who I was outside my neighborhood, and that might make my life more complicated.

Still, I couldn't fret about that when we were on the downhill run. Against the odds we had stayed alive long enough to get Stavros's men to flip on him. To make the day even better, Thorne found a place for us to clean up. It wasn't much, a public bathhouse, where an enterprising old woman sold purified rainwater, homemade soap and buckets, but after so long, I took it gladly. While he kept watch, I washed up, then donned a clean outfit. My clothes were all dark, nondescript, well-suited for my line of work, but not all of them smelled so ripe.

Then I stood guard for Thorne, making sure nobody crept up on us. This was the longest we'd stayed in a public place since the hit on the mobile market in Hazmat Square. Fortunately, he'd traded for enough food to keep us going. Once we were presentable, we split again and ate breakfast on top of what had been an overpass at one point. The road was broken, shattered by one of the early quakes, and I perched at the edge of the rubble, legs dangling. It was a safe sort of risk, as the tectonic plates had stabilized years before—and I had good balance, no risk of me getting vertigo and tumbling over.

"Come away from there," Thorne said, low.

I shifted, brow raised. "Are you afraid of heights?"

"No. That's just…not a good idea."

Wow. The imperturbable Thorne Goodman was wigged out by high spaces. He would die if he saw some of my best aerial maneuvers. Oddly, it made me feel better. It was excellent to know he had a weakness. Nobody should be as cold and collected as he had been through this ordeal; it made him seem inhuman.

"Why?" I asked, testing him further.

I set aside my food and slid to my feet, nothing but air behind me. His face tightened, but he didn't move toward me. Watching his face, I took a step backward, my heels nudging the cement. Though he didn't know it, even if I started to fall backward, I wouldn't. I could flip onto solid ground through years of practice…but to someone untrained, it might look as if I was taking a foolish risk.

"Mari, so help me—" The words came out through gritted teeth, and then he bit them off entirely, his face pale. Sweaty.

I realized then that he wasn't just scared; he was on the verge of puking or passing out. The game lost its savor. I bounded toward him, light on the loose rubble, and he seized me when I got within reach. He pulled me to him, shaking, and I let him. For the first time, I put my arms around him when I wasn't on his moto. It was another turning point, but I didn't know what it meant. Thorne held on to me like his knees might give out if I wasn't there to prop him up. *Damn.* I hadn't meant to do *this* to him, just screw with him a little.

Worried, I stroked his back; that he permitted it spoke volumes on his state of mind. "Did you see someone fall?" I asked.

Thorne shook his head, eyes shut. "She jumped."

And I made you relive it.

This, I knew instinctively, was the grudge he had against Stavros. By dying, the mysterious, unnamed female had given him reason to go to war. Something Stavros had done had driven her off a ledge. Not a romantic interest, I thought, but someone Thorne had felt protective toward. If she had been his lover, then Stavros wouldn't buy my role in this drama.

"Who?"

"Veronica." The name grated as if it was crafted of broken glass, too painful to speak.

"I was never in any danger," I said, but he wasn't listening.

His eyes opened, livid with fear, anger and something else that sparked like lightning, an emotion I'd never seen before. I couldn't have named it. He ran his hands up my arms to my shoulders and then cupped the back of my head, fingers lacing in my still-damp hair. His touch burned with insistent heat. For a wild, pulse-pounding moment, I thought he would kiss me. Thorne gazed at my mouth, his breath coming fast.

Then he opened his hands and stepped back. "You got me. It usually takes more to get me going…but I guess I'm on edge."

Disappointment tasted bitter at the back of my tongue. With some effort, I banished it. "I'm sorry. I didn't know that was your trigger."

He shrugged. "Never has been, but I never saw anybody dare gravity to kick their ass before, either."

I changed the subject. "I'm done eating. We should go pick up the meeting info, right?"

"Yeah. This is almost over. Soon everything will be back to normal."

Which meant Thorne taking over for Stavros and me never seeing him again. The prospect didn't fill me with as much joy as it had in the beginning. Damn him, anyway.

That night, we showed in good faith, knowing these nego-tiations would decide the future of Snake Ward. Thorne ar-rived early, and I verified there was nobody lying in wait by going to the top of a couple buildings and scouting that way. He was tense the entire time.

"It's clear," I reported when I got back.

That left us to wait for Henry, who arrived soon after. As promised, he came alone. "Stav's out of control," he said in lieu of greeting.

Thorne's mouth firmed. "I saw it when Veronica died, but nobody else seemed to agree."

"We noticed, brother, but changes in management can be complicated...and bloody."

Given the body count Stavros had thrown at us, I had to concur. I kept quiet because it was the role Thorne had as-signed me early on. As if he was thinking the same thing, he reached for me, encircling my shoulders with his arm.

"So what's your play?" Thorne asked.

"I'll bring him to you. I expect you can handle the rest."

"Stav still trusts you enough to make this feasible?"

Henry laughed. "Shit, I'm the only 'loyal' gun he's got left. The ones he's got beating the bushes for you are hired help, hoping to sign on if they bring you in."

"What about the others?"

"Mike's dead," he said flatly. "He was my boy, you know.

I told him no good would come of going head-to-head with the bossman, but he wouldn't stand down."

"Because of the people Stavros was killing?" I asked, speaking for the first time.

Henry cut his eyes to me. "Yeah. Mike didn't approve of taking out families for no reason. Neither do I, truth be told, but I wasn't brave enough to speak up. Maybe if I had…"

You'd be dead, too, I thought, *unless you were willing to drop Stavros then and there.*

"Well, it don't matter now. Bossman'll get what's coming to him."

Thorne nodded. "You said you're the only one left. The others dead?"

"Gone to ground. When the dust settles, they'll be back."

"Prepared to support me?" Thorne wanted to know.

That was key—and the whole reason he hadn't executed Stavros the first night. He needed physical support for his coup. Taking over Snake Ward wasn't a small job or somebody else would've knocked Stav off his throne years ago. People didn't love the bossman, but they feared him, which was the next-best thing to popular approval.

Henry inclined his head. "They all know and like you. Back in the day, you tried to reason with Stav…and sometimes you succeeded. We remember that."

"Your word's good with me." Then he smiled, but it was chilling. "If you play me, Henry, they'll find you in pieces."

"You think I'd sell you to Stav, after what he done to Mike?"

"No, but you might make a move of your own. Let me deal with Stavros, and then step up yourself with the men behind you."

To my surprise, Henry laughed. "Shit, brother, you think I want the weight of this ward on my shoulders? What do you think drove Stav so crazy? I need liquor, food and a warm woman, that's all."

"I have only your word for that, but it'll do until you prove otherwise." Man, Thorne could be scary when he tried.

"You'll see what's what when it all shakes out. After I talk to the boys, I'll set things up with Stav and leave word for you in the usual place."

"You'll tell him you found us?" I guessed.

Henry inclined his head. "That's the only way he's coming out. I'll say you're too wounded to move, likely to die in transit."

Yeah, the prospect of being denied personal retribution would piss the bossman off. He'd been running Snake Ward so long it had given him a God complex. I hoped like hell that didn't happen to Thorne. He might not be a good man, but he wasn't insane, so far as I could tell—at least, not more than anybody else in the Red Zone.

The meeting concluded shortly thereafter. Thorne found us a bolthole near the drop point. He could keep watch from here, making sure only the messenger came and went. If he saw any unusual activity in the area, we'd bail. At long last, the waiting was almost over. But oddly, he didn't seem more relaxed. He radiated tension, pacing our little hideaway with raw nerves.

"You all right?" Clearly he wasn't, but the question was invitation.

"No." He sat down opposite me with no warning, his gaze burning and intense. "I can't stop thinking about what Henry said…how he doesn't want this responsibility. I don't either. This isn't justice, Mari. It's payback."

"So it's more about taking Stav's life than his property."

He jerked his chin in an agitated nod. "But somebody's gotta drive the bus, right? We can't all be passengers."

"Maybe," I said slowly, "you could be a different kind of bossman. Instead of taking, maybe you could give back. Build something."

That was a pipe dream. Nothing like that ever happened in the Red Zone. Life had long since devolved into every man for himself. Sometimes people made friends, as I had with Nat, Seline and Edgar, but there were no larger connections. No public services or support network.

"I'm not a hero. Don't paint me as one." But I noticed he didn't reject the idea.

Maybe it was so stupid he thought the 'no' didn't need to be spoken out loud because the impossibility went without saying. But I let a little spark of hope kindle inside; I'd nourish it and keep an eye on the future. Maybe Thorne could drive the bus someplace better. Unlikely, but improbable optimism got me through the bad patches. In all honesty, Elodie shared that trait with me, which was part of why I found her so irritating.

"I'm not. It was just a suggestion." One I hoped would work on him down the line.

"Duly noted." He seemed calmer.

"If you want some free advice, don't worry about the future. You worked, sweated and bled for this moment. Let yourself enjoy it."

Thorne's brow went up in sardonic inquiry. "How?"

I realized he thought I meant something personal, him and me, so I stumbled over my reply. "Just…savor the impending triumph. By this time tomorrow night, it will be over."

"I can't help wondering what comes after."

"Sometimes it's best not to," I said.

He studied my face for a few seconds, expression unreadable. Thorne had a killer poker face, and I was pretty good at reading people. These days, it was a survival skill, knowing who to trust, who would screw you and when to run. Yet I couldn't tell what he was thinking.

"Yeah. Sometimes it's better not to realize what's coming." Then he ran a fingertip down my cheek, a gesture that was beyond me to interpret.

I didn't sleep well that night for oh-so-many reasons.

16

In the morning, we picked up the particulars from the drop site. The confrontation would take place near the Burn Ward border, along the river. It was a fitting backdrop, I thought. Today, the natives were restless. People stared as we sped along. Some raised their hands, calling out to acknowledge the new crown prince. Thorne didn't wave back.

Not yet. He had unfinished business.

Wind whipped my face through the helmet, burning my skin with dust particles. But that speed couldn't last, as our juice was limited. We needed to find a high, safe spot to power up the bike. Because we'd been moving so much, the panels never got more than a half charge, and Thorne had to hide it along with us. If he left it unattended, it would be gone.

It would suck to have a master plan derailed through lack of voltage.

He found the perfect spot in what used to be a parking garage. Or at least, that was what it looked like. Many of the ramps had collapsed, so it was unstable at best, yet he didn't hesitate in taking the corners with a little too much speed. I held on tighter as he jumped a small gap in the cement, then curled higher, until we reached the very top level. Raw metal girders were exposed, along with tumbled concrete, but there was no barrier between the sky overhead and us, exactly what the bike required.

There, we set up a primitive base camp. It was a hot day, muggy, with smoke circulating in the air. I'd probably get a lung infection after all this exposure. Oh, I knew my house offered only psychological protection, but maybe the power of my mind kept me healthy. I didn't encourage my sibs to spend a lot of time outdoors for various reasons.

"Is it getting enough light?" I asked. What I really wanted to know was, *will it have enough power to get us out of trouble?*

Thorne nodded. "It'll be fine by tonight."

When everything goes down.

"What's my role in this?"

"You played it…and well, I might add."

Shock reverberated through me, then anger rushed to fill the gaps. "I don't think so. I might play a damsel in distress, but I am *not* one. I'm in this with you…we'll finish it together. You know my strengths…now tell me what you need me to do."

To his credit, it didn't take him long to reevaluate. "Backup then. You still have the gun. I'll need you to find a good perch and cover me."

"I can also scout the meeting site. Tell you where he's likely to post gunmen."

"Can you take them out quietly?" he asked.

Given what he'd seen of my skills, it was a reasonable question. While he'd been on the ground, he had watched me kill a man. My stomach roiled at the thought of doing it again, but I nodded. "I can. Is that on?"

"If he's got guards, I want them out of the way before I move in. This ends one-on-one."

I could live with that. Thorne needed to kill Stavros personally to assume control of his territory. It was primitive street law, related to possession and power. As long as you could hold something, you owned it…and if somebody stronger came along, you lost everything.

"Then I'll back your play." I'd never said that to anyone before.

My jobs tended to be quiet and lonely. I slipped in, stole whatever my client wanted, and got out fast. Usually it was routine. No excitement.

But then, I'd never broken into a fortress before. My specialty was braving buildings that were deemed unsafe for human habitation. Too old, unstable, likely to collapse at any moment, but that didn't stop the rich from wanting to collect whatever old thing they had heard about…. That was primarily how I'd fed the family for the past three years, and before me, Dad had done the same.

I suspected my father wouldn't approve of this job at all. In my head, I heard his shocked voice: *I didn't teach you to kill, Mari.*

No, Dad. That, I learned on my own. When survival math came down to them or me, the calculation was simple. And Stavros had made it so we couldn't exist without some subtraction.

Thorne leveled a somber look on me. "Can you really do this? Before, it was more fight-or-flight. They attack…you respond. This time, you'll be hunting men. Executing them. I won't ask for anything you can't handle."

I understood what he was saying. And he was right. The idea of being so cold, so calculating, horrified me. In the Red Zone, I'd fought for my life a few times. And I'd killed with the traps more than once, but this was different. This decision meant turning a corner—giving away a piece of my soul—and I couldn't go back. Could never return to relative innocence.

"Do I want to?" I shook my head. "Not at all. But I can. I *will*. And I'll find a way to deal, afterward."

Though he didn't look delighted, he accepted my response. He could see I understood the risks…and the potential for damage in my own head. "Then it's settled."

"Did you seriously think you could stash me and play the endgame without me?"

"I must've been crazy."

I frowned, sensing sarcasm.

Apparently he read my look better than I could his. "No, I mean it. You've been amazing, Mari. No complaints, all-in from the jump. I know it wasn't personal…you were looking out for your brother and sister. But still, I appreciate it."

Wow. That's unexpected. True, in the beginning, everything I'd done had been motivated by the desire to protect my sibs. But now? Honestly, I wouldn't leave Thorne swinging in the wind even if the kids weren't a factor. But I wouldn't tell *him* that.

"We make a good team," I said, and then I wished I hadn't, because he enjoyed putting a personal spin on everything.

This time he didn't; he just nodded. I didn't know whether to be offended or relieved. His teasing disconcerted me because I didn't know how to take it. Men typically didn't pay me much attention, and I preferred it that way. Because Nat was beautiful, she dealt with unwanted moves all the time, and I dreaded the day when Elodie developed to that point. It wouldn't be long, a year or two, until the creepers noticed. Then I'd have to get good at killing them. So maybe this practice run was for the best, another life skill to acquire. Of course, knowing my sister, she'd knife a guy for looking at her wrong. She wasn't the sunny-natured angel she appeared.

"What?" he asked.

I turned to Thorne. "Hm?"

"You're smiling."

"I was just thinking of Elodie."

His expression softened, a look I'd never seen before. "Ah. It's amazing the way you've kept them safe. I can't even imagine."

"What?" I raised a brow.

"A family who gives a shit."

"These days it's pretty rare, I know."

"You know why my mother named me Thorne?"

"Because that's what you were to her?"

"Good guess." His tone was bleak.

Though I didn't say so, it could always be worse. There were women who did everything they could to abort. Sometimes it didn't work, and the baby was born...wrong. There was no recourse for such children. Abandoned by their mothers, they died in Junkland, whimpering their last breaths in such a way that I didn't know how the permanent residents bore it.

"At least she named you. Kept you."

"I'm still not sure why." He got up then, ostensibly to check how the bike was charging, but the move was more to be sure I understood this conversation was over.

I wished I could comfort him, but that would require intimacy and attachment. Apart from my sibs, I was allergic to both. So I let him withdraw, and the silence stood, until dark fell.

Then it was time to roll.

17

"You set?" Thorne asked. We had arrived a few moments before.

I nodded, swinging off his bike. "Good to go."

He scoped out the view. "If we're early, Stavros will be, too. He'll need time to make sure he can dominate, even if he thinks I'm dying. But he's not counting on you helping me."

That was surprising. "He thinks you're alone in this?"

"I don't have the resources to contract outside help." I heard the unspoken 'yet.'

"And it took all your savings just to keep us alive and fed while we were running."

Thorne nodded. "I'm banking on you, Mari."

Just what I don't need to hear. I had no idea why he trusted me at his back, but as I pulled off the helmet, I resolved to haul my weight.

"Do you think he trusts Henry?"

Thorne considered. "Not wholly. But enough to come, I think. Stav won't want to accept that he's got nobody left in his corner."

Yeah, that would be hard to hear. I drew my blade. "I'll see you soon."

I didn't know this terrain well, so I needed time to scout. When Thorne turned his head, I slipped into the shadows, second nature now. Sometimes survival stemmed from going unseen. He spun in a slow circle, searching for me. I could tell he was surprised and maybe a little impressed. Which was exactly what I intended.

I lifted my feet and placed them with care. The ground could give me away—loose gravel, broken glass, those were the enemies of stealth. He was still looking for me, but from this distance, there was no way he'd find me. I took satisfaction in that. Many times, I'd crept away from trouble while it stormed around, screaming impotent threats. They could hurt you only if they found you.

It was a dark night; no shine through the smog canopy. Occasionally the miasma parted to shower a glimmer of moonlight, but gloom hung heavy, as if even the night knew somebody would die, and so the stars turned their faces away. In short, it was perfect for an execution.

The ambush site was wide-open, an expanse of pocked cement with high sloping sides. If I were posting guards, I would situate them up along the top. There was little cover, too, which left Thorne as a clear target. Lack of light would factor into distance shooting; so would the wind whipping down the culvert, spraying the stagnant water pooled at the bottom. However, when Stavros came, he would come heavy, which meant bringing his best equipment. His men on the high ground would be ready to ice Thorne without hesitation.

He was counting on *me* to secure the area. I wouldn't let him down. The knife handle felt slick in my palms, sweaty with nerves. I'd never played a role in something so major before. I had assured Thorne I could handle this, but the truth was, I wasn't a professional hitter. I was a thief, not a killer— or rather, I was a thief who *would* kill, when driven to it.

I had never hunted men before.

Yet I had the skills. So I crept through the water, checking each potential perch. At the third site, I found my first target. He had his back to me, rifle on his shoulder, and he was watching Thorne, who stood where I had left him, casual, as if he had nothing to fear. It was a show of strength, daring Stavros to do his worst. In the murky air, I couldn't make out anything apart from his form, but the man before me was looking through a scope.

I watched where I stepped, each movement measured like a heartbeat. Slow motions were more likely to go unnoticed in peripheral vision; people sensed someone running up behind them. Knife in hand, I went for the kidney shot again, but I didn't want him calling out, so as he fell, I slashed his throat, too. When you didn't care about mess, that cut was the quickest way to silence somebody if you didn't have the physical strength to choke him out. My dad had taught me a lot about how a small person could neutralize a bigger one, though his lessons hadn't been lethal. The body made a muffled thump, not enough to carry on the concrete. The night swallowed his death.

A thief by nature and necessity, I rummaged through his pockets, removing everything of value. The portable items I tucked away. I left the rifle. Provided we survived this encounter, I'd come back for it, as it would fetch a good price at market. Until then, it would only slow me down, make my footfalls heavier. Since I was striving to be a ghost, I didn't need extra weight.

I had a lot of ground to cover. If I missed even one man, Thorne wouldn't walk away—and then neither would I. Sooner or later, Stavros would find the kids, and he practiced scorched-earth politics. *No.* I cut the fear spiral right there and refused to let it grow.

You have a job to do.

The second sentry was posted farther on. This time, I got close, but he heard me. He spun, bringing the rifle up, but I dove at him. I wasn't strong enough to win a physical contest, but that wasn't what I was going for anyway. To beat him, I only needed to do the unthinkable—I stabbed him in the balls. Forgetting his mission, his weapon, everything but pain, he cried out, and I whipped my knife up and opened his throat. Heart hammering, I listened.

Are the others close enough to have heard that?

For long moments, I kept still, crouched above the corpse. Nothing. I shifted enough to peer down into the basin, where Thorne still stood. No shots rang out. There was no second figure yet, so Stavros must have been getting his men in place; he wouldn't reveal himself until he was sure he had cover fire from all angles. That meant I was racing the clock.

How am I supposed to know if it's safe, whether I found every-one? This job dwarfed me, sent anxious spikes into my brain. I didn't want to be the reason Thorne died. This dread I shut down, too. Daily worries had plagued me for years; this was just a bigger version.

Finish the job. Then you can go home.

18

The third man was an easier kill.

He was so absorbed in his rifle that he didn't notice me until I was on him. This time, I cut the throat straightaway. On most men, I wouldn't try, but he was short—around my height—making the maneuver feasible. He fell in a gurgling heap; didn't take long for him to die. An icy chill suffused me, dread over what I was doing and how I'd look the kids in the eyes thereafter.

It's necessary, I told myself, but each silent step felt heavier.

I continued down this side of the viaduct, but I didn't find another guard. If Stavros was consistent, there would be three on the other side. I had to hurry. Soon, the bossman would feel confident, and he'd come out of hiding. Thorne was vulnerable while I worked. Sure, he was armed, but there were rifles trained on him. He wouldn't be safe until all these thugs went down.

I picked a careful path, clinging to the shadows. Without cover, this was the hardest part of my task. Each step, each second, my body drew taut, waiting for a bullet to blow through my chest. This far down, though, maybe I only had to worry about one shooter, the guy directly across. Erring on the side of caution, I crept even farther, so I could circle behind him. Otherwise when I crossed the open space, they would see me for sure. Slow movement could take you only so far; it wasn't as though I was invisible. All the while, I was conscious of the ticking clock.

As much as I dared, I picked up the pace. The bloody blade in my hand haunted me. Though I knew they weren't good men or they wouldn't be working for Stavros, part of me balked. Thorne had worked for him, too, and he wasn't a horrendous human being. But when push came to shove, I had to fight for my own life—and for the kids.

That resolve carried me up to the fourth goon. I couldn't imagine what so much manpower had cost Stavros. This guy had put down his rifle; he seemed relaxed, right up until my knife sank into his back. I twisted the weapon, and then pulled it out swiftly. This one didn't cry out or require his throat to be cut. I was getting *better* at this, and it wasn't comforting.

Two to go.

I checked the center of the culvert, saw that Thorne had abandoned his bike. Yeah, that would lend credence to the impression that he was wounded. He'd only leave it if he was too weak. I made out the shape of him huddled against some rubble, as if he needed to hide. That, too, would draw Stavros out. Nothing attracted a predator like a wounded enemy. The bossman enjoyed gloating, a kick or two in the face for a man on the ground. His lackeys had learned the trick from him, no doubt, when they'd cornered Thorne days before.

That wouldn't happen tonight.

Number five awaited. Dropping back to a sneaking squat, I edged in his direction. I came up on him sooner than I expected; he was out of position, watching for trouble, not just staring at the basin. For a moment he just stared, wondering if I was really a person or just a trick of the smog and the half-light. He shouted when he made up his mind, and I came in low, slicing for the tendons behind his knees. Unfortunately, he blocked with efficient slashes of his palms. That meant training. I had to take him out fast, as he was bigger than me, stronger, and he'd been in more stand-up fights.

I bit the arm holding me and then stomped down. The combined girl-tactic put him off balance, enough for me to throw my weight at his torso. Close up, I was so screwed. My opponent took the fight to the ground. He slammed a shoulder into me as we rolled. I ended up underneath him, the worst possible position for someone my size. A meaty hand circled my wrist; a little more pressure, and he'd break it. Then I wouldn't be able to fight; I wasn't ambidextrous.

In a clumsy lurch, I slammed my head into his chin. He bit his tongue, hard. The blood sprinkled down on me. In pain, he loosed his grip just enough, and I cut my way free, jabbing the knife into his forearm. Wild with determination, I kept slashing. Not deep cuts but they stung like a bitch. He tried to stop me with a blow to the temple, but I saw it coming and countered, so I took only part of the hit. Still, it sent my vision sparkly, and I got lucky with a downward jab. I hit an artery in his thigh, so when I pulled the knife out, blood jetted in great gouts. He swung at me with one hand, covering the wound in the other, but he weakened too fast to be a threat.

I scrambled away, wondering if anyone had heard his warning shout. There were other noises, people fighting and crying in distant houses. While it might put Stavros on alert, I decided there was no way for him to be sure what he'd heard without coming up here. And if he did...well, I'd find a way to kill him, too. Somehow.

"Everything all right?" a male voice called.

Dammit. That had to be number six.

"Fine." I pitched my voice low, hoping it would pass.

I needed the last guard at ease, as I lacked the stamina for another fight like this. Huddled on my knees, I waited for footfalls heading my way, but I heard nothing. The goon probably had firm instructions from Stavros, and he didn't care to disobey, unless circumstances made that unavoidable. Then I waited a little longer, just to be sure, while studying the basin.

As I stalked toward number six, a huge man strode toward Thorne. *Stavros.*

The end begins.

19

Stavros stood a head taller than Thorne, more bulk in chest and shoulders. His size wouldn't help him tonight. From my close encounter, I knew he had one good eye, a bristling beard and a head of fierce red hair, liberally shot through with silver. He looked as if he'd rather kill you than look at you, and in his case, appearances weren't deceiving.

I shivered, recalling how scared I had been when his men dragged me out of the market to force his offer on me. It had all been downhill from the moment I'd accepted that I had the choice to work for him or let the kids starve. And he'd gotten off on my lack of recourse.

As I'd left, Stavros had touched my cheek with a huge hand and said, "Do this job right, and I'll make you a happy girl." His tone had made it clear what he'd meant, as if sex with him would be an honor.

He had a booming voice; tonight, it carried to me fine. "You don't look good, Thorne. Betrayal doesn't taste as sweet as you thought?"

That resonance meant he intended to give orders to his men this way, too. Good to know they didn't have some secret signals set up. In all honesty, that was too sophisticated for Stavros; he believed in stabbing, shooting, burning and bludgeoning, not necessarily in that order.

Thorne pushed to his feet, giving the impression of mortal wounds. He was still wearing his bloodstained clothes, too. "I don't mind."

"Heard you took a bullet." Amusement flavored the boss-man's tone. He hadn't realized just how screwed he was yet. In his world, there were six men with rifles trained on Thorne, ready to kill on his orders.

"I'll live."

"No, you won't."

Thorne straightened. He looked stronger then. "I think you got that backward."

"Uh-uh. There's no way you walk out of here. Even if you beat me down, my boys put a bullet in you on my word."

"Is that the message you're sending now, Stav? Doesn't matter how strong you are, as long as you've got numbers?"

The bigger man stirred, cracked his knuckles. "I've been looking forward to this."

"Bring it on."

Thorne rushed him. Though I'd seen fights before, this one was…riveting. Lean grace versus brute strength. Stavros threw a punch, but Thorne wasn't there. Even on his weak knee, he whirled around behind him, unleashed a flurry of blows against his back. I didn't know that much about combat, but that kind of onslaught did internal damage. If Stavros didn't recover, he'd be coughing blood soon. The big man spun, fists up in bruiser stance. He shook the pain off as if it was nothing and slammed Thorne hard, right in the chest. I winced in sympathy. Broken ribs, for sure. That would make it tough to—

Thorne moved faster than I'd imagined possible. He lashed out with a kick, but he'd forgotten his knee was weak and he stumbled in the recovery, showing Stavros where to strike. The bossman returned with a vicious sweep. Thorne went down, and Stavros fell on top of him. I knew exactly how that felt, too. There were bruises forming from the hits I'd taken.

He rolled out, preventing a lock, and Stavros growled, bass

frustration echoing in the night air. He'd expected to taunt a dying man, not fight a furious one. Thorne slammed an elbow into the bossman's throat and stole his breath. While Stavros was reeling, Thorne pressed the advantage, landing blow after blow. He had rage; the need to avenge a girl named Veronica drove him on.

"Shoot him!" Stavros shouted through bloody teeth. He took another fist to the face, breaking his lips. He spat blood. "Now, take him out now!"

Oh, shit. I got so caught up in the fight that I forgot about number six.

The bossman was expecting six gunmen to unload, though they'd better be damn good shots if they could keep from hitting the big man at this distance…in the dark. I didn't bother with stealth. Speed mattered too much, so I went running while the last thug sighted. I sank my blade into his arm to skew his aim. The shot went wide, and then I stabbed him again, without aim or precision, determined he wouldn't hurt Thorne. I didn't register when I struck the death blow, only that he dropped, and the rifle beside him. The knife slipped from my bloody fingers, and I ran down to make sure Thorne was safe. He knelt beside Stavros, who was struggling on the ground.

"Did he hit you?" I panted out.

"A few lucky shots, nothing serious." But his pained movements belied the words.

Those ribs, along with his leg, would plague him for weeks, if not months. Being a badass, he'd probably refuse to rest, refuse to give himself a chance to heal properly. After tonight, that wasn't my business anymore. Our fates were about to be unchained.

"Not him, the shooter."

Thorne shook his head. "You came through, Mari. Thanks."

The bossman stared up at me with bruised, disbelieving eyes. "Expect me to believe this girl took out all my men? Bullshit. Henry must be around somewhere, that lying rat bastard. *She's* just a thief…and not even a good one, or I'd have blown her block to hell and back by now. She's another whore, a worthless splittail, just like—"

Thorne shot him in the head before he could say, "Veronica." I still didn't know who she was, exactly, what had happened to her, or why she mattered so much. The bullet made no exit wound, so after the initial report, silencing Stavros's tirade, there was only quiet, punctuated by the distant sound of life in Snake Ward. The people arguing and weeping and laughing and cooking their food over open fires didn't know yet how much life had changed.

But from this point on, things would never be the same.

20

I stared down at Stavros's body. "You didn't have to do that for me," I said.

Since the bossman had been talking shit about me when he took the bullet in the face, it felt personal. But maybe it was for Veronica—to keep Stavros from sullying her name. Thorne watched me with a veiled expression. When he held his head like that, the shadows filled his face and obscured everything. "Maybe I didn't."

Mind games. Or maybe not. I had been the catalyst but not the cause of his private war. Whatever, it didn't matter; I was ready to tie up the loose ends.

"So, what now?"

"We move on."

The things I had done would linger like ghosts. This blood on my hands wouldn't wash out of my head so easily. "It's that simple for you?"

Since he'd worked for Stavros, it probably was. He'd killed the bossman. Saved my life. Though that outcome hadn't been his driving motivation, the fact remained. Personal debt left me feeling itchy, as if it would come due in some uncomfortable way. But in the Red Zone, you lived one minute at a time, and I'd learned that lesson well.

"Human life is cheap, Mari. I can buy a kid for far less than it costs to join one of the fortresses."

I remembered his mother had sold him to the man on the ground before us. So I'd guess he knew better than me about the going rate for a child. "Do they permit buy-ins?" I'd thought, due to population control issues, only people born into the system could live inside the walls.

"It's rare but it happens. Anything can be bought."

There was no reply to that obvious truth, so I bent. "Do we need to clean this up?"

Thorne took my hands, drawing me up. "There's no point. Henry will send someone in the morning to make sure we got the job done."

He strode off, and I followed, watching the street behind us. At this hour, even the scavengers weren't stirring yet. In time, they'd learn that Thorne had taken Stavros's place. And things might get better. *Since it's Thorne.* I didn't know why I thought that. He might not be different, after all; he was cooler, less brutal, more refined in his cruelties.

Part of me hoped he would be decent since I had suggested he could build. That might turn out to be the biggest joke of all. Regardless, I ran along behind him as he headed for the bike. I braced my hands on the seat, wondering what you said at a moment like this.

Without ceremony, Thorne swung on the moto, then he turned to me. "If anyone asks, you don't know what happened. Rumors will circulate about your involvement, but if anyone finds out how tough you are, they'll come gunning to make a name on you."

How tough I am? Really? Yet I still repressed a reluctant pleasure in the strange compliment, as it came with hard-won respect.

"I had no plans to brag," I muttered.

"We shouldn't linger. I'll get you to the bolthole, where the kids are hiding."

"Thanks."

A flash of surprise quirked his mouth; I guessed he had expected me to argue. "Let's go."

The night was fairly quiet as Thorne drove. I took care where I held him, gentle on his waist because of his ribs. He felt incredibly warm and solid in my arms. If I had been a different person, I would have been tempted to confide my troubles. Tell him how hard it had been, the past few years. Sometimes the burden felt like more than I could carry, but I wouldn't switch places with a street ghost who had nobody to care if they came home.

As we neared the hidey-hole, I felt as if I needed to say something, but what? It seemed wrong to thank him for killing a guy, even if it wasn't for me. And it felt as if it had been, at least a little. I'd seen how his face had tightened when Stavros had called me names, whore and splittail. He'd had the gun up even before the bossman had brought the other girl into the diatribe.

"What will you do now?" I asked.

"Clean house."

I was curious how he would reorganize, if he'd implement new policies or try to help instead of stealing from those who had so little already. "Will you change—"

"It's better if you don't know my plans," he cut in gently.

"Right. I dunno what I was thinking." My sarcasm was tangible over the purr of the bike.

To my astonishment, he laughed. In our short acquaintance, I wasn't sure he'd ever made that sound. Hadn't been sure he could, to be honest.

"I'm glad you're not afraid of me."

"Why would I be? You're no worse than anyone else."

"It doesn't feel that way. But thanks."

Why the hell does he think he's worse than Stavros? The ex-bossman had regularly had people's kneecaps broken, know-

ing they'd never heal right without medical treatment. I had
seen his thugs do terrible things, night after night, in his name.
Speechless with awakening fear and wonder, I finished the
trip in silence. Thorne didn't speak, either.

He stopped outside a rundown building, and I swung off
the bike, handing back his helmet. I couldn't wait to hug the
kids. They'd never know just how close they'd come to being
alone in the world, or how scared I was of letting them down.
I couldn't wait to tell them my part in Stavros's downfall,
though they might not believe it. And Nat would be *so* glad
to go home. Hopefully, she could tell me how to find the rest
of our neighbors, where they might be hiding.

"Will you do me a favor?" I asked.

"What's that?"

"Destroy the bomb components Stavros meant to use. I
won't rest easy, knowing somebody else could blow up my
block."

He nodded. "I'll take care of it, I promise."

"Thanks."

"It was a pleasure working with you, Marjolaine Thistle."
My full moniker was silly—and I hated it—a memento of my
mother's whimsy, when practicality would've served us better. Thorne raised a brow. "Don't make that face. Your name
suits you."

"Sure it does."

"I wouldn't lie to you," he told me. "Not after what we've
been through together. Keep safe, Mari. It's a rough world
out there." With a faint smile, he bent and brushed his lips
against my forehead, where the heat lingered like a blessing.

Then he got back on the bike and drove away, whistling;
soon, the smoky dark took him from sight, but the tune carried
back to me, growing ever softer, until I wondered whether I'd
heard it at all. Belatedly, I remembered he still hadn't called

for payment due. I owed him on so many levels, not least for sending someone to check on my sibs when I most needed that peace of mind.

Therefore, I hadn't seen the last of Thorne Goodman. I just didn't know when he'd turn up again…or what he'd ask of me when he did.

★ ★ ★ ★ ★

SUN STORM

KAREN DUVALL

For my supportive writer peeps in Bend, Oregon.
Your friendship means the world to me.
Thank you, Steph, Diana, Trudy, Paty, Mary, Julia, Linda and Beth.

● | ●

I stared out the hospital window at the heat-glazed street below, knowing I shouldn't be shocked to see brown lawns, charred rooftops and the sun-scorched branches of leafless trees in the middle of January. But I was. I'd never get used to a hot winter in Colorado.

Few people ventured outside in the daytime anymore. The risk of getting caught in a sun storm was greater now than ever before, and only a rare few survived the storm's lethal rain of radioactive sun sparks. Exposure killed you slowly with Sun Fever, or if you were lucky, it let you live with altered DNA that turned you into a freak. That's what had happened to me. The sun and I were connected now. I could predict when a storm was about to happen, and there was one coming this way.

I gripped the window blinds, my fingers like burning bands of iron as the premonition flowed through me. My entire body felt on fire from the inside out, and I wondered if exhaling hard enough would send flames dancing on my breath. But, no, I'd already tried that. The air from my lungs came out as red clouds of smoke instead.

I had a half hour to warn the town to take cover before the storm hit. It was time to sound the alarm.

Still vibrating from the effects of foreseeing a storm, I shook out my hands to rid them of the sensation of being pricked by a thousand needles. Wisps of crimson vapor curled off my fingertips. I hauled out the hand-crank siren from the bottom desk drawer in the hospital administration office and rushed out into the hall.

I almost had a head-on collision with a nurse carrying a loaded tray of meds. The second she saw me she dropped her tray, and pills of myriad colors and sizes scattered across the gray linoleum floor. Her hand flew to her mouth, and her shock revealed the whites of her eyes. My physical appearance during a forecast often had that effect on people. My eyes, which were normally pale blue like the sky, felt hot, and I was sure they glowed. It would be another minute or two before my body returned completely back to normal.

"A storm's coming?" the nurse asked. She knew of my ability to predict storms. Everyone in town knew. "Where?"

A storm could happen anywhere and always did, but my scope of detection was limited to a two-hundred-mile radius. This time it was closer to home. It *was* home, in the same town where I was born, and it would arrive in thirty minutes. I felt a twinge of disappointment that I'd miss the thrill of chasing it, but I'd still get my kinetic energy fix. I needed it to function. "Here."

"You mean Lodgepole?"

I nodded. "Notify hospital staff. If people don't make it indoors in time, we should be prepared."

She bent to pick up her fallen tray, and I kicked it away. "Leave it. Hurry, okay?" I ran past her for the exit.

After slipping in a set of earplugs, I gripped the red siren's handle in one hand and operated the crank with the other. The wailing alarm traveled through the streets and echoed off buildings, alerting the tiny population of Lodgepole that a storm was coming. As long as they took shelter, everyone would be safe.

The impending storm made me anxious and eager all at once, yet I felt concern for anyone who chose not to heed my warning. I prayed there'd be no casualties this time. We had only two doctors left, and I served as a hospital orderly in exchange for room and board, as well as medical care for my ailing father. Frequent heat strokes had wreaked havoc on his brain, as had the depression that set in after my mother died of Sun Fever. My father and I both lived at the hospital now.

Like a football player hit so hard he hears ringing in his ears, the world had its bell rung when the biggest solar storm in history permanently blacked out half the northern hemisphere. We still heard echoes of that bell ringing as repeat storms sent radioactive sun sparks to infect hundreds of thousands of people with the deadly Sun Fever. Subsequent storms nudged the planet's poles a little at a time, causing earthquakes and tsunamis around the globe. Electricity, and therefore clean water, was difficult to come by. I held out hope that given time, the world would return to normal. My mother had always told me to never lose hope, and as long as I believed conditions would improve someday, I would have something to look forward to.

My attention was drawn to a bulletin board on the wall behind the vacant nurse's station. A number of newspaper headlines had been tacked there as the hospital's historical record of what was now known as the Bell Ringer. The clippings looked older than they were, having been yellowed and turned brittle by the hot dry air.

Bell Ringer Blacks Out Canada

Radioactive Sun Sparks Cause Lethal Fever

Electronic Communication Ends for Ninety-Five Percent of the World

Solar Storms Cause Heart Attacks, Short-Circuit Pacemakers

Dry Conditions Cause Fires, Entire Cities Burn to the Ground

My hands balled into fists as I reread these headlines for the hundredth time. Chain reactions between events had caused as much destruction as the solar storm that had started it all. Frustration with what I couldn't change raised the hair on the back of my neck. I slapped the board and left a sweaty handprint that smeared the ink on the clippings.

"Sarah!"

I swung around to face whoever had called my name. One of the nurses stood by a window that looked out onto the street. She pointed outside, her face contorted with worry. "Sarah, come here, quick! It's your father."

What the hell? I ran over to stand beside her and peered out the window. My dad, wearing only his plaid boxers and a dingy tank undershirt, shuffled clumsily toward the empty lot across the street.

My father's tattered sandals seemed to weigh down his feet as he dragged them over the hot asphalt. Gulping dry air that felt like a mouthful of thumbtacks, I ran to my room, which was next to my father's, and jabbed my feet into a pair of rubber flip-flops with partially melted soles. My heart thudded with panic as I dug out the heavy anti-radiation blanket from a cupboard. I tucked a bottle of water in the waistband of my shorts. Practically tripping over my own feet, I raced down the steps for the front door.

Going outside was like facing a furnace blast. I gazed up at a too-perfect blue sky, the sun a blazing orange orb that always appeared brightest just before a storm. The bottoms of my flip-flops stuck to the asphalt as I trotted across the street. I remembered a time when the hospital parking lot was always full and both sides of the street had been lined with cars. Not anymore. Tumbleweeds, dried leaves and pieces of old trash had taken their place.

Dad, what were you thinking? But that was the problem. His thinking was far from clear, and I found him kneeling on the baked ground, his head bowed over the dirt as if in prayer.

I flicked a glance at the sky. Red sparks glistened in the sunlight as they floated toward Earth. Though my mother had been exposed to the deadly sparks that killed her, my father never had. I wasn't about to let it happen now.

"Dad?" Having already been infected and changed by the sparks, they couldn't hurt me, so I held the blanket over him and left myself exposed. I reached for his hand to help him up. Making an effort to keep panic from my voice, I said, "Let's go home."

My gut clenched when he emptied his bottle of water over the dry ground. "Your mother forgot to water her vegetables today."

"She'll be happy you took care of it for her." Glittering sparks fell around us, bouncing off me as if I were made of rubber, yet their touch on my skin made me tingle from head to toe. I felt like a vessel filling to the brim with energy, but it wouldn't last. My body buzzed with fallout from the storm.

It hurt to lie, but I had to. "Let's go tell Mom, okay?"

My father nodded. "Okay."

I helped him to his feet, and he clung to me for balance. I noticed his knees were blistered from contact with the hot ground, and sweat beaded on his shiny scalp. Not only did I have to protect him from the sparks, I also had to get him inside and cool him off.

"I don't feel so good," he said, then began to retch. He teetered on his feet, and I struggled to keep the blanket over him. Sparks were thick in the sky as the storm flooded the air with a hellish red glitter that dissipated on contact with the ground. I wasn't strong enough to pick up my dad and carry him in. I hated taking the risk, but I'd have to wait it out and hope a spark never touched him.

Just then I heard the crunch of quick footsteps over the sun-baked ground and saw a man with hair the color of maple wood running toward us. He wore gray scrubs, and his body was unprotected from the sparks.

"What the hell are you doing?" I yelled. "Being out in the open during a sun storm is suicide."

"I could say the same to you." The man stopped in front of me and attempted to grab my father, but I held on, not sure about handing my dad over to someone I didn't know. "Let me help."

I narrowed my eyes at the stranger staring at me, his strong features a stoic mask of confidence. His eyes were a deep shade of chocolate, his skin ruddy from countless sunburns, and his thoughtful scowl wrinkled the skin just above his nose. Despite the fierce countenance, he was a handsome man. His full lips expressed neither joy nor distaste, but a practiced neutrality. He had the look of a troubled man.

I blinked as I noticed the sun sparks bounce off him as they did me, which could only mean one thing. "You're a—"

"I'm a Kinetic, and I'd hazard a guess that you're one, too."

• 2 •

"Now, let me help your old man, okay?" The stranger grabbed my dad away from me and gently lifted him up to cradle him in his arms, taking care to keep the blanket in place.

"Are you a doctor?" I asked his back as I followed him inside.

"I'm the new janitor." He turned to face me, a long hank of hair falling over one eye. He jerked his head back, and the errant lock flipped aside to reveal a white scar that bisected his eyebrow. It suited him, and I was surprised by how attracted I was. I had no clue who, or what, this guy was, but I felt drawn to him in a way I couldn't explain.

"Thank you, mister…"

"Matthews. Ian Matthews, but please, call me Ian." The corner of his mouth lifted in a snarly sort of smile. My heart quickened. "I'd shake your hand, but my arms are full."

"I'm Sarah Daggot. Thank you for helping my father." I gestured for Ian to follow me to my father's room, where he laid my dad on the bed.

"Dad?" I took my father's hand and rubbed it between both of mine. I checked him for the telltale purple rash that came with exposure, but his skin was clear. My shoulders lifted with a deep sigh of relief. "Can you hear me?"

My father opened his eyes and nodded.

"Be right back, okay?" I stepped out into the hall, and Ian came with me.

"Will he be all right?" Ian asked.

"I think so. This isn't the first time he's collapsed from the heat. I'm just glad he wasn't infected. Thanks to you." I didn't like how flirty that sounded.

"Lucky I saw you two out there. I heard your warning siren and figured I should stick around to help." He still hadn't smiled, but I was intrigued by the firm set of his jaw and how the corners of his lips made shallow dints on the sides of his mouth. I had a hard time looking away.

"My dad has never wandered off before," I said.

"Dementia?"

I nodded.

"That's becoming more common in heat stroke victims."

"It's caused partly by the strokes, but also from depression after my mom passed away. Sun Fever took her from us about a year ago."

His eye made a sudden twitch, and he looked away from me to focus elsewhere. I think he knew what it was like to lose someone to the fever. I waited for him to say so, but he didn't. So I did. "Has anyone close to you died of Sun—?"

"I should let one of the doctors know about your dad," Ian said. "I need to get back to work, but I'm sure we'll run into each other again." He started walking backward down the hall toward the stairs. "We'll go out for a drink. What do you say?"

I'd say I felt flustered. Was he asking me on a date? "Okay, sure. We could meet at—"

He waved goodbye, then turned toward the stairwell and disappeared.

In spite of feeling shell-shocked by our brisk encounter, I found myself looking forward to seeing him again. I'd never met another Kinetic, though I'd heard about them from folks passing through town on their way to anywhere but where they'd been. Everyone was looking for the ideal place to set down roots, yet rarely seemed to find it. I wondered if the same went for Ian Matthews. I allowed myself a small smile. He was a freak like me. Maybe I wasn't such an odd duck, after all.

I should try to sleep, but I wasn't tired. I never slept well anyway, especially not in this heat, and I was too hopped up on adrenaline from the storm to relax. It always took me a while to come down from the high. Once I did, anticipation for the next storm would string me out like an addict jonesing for her next fix. Not only did I *want* to chase a storm, I had to.

My connection to the sun took its toll in hours spent on the road chasing storms, but the kinetic energy I absorbed made up for it. I had a love-hate relationship with my ability: forecasting and chasing sun storms gave me a rush, but it also depressed me because of how dangerous they were for others. People died; I lived.

I wondered how Ian handled his own kinetic ability, and what that ability was. Could he control fire? Turn water to ice? Or maybe he had the ability to move objects or read minds. A traveler once told me about a Kinetic he'd met who could alter his physical form and become any animal he wished. Was Ian a shape-shifter? That would be freaky. Whatever he was, we shared a connection to the malevolent sun responsible for our change.

My dad lay supine on the bed, his skin still red from overheating. I wiped a damp washcloth over his face, remembering what he'd been like back when weather patterns were normal. Ever since I was a child I had an uncanny talent for predicting severe weather, which had encouraged both my parents to get in the business of chasing storms. Usually tornadoes, sometimes thunderstorms, even a few hurricanes. My dad had loved the thrill and adventure of tracking killer storms, and he'd charged people money to take them along in his storm-proof SUV on what he called storm-chasing tours. Our storm-chasing days were over now, but my ability to forecast the weather was not. Only now the type of weather I predicted went beyond the boundaries of Earth's atmosphere.

I didn't get a chance to contemplate when the next storm would happen because the sun was already sending me that message. Bracing myself against the foot of my father's bed, I let the premonition overtake me. My body heated up, my tongue like lava hot enough to melt the fillings in my teeth. I clenched my jaw as power surged through my veins, my eyes burning. A mental map formed in my mind. I wouldn't have far to go to chase this storm, either. It would strike in two hours, in downtown Denver. And I would make sure to be there when it happened.

I was lucky to still have my father's old storm-proof SUV. It looked like a bucket of bolts, its body dented and blotched with primer, but it was still a serviceable vehicle. I kept it in the hospital ambulance bay that had become an emergency vehicle graveyard. Old Stormy no longer ran on combustible fuel. It was solar power all the way.

The Storm Trooper sat slightly lopsided, which was probably due to having uneven tires. To prepare the Trooper for today's trip to Denver, I'd have to replace the solar battery with the one recharging out in the sun. But first I examined the vehicle for possible damage done by any attempted break-ins. There was always someone trying to steal it, and I wasn't surprised to see a crowbar lying on the ground nearby. A few new dents had been added to the severely dimpled door, but the modified SUV was solid as a tank. If it could withstand a tornado, it had no problem repelling the most persistent thief.

I opened the back hatch and replenished my supply of bottled water, adding a box of stale energy bars that were over a year past their expiration date. I didn't care. Food was food, and scarce as it was, I knew better than to be particular.

Now for the battery. I hated this part.

I wouldn't exactly call myself petite, but the strength required to lift the solar battery that weighed almost as much as I did was more than my spindly girl arms could muster. However, I'd devised a system using a dolly and a jack that enabled me to get the job done.

Wincing at the clock on the dashboard, I realized I was cutting it close. It would take me a half hour to get the recharged battery installed and hooked up properly. I slid the dolly under the battery and started wheeling it over to the Trooper.

"Need help?" asked a voice from behind me.

I let go of the dolly, and the battery slid off. "Shit!" My heart pounded in my ears.

"I'll get it." Ian stepped out of the shadows and crouched down to reseat the battery on the dolly's flat metal platform. He stood and effortlessly rolled it toward the Trooper. "Is this where you want it?"

"Yeah," I said, shaken by his surprise visit. I hadn't even heard him coming. Maybe he was an auditory Kinetic with the ability to control sound. It made me surprisingly happy to see him again so soon. "Thanks for getting the doctor for my dad."

"No problem. This your rig?"

I nodded. "It's actually my dad's. He built it from two retrofitted pickup trucks."

"Wow. I'm impressed."

Smiling, I said, "He used to be quite the mechanic. And an incredible storm chaser."

Ian arched his eyebrows. "Storm chasing, huh?"

"It was the family business."

"I just found out your kinetic ability is predicting storms, so the connection makes sense." His gaze darted around the garage as if he looked for someone.

"We're alone." And I wasn't so sure I liked that he was concerned about that. Did I want to be alone with this man? Part of me said yes, oh, yes. He made my insides go all warm and melty, or maybe it was his kinetic energy that did that. Also, how could I not like the man who had saved my father's life? But despite my desire to touch the broad muscles bunched beneath his thin tank undershirt, the reality was that Ian was a stranger. He seemed harmless on the outside, and God knew my mother had always preached the importance of seeing the good in people, but no one could be too careful. I'd encountered too many desperate people since the Bell Ringer, and desperate people did desperate things. I needed to know what kind of man he really was.

"Going somewhere?" He eyed the vehicle.

"As a matter of fact, I am. Another storm is coming, to downtown Denver this time, and I'm kind of in a hurry to get there before it hits."

He scowled, his delicious brown eyes getting lost in his squint. "That's dangerous."

"Not for me. But it could be for the people in Denver if I don't arrive in time to warn them." I flipped up the Storm Trooper's hood and angled my jack under the battery to lift it from the ground. The higher I could get it, the less distance I'd have to carry it.

"Let me do that." He crouched down, scooped up the battery with a grunt, and carried it the rest of the way to the vehicle. I was about to explain where it needed to go, but there was no need. He plunked it precisely in place and began hooking up the cables.

"How did you know—?"

"Your dad and I have something in common." He hunkered over the engine, checking lines and pistons and electrical cords. Ian knew his way around a solar-powered car. "I was a mechanic in Boston. That's where I'm from."

He seemed too good to be true, which spiked my suspicion meter. I seriously liked this guy, so why did I resist trusting him?

"All set," he said, as he wiped his hands on his scrub pants. "Ready to go?"

I frowned. "Are you inviting yourself to come with me?"

"Don't mind if I do." He smiled and I had to admit his charm was disarming. There was real heart in that smile. His eyes had a genuine twinkle, but they also hinted at what remained unspoken. I sensed his discomfort, which made me uncomfortable, too. About him.

I couldn't think of a better way to find out more about him than to take him along, but only on one condition. "Before you hop in, I need you to answer a question for me."

His smile faded to a barely discernible grin. "Sure. What do you want to know?"

"What kind of Kinetic are you?"

His grin broadened to the snarly one I liked so much. "I'm the weatherman."

Ian *controlled* weather. I *chased* weather. The combination was uncanny. I thought about the good he could do for farmers and their dying crops. Hardly anyone grew fruits and vegetables anymore, unless it was in a controlled terrarium or greenhouse. The yields were rare and precious, and only available to the wealthy.

Now that we were both buckled into our seats and on our way out of town, I decided to ask more about what he could do. "If you can make it rain, you have the power to change the world."

He squinted as if that would help him see me better. "Not really. To make rain I need a water source to draw from, so I'm more like a human sprinkler system."

"Oh." I'm sure he must have heard the disappointment in my voice. "What about wind? Lightning and thunder?"

"Wind, yes. The lightning and thunder falls outside my jurisdiction. That would be electro kinesis."

"Sun storms?" I asked, feeling hopeful.

He took a long pause before finally saying, "I doubt it. My powers aren't that strong."

Of all the weather to control, sun storms were the only storms that made a difference. Stopping them could potentially save the planet. "You're kidding, right? You should give it a try. The only weather we have anymore are sun—"

"Does the air conditioner work?" Ian tapped the vents where cool air should be pouring out. A hot breeze blew from them instead.

I frowned at his sudden change of subject. If he didn't want to talk about his ability, I could respect that. Maybe he'd open up once he got to know me better. I let the subject go for now.

I shifted gears as the highway opened up, but I kept my speed low. Road hazards were plentiful, and you never knew what, or who, you might run into. "Air conditioner?" I asked, lacing my tone with exaggerated wonder. "What's that?"

He gave me a horrified look, and I laughed.

"I'm kidding. No, the air conditioner does *not* work."

"I could fix it for you," he said. "I can't *make* coolant, but I know where to find it."

I looked at him sideways. "Okay, you're on."

He paused before asking, "Mind if I grab a bottle of water from the back?"

"Help yourself."

Ian reached between the seats to take a bottle of water from a box on the floor. Water was rationed, but I knew my quota and had no problem sharing. After screwing off the tops of two bottles, he handed me one and kept the other for himself. My eyes followed him as he took a long, deep swallow. I couldn't help watching his lips move as they sucked in the water. The corners of his mouth glistened with moisture as he set the bottle down between his legs. He smacked his lips and released a loud *ah* of satisfaction.

I blinked and shifted my focus back to the road. Another distraction like that and I'd roll the Trooper.

I checked the sky, and the sun looked its usual ugly orange self, no brighter and no dimmer than normal. The storm was at least forty-five minutes away, and we'd be in the city within a half hour.

The on-ramp to the Interstate looked like ruins after a bombing and that probably wasn't far from the truth. It's what a lot of angry, bitter people were prone to do these days. So many had lost everything and everyone they'd ever loved. Desperation and depression combined with unstable energy created by the storms tended to mess with neurons in the brain. The people affected most became more animal than human, acting purely on the heat of their emotions. We had a name for them: *Berserkers*.

If he didn't want to talk about kinetic abilities, I had other questions I could ask. "So tell me, Ian, what brought you to Lodgepole?"

He shrugged. "I've traveled all over the country. Lodgepole seems like a pleasant little town that's not too badly rav-aged by the storms."

I was about to ask him how the conditions were in the other places he'd seen, when a loud pop like a gunshot rang out, and I lost control of the SUV.

3

Gripping the steering wheel with everything I had, I couldn't hold it steady, and the vehicle seemed to have a mind of its own. It swerved off the highway and sideswiped what was left of a chain-link fence. We rumbled over the ground as if it were made of boulders rather than cracked asphalt, and my head bumped against the ceiling a half dozen times before the Trooper came to a complete stop.

Dazed, Ian and I both sat staring out the filthy tinted window. I saw the city skyline ahead of us, too far to walk to and arrive in time to warn its residents of what was coming. If anyone got caught out in the open, they were doomed. And it would be my fault.

I slammed my fist against the steering wheel. "Damn it!"

"You blew a tire," Ian said. "I'll change it for you."

"I used my only spare last week." Tears stung my eyes, and I slapped the steering wheel two more times just to feel my palms hurt. It helped mute the pain inside my heart. People were going to die, and I'd miss my fix. No one had to tell me which was worse, but my body and mind leveled both as equally tragic. I felt guilty as hell about it, too.

"I'll take care of it." Ian opened the car door and climbed out to stand within the blaze of daylight.

I joined him, happy to fry in the heat. I could call it poetic justice for any lives lost today because of me. "You can't replace it in time, Ian. And, besides, where would you find a tire?"

He pointed down the hill to a truck turned over on its side. "One of those should do fine. And you're right, we won't make it to the city in time. You can't stop the storm, so don't beat yourself up about it. Let it go." He trudged down the hill toward the abandoned truck.

Let it go? He made it sound so simple. "You don't understand," I yelled down to him. "Chasing storms is what I *have* to do. There's no choice involved. The storm's victims aren't the only ones who suffer if I don't reach them in time." If I didn't chase the storms I predicted, I'd be left empty inside. It was like jonesing for heroin, and the withdrawals left me weak and shaking until the next storm.

Ian had found a crowbar and jack in the bed of the truck and was already removing the lug nuts. "You can't save the world, Sarah. You can't be everywhere at once."

I gritted my teeth against the emotion that clogged my throat. Of course I couldn't save the world, but I was compelled to try.

Ian rolled the tire up the hill, avoiding my eyes the whole time. He made an effort not to look at me, his brows furled over squinted eyes that hid from the sun. I wanted him to see me, to acknowledge the need in my eyes so that he would understand, but he wasn't ready for that. He didn't know me, at least not yet. I hoped to change that.

I gazed at the sky over Denver. It was as bright as a high-wattage light bulb, and it shone down on a glittering wave of sun sparks that hovered over the city. So beautiful. Like Christmas. And deadly as hell. The sparks fluttered toward the ground like millions of flaming fireflies, and all I could do was watch.

A hand curled over my shoulder, and I jerked at the sudden contact.

"You have a gift, but you can only do so much," Ian said softly as he draped his arm around my shoulders. His fingers felt so warm on my skin, and his voice, with that subtle edge of gravel, sounded smooth as velvet in my ears. "Don't blame yourself for what you can't control."

He was right, but needing the storms was wrong and that's where my guilt came from. Yet I knew another storm would come along, and another after that. I leaned into Ian, and he held me close, comforting me. His firm touch infused me with a sudden burst of strength. It was unexpected and made me a little light-headed. The longer our bodies stayed in contact, the more intense the energy became. It reminded me of what I got from the sun, only to a lesser degree.

"Do you feel that?" I asked him.

He let go and shot me a puzzled look. "Yeah. What was it?"

I shook my head. "I don't know." But I felt better. Whatever had happened between us had diluted my sense of loss at having missed the storm. I wasn't feeling sick, either.

I gazed at the skyline again, which was now clear of sun sparks. The danger had passed, but a few casualties might have been left behind.

"The tire's changed. Ready to go back?" Ian asked.

"No." I slid onto the driver's seat, my back stinging from exposing my skin to the sun for too long. "We need to go into the city."

Ian plopped onto the seat beside me. His eyes filled with concern, he said, "You'll only torture yourself, Sarah. You can't undo what's been done, and you can't heal whoever got infected."

He thought I should *let it go*. But that was impossible. "Exposure knocks people out, and if they can't get out of the heat, the sun will cook them alive."

"Maybe that would be a more merciful death than slowly wasting away from fever," Ian said, the shadows beneath his eyes making him look more tortured than tired. He obviously knew something about what the fever was like. Had he lost friends or family to the disease? I made myself a mental note to ask him later.

I turned the key in the ignition, and the Trooper hummed to life. I prayed the frame hadn't been bent by the accident. Rolling the vehicle forward, the ride felt smooth and even. Ian had done a good job with that tire. "We're going in," I told him. "It's not up for debate."

He remained quiet but tense for the rest of the drive. His gaze darted side to side as we drove through desolate streets flanked by charred trees and a variety of refuse, from gutted cars to dented Dumpsters. He jerked in his seat a few times, his lip curled and eyes feral. He was on the alert for something, and based on his angry scowl, it wasn't storm victims. I inched along, peering up and down each street as we got closer to the State Capitol. What had once been an emerald carpet of perfectly manicured lawn in Civic Center Park was now a vast field of abandoned cars and hollowed-out fire pits dotted with mounds of trash and partially burned furniture. I spotted a few tents, too. If they hadn't been zipped tight to keep out the sparks, the occupants were goners.

I slowed the Trooper and pulled to the curb.

"Why are we stopping?" Ian asked.

"Those tents over there." I pointed at the park. "There could be people inside."

"If they're inside, they're protected from the sun."

"But if they were infected, they'll need medical attention. There's an infirmary inside the Capitol Building."

Ian looked agitated, but he apparently wanted to help. "What would you like me to do?"

Rather than tell him, I got out of the SUV and led the way to the cluster of tents. All but one was vacant. I peered inside and found a young couple that looked to be in their early twenties. The woman cradled the man's head in her lap, her eyes round as she stared up at me while gently combing her fingers through her companion's hair.

My heart dipped when I saw the purple rash that covered the man's face. The sparks had infected him.

"Please," the woman said, her voice shaking. "Tell me there's a cure now. You can make him better, right?"

I held my composure as I knelt on the floor of the tent. *My fault, my fault.* "No, hon, I'm afraid not."

Ian hadn't come inside but stood looking through the open tent flap. "I'll go back to the SUV and get them some water. I'll need the key to get inside." I tossed it to him, and he vanished from sight, his fading footsteps crunching over dry brittle grass.

Tears welled in the woman's eyes, and her lower lip trembled. "It happened so fast. We'd been at home in bed, in a basement apartment two blocks from here, but I woke up and couldn't get comfortable enough to go back to sleep. I thought a short walk might help." Her hands absently rubbed her bulging belly, her unborn child a pillow for her husband's head. "We'd just rounded the corner when my husband spotted the sparks. He got us to this tent before they fell. He pushed me in ahead of him, but he didn't make it—" She choked out a sob. "The sparks touched him."

I held my breath to keep from screaming. I had to help this woman and her husband. They were my responsibility now. "My friend is getting you water, and then we'll help you both to the infirmary across the street. I hear there are good people there."

She nodded. "I heard that, too. Maybe my husband will get better on his own. It can't be that bad, can it? Only a couple of sparks touched him."

I smiled. "Maybe." Though I knew the number of sparks didn't matter when it came to exposure, but I couldn't tell her that. Not now when her grief was still so fresh. It could be a blessing that the fewer the sparks, the less aggressive the fever. He could last as long as a month and might even see the birth of his child. "We can hope, right?"

"Yes," she said, her smile shaky as she wiped a tear from her cheek and kissed the top of her husband's head. "And believe in a better future. For my baby."

Believe. The word echoed between my ears, and the voice saying it sounded like my mother's.

Ian should have been back by now. "I'll just go outside to check on my friend," I told the woman, and left the tent. I glanced at the street where I'd parked the Trooper. Both Ian and the SUV were gone.

4

"Ian?" I called as I trotted to the curb where I'd parked the SUV. But it wasn't there, and neither was Ian. Had he really stolen my car? I glanced up and down the deserted street, then ran to the next block and checked there, too. Not a trace.

"That son of a bitch," I muttered between gritted teeth. I knew he was hiding something, but I never would have taken him for a thief. He'd seemed genuine, sincere. When would I learn to stop being so trusting of others and simply trust my own instincts? Opportunists were everywhere.

I paced the sidewalk in front of the park. How would I get home? And how the hell would I chase storms now? My heart pounded with panic. As my mind raced with strategies to get me on the road, I started back toward the tent with the storm victim inside. The least I could do was help that couple get to the infirmary. I'd work out my own issues later.

Halfway across the park, I heard someone yell, "Interloper!"

I turned around, looking left to right, and saw no one. Then I glanced up into a charred cottonwood tree. I spotted a man wearing a black mask and black cape. His flabby bare chest was hairless and sunburned. Wearing faded swim trunks and a pair of trashy work boots two sizes too big, he looked like the ghetto version of a superhero. Since he was obviously a nut job, I ignored him. I wasn't in the mood to be messed with.

I kept on walking, and again he shouted at me, "Interloper! Trespasser! You don't belong here."

I stopped and narrowed my eyes at him. "Who put you in charge?"

"I did."

"Yeah?" I shook my head and tossed another hopeful glance at the street. Still no Trooper and no Ian. "Have fun with that."

"Get out."

"Excuse me?"

"I said, get out of my city!" He flung his arm toward me, and it felt as if I'd been kicked in the stomach. My body flew up and backward, landing just short of a very nasty metal couch frame. He was a Kinetic. Crap.

"I'm The Law and you're a puny human." He spit on the ground. "Get out of my city."

This could be a problem. Not only did I have no means of leaving, I took issue with getting pushed around by some deluded freak with a God complex. If this were to be a battle of kinetic powers, I'd lose before putting on the gloves. I had nothing to fight with.

"Okay," I said, hoping to placate him. "I'm leaving." I waved him off and resumed walking toward the tent.

Suddenly unable to breath, I gasped for air as invisible fingers crushed my windpipe. Standing on the branch of his mighty cottonwood, the man glared down at me while leaning against the trunk and holding out both hands clenched into fists. He was going to kill me for trespassing. Instead of hitting me, he choked me, hands-free.

Panic overcame me as I dropped to my knees, my eyes swelling in their sockets and my hands desperately grappling at what wasn't there. My fingernails dug into my neck in a desperate attempt to free myself from the stranglehold. Skin slick with my own blood, my hands slid over my throat as they searched for the tightening band that cut off my air. The light around me dimmed. I was about to pass out.

The squeal of braking tires sounded in the distance and was followed by the patter of running feet. Strong arms grabbed me around the waist and lowered me gently to the ground. Whoever it was yelled something I couldn't make out, but I managed to catch a few words: die, kill, crazy bastard. A sudden wind whistled in my ears and tousled my short hair. I blinked, my vision clearing as the choking sensation faded, and I could finally breathe again.

I gulped in air and saw Ian standing over me, his hands whipping in circles above his head. He'd created a cyclone, and it had lifted my assailant from his tree branch, holding him about twenty feet aloft. His superhero mask had slipped off, and his huge, frightened eyes begged for freedom, but Ian wouldn't give it to him. I could tell by the expression on Ian's face that he was dangerously pissed off.

"Ian," I rasped, though I wasn't sure he heard me. "The guy is sick in the head. He can't help himself. Don't kill him."

Ian's gaze swiveled to mine, and I saw his fury and his pain. I wondered if his anger was meant for someone else. I added that question to my "Ask Ian" list, if I ever talked to him again.

The cyclone spun the unmasked fraud toward the Platte River. I had a feeling it might be a while before he came back.

Ian dropped to the ground beside me, his face pale and sweating. The power he had used to create the twister had apparently sucked a good amount of energy from him. He lay back on the hard ground and closed his eyes.

I should have left him right where he was. But at the moment, I was as exhausted as he was. My throat felt bruised, and I touched my neck, my fingers coming away bloody. I'd clawed myself good.

"You're bleeding," Ian said, still catching his breath.

I glared at him. "You noticed, huh? Did you also notice that I'd have no way to get back home without the SUV you stole from me?"

He looked away to stare at a heap of trash behind the tents. "I didn't steal your car." His tone wasn't convincing.

Though I'd stood at death's door only minutes ago, I forced myself to my feet. "Enjoy what's left of your life, Ian."

"I came back," he yelled at my retreating back. "Doesn't that count for anything?"

I stopped and turned to face him. "Why come back? And why run off in the first place?"

"It's complicated."

I folded my arms across my chest. There was no excuse for what he'd done. Or almost done. I waited for an explanation.

"To be honest—"

"Oh, let's, shall we?" I glowered at him.

He stood and brushed pieces of dead grass from his pants. "I spotted an auto parts store down the street and thought I'd make a quick run to get a can of coolant for your air conditioner. As I was driving back, I had an overwhelming urge to get away."

"Get away?" That was crazy. He wasn't anyone's prisoner, least of all mine. "Ian, you're a free man. You can go anywhere you want."

His dark eyes were full of misery. "I'm free now, but I haven't always been. Someone's after me, Sarah. He wants to use me and any other Kinetic he can get his hands on. If you're not careful, he'll take you, too."

Ian helped me get the couple out of the tent and into a building a block away that had an infirmary. I treated the scratches on my neck while we were there. Ian remained silent the entire time, and I was bursting with questions that I couldn't ask until we were alone. I probably shouldn't have agreed to take him back with me, but I wasn't cruel enough to leave him stranded. Now that I knew what he was capable of, I'd be watching him carefully. Duplicity aside, his ability could help people.

"How could you not tell me any of this?" I asked Ian on our drive back to Lodgepole. "Being stalked by a kidnapper is not a healthy secret to keep, not for you and definitely not for me."

He sat slouched in the passenger seat, eyes averted from mine.

"I want answers, Ian. Right. Now."

He rubbed his forehead as if it hurt. "I know how it looks, but it's not what you think. I'm not a criminal."

"Convince me."

"I will," he said, sliding his gaze to give me a hopeful look, then glancing away again. He licked his lips and swallowed. "First, I need to make a confession."

I swung my head around to look at him, nearly giving myself whiplash. "What?"

"I knew about your SUV before I knew about you."

A liar and a thief. I really knew how to pick 'em. "So you'd planned to steal my car all along."

He sighed. "Before I met you, I saw it in the ambulance bay and tried breaking in to steal it. I was desperate for a way to put distance between me and the guy who's after me."

Desperate. I really hated that word. "Yet when you got the chance to steal my car, you didn't. Why not?"

He swiveled in the seat with his back to the window, his attention only on me. "Several reasons. One, I'm not a thief. Two, I couldn't leave you stranded. Three, we're both Kinetics, which means the guy after me will come after you, too, and I don't want you getting hurt. And four…"

I waited. "What's the fourth reason?"

"I like you too much to leave you."

• 5 •

The blush sizzled up my neck to my cheeks. My spine tingled at knowing how Ian felt because the feeling was mutual. I think I liked him more than was good for me. I wanted to trust him, I really did, but reasons not to were stacking up. Rather than respond to his admission of affection, I redirected back to why he felt the need to steal my SUV in the first place. "Who is this mysterious Kinetic kidnapper anyway?"

Ian faced forward again and tilted his head back, eyes closed. After a short pause, he said, "After my…" He waved his hands up and down the front of his body. "I discovered I could do things with the weather. So I started to experiment. I made the mistake of making it rain on an old woman's backyard garden. That action attracted the attention of a Secret Service agent who was rounding up Kinetics for the government."

The existence of Kinetics was no secret, though it stirred up hard feelings for anyone who'd lost a loved one to Sun Fever. Many Kinetics kept their abilities private to deter resentment. If the government sought us out, they'd have to do some digging to uncover all the ones staying under the radar. "Why would the U.S. government have any interest in us?"

"According to Agent *Sam Nichol*," he said, putting emphasis on the man's name as if it left a bad taste in his mouth, "there's a plan to use us to heal the planet."

This news was encouraging, but Ian's grimace expressed the opposite.

"How is that a bad thing?" I asked.

"I'm not sure that it is, but I'm positive Nichol is. Bad, I mean."

"What did he do?"

"He started out okay," Ian said. "A genuinely nice guy doing his duty for his country. When he first told me about the plan to collect all the Kinetics and house them at the military base inside Cheyenne Mountain in Colorado Springs, I was on board. I believed him. Then he lost his wife and kids to the fever. He was grief-stricken at first, then bitter, then crazy, and then he got mean."

I could see how that would happen, especially to someone whose job must have been stressful. The electromagnetic interference from the solar storms affected *everyone* in some way. Personality and mood changes were only the half of it. Add to that the vitamin and mineral deficiencies in a poor diet of rations and you got a stew of dysfunctional people.

"Had you and Nichol become friends?" I asked.

"No." He pressed his lips together before grinding out, "Enemies."

"What did he do to make you hate him so much?"

"He drugged me, beat me and kept me chained up in a trailer while he went from town to town, selling my services to the highest bidder." Ian flipped up the hank of hair that usually covered the scar on his right eyebrow. "He gave me this. Threw a whisky bottle at me when I couldn't make enough rain. I'd drained the reservoir, but it wasn't enough, so he busted my head open." He dropped the hair and hunched forward, his body stiff with rage.

My chest tightened as I considered what it must have been like for him: treated as a slave and forced to perform weather tricks like a trained monkey. Ian had amazing control over his ability, and those who used him had probably made it a habit of demanding the impossible. For Ian to be so traumatized by his experience, I had to wonder what else he'd had to endure when he failed to deliver to Nichol's satisfaction.

"How did you get away?" I asked.

"The same way I got caught. I used weather." He lifted one hand and waved it in a small circle.

"Ah. You made a cyclone."

He nodded and dropped his hand. "It wasn't a big one, but strong enough to create the distraction I needed. I've been running ever since."

That's why he was always looking over his shoulder. "You haven't seen this Nichol guy since?"

Ian shook his head. "I doubt he's far away. He won't stop looking for me because I made good money for him. He has a pimped-out SUV like yours, only faster and with more modifications. I figured I'd have a better chance eluding him if I had one, too." He dipped his chin and stared down at his lap.

My mind kept scrolling back to what he'd said about the government. "What do you know about this plan to heal the planet?"

"Not much. Only that Nichol said that the conjoined powers of Kinetics would be strong enough to stop the storms. He also said he didn't believe it."

The theory made sense. Ian and I had felt the surge of power between us when he'd held me. He'd passed some of his kinetic energy to me, which is why I hadn't gone through withdrawals right after I'd failed to chase the sun storm in Denver. Or at least I hadn't suffered them yet. A faint pounding in my ears and a twitching sensation in my legs told me I wasn't off the hook. The withdrawals were just delayed, and I hoped they wouldn't be severe.

Ian shot me a concerned look. "Your hands are shaking."

I glanced at my fingers gripping the steering wheel, knuckles white as bone. Hard as I tried, I couldn't hide their trembling. "So they are."

"You okay?"

"I will be as soon as I can chase another storm." I wiped my sweaty palms on my T-shirt.

"I understand."

I doubted he really did. He didn't know what it was like to be a monster that fed off the source of other people's suffering. The pain of withdrawal was my just desert, and I was okay with that.

My vision blurred and I almost ran off the road.

"You better let me drive," Ian said.

"Not a chance," I told him, blinking hard to stay focused. We had only a few blocks left before reaching the hospital. I barely managed to get us there without wrecking the Trooper.

I parked the car inside the ambulance bay, and we sat in silence for a minute while I gathered enough wits to open the door and climb out. Ian did, as well. His slouched posture revealed his guilt for what he'd done, but at least now I understood why. He wasn't a malevolent man, just a reckless one.

"Want to get that drink?" he asked me, a hopeful glint in his eyes.

"Look, Ian, I can forgive what you did, but it might be best if we—"

"Kept our distance," he finished with a nod. "I get it."

I was going to say waited a few days, but perhaps distance was the better plan. After today, I doubted he'd stay in town much longer anyway. Best to cut the connection now because it would be much harder to do if I started liking him more than I already did.

"Thank you for saving me today," I told him, but he was already on the other side of the garage. The heavy thud of a closed door echoed against the concrete walls and inside the hollow chambers of my heart.

I felt no better after waking from my short nap, just hungry. I craved something salty. Tonight was a good night to treat myself to some real meat, even if it was tough as an old tire.

After taking a quick bath, I headed out into the cooler, eighty-degree night to get a meager meal of jerky and dried fruit. Eating should boost my energy by at least a watt or two.

I stood at the intersection in the middle of town, facing Martha June's General Store. I saw the abandoned Quick Stop gas station on the corner next to the hardware store, and the empty Java Jungle drive-through in the parking lot. It was twilight, and people were just leaving their homes to start their day. Children went to school at night, during the same hours their parents went to work. The town came alive when the sun went down.

Evening wasn't as dark as it used to be before the solar storms. Though the sun wasn't visible, it left its imprint with charged particles that collided with atoms to create a natural light display. There'd been a time when such displays could only be seen in the far north, but now they were everywhere. They used to be called Northern Lights. Today we called them Night Rainbows.

Hardly anyone drove a car anymore since gasoline was rare to nonexistent, and decent solar batteries were hard to find, but almost everyone owned a bicycle or rickshaw. Even with the population sparse as it was, the streets teemed with cyclists tonight.

A mild wind blew through town that started out as blustery gusts. The pleased looks on people's faces expressed their relief at the change in weather, and I had to agree with them. The air was inert most days, so having it brush through my hair like ghostly fingers felt wonderful.

Scraps of paper and dead leaves blew across the street and collected in dry gutters. Women had to hold down their skirts and dresses to keep them from flying up over their heads. What started out as laughter quickly turned to shouts of alarm as tree branches, cardboard boxes and garbage cans rolled over the ground at incredible speed. Someone was struck by flying debris and fell in a rolling heap to the ground.

Taking cover in the wide doorway of a building, I watched helplessly as people were snatched by the maelstrom and tumbled through the streets, their cries swallowed by the wind. The air was hazy with dirt and debris, but I clearly saw a rusted metal lounge chair hurtle toward the general store and smash through its plate-glass window. A man went running toward the building with a child in his arms and a woman slung over his shoulder. He disappeared inside, then came out empty-handed. He vanished into a cloud of swirling dust and trash, but returned with two more children that he deposited inside the store.

When the man came out again, he doubled over, coughing and wiping a sleeve across his forehead. He lifted his face, and the dust cleared enough for me to see who it was. I was struck by his scowl of determination, how tight he clenched his jaw, and the white scar that bisected his right eyebrow. Ian Matthews straightened and squared his shoulders, his chest puffed out as if he'd just taken a fortifying breath. Then his posture changed. He jerked his chin up and stood squarely to face me.

My gaze locked with Ian's, and though we were at least fifty yards apart, I could feel the pull of his power. He appeared calm, yet fierce, and my heart thrummed against my ribs as his strength attracted me like a magnet.

I had to go to him. I mean, I really had to, as in I was *compelled* to join him. To join *with* him. Letting go of the door frame, I crouched low to the ground to create drag and slowly made my way across the street. Ian's eyes grew wide with surprise, and he shook his head, waving for me to go back. He had no idea the command he had over me just then. I could *not* refuse his silent and subconscious call.

A shadow of worry darkened his face, and his eyes began losing their glow. He started walking toward me.

I shook my head. "Keep at it!" I shouted. "Stop the wind!"

I doubted he could hear me through the roar of whirling air that tossed around pebbles like popping corn. But he understood because he halted his advance, and his eyes began to glow again. I ran the last ten feet and flung my arms around him to stop myself from blowing away.

The second our bodies touched, there was that same power surge as before. My head against his chest, I heard his heart beat strong and steady. My own heart beat in rhythm with his, like a melody in perfect tempo.

We were encased inside an invisible bubble that repelled the wind. The bubble grew, shoving the maelstrom farther and farther away until not a single twig blew in the street. The storm was over.

Ian and I continued to cling to one another, both of us thinking the wind might come rushing back. But after a few minutes, the calm continued. We were safe. And so was the town.

I blinked at the sudden realization that my withdrawal symptoms had vanished, as well. He had channeled kinetic energy through us both, and that was enough for the fix I needed. At least until the next storm.

"That was incredible," Ian murmured.

"I know." I slowly released him and stepped back. "The power…" I was conflicted about our connection. As good as it felt, surrendering myself to his control didn't sit well with me. I wasn't ready. Being that vulnerable with another person, especially someone I hardly knew, someone who had deceived me, wasn't easy to accept. I wasn't sure I ever could.

"You look amazing, Sarah," he told me. "You're glowing."

"Oh, no." I sucked in a breath. My fingers traced over my face. "Literally?"

He smiled. "No. As in healthy."

I closed my eyes in relief. "Look, Ian. What just happened was amazing, but I haven't changed my mind about how I feel. We need distance from each other."

A frown replaced his smile. He studied me for a minute, his piercing gaze trying to read what was in my mind. "So you're telling me I should move on."

I knew this would happen sooner or later. I didn't want him to leave, but that might be best for both of us, at least for the time being. "It doesn't have to be forever. When the world returns to normal—"

"For better or worse, you and I both know the world will

never be like it was," he said, his dark eyes intense. "And neither will we. What we've become is never going to change. Tell me what scares you, Sarah."

He scared me. I was afraid of what he'd done to me just now, whether he'd meant to or not. "I give myself over to my ability with every premonition I have," I told him, biting off each word. It was important that he understand. "Losing control to you, too, is more than I can handle."

Bewildered, he said, "You still don't trust me."

Not after he'd lied and tried to steal from me. "I'm sorry, but I can't. Not yet."

His expression abruptly changed. It was as if he'd erected a wall between us, his eyes hard and his lips pressed tight together. He narrowed his gaze and cocked his head slightly to the side. "It's just as well. Once news about how we stopped the windstorm reaches Nichol, he'll come here looking for me, and when he does, I don't want him near you. I'll keep my distance, but I'm not leaving town. I'm staying to protect you."

My pulse jumped. Part of me was glad that he'd be staying. The other part knew how hard it would be not to get close to him again.

After three days of avoiding each other, Ian and I both performed the job of a hospital orderly. We helped feed patients, bathed and dressed them, read to them and assisted them in any nonmedical way we could, all without coming in direct contact with one another.

The hospital was small and had only a couple of wings. On the rare occasion that our paths crossed, Ian appeared closed off, guarded, always looking over his shoulder. It drove me mad to know he lived in the hospital basement, and I was a mere two floors above him. I longed for a better compromise than distance, but separation had been my idea. That made it my problem. Not his.

I sat in an armchair positioned by the window, the blinds only partially drawn since blessed twilight had taken the burning sunshine away. I was reading to a patient in hospice care. Night Rainbows undulated like waves of fairy dust in the distance, their beauty a contradiction to the destructive force that made them.

Sally Gardner lay in a coma on her hospital bed. No medicine existed that could bring down her fever, and it hurt to see her like this. She reminded me of my mother. I hoped the sound of my voice gave her comfort. I wanted her to know she wouldn't die alone.

Ian walked in and stopped when he saw me. "Sorry, I just came in to change her bedding. I'll leave you alone." He turned around to leave.

I closed the book in my lap. "Don't go. I'm sure Sally would appreciate the company." And so would I. Realizing I was violating my own rule, I expected him to walk out the door and not come back.

His gaze shifted away from the dying woman on the bed to study the floor. "I remember you saying that your mother died of the fever."

I nodded, pleased that he hadn't walked out. Maybe it was time to lift the moratorium on our fragile friendship. "But my mom died at home with my father and me at her bedside. This poor woman doesn't have anyone."

Head still lowered, he gazed up at me, his eyes tender with meaning. "So you know what it's like to lose someone you love."

"Do you?"

He approached the bed and ran the backs of his fingers gently down Sally's arm. "I lost them both the same day."

My hunch about something troubling him was right. I imagined it was hard for him to talk about, but maybe all he needed was to get it off his chest. He must have a lot of pain buried inside. "Your parents?"

"My wife and daughter."

Hearing that was like a punch to the gut. His grief explained a lot about his behavior. I'm not sure why, but I never would have guessed he'd been married and had a child. To hide my surprise, I flipped through the pages of the book in my lap. "I'm sorry for your loss."

"Lacie was only four years old. She and her mother had suffered terribly, and the mercy of death released all three of us from the pain of hanging on. They died at the exact same moment. I held them both in my arms when they drew their last breath. It was a miracle."

Hearing the love in his voice made my heart swell with affection for him. "I didn't understand why I'd survived the fever and my family hadn't. I felt guilty. That's why I left Boston, to search for answers."

Survivor guilt. It was a common affliction among the living, and I understood what he'd gone through. "Did you find them?"

He shook his head. "What started out as a quest for truth turned into a desperate fight for freedom after Nichol took me. Since my escape, I've focused so much on not getting caught again that I almost forgot what had sent me on the road in the first place." His haunted eyes swiveled to look at me. "Until I came here."

My pulse quickened. Why couldn't he have just been an ordinary man? I think even without his kinetic powers he'd be special. I was glad he'd come to Lodgepole and was about to say so when a flash of light brightened the window. Then came a boom loud enough to rattle the blinds.

"What the hell?" Ian ran to the window, and I left the chair to stand beside him. Two blocks away, the community center flickered with flames as smoke belched from its broken windows.

• 7 •

I watched as people ran from the flaming building and a siren blared. The only fire truck the town had pulled up in front of the burning structure and three figures climbed out. I wondered how long it would take for the water to get turned on, or even if it would. The hydrants had been disconnected months ago. All anyone could do was evacuate the building, and I just hoped no one was left inside.

By the time Ian and I made it to the first floor, the lobby bustled with chaos.

"Anyone know what caused this?" Ian yelled into the crowd.

"No," a man answered. "We were playing pool when the roof exploded."

"Lightning strike," someone else called out.

A man pushed his way to the front, his black skin even blacker with smears of soot. He gasped in air and coughed, his eyes streaming tears that I hoped was only from the smoke. "The fire's spreading to other buildings."

"Is anyone inside?" Ian asked.

"We all got out of the center in time," the man said. "But there could be people inside the buildings next door. The fire's spreading fast."

My heart jerked as I caught my breath. We needed water to put out the fire. The water tank was only half a mile away, but bringing the mountain to Mohammed wasn't going to happen. Unless…

I ran to Ian and clutched his arm. "You can help."

He looked down at me as if I'd just grown a third eye. "What?"

I yanked him toward me so that I could whisper, "Rain."

He gently pulled away. Regret glimmered in his eyes as he shook his head.

"Why not?" A sense of panic and frustration overwhelmed me. I was helpless to do anything. The town could burn to the ground, and Ian had the power to prevent it.

"You know why," Ian said without looking at me.

Of course I knew why he wouldn't *want* to make it rain, but not why he'd flat-out refuse to save an entire town. He'd always proven himself helpful before, so I didn't understand why the sudden change. I glared daggers at him and growled, "You're a selfish bastard." I ran out into the hot night made even hotter by the fire.

I think everyone in town came out that evening. Cycle rickshaws peddled toward the fire, their carriages loaded with buckets. Some even had cases of bottled water the owners were willing to sacrifice just to put out the flames. Lodgepole, and the people who lived here, was all we had left of our old lives. We'd do whatever it took to save it.

I'd barely sprinted one block when the distinct buzz of a motorcycle approached from behind. I turned my head to see Ian whiz by at top speed. Was he hightailing it out of town already? Tears of disappointment stung my eyes. I'd always considered myself a good judge of character, but maybe I didn't have a clue. Ian being a Kinetic had clouded my judgment. He cut sharply around the corner where the community center flickered with flames, then vanished from sight.

The heat grew so intense that I stopped running about fifty

feet from the curb. I couldn't stop the fire, but I had basic first aid skills I'd put to good use if anyone got hurt.

I glared at the colorful Night Rainbows that rippled on the horizon, my fury aimed at the brilliant star responsible for making our lives a living hell. It had killed my mother and warped my poor father's mind. It had forced us from our homes, our jobs, and in some cases, even our families. The sun was a bully, and I hated my addiction to its power.

I clenched my fists, my nails cutting into my palms, when I felt a wet drop land on my curled fingers. It was followed by another one, then another. I gazed up at the fluffy gray cloud hovering above the community center. It opened, and rain poured down, splattering the asphalt and sizzling into steam as it came in contact with the fire.

Ian had made it rain, and I was thankful for it.

The street swarmed with people, their upturned faces catching drops of rain as a low cluster of dark clouds continued to dowse us with water. Everyone acted as if they'd never seen rain before. It had been at least a year since little more than a shower had drizzled over our town.

The air was cleansed of acrid smoke, and the community center fire waned, the flames sputtering beneath a sheet of gentle rain.

I heard the whine of Ian's bike coming toward me. He slowed to a stop about twenty feet away and cut the engine. Amazed by what he'd done, gratitude overwhelmed me and I ran to him, throwing my arms around his neck to give him a fierce hug. It didn't matter that his power could overtake me again. I just wanted him to know how thankful I was.

"Thank you," I said, my words muffled against his warm neck.

His hands gently grasped my wrists as he pushed me back. "You called me a selfish bastard."

I heaved a sigh of shame. "I'm sorry, but I was upset—"

"You know what this means?"

"Of course I do. It means you helped save this town from burning to the ground."

"Possibly at the cost of our freedom. I was thinking about you, Sarah. I don't want you getting hurt the way I was."

I shook my head. "You don't know that will happen. No one here knows you did this." I gazed up at the sky and let drops of moisture refresh me before facing him again.

He scowled, his jaw tight and his muscular shoulders tense as they bunched beneath his scrubs. "Don't be so sure." He stomped down on the throttle, and the bike's engine roared to life.

"Wait!" My wet hair stuck to my face and sides of my neck, the cool rain bathing the sweat from my skin. I blinked up at the cloud that began to dissipate and heard a moan of disappointment erupt from the crowd still loitering in the street. "Where are you going?"

"I said I'd stay to protect you in case Nichol shows up, but if I leave now I can lead him away."

"Ian, don't go." I grabbed his hand, and when our fingers touched, a surge of energy leaped between us. Could I resist him? I didn't even try. The cloud above re-gathered itself, and it began raining again.

He looked amazed. "I…I didn't do that."

I was just as surprised. "Where's the water coming from? The town water tank?"

He shook his head. "There's a honeycomb of aquifers running deep underground. I tapped into one to make it rain." He pulled away from me, and the rain became a light drizzle.

We'd proven to ourselves that Kinetics were stronger together than they were apart. A project for using the combined powers of Kinetics could be a powerful weapon. I wanted to find out more and wondered who we could contact. It obviously wouldn't be Agent Nichol.

"Look what we can do together, Ian," I said, and hastily snatched hold of his hand again. The rain picked up, and he shook his fingers loose from mine. "We need to explore the extent of our power."

"And put you in danger of getting nabbed along with me? That's not going to happen." He twisted the throttle, and the bike jerked forward. He sped away down the street.

Would he really leave town? I pressed my lips firmly together and squinted in the direction where he'd disappeared. No. He couldn't. I wouldn't let him. I had an idea that would turn the tables on Ian's kidnapper, but it would have to wait until the next sun storm.

• 8 •

By the time I arrived back at the hospital, the sun had risen like a glowing orange slice on the horizon.

"Dad?" I found him in his hospital room sitting cross-legged on the floor with my mother's nightgown in his lap. He held it up to his face, his scarred fingers clutching the fabric as he nuzzled the folds while taking long, deep breaths.

I bent to gently pull the nightie from him. "Come on, Dad. You need to take your medicine and your water ration before going to bed."

He gripped the garment more tightly, the skin beneath his dirty fingernails turning paper white. "In a minute, Sarah. I have to help your mother put on her nightgown. You know how hard it is for her to lift her arms."

Sighing, I nodded and let go. Ever since my mother had died, it comforted him to carry the gown around like a child's security blanket. If it helped relax him long enough to sleep through the day, all the better.

I reached down to clasp my hands around his thin upper arms and helped him to his feet. My father had once been a robust man, thickly muscled and youthfully handsome. He was only forty-six years old, but he looked more like sixty-six now. He wobbled on his feet when I finally had him standing. Smiling down at me from his six-foot height, he draped an arm over my shoulders. "You look so much like your mother. Did I ever tell you that?"

"Yup." I steered him toward the bed.

"Her hair was golden, just like yours. Thick and shiny." He frowned as he lightly touched my hair. "But not this short. She never cut it this short."

I nodded, remembering my mother's beautiful hair.

"Are stars out tonight?" he asked as he swallowed the pills I'd given him to help with his dementia.

I nodded, not bothering to correct him that it was daytime. I wasn't lying, either. There really was a star out, a great big one, and it was burning our planet alive.

The hellish orb drew my attention to the window, and heat began to gather at my core. It spread, filling my veins with liquid sunshine. I was elated to receive the premonition as I fed on its power, my arms and legs shaking with it. The need grew in me, and I almost passed out from the pure pleasure of getting my fix.

"Sarah?"

Oh, God, I thought he'd fallen asleep. I spun around to face the wall, so he couldn't see my face. My father had never seen me transition. I hadn't wanted to scare him.

"What's happening to you?" he asked, voice shaking. "Why is there red smoke coming from your hands?"

I curled my fingers and hugged my fists to my chest so that he couldn't see them. "I'm fine, Dad," I said, though it came out a raspy whisper. My throat was almost too hot for me to speak. "Really. Now go to sleep."

My legs like lead weights, I tried dragging my feet toward the door, but I could hardly move. A time stamp imprinted itself in my mind. Three hours. Then came the mental map. Destination: Black Hawk, Colorado.

The bed creaked behind me.

"Dad, get back into bed." I tried again to leave the room, but my feet felt glued to the floor. "I told you I'm fine—"

His bony fingers closed around my upper arms, and he screamed, then quickly let go. I spun around to see what was wrong. His terrified eyes stared at me as he continued to yell and back away toward the bed. His hands fanned out from his sides, and I saw that his fingers were an angry red. My skin had burned him.

I tried to move forward just to see how bad it was, but he screamed even louder. He held his hands out in front of him as if to ward me off.

"Demon!" He pointed at me. "You possessed my daughter!"

I shook my head, and tears dripped from the corners of my eyes. I felt normal now, so I knew I must look normal, but it was too late. "I'm not a demon, I'm still your little girl."

"Will he be okay?" I asked the doctor who rushed into my father's room.

"He should be. I doubt he'll even remember what happened."

He was right. With my dad's mind slipping more and more each day, he seemed only to remember the distant past. His short-term memory was just about shot.

The doctor's brow crimped with concern. "Will *you* be okay?"

I had to smile at that. I'd be more than okay as soon I arrived in Black Hawk a couple of hours from now. A storm was coming, and Ian and I were about to give Agent Sam Nichol a personal invitation for a front-row seat.

"I won't do it." Ian paced in front of the Storm Trooper, while tossing an empty can of coolant from one hand to the other. I'd asked one of the nurses to deliver him a message to meet me in the ambulance bay. After he refilled the reservoir for the air conditioner, I told him about my plan and was having trouble convincing him to go along with it. "I don't want you anywhere near that son of a bitch."

"I won't be," I assured him. At least not too close and not for long. We just had to time it right. "I know when and where the sun storm is coming. Nichol doesn't. I'll use you as bait to get him out in the open and then we'll trap the bastard so he has nowhere to run. See how he likes having his freedom taken away."

Ian's lip curled, and he offered me that snarly smile of his, but he shook his head at the same time. "You underestimate the guy. He's sly. Anyway, what will we do with him if we catch him?"

"You mean *when* we catch him," I said. "He's a criminal. We tie him up and turn him in to the military base at Cheyenne Mountain. Let them deal with him."

"It'll be his word against ours. Who do you think the government is going to believe?"

He had a point, but I had a counter one. "Okay, fine. We'll turn ourselves in along with Nichol. That's his assignment, right? To round up all the Kinetics? This way we'll be under the government's protection. Without access to you, Nichol's profiteering days are over." And, ironically enough, the agent would look like a hero for bringing us in. The guy should rot in hell for what he'd done, but if Ian and I could be protected from him and others like him, that's what mattered.

A dark look settled over Ian's face. His pensive stare at the SUV made me wonder what he was thinking. "Your plan could work," he finally said.

A flutter of anticipation rippled up the back of my neck. The next step was contacting Nichol. "He has a satellite phone in his vehicle, right? Do you remember the number?"

"I'll never forget it."

Of course the agent would have a satphone. The only people with satellite phones were government, law enforcement, fire stations and hospitals. The rest of us had to use couriers and an extremely slow mail system. The days of cell phones and email were over, at least until more communication satellites came back on line.

We no longer had a mayor in Lodgepole, but because I'd managed to save the town from the sparks of numerous sun storms, I'd earned the proverbial key to the city, and it came with privileges. One of those privileges was use of the hospital's satphone. I'd never needed it before now, but I knew where it was.

"Meet me on the roof," I told Ian, and went to retrieve the phone from the bottom desk drawer in the administration office. When I emerged on the rooftop, I noticed the sun was exceptionally brutal. There was a shady spot created by what was left of a plywood shack someone had constructed years ago. There'd be no rain today, but the shack at least provided shelter from the sun's cruel rays. Ian was already standing beneath it, waiting for me.

"You okay with this?" I asked, my stomach tightening with dread in case he wasn't. He was a crucial component in this plan, and I knew it made him uncomfortable.

"Of course I'm *not* okay with it." His gruff tone made that obvious. "But I get it. It's a smart move."

"And not without risk, but it's our best chance of stopping this guy. Does he carry weapons?"

"A Stunner that shoots extremely effective electric bullets." Ian rubbed his chest as if recalling just *how* effective.

"He could use it to kill if he wanted to, but I was worth more to him alive."

I opened the case and pulled out the satphone. "What's the number?"

"What if he's not there?" Ian asked, trying to sound as if he didn't care one way or the other. But I knew better. "The storm will strike in less than two hours."

"Then we wait until the next storm and try again." It was even possible his location put him too far away from Black Hawk to make it there in time. "How fast is his vehicle?"

Ian snorted. "Damn fast for a solar-powered car, and he drives at top speed. It's not like he has to worry about getting a speeding ticket."

He gave me Nichol's sat number, and I punched it in. My pulse quickened as my anxiety mounted with each ring. I breathed deeply, concentrating on the speech I'd rehearsed inside my head. If the agent answered, I had to be convincing, and I wasn't terribly confident of my acting skills.

"Yeah," said a tenor voice on the other end.

I nodded at Ian, who stiffened and began to pace in a circle, his dark eyes filled with malice.

When I didn't respond right away, Nichol said, "Who the hell is this?"

I swallowed hard. "A friend."

He paused. "Wrong number. I ain't got no friends."

"You do now. Especially when you hear what I have to say."

"And what's that?"

"Two words. Ian. Matthews."

The pause drew out too long, and I thought we'd been disconnected. Finally, he said, "Don't try to bullshit a bullshitter."

"It's not bullshit, Agent Nichol. I have him right here."

"Where's here?"

I let a smile seep into my voice. "I'm not stupid enough to answer that. You're not welcome where I am, and you don't need to know."

"What do you want for him?"

"A partnership. You and me. Fifty-fifty." He seemed the type who liked being the one on top in a relationship.

He laughed, long and hard. "The hell you say. Look here, missy, I'm a busy man. I don't have time for idiots. Good luck with your *business* dealings."

"Wait!" He was supposed to jump at the opportunity I offered. What the hell had just happened? Ian frowned and mouthed *what's wrong?* I shook my head and refocused on my conversation with Nichol. "Okay, fine. Just give me money. I'll sell him to you."

Ian's tortured expression tore at my heart. He knew I didn't mean it, but hearing me say it couldn't have been easy.

"You know what he can do?" Nichol asked, a shrewd edge to his voice.

"He told me." What better way to lie than to use the truth? "We got friendly, if you know what I mean." I gave Ian a sideways glance, and he looked appalled. I shrugged and kept talking. "Pillow talk can reveal all kinds of things. He told me all about you."

"That so?"

"How do you think I got this number? Found it written down on a piece of paper stuffed in his duffel bag."

A growl rumbled through the phone. "You're not as dumb as I thought."

"Damn right. I'm also a nurse. I drugged him, and he's weak as a kitten, but not for long. Meet me at the Black Hawk statue off Highway 19 near Main Street in exactly one hour and forty-five minutes. Don't be a minute late or the deal's off."

Nichol hesitated. "That's in the Rocky Mountain foothills."

Damn. What if he wasn't in the state? I just assumed that since the military base with the Kinetics was in Colorado, he would be, too.

"Lucky for you I'm in Fort Collins at the moment. I'll be there." He ended the call.

"He bought it!" I wanted to rush to Ian and hug him, but one look at his stone-cold face told me that wasn't a good idea. "Something wrong?"

"I don't get why you're doing this. It's not your problem."

"Because it's worth doing."

His snarly smile was both beguiling and successful at hiding what he was thinking. It made him hard to read. "But you don't trust me. So why help me?"

He asked the hardest questions. "I've changed my mind. I *do* trust you."

His chin wrinkled when he jutted out his jaw. "Since when?"

I jumped at the sudden hike in volume when he spoke. "Since last night. You were willing to sacrifice your freedom to protect me, and to save this town from a fire we had no way of putting out. I admire and trust a chivalrous man."

Eyes less hard than they were a minute ago, he asked, "Does that mean I'm forgiven for being a deceitful bastard?"

I let a few seconds pass before I said, "Yeah."

He smiled.

While smiling back, I tried to ignore the seed of doubt that wedged in my gut. I didn't doubt him, I doubted myself. It was possible I was in way over my head.

• 9 •

The sun was high in the sky as it approached noon. Cool air poured from the Trooper's vents, and I angled my head to bathe my neck in pure refreshment.

"Keep your eyes on the road," Ian said. "Or would you rather I drive?"

Actually, I would. For one thing, it would prove that I trusted him. For another, I was so tired, my eyelids felt weighted with bags of sand. I hadn't slept today. "The only reason I'm not handing you the reins is because I know where we're going and you don't."

He harrumphed. "Have it your way, but I'm a great driver."

"I'm sure you are." I glanced at his bouncing knee, an obvious sign of his anxiety. I wished I knew how to settle him down. Did I dare touch him? I let one hand fall from the wheel and reached over to pat his arm. I didn't tell him not to worry. He had every right to do so. I just wanted him to know I had his back.

He turned his head slightly to peer at me from the corner of his eye. Without speaking, his hand gently covered mine, his warmth seeping into me and making *me* feel safe rather than the other way around. Maybe it was mutual. At any rate, I didn't experience the overwhelming charge between us that had happened before. Heightened emotions must trigger the surge. Good to know.

The highway snaked through the foothills that had once

been lush with majestic pine trees and myriad wildlife. Now it was a blackened thicket of destruction.

I hadn't been to Black Hawk since before the storms, so I remembered it as a popular mountain community with several gambling casinos and historical attractions like a steam locomotive and museums. Tourists used to love the old mining town where they could pan the creek for gold. But now there was no creek, and not much of a town to speak of. Just empty streets with gutted buildings and old signs that didn't mean anything anymore.

I searched for the sculpture of the giant black hawk where I'd told Nichol to meet us, but it was no longer there. I stopped on the bridge connecting the highway to the road leading into town. "I wonder what happened to it," I said.

Ian got out of the SUV and peered over the railing. Turning to look at me, he said, "It flew off its perch." He pointed down at the dry creek bed. "It's down there."

Flown? More like hurled. Seeing the gaping cracks in the pavement, I guessed one or more earthquakes had sent the fourteen-foot iron hawk over the edge. The location where we had agreed to meet remained the same, so even without a hawk, Nichol would have no trouble finding us.

I parked the Trooper and gathered the few props we'd need to put on our show. Ian had found a comfortable spot to pose for our ruse in the shade of a demolished building. He'd put himself far enough from the road that Nichol would have to walk a hundred feet or more from wherever he parked. That would draw him out into the open.

We'd arrived early so that we could set up. I unwound a length of rope and began tying Ian's ankles.

"Do you have to?" he asked, sounding annoyed, and I didn't blame him.

"Yes, but I'll keep it loose. You can easily kick free." The plan was for Nichol to think Ian was incapacitated; an easy capture. When the storm started, he'd panic and agree to anything we asked if we promised to save him from exposure. Ian would trap him in a cyclone until the sparks passed, then we'd tie him up and take him with us to the base in Cheyenne Mountain. I'd threaten to throw him under the sparks of the next storm if he gave us any trouble.

I wrapped duct tape around Ian's wrists, but left a large gap that Nichol wouldn't see. The bond was so flimsy a toddler could have broken free. Even so, I could tell the sweat beading on Ian's forehead wasn't just from the heat. "You can do this," I told him.

"Never said I couldn't." He glared up at me, then leaned his head back against the broken slab of concrete holding up what was left of the building.

I'd grabbed a syringe from the hospital's drug supply and planned to jab our captive with a strong sedative once we caught him. I was just filling it up when I spotted a black SUV. It was shiny with solar wafers that covered its hood, trunk and roof, and it rolled slowly over the bridge before stopping behind the Trooper.

Every nerve in my body snapped to attention as adrenaline pumped through me faster than I could blink. Nichol finally emerged from the car and stood at the edge of the bridge wearing a slick black raincoat, a driver's cap made from the same shiny material and glasses with moderately tinted lenses. "It's so hard to find a good parking place these days." Flashing a grin, he added, "Where'd you get the solar mobile?"

Getting chummy to soften me up would never work. "None of your business."

"Is that any way to talk to your new 'friend'?" he asked, faking disappointment.

I tossed a quick look at the sky and clapped my hands. "Chop-chop, Nichol. I don't have all day. Give me the money, and you can take your prize."

He frowned. "A girl of so few words. I like your style, uh… You never told me your name."

"Sarah." I didn't see the harm in telling him. "Sarah Daggot."

His eyes squinted in thought. "Now I recognize the rig. Your dad is George Daggot, right? The storm chaser?"

I swallowed. How the hell would he know who my dad was? "Okay, time's up. My prisoner and I are leaving."

"Well, I'll be damned. My solar car is modeled after your dad's design. That jalopy there," he said, sweeping his hand at my Trooper, "is the original prototype?"

"Going once," I said, edging over to Ian and crouching down as if to drag him to his feet. "Going twice—"

"You young people have no patience." He trudged down the hill toward us.

When he got halfway, I said, "Stop right there. You have the money?" I flicked a glance at the sky and saw brilliant red glitter floating slowly toward us. Just another minute or two. "Let me see it."

"Or what?"

I showed him the syringe. "Or I kill him."

"You're one cold bitch." He tossed an envelope on the ground at my feet. "How do I know he's not already dead?"

I nudged Ian with my foot, and he groaned. "See? He's not dead. Not yet, anyway." I picked up the envelope and thumbed through the bills. Wow. Money could still buy a lot of stuff, like food and medicine. Lodgepole would put this to good use.

Nichol glared at Ian. "You have him trussed up a bit tight, don't you think?"

"Had to," I said. "He's a Kinetic with the power to make weather. I can't be careful enough."

He frowned at me. "You keep checking the sky. What do you see up there, huh? I haven't seen a wild bird in—" Nichol shot a look above him and bent backward to look higher. His hat fell to the ground, unveiling his shiny, hairless scalp. "Holy shit! Sparks!" He twisted around and ran for his vehicle.

Ian whipped his hands free of the tape, and they became a blur of motion as he made circles in the air. A gust of wind spun a dust cloud tight around Nichol's ankles, holding him in place. The sparks were closing in.

Nichol couldn't break out of the cyclone that spun around him the way cotton candy twists around a paper cone. His eyes widened as he stared at me. "You planned this. You're a Kinetic like him."

"Not quite like him, but the sparks can't hurt me."

"You knew when and where this storm would hit. That makes you…" He laughed. The crazy bastard laughed while lethal radiation was about to sprinkle down on his head. "You're the one. The two of you together, that's what's supposed to do it."

I was dying to ask *do what?* but the sparks were dangerously close to him now. "Ian, close up the cyclone. We got his attention."

"Do you think so?" Ian asked. "I'm not so sure. He doesn't look compliant to me. Are you compliant, Agent Nichol?"

Nichol smirked and stood perfectly relaxed, as if his life didn't teeter on the brink.

"Ian, seriously. We didn't come here to murder the man."

I stared hard at Ian, whose expression held rigid determination. "Ian? Don't do it."

"Why not? This asshole treated me lower than dirt. He abused me. Give me one good reason not to let the sparks have him."

"That's not up to you," I said, hoping my words sank in. I understood Ian's desire for revenge, but I hadn't believed he would act on it. If he killed the agent, Ian would be signing his own death warrant.

Ian's shoulders heaved with a sigh, and he nodded. The cyclone, thick with spinning dirt and small rocks, grew taller around Nichol, and was now up to his waist. Once it encircled him from head to toe, the sparks couldn't touch him.

Nichol's raincoat flashed open, and his hand dove into an inside pocket. He yanked out a square pistol and pointed it at Ian. Then fired.

The bullet hit Ian square in the chest. The cyclone evaporated in an instant. I screamed and ran to Ian, ignoring the fleeing agent, but Nichol's shouts jerked my focus back to him. He'd hardly taken two steps when a blanket of red sun sparks coated his body.

Agent Sam Nichol rolled on the ground as if trying to rub off the miniscule sparks that glommed onto him like fleas on a dog. His thrashing didn't last long. Within seconds, the storm ended, and the remaining sparks vanished into the ground. He lay unconscious.

The electric bullet stuck to Ian's chest like a wasp with an embedded stinger. It pumped him with current, and the voltage twisted his muscles, forcing him to convulse. I yanked the bullet free and tossed it away as far as I could.

"Dead?" Ian asked, the word like a harsh whisper.

"You? No. Nichol? Not yet, but he will be in a matter of

days." How could our plan have gone so wrong? As much as I disliked Nichol, I didn't want him dead. It was apparent, however, that Ian did. "Were you *trying* to kill him?"

"No," Ian said, but his denial sounded fuzzy around the edges. "I was mad enough to kill him, but I've never taken a life and don't intend to start with a bottom-feeder like Nichol."

We locked eyes, and I saw the truth there, and the regret. "Why did you wait so long to close the cyclone?"

"I wanted him to feel as helpless and trapped as I was when he used me as his personal weather-maker."

"But he never tried to kill you, did he?" I asked.

"He needed me alive, but there were times I'd wished I was dead." He stood over Nichol and stared down at the un-conscious man. A purple-veined rash covered Nichol's face and scalp. "He drugged me, starved me, even withheld water when I didn't do what I was told. He's a monster."

I gazed down at the sick agent, whose exposure was acute. He wouldn't last a week. "We have to take him with us."

Ian jutted out his chin and clenched his jaw. I knew bring-ing the agent along was the last thing he wanted, but we couldn't leave the man here in the middle of nowhere. He was a dead man walking, but it would be inhumane to make him suffer any more than he had to.

Ian rubbed his chest. "That bullet was set to kill," he said. "If you hadn't yanked it out when you did, it would have juiced me with enough current to stop my heart."

So I guessed Nichol hadn't wanted Ian as badly as we thought he had. Or, more likely, the shooting had been a desperate act of last resort. If Nichol couldn't have him, no one would.

"We'll take him to the hospital," I said. "The staff there will make him comfortable as possible until he slips into a coma."

Ian eyed the black solar car. "That's mine now."

"As it should be." After what Nichol had put him through, Ian deserved compensation. "We'll sedate him and tie his hands, just in case. Irrational behavior often comes with the fever, and from what you told me, he's crazy enough as it is."

"What happens to us once he's taken care of?" Ian asked.

"We head south to Colorado Springs." We might as well join our fellow Kinetics and get the answer to what Nichol was babbling about. *You're the one. The two of you together, that's what's supposed to do it.* The one to do what? I really wanted to know.

I followed Ian back to Lodgepole and tried not to worry about him driving off to parts unknown, then dumping the agent in a ditch along the way. We hadn't known each other long, and he'd deceived me once, but since then he'd proven to be a man of his word. He wouldn't try to trick me again. In an odd sort of way, Ian and I were partners.

He pulled the agent's solar car into the hospital's emergency entrance and parked it there while he went inside for a wheelchair and to alert staff of their new patient. While he did that, I checked on Nichol, who was now semiconscious.

"How are you feeling?" I asked, knowing full well he felt like shit. He was at stage one of the illness, his fever only starting, and the rash must have been itching like crazy. But he didn't scratch. He grimaced as if he wanted to, but some apparent deep-seated determination helped him resist the urge. His tolerance was impressive.

"Not good," he said, his voice barely above a whisper. "Thanks to you."

I shook my head. "If you'd stood down, we could have protected you from the sparks."

Eyes narrowed with suspicion, he said, "Matthews wants me dead."

"Can you blame him?'

Nichol glared at me.

I started to walk away, but he reached out to grab my arm, his fingers pinching me hard enough to bruise. "It's been scrubbed."

"What's been scrubbed?" He was talking nonsense now, a symptom of the disease. I peeled his fingers off and shoved his hand away.

"Kinetic program. Hundreds of them." He paused to take a breath. "Need only a weather Kinetic. And a storm forecaster. Stop the storms."

He was making no sense. "What do you mean *stop* the storms?"

A medical technician came out to help Nichol into a wheel-chair.

Completely bewildered, I followed behind the tech as he wheeled Nichol into the hospital. "Agent Nichol, I don't understand. Are you talking about the base in Cheyenne Mountain? The plan for the Kinetics there?"

He was weak and had trouble holding his head up, but he managed to look at me sideways. He smiled. "If they only knew. About you."

I wasn't a secret, but it wasn't as if there was any kind of mass media anymore. I was tabloid news, and the tabloids had been extinct for some time. A freak in a dying world wasn't much of a *real* news headline. "Then maybe I should tell them."

His broad grin revealed bloody teeth. That was just the beginning of his hemorrhaging. There would be more. "Go ahead," he croaked. "They'll take you apart just like the others. See what makes you tick." He chuckled and began to cough.

"Sarah," the staff doc said. "He needs rest."

That was the doc's polite way of telling me to leave. "Okay, I'm going, but this man is a criminal and needs to be restrained."

"This man has Sun Fever. He's not strong enough to be dangerous to anyone."

"I'm not so sure about that," I told the doc. "He's sly and he's smart. You'll need to strap him to his bed."

"I'm not strapping down a dying man." The middle-aged doc looked down at me through glasses perched on the middle of his nose. "We'll sedate him for his own comfort. He's not going anywhere."

Sedation would have to do, but I doubted it would be enough. Nichol wasn't the type to give up.

After parking the Trooper in the ambulance bay, I saw Ian walking circles around Nichol's SUV, rag in hand, as he wiped road dirt from the rig's solid steel body.

"Nichol has been admitted."

He grunted. "That psycho should be *committed.*"

"Probably, but this will have to do." I walked around the shiny black solar car, admiring its sleek design. So this was fashioned after my father's storm-chaser. I never would have guessed. I hadn't paid attention to the interior while focused on Nichol, so now I took the time to gaze through the tinted windows and get a closer look.

When I glanced up at Ian, he melted my heart with his lopsided smile. "Want to sit inside?"

How could I resist? "Sure do."

He opened the passenger side door for me to slide in. The upholstery was black leather with thick cushioned seats, and the dashboard had more dials and buttons than a jet cockpit. "Wow."

Ian got in on the driver's side. He slipped a key into the ignition and the engine whirred to life. Cool air poured from the vents in the dash. I could live in this car.

"What do you say we give your dad's vehicle a rest and take this one instead?"

"Sounds good to me. Where are we going?"

"Where you suggested we go, the military base in Cheyenne Mountain."

I immediately thought of what Nichol had told me just now. If there was a thread of truth to what the agent had said, going there could be a mistake.

After I told Ian what Nichol had told me, he said, "Sarah, you should know better than to believe him. He's a chronic liar."

"I didn't say I believed him, but it got me to thinking. I'd rather not take a chance of getting captured and used as a guinea pig for a government experiment. Or worse." And getting locked up at a secure base inside a mountain would keep me from chasing storms. I'd go mad.

"We should at least go to Colorado Springs, maybe ask the locals what they know about the base. Couldn't hurt," Ian said. I could tell by the look of determination on his face that he wasn't going to take no for an answer. He was a stubborn man. "We won't get caught. I promise."

I sighed. "Deal. But if a storm pops up in the meantime, I'm chasing it." I gave him a piercing look to let him know I meant business. "Since you'll be driving, you have to take me to wherever the storm hits."

He nodded, his eyes gentle with understanding. It felt good not to have to go into long explanations with him. We were on the same page.

He tapped one of the glass-domed gauges. "The level of

juice is above the green line, so I imagine the solar tank is full. I have no idea how long it will last in a rig this size."

"There's no shortage on fuel," I said, squinting out at the cloudless blue sky on the horizon. "Recharging won't be a problem, but Nichol's SUV is larger than mine. It may require more power than what we're used to."

He shrugged. "We'll take our chances."

We retrieved our supplies, including the alert siren, from the Trooper and packed them in the agent's car, which now belonged to Ian. It felt odd to be traveling in a strange vehicle, and odder still not to be the one driving.

We'd barely driven through the alley behind the hospital when the heat of warning from a coming storm sizzled inside my skull. My heartbeat picked up speed along with the car as we headed out of town. The energy felt amazing, and my body lapped it up like a cat lapping up milk. My hands shook from my premonition, and I gazed down at the red smoke curling from my fingertips. I couldn't stop it, and I couldn't excuse it to Ian or anyone else. This was who I was and if Ian had a problem with that, well…

"You okay?" he asked, giving me a sideways stare that showed curiosity rather than horror. The light of understanding shone in his eyes. "Ah, I see. You're forecasting."

As soon as I was physically able to speak, I said, "A typical day in my own personal freakdom."

He chuckled and returned his attention to the road.

"It doesn't bother you? My transformation?"

Shaking his head, he said, "Nope. I think it's hot."

My smile widened. He thought I was hot. Still flushed from my premonition, I don't think he noticed my blush. His compliment flustered me, but my forecast took priority over everything else I was feeling. "The storm will strike in Morrison." I consulted my mental map that showed grid lines and topography, as if it was imprinted on the inside of my eyelids. I knew the area well. It was on the way to where we were going. "It's a small town just south of here. Maybe ten miles at most. The storm won't hit for another three hours, so we have plenty of time."

"I know where it is," Ian said. "I stayed there a few weeks before moving on to Lodgepole."

"I haven't been to Morrison since my mom was alive. What's it like now?"

He hesitated. "Dirty. Broken. Mostly empty."

I figured as much, which meant the people there must be warned about the coming storm. "But someone lives there, right?"

Tilting his head from one side to the other, he said, "Not sure I'd call it living." He coughed and jerked his chin toward the backseat. "Can I get a water?"

I turned around to grab a couple bottles from a case on the floor. There was also a plastic basket with a lid. After handing Ian his water, I turned back around to investigate the basket. "Berserkers, huh?"

"Yeah. Quite a few." He took a swig from his bottle.

There were apples in the basket. Real apples! And ham sandwiches made with white bread and green lettuce, wrapped in plastic. Nichol had packed himself a lunch. He must have had connections. I wiped drool from my lips as I turned back around to sit with my treasure in my lap.

Ian slowed the car while turning down a wide street I recognized. It led through a suburban neighborhood on the way to the outlet mall. I remembered hearing about the homes here having suffered a severe fire. It didn't look like the same suburb. Husks of houses with charred frames and exposed plumbing poked up from the blackened earth like rows of broken teeth rotted with decay. A child's plastic tricycle sat in the middle of the street, its melted wheels fused to the asphalt.

I gazed, horrified, at the devastation that went on block after block. "Ian," I said weakly, my mouth dry even after taking a sip of water. "Tell me about the people here."

His attention remained on the road ahead. "The few I've seen may look like people, but I'd hardly call them human. They were closer to being animals."

Berserkers to the extreme. I'd never seen them that rabid. The ones I'd encountered had a mob mentality, but I hadn't considered them especially dangerous.

Ian steered the car down another deserted street that was as burned out as all the others. I got a view of the mall at the other end. "I've seen it before, in other towns I've passed through." He twirled his finger beside his head. "Their brains are scrambled worse than Nichol's. Some people just snap."

I thought of my father, who hadn't snapped, but his mind had been adversely affected by the storms. I think having me with him kept him sane. "I wonder why news of the Berserkers never hit the monthly newspaper."

"My guess is that our government wants to avoid national panic."

I was stunned it had been kept secret from the public for so long. "It could have been prevented if someone cared enough to do something for these poor people."

"Maybe, maybe not." He angled the car toward a deserted gas station on the corner. "But from what I've seen, it's too widespread to stop. Some cities have even rounded them up to segregate them from the rest of the community. The hordes of Berserkers either killed each other or starved to death."

I stared down at the basket of food in my lap and no longer felt hungry. "I had no idea."

"I didn't think you did. Few people do." Ian drove into the open garage bay and parked the car over a hydraulic lift, its engine still running. "I need to check something."

"What's wrong?"

"The brakes feel mushy. Could be the pads."

The last thing we needed was for the brakes to fail and cause a crash that totaled the car. I'd be screwed without transportation. "Can you fix it?"

"If the parts are in this garage I can."

I peered out the window, expecting a crowd of Berserkers to storm the car. We were tucked into the shadows, not visible from the street. Even so, I didn't feel safe.

Ian must have noticed my tension. "They have enough sense to stay out of the sun. We're okay for now."

I blinked over eyes that felt covered by sandpaper. "Good, because I'm not sure I can keep my eyes open much longer." I yawned and added, "I just need a short nap until the storm comes. My energy is way low. Can we keep the air going?"

He patted the dashboard and checked the voltage meter. "The dial is still in the green. We should be fine running the engine for a couple more hours." He grabbed an apple and a sandwich from the container in my lap.

My stomach growled, begging for food, but the call to dreamland was much stronger. The hum of the fan blowing cool air in my face was like a lullaby that soothed away all conscious thought.

I heard ringing, like a phone, and figured I must be dreaming. I roused from my doze with the instinctive need to make it stop. Where was it coming from?

Ian's hand grabbed a black, rectangular object from a cubby in the console.

"Satphone." He turned the ringing phone over in his hands. Someone was trying to reach Nichol. "You should answer it."

He stared at the tiny screen that lit up with a name. "Charles Jaginski."

I blinked as adrenaline chased away my need for sleep. Widening my eyes, I said. "Maybe he's a friend of Nichol's."

"Let's find out." Ian pressed a button with his thumb. "Yeah," he said into the phone, his voice sounding generic and a touch higher than normal for him. I tried to remember what Nichol sounded like. I think Ian got pretty close.

"Nichol, I'm in." The curt male voice spoke through a speaker in the car's dash.

Ian looked at me and shrugged, so I motioned for him to keep going. "Yeah?"

There was a brief pause, and then, "I know you've gone rogue, man. The scene at the base is bullshit. I'd rather do business with you than with these jarheads. I have a bead on some Kinetics here in Wyoming we can nab and sell. Deal?"

So Nichol wasn't the only scum in the bottom-feeding pool. Ian paused, his disgust palpable. "Yeah."

"What's wrong with you? You never talked much when we were partners, but I need more of an answer than 'yeah.' I'm putting my ass on the line for you."

Ian coughed but didn't reply.

Jaginski sighed. "Every time we talk you're like a different guy. I think you're touched in the head, becoming one of those Berserkers. Maybe doing business with you isn't such a good idea. I'll wrangle these Kinetics on my own."

Ian hesitated before finally grunting something I couldn't make out.

The man on the other end said through gritted teeth, "That's how you wanna play it? Fine. I'm juicin' up my rig and keepin' these Kinetics for myself. One's a geokinetic and the other is pyro. What do you think of that, asshole?"

If anyone could tell us about the Kinetic program, it would be this guy. I grabbed the phone from Ian, but he wrestled it out of my hands. He looked furious, his scowl pinching his brows so close together they'd become a single ridge. Shaking his head so hard I was afraid he'd break his neck, he mouthed the words, "Don't speak. He's a slaver." I bit my lip to stop myself from talking.

"Nichol? What the hell's goin' on?" Jaginski sounded suspicious. He was no idiot. It took him barely a second to figure it out. "Shit!" Then came a click followed by dead silence.

"Damn it," Ian said, a sneer curling his lip. "If Nichol's SUV has a GPS tracking device, it's only a matter of time before his ex-partner finds this car and discovers us." Ian rolled the window down to toss out his apple core. A blast of hot air shot inside before he got the window closed again. It smelled like dust and metal and old motor oil. "If the GPS is here, I'll find it."

"Charles Jaginski and Sam Nichol are anything but friends. You heard what he just said. He thinks Nichol is crazy. It's possible Jaginski's nothing like his partner."

"Come on, Sarah. He's a slaver like Nichol. He just said so himself."

"Not necessarily. Could be extortion."

Ian snorted. "And that's better? I've never met the guy, never heard a word about him from Nichol. But birds of a feather…"

"The enemy of our enemy is our friend."

"At least he's in Wyoming, which means he's five or six hours away." He twisted in his seat to look at me. "Where does this Suzie-Sunshine-who-loves-everyone attitude come from?"

"I don't *love* everyone." And I certainly wasn't feeling much love for him at the moment. "My mother raised me to see the good in people and to think of my glass as half full, not half empty." I wanted to add something about how his pessimism made him so lonely, but that would hit a nerve that was better left untouched. "You're missing out on getting to know people who can help you."

"I don't need help."

"Yet you offer it all the time."

He hadn't shifted his gaze away from me since we'd started this conversation, and even now he gave me a look so intense it felt as though he read every thought inside my head.

"Can I ask you something?"

He broke eye contact and made a show of rechecking the gauges on the dash. After a few seconds, he said, "Okay. Shoot."

"You could have taken Nichol's car and left town, gone anywhere you wanted." I watched him for a change of expression, but he switched his attention to the sandwich he was unwrapping. "Why didn't you?"

Laying the uneaten sandwich in his lap, he sighed and peered out the window at a rack of dirty tools mounted on the wall. "Maybe I finally found what I was looking for."

"And that is?"

He focused on me again. "A place to call home."

10

Why had Ian turned the engine off? The heat inside the car woke me from my nap. I opened heavy eyelids to gaze at Ian, who leaned back against the seat with his eyes closed. His chest rose and fell in the slow rhythm of deep sleep, and his profile revealed a straight nose with nostrils slightly flared, full lips relaxed and chin angled downward. Such a peaceful picture, and yet I sensed the tense soul inside him that longed for the normal life he must have once had. I wished he could have it back. I wished we all could.

The clock on the dash said thirty minutes had passed. A bundle of nerves at the base of my spine let me know the sun storm was close. I could almost taste the sparks. I grasped the door handle with one hand and reached for Ian with the other. As much as I hated to disturb him, I didn't want him waking up to the blaring scream of my alarm.

"Hey, it's time," I told him as I pushed open the door. Just as I swung my legs out, Ian yelled, "Stop!"

Instead of solid ground, my feet met empty space.

When I slipped off the seat, my legs kicked the air and one arm flailed as the other clutched the door handle. Looking down, I realized the car had been raised by the hydraulic lift and was now poised about ten feet up in the air. I could drop without hurting myself, but when I glanced up again, I saw Ian's hand reach for mine. My fingers sought his and just as we were about to touch, someone's hand grabbed my ankle.

Bony fingers dug into my skin and tugged, but the effort was too weak to dislodge me. Ian got hold of my forearm and pulled. Another pair of hands gripped my other leg. I felt like a rope in a game of tug of war.

"Ian!" I yelled.

"Damn it." His grip tightened. "I was afraid this might happen. That's why I lifted the car."

"Why didn't you tell me?"

"I did, but you must not have been as awake as I thought you were."

I kicked at the feeble hands holding me. Glancing down, I saw two dangerously thin women covered in grime from head to toe. Their skin was so burned that their eyes seemed overly bright within the dark circles that haloed their sockets. *Berserkers.*

"You took my Johnny!" one of them screeched.

"No!" I kicked at their hands, which briefly fell away only to latch right back on. Who the hell was Johnny? "I didn't take anyone. Let go!"

"You burned down my house," the other one said.

My heart went out to them. These confused, wretched creatures were mad with grief. What would they do to me if I fell? Maybe I could outrun them. I considered releasing the car door, but just as I began to relax my hold, there was a sharp pain on my heel. One of them had bitten me!

Panic scrambled up my spine, and I kicked even more forcefully now. A breeze stirred beneath me, gathering in strength and sucking at the air around the women. I heard shouting nearby and guessed reinforcements were on the way. I could hold out against these two, but add a couple more and I'd be done for.

I gazed up at Ian, who was holding my hand, his eyes bright

with the power he used to create the mini cyclone. Little by little, he siphoned strength from me to grow the weapon he was creating. The two women screamed in frustration as the cyclone pulled them away from me and carried them outside the garage. Three more Berserkers on their way in stopped when the human pinwheel tumbled past them. They turned and ran as if the hounds of hell nipped at their ankles.

Ian released me, and I fell to the floor.

He dropped down from the other side of the car. "Sarah!"

After helping me to my feet, he wrapped an arm around me to hold me up, his hand sliding up my rib cage and settling just beneath my breast. I could feel his warm skin through the thin fabric of my shirt. If it had been anyone else, I'd have slapped his hand away. But not Ian. I'd come to trust him too much to think he'd want anything other than to help me.

"Will they come back?" I asked.

"Probably." He held me close, and I leaned into him, comforted by how safe he made me feel. "But not right away. The cyclone scared them enough for now."

"What do they want?"

"I don't know, and I'm not sure they know, either. They have little left of themselves but their instinct to survive."

"We can help them do at least that much," I said, grabbing up the siren that had fallen out of the SUV with me. I trudged outside, seeing the sun lower in the sky as it prepared to set, but its radiance wasn't diminished by the late hour. If anything, it was stronger because of the descending storm.

I cranked the siren, not sure if I was warning the Berserkers of danger or calling them out of hiding. If they had the sense to stay under cover during the day, they surely knew the significance of an alert. I gazed up at the blanket of flashing red sparks falling toward us.

I wanted the sparks to touch me, but I also wanted to try something. With Ian.

He stood beside me, watching the sky. I turned to him and said, "Make the wind blow."

His eyes lit up at the suggestion. "Of course," he said, his tone deep with wonder. He knew what I was asking without me having to say it aloud. That's how connected we were. "I've wanted to try it before, but I was always too late because the sparks had already fallen."

"Now you won't be." I held out my hand, and he folded his around mine, his fingers warm and rough with calluses. Vines of energy twined where our flesh touched, and I felt their power travel up my arms, across my shoulders and up the back of my neck.

A wind began to form, one that was like the gale that had attacked Lodgepole just the other night. Only this wind was completely under Ian's control. It felt warm and billowed like silk that wrapped loosely around us. Ian sent it upward, high enough to reach the sparks fifty feet above our heads.

The invisible shield Ian created was also a battering ram that pushed the sparks back to where they came from. We watched as the sparks grew smaller and smaller while returning to the sun that spawned them.

"How high will they go?" I asked.

"Beyond the bubble of Earth's atmosphere. The vacuum of space will take them from there."

"I wish you could do this to every storm." Then no one would ever have to fear exposure to sun sparks.

"I would if you could tell me when they were coming."

"I can't foresee them all, though I wish I could."

"I know."

Our team approach might be the answer to stopping the

deadly sparks for good. My thoughts wound back to what Nichol had said in Black Hawk. Was he telling the truth? I supposed we'd find out once we arrived in Colorado Springs.

My knees felt weak, and I held on to Ian for support.

Anxiety made his dark eyes even darker. "You needed those sparks."

I smiled. "Actually, the energy you gave me works almost as well. I'm always a bit shaky after a storm. I worry about taking too much from you."

"You won't. I have plenty to give, and I always get it back."

He did. Time was all he needed to replenish himself. I had to rely on the sun for that.

It was approaching twilight, and if Berserkers lay low in the heat of day, they'd be out in the relative cool of night. I'd rather not confront more than the two I already had. "We have to find a new hiding place." I wasn't all that crazy about this dark and stinky garage anyway. "Lower the car and let's go."

He hesitated. "About that." He stepped away from me while folding his arms across his chest. "We can't take the car."

Confused, I asked, "Why not? Couldn't you fix the brakes?"

"Oh, I fixed them good as new, even found the tracking device, not that it matters now." He looked guarded when he added, "There's no voltage left. The air conditioner ate more energy than I thought it would."

My heart dove into my empty stomach. "You mean we're stuck here?"

"Only until we recharge the battery, but it takes sunlight to do that."

I peered out at the darkening sky streaked with Night Rainbows. That would be hours from now. Hands held out to my sides and palms up in a pose of surrender, I said, "Fine. Just get the car down, and I'll help you push it outside."

He stepped over to the wall of tools and flipped a switch. "The lift is powered by a generator I found. We're lucky it still works."

The hydraulic motor hummed and creaked like an orchestra of tortured metal.

"Oh, no." Ian pulled me away from the lift and backed us up a few steps.

"What's wrong?"

"The generator's working, but I think the compressor is faulty. It sounds like—"

The posts holding up the car suddenly dropped into the floor like a broken elevator. The car followed, crashing on the ground with such force it cracked the concrete under its popped tires. The solar panels on the vehicle's roof shattered, spraying shards of glass in every direction. Ian pushed me to the ground and sheltered me with his body.

"Ian?" Heart pulsing in my ears, I slid carefully out from beneath him. He remained facedown on the concrete, and I could see why. The back of his shirt was a bloody mess from glass splinters that had sprayed from the crash.

"How bad is it?" I crouched beside him on the garage floor, my hands shaking as I gently touched his bloody shoulder. "Ian?"

"It just stings a little. I'm fine."

My breathing quickened, and so did my worry. I checked his back, looking for gaping wounds, but didn't see any. They all appeared superficial. "Don't move." I peered out the open door of the garage in search of lurking Berserkers. We were still alone. "Berserkers aren't attracted to blood, are they?"

"Blood? Of course not. Why?"

Images from a dozen old horror movies flashed behind my eyes. One of those women had bitten me, so I couldn't help conjuring up thoughts of zombies and vampires. "Just curious." I walked through the broken glass toward the ruined solar car.

"There must be a first aid kit inside the car, and I need to get us water." It took a few hard tugs on the door handle before it finally opened. I grabbed the case of water, then rummaged in the glove box until I found a kit that contained antiseptic, gauze, tape, tiny scissors and tweezers.

Shoved in a corner of the garage were some old packing blankets like the kind movers used to protect furniture. They were ripped and filthy, smelling strongly of motor oil, and also a bit chewed by rodents…or something. But they would serve my purposes. I folded one up to put under my knees, and the other I slid beneath Ian's upper body. He lay facedown, his arms tucked tight against his sides. He may not have been in much pain now, but he would be. I had to tweeze the glass out of his skin.

I went back to the car and searched beneath the front seat. A man like Nichol impressed me as the self-entitled type, so I was fairly sure he kept his vices close at hand. My fingers encountered something cool and smooth. A bottle. I slid it out into the open and sure enough, a fifth of vodka. Ian would need this.

I twisted the cap off before handing it to him.

He shook his head. "I don't drink. It slows the reflexes."

"This isn't drinking, Ian. It's anesthetic."

He grunted and accepted the bottle, then took a long pull. This obviously wasn't the first time he'd ever indulged, though probably never under these circumstances.

"I used to drink too much," he admitted. "After my family…"

After his wife and child died. I could see how such tragedy might motivate a person to drown his grief in alcohol. "That's understandable."

His lips relaxed in a soft smile. "Those memories don't hurt as much now. Moving around brought me peace, and helping those who needed what I could do did a lot to ease my mind."

"You have nothing to feel guilty about," I told him. "You didn't cause the storms."

"But what if I could have stopped them?"

I shook my head. "Not then, but you might be able to now. After what we just did together, I'm willing to explore how far we can go. We're strongest when we work as a team."

Too distracted to consider much more than dulling his pain, he ignored me and guzzled more vodka.

Using scissors from the kit, I snipped away his shirt and gently peeled the fabric from his skin. He hissed in a lungful of air, and his whole body tightened like a coiled spring. Once I had the shirt off, he exhaled a slow breath of relief, his muscles going slack beneath my hands.

He didn't squirm or yell, not even when I used a bottle of water to clean the blood away, and then antiseptic to sterilize his wounds. There had to have been more than a dozen cuts, but none were especially deep. The powerful muscles of his back rippled as I plucked the offending splinters from his tan skin. My fingers skimmed lightly over his flesh, and he shivered.

"Tickles," he mumbled into the pad where his face was buried. He didn't laugh. His tone was matter-of-fact, as if stating what time it was or pointing out the color of the sky. I liked that about him. Ian was a straight shooter, and despite his bitterness, he had a good heart. As my mom would say, a good heart trumped everything.

When I was finished tending to his back, I cocked my head to admire my work. Not bad. "How does that feel?" He answered me with a muffled snore.

11

"Why did you let me drink so much?" Ian groaned as he sat holding his head.

"You were in pain. Then you passed out. I thought you would sleep it off," I said, pacing the garage floor.

He smirked at me. "Do you know what a hangover's like?"

"No." And I hoped I'd never find out.

He shifted his position and winced. His back had too many puncture wounds to bandage properly, so I'd left them uncovered, allowing them to scab naturally. Only problem was that whenever he moved, the wounds split open and he'd start bleeding again.

My focus shifted to the heap of metal that had once been a powerful solar car. "We need another one of those."

Ian snorted. "We walk back to Lodgepole to get your father's SUV, or we use bicycles to get there. Two wheels are better than none."

I jerked my head at the open doorway. "Let's go find us some bikes."

He grimaced. "We should wait until daylight when the Berserkers crawl back into their holes. We've had enough trouble from them for one day."

Point taken. Besides, he was in no condition to fight off wild people. "Okay, but in the meantime I want to figure out a way to channel the power of the sun."

Ian's thoughtful scowl made the scar through his eyebrow

more pronounced. "You're looking for a way to end your addiction."

He understood the feeling of helplessness that came with being out of control, so he knew what I needed. I seated myself on the floor beside him. "If I can tap into a direct source of power, I won't have to siphon off yours, and I won't have to depend so much on the sparks."

"You want to use the sun itself?"

I nodded. "I can't control my forecasts, but if I miss a storm, I shouldn't have to go through withdrawals every time. I want kinetic energy when I need it and not be forced to accept a few paltry sparks that come and go on a whim." I warmed up to my own conviction as I imagined how my life would change. I could choose which storms I chased. I could end my slavery to the sparks.

"And you need my help."

"We're far stronger together than we could ever be apart. Come with me."

He frowned. "Where are we going?"

"To the surface of the sun."

His snarly smile gave me goose bumps. "Do you have a supersonic, heat-resistant rocket ship I don't know about?"

"Sort of." I pointed at my head. "It's in here."

He laughed. "It must be, because you have quite an imagination."

"Except that it's not my imagination, Ian. When I forecast, I get visual messages from the sun inside my head: a time and a place. So why not visit the sender the same way?"

Looking puzzled, he asked, "With your mind? But I don't receive messages from the sun."

"Doesn't matter. You're a powerful Kinetic who got your

power from sun sparks. Whether you like it or not, you're linked to the source of those sparks. You can join me."

"Inside your head?" he asked, his tone incredulous.

"You and I have a bond. We've both felt the power working through us when we engage our emotions through physical touch. That's what triggers it." The thought of his consciousness merged with mine gave me an unexpected thrill. "With your weather ability, you may even discover a way to stop the storms. Trust me, okay?"

"Of course." His grin told me he'd go along with whatever I wanted, but it didn't necessarily say he believed me. I'd just have to prove to him, and to myself, that I was right.

We both sat Indian style, and I swiveled around to face him, motioning for him to turn his body so that our knees were touching. "I'll let my mind touch the flares on the sun's surface, extract their energy. Once you and I merge, you'll be able to watch."

He whistled. "That's a tall order for something you've never done before."

I shrugged. "Who says it's never been done? It's just never been done by me. Or by you." We both knew there were other Kinetics, so it wasn't a stretch to believe that one or more of them had tried tapping energy from the sun. And possibly succeeded. "Ready?"

I closed my eyes and held my hands out to him. He laced his fingers with mine, the heels of our palms pressed together. The sensation was electric, and not just because of our abilities. It went further than that. I was connected to him in a way that went beyond the twining of kinetic energy. I sensed his heartbeat through my hands, and it thrummed in rhythm with my own. It felt good. It felt right.

I opened my eyes for a split second, just to see his face. He stared at me, his eyes smiling, though his lips were not. There was a liquid sheen to his gaze that gave my heart a jolt. He felt what I did. And best of all, I saw the joy it gave him.

My eyes closed again as I summoned calm to my quickening heart. I focused on the sun, saw it as a place rather than a symbol of death. Its purpose was to give life, not take it away, and I sought the positive energy that had given me the gift to forecast its storms.

Ian's power flowed into me like water from a faucet. A hum of energy slithered over my skin and tingled down my spine as it tugged my consciousness upward, through the ceiling, above the building, hurtling me high into the sky toward outer space. The feeling of weightlessness was unlike anything I'd ever experienced: Free from my body and from the baked planet that died little by little every day. But I wasn't free of my need for sparks.

As my consciousness approached the giant, flaming orb at the center of our solar system, I wasn't afraid. It was as if part of the sun lived inside me and was returning home to visit. I felt no heat, no cold, no physical sensation of any kind. I was pure energy, and the sun embraced me like a mother embraces her child.

Ian was there with me. I could feel him settle calmly inside my head, watching everything I saw. I sensed his wonder but also his acceptance of what was happening. He shared in my experience and had the same sense of familiarity as I did. The sun was inside us both because it had made us what we'd become.

Giant flares shot from the sun's surface like graceful fountains of fire. It reminded me of volcanic eruptions.

This incredible journey fed me what I needed. My soul gobbled up the sun's fire like a treat I couldn't get enough of.

I felt Ian reach out beyond our link to explore the fiery surface, testing the limits of his power, but he must have gone too close. He yanked back, and our link snapped like a rubber band.

My consciousness plummeted back to earth. The force of my return jolted me loose from Ian, and I sensed something wrong. One look at Ian's hands and I nearly screamed. He had blisters on his fingers.

"Oh, my God! Did the sun do that?" I asked, knowing it couldn't have happened any other way. "I had no idea…"

He grimaced and held his hands out, palms up. "I shouldn't have gone so close."

"This is all my fault." I grabbed the first aid cream from the kit and started applying it to his hands. "I didn't think this would happen."

"My power isn't strong enough to stop the storms, even combined with yours. I need more…" He seemed to struggle for the right words, but I wasn't sure there were any. "Juju? Mojo? Hell, I don't know. Just…more."

I blew on his fingers. "How does that feel?"

He grinned. "Better. Don't stop."

The smile I gave him was a half-hearted one. I should have known this wouldn't be easy. It was mind over matter, and I had no clue how that worked. I understood, though, what he meant when he said he needed *more*. For the two of us to take on stopping a sun storm, we needed backup. We needed *more* people like us. And there was only one place that could provide them.

That clinched it. We couldn't afford to wait until daylight to find bicycles for peddling the ten miles back to Lodgepole. We had to step it up and find the bikes now. Had tapping into the sun cured my addiction to sun sparks? Probably not. I felt stronger, yes, but my energy was already starting to drain. If I got hit with a premonition for a new storm, I no longer had the means to chase it. Getting the Trooper was my only hope.

12

"One of the stores at the outlet mall used to sell bicycles," I told Ian as we walked together down the sidewalk. I felt thankful for the light offered by the Night Rainbows.

"It's dangerous to be out in the open at this time of night," he said.

"I know, but we need to be mobile soon as possible. How are your hands?

Ian stretched his greased-up fingers. "Not bad. There are only a couple of blisters on each of them, and they don't burn anymore." Which was odd considering it had happened less than an hour ago. Maybe it was because the burns were psychosomatic and not physical.

We'd abandoned Nichol's solar car after retrieving every useful item we could carry. The agent had had two backpacks in the trunk, one filled with clothes and the other with food and water. If we could just find a couple of bikes, we'd be set.

"Discount Mart!" I pointed at the stark rectangular building without a single window intact. "My mom and I used to go there all the time for school clothes when I was a kid. They carry everything you can think of, including bicycles."

Ian tossed me a quick look and kept on walking. "Yeah, I know. There's not much left in there now. It's been ransacked, but we'll take a quick look. I want to show you something inside anyway."

"What?"

"You'll see."

We stepped over jagged chunks of glass that had once been display windows. Even the carpet inside had been ripped up. However, most of the signs inside were still standing.

I stepped quickly through the women's clothing department. Broken hangers were strewn across the floor and wedged under display shelves. I had a sudden memory of when my mother and I were browsing through dresses, looking for something new for her to wear for my parents' anniversary dinner. She'd been so happy back then. "Hey," Ian said gently. "You okay?"

My eyes stung with unshed tears. I wished I could be strong the way my mother had been, to see the good in everything the way she had, to imagine a bright future when the world would be normal again. My throat clogged with a sudden surge of grief. I grieved for my mother, for friends I'd lost to either disease or disaster, and for the town I'd called home since the day I was born. Most of it was gone now. My sick and confused father was all I had left, and I loved him dearly.

Though I missed my mother, I hadn't cried for her since the day she died, but Ian's concern touched me to the core, and I couldn't hold back any longer. I let the tears flow, silent and hot, and the release was like a long-needed cleansing of the darkness I'd bottled up for too long. He wrapped an arm around my shoulder and pulled me close. I buried my face in his chest and sobbed, as if wringing every last bit of loss from my heart.

The pounding of feet brought me up short, and I jerked away from Ian to peer in the direction it was coming from. A small group of half-naked, filthy Berserkers trotted our way.

I'd had as much as I could take from these people. They were pathetic, yes, but they were also dangerous, and I'd be damned if I'd end up collateral damage in one of their savage tantrums. Rage flamed through my veins, and I shook all over. I grabbed a bent clothing pole off the floor and hoisted it over my shoulder like a baseball bat.

I hardly recognized my own voice when I screamed, "Bring it on, bitches!"

The Berserkers gawked at me in surprise. Maybe they thought I'd become one of them, and at the moment, they weren't far off. All I knew was that I refused to add one more tragedy to the toppling stack that had become my life. I swung my metal pole at the air in front of them.

"I didn't take your Johnny!" I screamed, then swung the pole in the other direction. "I didn't burn down your freakin' house!" I pounded the pole on the floor, releasing the frustration of having lost so much and knowing I'd never get it back.

The little group actually backed up a step. I lunged forward, growling like something feral, and they turned to beat tracks out of the store.

I blinked at their retreat and tossed the pole down, my chest heaving and my blood pounding between my temples. I thought my heart would bang its way outside my chest.

I heard clapping from behind me and twisted around to see Ian grinning.

"Well done. Remind me never to go berserk around you."

Dazed by my own outburst, I felt suddenly drained. I wobbled on my feet, and Ian rushed over to steady me. "Let's get you someplace where you can calm down."

I nodded and let him guide me toward the back of the store and a set of stairs leading down to a stock room. He slid a flashlight out from his backpack and aimed the light at the shadows. There were mostly empty boxes and trash down here, but the smell was horrendous. We came upon a closed door with a metal bar wedged across the frame and a heavy padlock attached to a chain that held the whole thing together. Ian dug in his pocket and withdrew a key that he slipped in the lock. The shank popped free.

He opened the door and ushered me inside. Peering out into the stockroom, he swept the flashlight's beam from one end to the other before slamming the door shut and relocking it from the inside.

"Wow, you have quite an elaborate safeguard."

"One can never be too careful when keeping out Berserkers."

"I'm guessing this place is yours?" I took in the sparse furnishings of a room that appeared well lived in. It was filled with all the comforts of home: bed, dresser, table, kitchen area. "You did this?"

"Yep." He shrugged off his backpack and gestured for me to hand mine over. He tossed both in the corner of what appeared to have been an employee break room. There was even a three-legged vending machine leaning against the wall. "I lived here before moving to Lodgepole. I had to fight a few Berserkers for it, but I can be quite persuasive when need be."

I knew that for a fact. "Why did you leave here?"

"I was looking for someplace to call home, a community to live in." He turned a slow circle where he stood. "Living in the basement of an abandoned store in a town full of Berserkers isn't my idea of home."

I couldn't blame him for leaving. I wouldn't want to live here, either. "It's a lot more comfortable than the garage."

He shook his head. "This place is crawling with Berserkers. I figured a locked car with AC would be safer than this dump."

I gave him a dubious look. "Really?"

He nodded. "There was no telling what would be waiting

for us in here. We're damn lucky we didn't get ambushed."
He waved a hand at the chair and the cot. I chose the cot and
flopped down onto it with my forearm slung over my eyes.
He handed me a bottle of water. "Make yourself at home."

"Thanks."

He sat in the chair across from me and pulled the fifth of
vodka from one of the backpacks.

"Are you really going to drink more of that?" It bothered
me that he felt a need for more alcohol so soon.

"No." He twisted off the cap. "You are."

When he offered me the bottle, I pushed it away. "I'll pass,
thanks."

"I'm not trying to get you drunk, if that's what you're worried about."

I gasped. He presumed way too much. "I already told you
I trusted you. What makes you think I changed my mind?"

Ignoring my question, he waggled the bottle at me. "Just
a couple of sips. Your nerves are frayed, and you're wound
tighter than Ebenezer Scrooge at Christmas. Consider it medicine."

I'd only ever had one drink my entire life and that was
at my high school graduation party nearly eight years ago. I
hadn't gotten drunk, but I did end up feeling warm and fuzzy
all over. I could use some of that right now. "Just a sip." I accepted the bottle and tilted it to my lips. The vodka felt cool
against my tongue and tasted kind of sweet, but once it reached
the back of my throat I almost choked on my tonsils.

Ian joined me on the cot and gave my back a couple of pats.
"That wasn't so bad, was it?"

I shook my head, still sputtering, and thrust the bottle back
at him. "Yeah, it was. I've had enough, thank you."

I closed my eyes, and the pounding in my head began to

ease. A hazy glow settled in my stomach, making me glad I'd only taken one sip. That was plenty. In fact, it was just right.

"How do you feel now?" Ian asked.

"Mmm…" Thirstier than usual, I gulped from my water bottle. "Relaxed. Fearless." I took his hands gently in mine and inspected his burns. I ran my finger lightly over one diminished blister. "I think I should tap into the sun again. Want to come with me?"

"You can't be serious."

"I'll be gentle. I promise."

His expression grew solemn. "I believe you. You're one of the gentlest people I know."

I felt suddenly less playful than I had a minute ago. The vodka had calmed my nerves, but it wasn't enough to drive away the sinking feeling in my gut. The world wouldn't get any better without help. "You don't want to join me?"

He shook his head, his gaze burning into mine. He skimmed his fingers over my bare arms, and I shivered. "But there's something I *do* want."

My heart thudded in my throat. His skin touching mine made me tingle in all the right places, and I wanted more. I sensed his desire, and I felt the same toward him, but I wanted to hear him say it. "And that is?"

His hand slid over my shoulder to my neck, where he cupped the back of my head. Leaning forward, his chin slightly tilted, he pressed his lips to mine. They were firm, yet supple in how they molded to the shape of my mouth, and there was a lingering scent of vodka on his breath that didn't bother me. I wondered if the smell combined with the small amount I'd sipped was responsible for the dizziness inside my head.

He drew me in like a magnet, but this time I didn't overthink it. I knew him better now, and I wanted to surrender myself to him. It wasn't about control or lack of it, but about filling a need we had for each other. I was more than okay with that.

I caressed the side of his face with the palm of my hand, moving my lips against his, as his mouth parted and he stroked me gently with his tongue. Our upper bodies were pressed tightly against each other now, his heart thrumming against my chest. It created a primal melody that quickened my breathing.

A sudden yearning to get closer had me leaning into him harder. He moved backward on the cot, lowering his back to the thin mattress, and I followed. I was on top of him now, and the thin barrier of my shirt lay between my breasts and his naked chest. Unable to stand the separation, I peeled my shirt up over my head and tossed it to the floor. We both moaned as our bare skin slid against each other, our kisses becoming fevered with need.

Our hands roamed over the hills and valleys of each other's bodies, exploring and pleasing, savoring and wanting. I could get happily lost in time right here and never leave this room. If only I could lose myself in passion, to feel alive and forget the horrors outside these walls. For this moment, it was just Ian and me, in a world inside an abandoned employee break room. A world we made just for us.

My light head felt nice at first, but then it became filled with heat, and not the passionate kind. A poorly timed premonition was on its way.

I relaxed against Ian, letting the sensation wash over me, but I focused on staying in control of it this time. "Ian," I whispered against his mouth.

"Hm?" His chest heaved against mine, and desire swelled

beneath my skin, just as his desire made him hard. But I had
to resist. I had to pay attention.

"A premonition," I said.

"Now?"

"Yes."

He started to sit up, but I pushed him back down. "Don't
move. I need you with me. I need your strength to tap into
the sun before it taps into me." I laid my head on his chest,
letting his heartbeat lull me into a meditative state. I saw the
date stamp, two days from now, but the location was unclear.
No map presented itself, but the entire Earth loomed like a
giant hot air balloon.

"Tell me what you see," Ian said softly.

I was looking down at the state of Colorado from a far
enough distance that the Rocky Mountains appeared as
scribbles in the sand. This was well beyond my ability's two-
hundred-mile limit. My focus on the entire North American
continent, I held the image in my mind and watched. A solar
flare shot through the atmosphere, and I sensed more than
saw the surge of energy it sent to the earth's magnetic poles.
That's how the Bell Ringer had wreaked havoc the first time,
only what I was seeing now appeared much worse.

"What's happening?" Ian asked.

"The apocalypse." I sucked in a breath as I witnessed the
unfolding devastation. The Earth jerked on its axis, causing
earthquakes, tidal waves, windstorms, volcanic eruptions and
incredible floods all around the planet. Volcanic ash spewed
into the atmosphere, blocking the sun. The Earth shook, and
chunks of mountains crumbled like rocks made of sand, while
giant tidal waves enveloped every shoreline. Massive fires
sprang from every location not covered by water, and powerful winds fed the flames to make them ferocious devourers

of anything left standing. Nothing could survive such a catastrophe. There wouldn't be a single living thing left when it was over.

Tears filling my eyes, I told Ian what I foresaw.

13

I couldn't get out of there fast enough, and not because I didn't want to be with Ian. I wanted him more than anything. But because I felt desperate to return to Lodgepole.

Ian looked bewildered. "Where are you going?" he asked as he watched me tug my T-shirt over my head and shrug on one of the backpacks.

"Back to the hospital for my father's SUV." I threw the other pack at him. "We have to get to the base as quickly as possible. If they don't know what's about to happen, I have to tell them." And could they stop it? That's what I had to find out.

Ian said nothing. He couldn't tell me not to worry, that I was imagining things, because we knew for a fact it was real. I'd seen it with my mind's eye, and there was no obvious way to stop it. The apocalypse was coming, and she was a raving bitch with murder on her mind.

"We still don't have bikes. How do you plan to get there?"

"Walk. Run. I don't care, I'm just going." I yanked at the barred door. "A little help, please?"

Ian narrowed his eyes. "Sure." He brushed passed me and unlocked the door, then opened it wide. Stepping aside to make room, he crossed his arms and waited.

"You're coming with me, aren't you?"

Scowling, he said, "Are you inviting me? Or commanding me?"

I massaged my temples and struggled to adjust my attitude. I needed to lighten up. "I'm sorry. It's not like me to bark orders. You've done so much to help my father and me, and here I am being a total bitch. But after what I saw in my premonition…"

He hesitated. His expression softened as he drew me into his arms. "I know, and it's okay. We're both on edge. If we start walking now, we should arrive at the hospital in about three hours."

I heaved a relieved sigh. "You mean more to me than I ever imagined anyone could. I don't want to lose you."

He kissed the top of my head. "You won't. I'm here for as long as you need me."

I needed him forever, and forever was just about up.

After an hour of walking on the deserted highway, I had to stop and rest. Ian and I hadn't spoken much since our special time together that had ended way too soon. We both kept our own counsel as we reviewed our separate lives and made peace with a world that was drawing to an end. I had no major regrets other than meeting a man I could fall in love with if given half a chance. But instead we'd be saying goodbye forever.

The two of us sat in silence on the warm asphalt at the center of the empty, silent highway. Night Rainbows lit up the horizon on all sides, and the hypnotic waves of color helped soothe my agitated mind.

"What are you thinking?" Ian asked.

I shrugged. "How tired I am. And that I'm relieved my father doesn't know what's about to happen. Ignorance really can be bliss."

He reached for my hand and pulled me closer so that I could lay my head on his shoulder. He whispered, "Thank you."

I lifted my head to stare into his face. "For what?"

"For opening my mind to the possibility of a brighter future."

Nearly choking on the water I sipped, I said, "You do realize the end is coming, right?"

He nodded, and in his usual calm, matter-of-fact tone, he said, "Yes, but you gave me a taste of what the world has to offer, even when there are only a few good things left in it. When it comes to you, Sarah, I'll gladly take a few days of wonderful over a lifetime of horrible. Now I can die a happy man."

Why did he have to be so amazing? I blinked and held my breath to stop myself from weeping. My smile wobbled, and I couldn't control the quaver in my voice. "I...I don't know what to say."

"I don't expect you to say anything. I just wanted you to know."

I wanted to kiss him again, to hold him close and breathe him in, taste his skin, and do a lot more than touch him. But my fantasy was cut short when a flash of headlights shone up ahead. A car? Here? It was coming fast, too.

Ian and I jumped up and scrambled to the side of the road. The driver had seen us and was slowing down. I had a bad feeling all of a sudden, and from the way Ian gripped my hand, he was feeling it, too.

"Run!" he said.

We tore off into the barren field that ran alongside the highway. The ground was rocky and uneven, and I struggled to keep up. Ian tugged me along, and I knew I had to be slowing him down.

I tripped over something in our path—a stump or a rock, I couldn't tell—and went flying. I landed on my shoulder.

When I rolled onto my knees, preparing to get up and run again, I had an abrupt change of heart. It was pointless to run. There was nowhere to go.

Ian trotted back to where I sat with my arms wrapped around my knees. He helped me to my feet. "What are you doing?"

"Giving up."

We both glanced back at the highway. The car that looked exactly like the one we'd stolen from Nichol had driven off the road and was rolling toward us at walking speed. The person driving wasn't too concerned about us running away.

The car door swung open, and a tall man stepped out wearing the same style shiny black raincoat that Nichol had worn. He had on a hat, too, but his was a fedora. His gray chinstrap beard was in dire need of a trim, and he wore a gold hoop in one ear. It didn't take a mastermind to figure out this was Nichol's partner, Charles Jaginski.

"You almost missed us," Ian said, his voice laced with sarcasm.

"GPS tracking is genius. You stopped the signal, but not before I locked onto where it originated. I took a chance you'd still be in the area, and here you are." The agent held up what looked like a rifle big enough to take down an elephant. "I'm not gonna have to use this on you, am I?"

"Depends," I said, feeling either brave or stupid. Probably both. "Does it electrocute people?"

"What?" Charles Jaginski looked genuinely perplexed. "Why the hell would I want to electrocute anyone?"

I glared at him. "Your partner is into it, so I thought you were, too."

"That's *ex*-partner. Nichol is a damn idiot who's lost the few marbles he had rolling around that nearly empty head of his." Jaginski set the rifle on the ground and leaned it against the car. "Stunners are for self-defense only. We don't hurt people. Our mission is to help them."

"You're a funny man, Agent Jaginski," I said. "We know you're a slaver. You spilled the beans in the phone conversation we weren't supposed to hear."

"Call me Jag," the agent said.

"You going to sell us to the highest bidder now?" I asked.

Arms crossed, he said, "All depends on what you can do. You're both Kinetics?"

"You wouldn't be here if you didn't suspect we were," Ian said.

Jag retrieved the rifle from the ground and cocked it. "Wanna see what *this* can do?"

"Sure." I stiffened, ready for anything. "Shoot."

"Like hell," Ian said, standing in front of me to block Jaginski's target.

Jaginski aimed the gun to the side of me and pulled the trigger. A giant net shot out of the barrel and landed harmlessly on the ground beside me.

"Nichol obviously gave you the wrong impression of our branch of the Secret Service." Jag spat on the ground. "The net's for rounding up Berserkers, but I admit to using it on a few crazy Kinetics with delusions of grandeur."

My thoughts immediately spun back to the run-in I'd had in Denver. I scrutinized the agent. "I thought you wanted to go into business with Nichol, be a slaver like him."

He barked a laugh. "Sounded convincing, did I? That was bullshit. I've been trying to bring Nichol in for months. He wouldn't listen to reason, so tricking him was my next option."

"There's no need," Ian said. "He's been exposed to the sparks."

Jaginski's eyes squinted in the light of the Night Rainbows that cast eerie lines of color across his face. "Damn. No kidding?"

"No kidding," I said, feeling a mild twinge of guilt for my part in Nichol's encounter with the sparks. "So our question to you is, what's up with the military base in Colorado Springs? Is the government experimenting on Kinetics?"

He grinned, showing brilliant white teeth. "Hell, no. Is that what Nichol told you?"

Ian and I shared a look, then Ian said, "You knew we were Kinetics before you even came looking for us. Why else would you bother?"

"For one thing, I came to retrieve the quarter-million-dollar car you stole. It's government property," Jag said.

A quarter-million? Wow. I had no idea my dad's design was worth so much.

Combing his fingers through his hair, Ian circled in place, which I knew to be a sign of his discomfort. "About the car. It's totaled."

The smile dropped from Jag's face.

"Sorry," Ian added.

The corners of the agent's mouth turned down as if he'd just tasted something bitter. He cleared his throat. "Forget the car. I knew you were Kinetics because that's the only reason you'd associate with Nichol. I suppose you could have been one of his customers lookin' to hook up with a Kinetic, but those people have all kinds of money and wouldn't need to boost a car."

"Deductive reasoning," I said, admiring how Jag's mind worked.

"So..." Jag drew out the word as he looked from Ian to me and back again. "You have no vehicle. You're both Kinetics.

Therefore, I'd like to offer you a place to live where you'll be guaranteed protection from people like Nichol."

"What would be the point?" I asked.

He looked puzzled. "The point would be a better life for yourselves."

Ian glared at the agent. "A life that will last only two more days."

Jag jerked his shoulders back. "What are you talking about?"

From the look on his face, he knew *exactly* what we were talking about. "The end of the world."

"You shouldn't know anything about that." Jag scowled down at the ground as if it had disappointed him. "No one but the precogs know, which means one of you is precognitive if you saw what's coming. The Bell Ringer is a flash of static compared to this monster." He lifted his gaze, eyes questioning.

Neither Ian nor I spoke up. Should I trust this guy? I really wanted to. He was the enemy of my enemy, which made him a friend. Right? "I'm—"

"Don't tell him what you are," Ian said to me. He looked at Jag. "First, we need proof you're one of the good guys."

"I can tell you exactly what you saw in your vision. Will that prove it to you?" So he did. He described the volcanic eruptions, tidal waves, earthquakes and floods, where they would happen and the destruction they'd cause.

My breathing hitched, and I had to sit back down in the dirt before I fell down. It was as if he'd witnessed it right along with me. "You saw it, too?"

Jag shook his head. "We have ten precogs at the base, and they all saw the same thing. They were interviewed separately, and then each agent was briefed with their intel. Our mission is to find the only two Kinetics able to stop it. There's been a full-scale search for weeks, but no one's had any luck. We hope to find them before it's too late."

Two days isn't enough time to do *anything*, let alone find two needles in a haystack. The air suddenly became too thin to breathe. "What kind of Kinetics?"

Jag gave me a solemn look and answered, "One who can control weather, and a forecaster who predicts sun storms."

My stomach lurched. A forecaster of sun storms. A weather Kinetic. He claimed that's who they needed to prevent the apocalypse, but what did that entail? Hurling us into a boiling volcano? A blood sacrifice to the sun god?

Ian asked the same question that was churning inside my head. "Why only those two?"

Jag sighed and rolled his eyes. "It's damn spooky if you ask me, but all I've been told is it has nothing to do with science."

"Then what does it have to do with?" I asked.

"Astrology. Numerology. Theology. Mythology. And a few other 'ologies' that don't make any normal kind of sense. In my opinion, explanations should be cut-and-dried, black and white. The only thing gray about me is my beard." He looked between us again. "So which one of you is the precog?"

I lifted my hand, then dropped it. "I'm not really precognitive. I can only predict…certain things, so it's not the same."

The big man held his hands up, as if preparing to give a sermon. "There are several types of clairvoyant Kinetics. Some can forecast earthquakes, tidal waves and volcanoes, but it's unusual for them to have visions like the precogs do, except that's exactly what's been happening. The impending cataclysm is global, and not a single forecaster has been denied a preview. I bet even the forecaster of sun storms got a good glimpse of what's coming." He gave me a shrewd stare. "I've heard rumors there's one here in Colorado."

I swallowed. A deep flush heated my face from the neck up, and I locked eyes with Jag. He knew. He'd known before he even got here. "When did you realize it was me?" I asked him.

"I had my suspicions, but didn't know for sure until just now." He directed his attention to Ian. "Weatherman?"

Ian smiled and held up one finger. "The gang's all here."

"Then what are we waiting for?" Jag opened the passenger side door. "Hop in and let's go!"

I thought about my father. I wanted him with me. Plus, I doubted Jag realized Nichol was still alive and in Lodgepole. "Nichol's not dead."

"He's not? Good lord," Jag said and leaned against the car. "Are you telling me he's a Kinetic now? We're all in for a world of hurt if he is."

Well, crap. I hadn't considered the possibility, but he could be. Nichol's fever had barely started when we'd left him. I watched Ian circle where he stood and knew he was thinking the same thing.

"We don't know if he is or isn't," I told Jag. "He was very sick the last time we saw him, but that's how it always starts. I had the fever for a week before I got better and turned into… this."

"How long's it been since he was exposed?" Jag asked.

"Less than a day," Ian said.

"Then we still have time. Get in." He climbed in the car and started the engine. "He's sick now, which means he's weak. I want to get him back to the base before he turns, *if* he turns. Who knows what kind of a Kinetic he'd turn out to be?"

Jag called ahead to let the base know we were coming. They'd have sent a helicopter to get us if one were available, but instead they were sending backup just in case something went awry with Nichol's transport. Their main concern was getting Ian and me safely ensconced at Kinetic headquarters. They even said my dad was welcome to stay with me.

It was approaching daylight, so I didn't expect to see many people on the street, but as we drove slowly through Lodgepole, I sensed their absence. No messengers peddled bikes over curbs and around the sharp corners of buildings, no one rushed home from work to beat the sun, no kids played kickball in the street. It was like a ghost town.

"Not many folks live here, huh?" Jag said as he drove us through the alley in back of the hospital.

"A lot of them have moved away." I let myself remember my missing friends and neighbors, and wished there had been a way to keep in touch. I didn't even know where most of them had ended up, or even if they were still alive. "The grass always looks greener somewhere else." *Grass?* I laughed silently at the irony.

Jag grinned. "With only one randomly published newspaper, it's natural for people to seek out other ways to get their news, or whatever else they're looking for."

"Speaking for myself, I drifted from town to town for a long time looking for answers," Ian said.

"And it appears you found them. Right here." Jag winked at me, and I feigned interest in the closed garage door of the ambulance bay. Not that it mattered, but was it that obvious how Ian and I felt about each other?

"Okay, here's the plan," Jag said. "I'll bring Nichol out through the back. I'd rather not alert the public just in case he's already turned. I don't anticipate any trouble, but I like being prepared."

He parked the black SUV alongside the chain-link fence opposite the garage bay. He looked at me, then at Ian. "Ready to go in?"

"The sooner we get this over with, the better," Ian said, and followed Jag out of the car.

I got out and trotted to catch up with them but stopped with a sudden afterthought. "You go on ahead. I need to get something from the car first."

"See you inside." Ian gave me his lopsided smile, and I blushed. He knew how to push my buttons.

I rummaged through my backpack until I found the apple I'd saved from the lunch Nichol had inadvertently left for us. I wanted my dad to have it. The last time he'd seen me he'd thought I was possessed by a demon, and I might have to bribe him into leaving with me. An apple could do the trick.

I was just zipping up the pack when an explosion nearly burst my eardrums. I ducked down and saw pieces of concrete and wood fly by, some of it hitting the car and rocking it so hard it balanced briefly on two wheels. It fell back down with a jarring thud. Thank God the car was storm-proof and could repel just about anything. What the hell had just happened?

I lifted my head to peer out the window. The garage door had exploded off the bay, and flames engulfed the inside.

14

"Ian," I gasped, the air clinging to my throat without making it down to my lungs. "Ian?" I leaped out of the car and hit the ground running, stopping before I reached the inferno that sucked all the oxygen from the air. Smoke billowed from the gaping hole left by the explosion.

I coughed and tried to get closer, squinting my eyes against the acrid fumes of burning car parts and tire rubber. Another explosion knocked me off my feet, and I rolled over backward to get clear of flying shrapnel. "Ian!" I screamed into the fire that gobbled my words like candy. "Ian!"

Staring into the flames, I tried to make out any figures inside, but no one could have survived such a conflagration. Fire filled every inch of space there was. The brilliant orange-and-yellow flares reminded me of the sun that hovered just above the horizon like a neon sign that announced: Ian is dead.

"No!" I screamed. "No, no, no!" I again tried to brave the flames but smelled burning hair and realized it was mine. Brushing away the sparks, I stumbled backward to get clear of the inferno.

I stood paralyzed, staring into the blaze. Just as we were about to mend the world and have a life together, I lost him. Ian was gone.

The flames shot higher, spreading up the sides of the building. I had to get inside and help people get out. I had to save my father!

I willed my feet to move, tears clogging my throat as my grief threatened to overtake me. I wouldn't let it. I couldn't. Ian would have never let his emotions get in the way of doing what had to be done. He was selfless, and that's what I had to be.

My eyes filled and blurred my vision, but I could see well enough to run to the front of the building.

Inside, over a dozen people rushed up and down the halls, pushing wheelchairs filled with patients, some of them victims of Sun Fever. They wheeled past me as if they didn't see me. Their obvious goal was to get outside and away from the fire. Smoke billowed up the stairwell leading from the basement and ambulance bay. I was certain fire would soon follow.

I flew up the stairs, taking them two at a time, as I raced to my father's room. Heart pounding with adrenaline and pain, I found my father lying on his bed asleep. How the hell could anyone leave a sick man sleeping inside a burning building? I spotted a wheelchair out of the corner of my eye, but it already had someone in it. The uniform told me it was a nurse, but she was too still, her head drooped forward and her hands folded in her lap. I went to nudge her awake, to yell at her for neglecting my father, but when I grabbed her shoulder, her body collapsed limply to the side. Her head leaned in the same direction, and that's when I saw the hypodermic syringe protruding from her neck.

The door to the room abruptly slammed shut, and someone behind me said, "I'm surprised you made it."

Agent Sam Nichol stood in front of the closed door inside my father's room and glared at me. He looked more ill than when I had seen him last. The rash had spread, and the top of his head appeared covered in purple paint. Bloodshot eyes glowered from shadowed sockets, and dried blood encrusted his lips. How was he able to even stand?

"The doc was supposed to keep you sedated." My gaze flicked to my father and back to Nichol. "Did you cause the explosion?"

"One thing at a time." He held a cell phone in one hand and a hypodermic syringe in the other. His voice was a graveled croak that I could barely understand. "I told your doc I was afraid of needles so he had a nurse give me pills."

Pills he hadn't swallowed. Never underestimate a dying man desperate for revenge. I made a move toward my father, but Nichol stepped in front of me and sat on my father's bed. "So this is the inventor of our storm-chasing solar cars, eh?" Without a glance at my dad, he added, "It's an honor to meet you, Mr. Daggot."

My dad didn't move or speak. "You better not have hurt him."

"Nah." Nichol jerked a look at the cell phone in his hand. "Your dad's a sound sleeper. He didn't even flinch when I helped Nurse Nightingale over there take a nap."

Nichol was probably too weak to fight me off, but he'd positioned himself too close to my dad, and I was afraid of what he'd do with that syringe. I knew he'd use it if I tried to leave the room. I was stuck.

The madman studied me. "Someone's been crying."

Bastard. I swiped furiously at my face.

"That explosion was meant for both of you, yet you survived and your boyfriend didn't." He grinned.

His image was distorted by the tears standing in my eyes. I gritted my teeth and said, "You can hardly walk. How did you make it down to the basement to set a bomb?"

"I get around pretty good when I ignore the pain. No one

here expected a dying man with Sun Fever to wander, but I did." He grimaced, and his eye twitched. "The Secret Service is trained well in all types of combat, including how to make explosives. A hospital is loaded with every ingredient I need to make a bomb powerful enough to blow half this town off the map. The bomb downstairs went off when the bay door opened. What I have here—" he held up the cell phone "—is a remote detonator that will explode a bomb set to blow this building sky-high."

I panted, my shock and terror driving the breath from me. "And you along with it?" To hell, I hoped.

"Of course," he said calmly. "I have nothing to live for but this moment. I'm already dead. Now you will be, too."

I didn't get how his sick mind worked. "Why?"

"Because you're who the agency needs to fix the world. You *and* your boyfriend." He chuckled. "Who's dead now, thanks to me, but you'll be joining him soon. I knew you'd come back for your old man." He held up the cell phone to make his point, his thumb poised to press a button on the keypad. "Now you have the unique privilege of dying with me."

I shook my head. "I'm not the only one you'd be killing. Everyone in the world will die."

He smiled a rictus death grin. "I know. They'll all die anyway because the two of you were a package deal. The agency's plan won't work now. It's a lose-lose situation for us all."

My mind buzzed with panic. Did I want to die? No, but if it had to happen, I'd rather die in the apocalypse than get blown up with Nichol. "Are you sure you're dying?"

"Have you taken a good look at me lately?" He turned side to side, mocking a model's pose. "I'm the picture of death."

"How do you know you won't recover?"

"From the fever?" He laughed. "No one does."

"I did."

"But you're a…" His glare softened to a look of realization. "Kinetic."

"You might be one, too." Did I think so? The possibility was there, but I'd kill him before he had a chance to transform. I owed it to Ian. "You'll never know if you blow yourself up."

His frown crimped the map of squiggly rash lines that covered his forehead. He licked his bleeding lips and said softly, "And now that wonder boy is dead, I've blown my chance at life after a full recovery."

The pun wasn't funny, it was tragic. "You know what else you've blown?"

He narrowed his eyes at me.

I abruptly thought of Jag, the kind and thoughtful agent who had obviously been killed in the blast with Ian. I was so torn up over Ian's death that it hadn't registered until now. The lump in my throat grew as my grief compounded. I breathed in deep before telling Nichol, "You blew up your partner, too."

"That's not possible. Jag's in Wyoming." Nichol's face contorted with rage, and he raised his voice a notch. "You brought him here with you?"

"He found Ian and me ten miles outside of town." I secretly enjoyed how this news was getting to him, but I pretended to act concerned. Jag hadn't deserved to die. "Jag was a good man trying to save the world. When we told him what had happened to you, he brought us here so that he could…" *Careful*, I told myself. I was poking at a madman's soft gooey center—if he had one—and it might explode. "He came here to see you."

"You're lying," Nichol said, his tone dangerously low. "Jag hated me."

I tilted my head to one side, a lie poised on my tongue. I

would tell Nichol what he wanted to hear. "He never hated you. He understood you and didn't think you should die without knowing someone cared. But now he's dead because you killed him."

Something on the window behind Nichol drew my attention. It looked like shiny diamonds glued to the glass, but they were moving. Wait. Not diamonds, water. It was raining. How was that possible?

The hand holding the detonator started to shake.

"Jag would want you to recover," I told Nichol, trying to appeal to his survival instinct. Tasting the words before I spoke them, they made my stomach roil with disgust. "It's not too late. We can find another weather Kinetic. There's still time to save the world—"

"There *is* no one else," he growled. "Ian Matthews was the only one." Nichol grabbed my wrist and yanked me to him, turning around so that we both faced the window. His chest pressed against my back, his arm surprisingly strong around my neck. With his other hand he held the detonator out to the side, too far for me to reach. "One of a kind. Both of you. And you're mine now."

I struggled to breathe through my constricted throat while I watched drops of rain slide down the windowpane. Nichol either hadn't seen it or didn't realize what it was, but I knew what it meant. A flash of joy lightened my heart. Rain could only come from one place. Ian. He was alive.

The stink of Nichol's fever-ravaged body was almost more than I could bear. His face felt hot against my cheek. I closed my eyes, thinking about Ian. I sensed his nearness. He used his power to make the rain, and his strong emotions drew me to him. He feared for my life, and I felt his rage directed toward Nichol. I wanted to break away and run, but if I did, the agent would trigger the bomb and we'd all be dead.

"You're crying again. I feel your tears on the side of my face," he whispered against my ear, his scabbed lips scratching my skin. "Don't be afraid. Death will come fast for us both. Like it did for your weatherman."

"Demon! Let her go!"

The unexpected shout from my father startled Nichol, and he dropped the detonator, but he didn't let go of me. He dragged me to the floor with him as he scrambled for his device, which skittered far under the bed.

Nichol made a loud "oomph" when my father landed on his back and encircled his neck with one bony arm that still had enough strength to hang on. "Leave my daughter alone, you freak!" He started punching the top of Nichol's head, and the agent finally released me.

I gasped in the oxygen I'd been denied while in Nichol's death grip. I remembered the syringe and checked the floor to see if he'd dropped that, as well. He hadn't. Nichol gripped it in his fist and swung it backward, stabbing it into my father's leg. My dad howled and rolled off onto the floor.

"Dad!" I rushed to where he'd landed against the wall. He clutched his leg with the syringe still embedded in his flesh. I yanked it free and held it like a weapon against Nichol if he came at me again. But he was still on his hands and knees, straining to reach under the bed for his detonator.

"I couldn't let that demon possess you again." My father's breathing sounded labored, and he slurred his words. I realized then that he'd thought Nichol was responsible for making my eyes glow and smoke trail from my fingers. That's how I'd looked the last time he'd seen me.

I started to tell him there was no demon, but before I could speak he slumped in my arms and went still.

My sense of loss was overpowering. I screamed and lurched to my feet, ready to spring at Nichol and tear his throat out, but I was cut short when the door suddenly banged open. Ian stalked in, his face hard with stone-cold rage. Nichol was still on all fours, half-hidden under the bed. Ian kicked him in the stomach so hard that the madman flipped over to land on his back.

Ian rushed to my side but turned to keep an eye on the agent. He glowered down at Nichol and yelled, "Get up!"

Nichol coughed a spray of blood. He grimaced and said, "You should be dead."

"You wish." Ian pointed the Stunner at Nichol's chest, his eyes still glowing with power as the rain continued to fall in torrents that splattered the window. His strength was directly linked to his emotions, which were off the grid. Eyebrows angled severely down toward the bridge of his nose, it gave him a devilish look that took my breath away. His lips were pressed so tight together they were almost white. The fury in his eyes frightened me. He was like a man possessed.

"I'd kill you if I hadn't promised Jag I'd take you in alive." Ian heaved in a breath, his expanding chest smeared with black soot. His arms were covered by angry red scrapes, and an open gash on his shoulder leaked blood. The explosion hadn't left him unscathed.

My voice cracked when I asked, "Jag didn't make it?" Ian's survival had me hopeful, but I knew the answer before asking. It was a miracle Ian hadn't been killed along with him.

He risked a quick look at me and shook his head, mouthing the word *no.*

Nichol staggered to his feet, empty-handed, and had to

hold on to the bed for balance. "Give me one reason to go with you."

Ian hesitated. "Before Jag died, he said there was a chance you could get help at the base."

The agent sneered. "The sons of bitches only want to take me down."

Neither confirming nor denying it, Ian held the Stunner a bit higher, its electronic muzzle aimed at Nichol. "How does it feel to be on the other side of a gun? I own your ass now." He motioned for Nichol to step in front of him. "Let's go."

The agent appeared to acquiesce by holding his wrists out, waiting for them to be tied. The sick man's face was totally wiped of emotion, and I thought perhaps he'd actually given up this time. I should have known better. He rushed at me, his hands stretched out in front of him, fingers curled, as he screamed at the top of his lungs.

15

Nichol didn't get more than two steps before Ian shot him square in the chest. The agent collapsed to the floor and went into spastic convulsions.

"Did he hurt you?" Ian asked, as he crouched to hold down Nichol, who kicked and thrashed his arms.

"He never touched me." I glanced over at my dad slumped on the floor. My chest tightened with grief. This was too much loss for one day. I glared at Nichol for being the cause.

Nichol's body relaxed and became still. "The charge must have been stronger than I thought." Ian turned the Stunner over in his hands. "I've never used one before. Jag had me get the gun from his car, told me what settings to use."

"I saw the explosion." The memory of it flashed in my mind and brought back the terror. "Everything inside the ambulance bay was on fire. I don't see how you could have escaped."

"I didn't. The impact of the explosion sent Jag and me flying across the room, and we landed under the stairs. I created a bubble around us both, just like I did for you and me during the windstorm."

"How bad was Jag hurt?"

"At first I didn't think he was any worse off than me. I dragged him outside to get us away from the fire and noticed a trail of blood on the ground behind us. He'd been struck by shrapnel. He told me he felt fine, said to get the gun and go inside to find Nichol. But when I went to check on him, he was dead."

I'd hardly known the man, but I'd liked Jag. And I'd trusted him. It made me sad that he was gone. "So you made it rain to put out the fire."

Ian nodded. "It was spreading into the hospital, and I knew you were in there with your father. You must have thought I was dead." Offering me an apologetic look, he added, "I didn't mean to scare you."

I smiled weakly, and my eyes began stinging again. "I'm just so happy you're alive."

He wrapped his arms around me and held me close. I buried my face in his neck that smelled of ashes and burnt tires. I didn't care what he smelled like as long as I had him with me again. It horrified me to think how close I'd come to losing him.

I pulled my head away so that I could say, "It's raining harder than I thought possible. I didn't know you could do that."

"I didn't think I could, but I tried what you did yesterday. I tapped directly into the sun."

I wasn't surprised it had worked for him, but I wished I'd been there to help. The fact he'd succeeded in creating a direct link with the sun was proof he could stop the coming storm. He just couldn't do it alone.

Ian returned his attention to Nichol. "He should be awake by now." He nudged the agent, who didn't respond. He rested two fingers against the pulse in Nichol's neck. "Damn. The man's dead."

"Are you sure?" I knelt on the floor and checked the agent's wrist. "Maybe his fever was too far along for him to take the shock to his system."

"Or…" Ian balanced the gun in his hand. "It's possible Jag had no intention of taking Nichol alive, but couldn't bring himself to tell me I'd have to kill a man."

"I suppose you could argue that Jag did the killing, not you."

"Even though I pulled the trigger?" He raised both eyebrows.

"There is that." I saw movement from the corner of my eye and turned to look at where my father lay. He lifted his head and groaned.

"Dad?" I crawled over to him and grabbed hold of his hand. "Oh, my God, I was afraid you were dead."

His voice a husky whisper, he said, "No, honey. I must have fallen asleep. How did I get on the floor?"

I smiled through my tears. Gut-wrenching grief followed by incredible joy wreaked havoc on my heart. I picked up the hypo I'd dropped when I'd leaped up to lunge at Nichol. The plunger was still extended. My father hadn't been dosed with whatever toxin was in the syringe.

Ian lifted my father in his arms and laid him gently on the bed. "How are you feeling, Mr. Daggot?"

My dad coughed and glanced around the room. "I don't know. I can't remember anything."

"It's okay, Dad," I told him. "You don't have to remember if you don't want to. We're leaving here now, moving to a new home. Starting over."

He scowled. "But your mother…"

I closed my eyes and heaved a sigh of disappointment. "You know that Mom—"

"Is dead?" A gleam of lucidity shone in his rheumy eyes. It was so rare for him to be this coherent, and I wanted it to last forever instead of minutes. "I know that, Sarah. But she wouldn't want us to leave Lodgepole. This has been your home since the day you were born."

I smiled and cupped his cheek with my hand. "We'll come back to visit, maybe even help rebuild the town when the world is back to normal." I wanted with all my heart to believe that wish would come true. Ian and I had the power to stop the total annihilation of the planet. But could we pull it off in time?

It didn't take us long to find the bomb Nichol had hidden. He'd been too feeble to expend much effort, so we discovered it taped beneath the window outside my father's room. The backup promised by the base in Colorado Springs arrived and defused both the bomb and its detonator. They also took Nichol's body away. Though reluctant to let us drive to the base on our own, they finally agreed to our using Jag's car as long as we stayed sandwiched between their two-car escort. My father's Storm Trooper hadn't survived the blast. Ian and I surmised that's where Nichol had planted the first bomb.

I clenched my jaw, feeling the pressure of the world on my shoulders. I had yet to experience a vision of what happened *after* the cataclysm to know if we would be successful. That made me anxious.

We were closing in on Cheyenne Mountain now. In addition to the base, there was a modern city deep inside the mountain, and Jag had claimed that if the storm could *not* be stopped, we'd still be safe there. In theory.

Ian was driving Jag's SUV, and the gentle hum of the car's electric engine had lulled my father to sleep in the backseat. It was after noon, and I peered out the window at the desolate landscape flanking the Interstate. Violence had become a way for storm-damaged people to express their grief.

Ian squeezed my hand. "Nervous?"

I nodded. "A little. If this doesn't work…"

"Then it doesn't work," he said. "We'll either live, or we'll die. Whatever happens will be better than struggling to survive on a dying planet. Best to get it over with, one way or the other."

I liked his way of thinking, which was just like Jag's. Black or white. No gray.

Less than twenty-four hours later, after a very long nap in an air-conditioned bedroom and an incredible meal that had included fresh fruit and vegetables, Ian and I were brought to the Kinetic Room. I'd never seen anything like it. The room was about the size of a football stadium, and at its center was an enormous chunk of ice about twenty feet tall and thirty feet long. I had a fair idea what it was for.

The room was freezing, probably to keep the ice from melting. Ian and I were given warm clothing to protect us from the cold. I'd forgotten what it felt like to wear a coat. We were directed to a platform elevator at the base of the iceberg and told that it would take us to the top.

I gripped Ian's hand. "Won't we fall when the ice melts?"

He looked up to study the platform's construction. "I doubt it will melt that fast, but I'm sure that's been thought through. From what I can see, the platform at the top is designed to lower us slowly, as the ice shrinks." Giving my hand a gentle squeeze, he added, "We'll be fine."

As the elevator lifted us to the iceberg's summit, I watched hundreds of men and women fill the room and take their places in a circle around the manmade glacier. These were Kinetics, all of whom had a kinetic power granted by the sun. I tried to imagine what they could do, and if all of them could be trusted to do the right thing. It seemed dangerous to have them all in one place, but it was their combined kinetic strength that would support us in our task. We needed them to help make this work.

"May I have everyone's attention?" boomed a man's voice from an overhead speaker. "Please clasp hands."

I was already holding Ian's hands, sensing his heat flow into me. We stood facing each other on top of the ice mountain, our eyes locked and our souls joined. His magnetism was too strong to resist, but I didn't want to resist. We shared each other's power, and I felt no lack of control, only surrender by choice. We'd come to know one another over the past several days, and the fusion of our strength was what enhanced the familiarity that grew between us. It was as if I'd known him all my life.

"I'm seeking," the voice said, and I wondered what he meant. "Forecasters, please seek with me."

Of course. He was seeking the source of our power. I focused on lifting my consciousness high above the atmosphere, up toward the sun that welcomed me as it had before. Only now I wasn't alone. There were other forecasters with me, some who could foresee earthquakes and others who foresaw tidal waves, but I was the only one with the ability to warn of impending sun storms. I sensed the strength from all of them pour through me, and my vision became so clear it was as if I could touch the sun's flares with my bare hands. The solar star's surface erupted in clusters of flaming geysers, which became explosive volcanoes that shot fiery streams of gas toward Earth. This is what Ian had to stop before it went too far and destroyed the planet.

I diverted some attention to my physical body and noticed that my hands were warm, but the ice beneath me drew the heat away. Ian's hands gripped mine more fiercely, and that's when I knew he was working to exert his control over the storm. The geysers on the sun's surface began to bubble and spurt fire. It was happening for real now, not a vision. And Ian had to make it stop.

The air in the room grew thick and heavy with power. My mind's eye still watched the sun, but my body registered every emotion coming from the Kinetics: excitement, apprehension, terror…Ian's fingers trembled in my hand but not in fear. He reveled in his power to take away the suffering and pain of all who had endured the wrath of the sun.

The surface of our solar star rippled, then smoothed as the flares were calmed from flames to sparks. There were no further eruptions. The danger had passed.

My mind leaped forward to a vision of the future, where thick puffs of cumulous clouds dotted a brilliant blue sky, and green meadows spread over hills like an emerald carpet. Trees waved leafy branches heavy with fruit, and backyard gardens burst with color. The birds were back, and so were all the other living creatures unable to survive without help in our sun-baked world. This wasn't the past as I remembered it, but the future of how it would be again. It finally made sense. I now understood the sun had purified our planet to prepare for a new beginning.

Together, the forecasters withdrew their consciousness from the sun and returned to Earth. The platform that held Ian and me was now on the same level with everyone else. A few exuberant claps grew to cacophonous applause when we noticed the iceberg had melted into a warm pond that lapped at our ankles. We'd done it. We stopped the apocalypse.

I turned to face Ian, whose wide grin expressed joy and pride in what we had accomplished together. His eyes still glowed, but I saw more in them than power this time. I saw love. He drew me into his arms, lifted me off my feet and kissed me long and deep. Our time together wasn't over. In fact, we had all the time in the world.

★ ★ ★ ★ ★

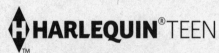

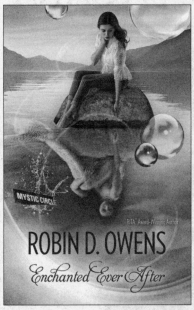

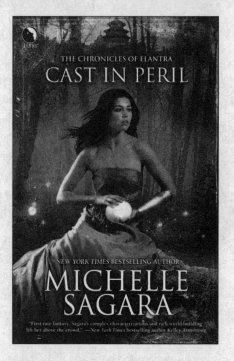

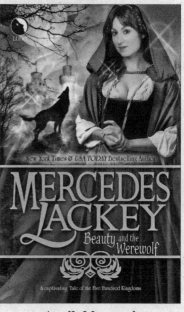